I0778738

Copyright © 2024 by Olive D Wilson.
All rights reserved. No part of this book may be used or reproduced in any form whatsoever without written permission except in the case of brief quotations in critical articles or reviews.
This book is a work of fiction. Names, characters, businesses, organizations, places, events and incidents either are the product of the author's imagination or are used fictitiously. Any resemblance to actual persons, living or dead, events, or locales is entirely coincidental.
Printed in the United States of America.

For more information, or to book an event, contact :
olivedwilson19@gmail.com
Book design by Olive Wilson
Cover design by Olive Wilson
ISBN - Paperback: 9798991029308
First Edition: July 2024

For those who use success as leverage and fame as vengeance.

A Life of
Morals
& Murder

Prologue

Tiesto hated his job.

The blasted museum was a hotspot for robberies of all kinds, and it didn't help that it was dead center in the most criminal infested city on the planet. Hanslack certainly was full of thugs. Some had paid him a visit last night, hooded with long fingers. They hadn't made a sound.

His security guard training hadn't done a thing against the two figures that had broken in yesterday. One's knives had pinned his tailored guard uniform to the wall while the other had kept him quiet with an arrow to the throat. All while they lifted the Olearian from its display on the near wall.

They were gone as soon as they came, not leaving a trace except for the missing painting. He never saw their faces, just the darkness lingering beneath their hoods. It was as if they were skeletons that had risen from their graves just to steal the blasted painting.

His boss had given him quite a talking to, but it wasn't going to do much. If the slums kept going after the museum, then one security guard didn't stand much of a chance.

To his disgust, he had been given a *second* night shift. The urge to quit right then and there had become overwhelming. He was surprised he didn't just hand his boss his uniform. But he needed this job, it may have been incredibly unpleasant, but it paid the bills. And he didn't want to sink to the low level of the dirty thieves that had robbed the museum the night before.

Now he was striding through the dark rooms, lantern in hand and knife strapped to his waist. The entire museum smelt of dust, and if he stayed there for too long he would break into a sneezing fit. Stars glittered outside the windows, teasing him about being stuck here this glorious night. No one came to this wretched place anyway, it was basically just a warehouse that was bound to get robbed until it was nothing more than a large, empty building.

Tiesto wandered into the exotic metals section. Through the eerie dark, he could see glimmers of gold and silver perched against the wall. A low grumble told him he was near the boiling exhibit, where metals were turned to liquid to show their boiling point.

His shoes padded softly against the floor as he approached the pot of hot liquid. As much as he hated his job, he did find this kind of thing interesting. Bubbles formed and exploded as the golden substance boiled. Steam rose like a river from the hot pot, showing how hot the material needed to be.

His head whipped around as he heard a screeching. He drew his knife as the sound got louder, making his ears ache. The sound was joined by his panicked breath, rising and falling in irregular patterns.

It's another robbery. He thought, his nerves soothing with those words. Honestly, he couldn't care less what this criminal stole, putting up a fight wouldn't do any good.

A figure appeared in the entryway. They stood cloaked, a small throwing star in hand that Tiesto guessed was dragging against the wall, making the terrible screeching.

He shrugged, barely acknowledging the figure in the doorway. "Take whatever you want." He told them, turning away. "I really couldn't care less."

Tiesto's eyes widened as he saw three identical figures in the other entryway, blocking his escape. Fear started to sting in his bones, crawling up his spine like a spider. "I told you." He said, mustering up all the courage he could. "I don't care what you steal, just let me leave."

"We aren't here to steal." The first one replied in a rocksalt rasp. "We're here for a *witness*."

On the last word, Tiesto was swarmed. Cloaked figures surrounded him, slamming his back against the dusty wall. He felt a scream rising in his throat, but it was as though something blocked it, not allowing it to escape. He tried to struggle but his limbs couldn't move. They were paralyzed with fear, only able to shake uncontrollably.

He felt a hand land on his quickly rising chest. The first cloaked figure was standing before him. They tipped their hood back to reveal a pale woman. Her face was sharp and jagged. The straightest hair fell down her head and onto her boney shoulders.

"Arrow." She commanded, holding out pale, long fingers. Another of the cloaked figures pulled one from his cloak and handed it to the woman.

She smiled, showing fanged teeth and wild eyes, then slammed the arrow into Tiesto's wrist.

He had never felt pain like this. A wail escaped his throat as the woman twisted the arrow deeper into his flesh. Hot, thick blood trickled down his arm like a river.

The woman let go of the arrow and pulled one of her throwing stars from her cloak. She pressed the cold metal to his throat, poking his sweaty skin.

"Don't cry." She rasped, tilting her head to the side. Tears slid down Tiesto's cheeks, uncontrollably leaking from his eyes. An innocent expression crossed her face, curiosity touching her lips. "You have no reason to. All I want to do is ask you some..." her expression shifted back to the dangerous lioness she came in as. "*Questions.*"

The blade pressed deeper into his skin, and anger dripped from the women's teeth like blood. "There was a girl that broke into here yesterday, what did she look like?"

Tiesto took a sharp breath; his lips quivered, barely able to open. "I-" he whimpered, more tears spilling from his eyes. "I didn't see her, she was wearing a cloak."

The blade twisted near his throat, he felt a small stream of blood leak from the puncture, dripping down his neck. "No." Her eyes flashed, "She's good, but not that good." The woman looked shaken. "I need *details*!"

Tiesto whimpered. Sweat dripped down from his pores, mixing with the blood from his open wounds. "Please." He begged through the massive lump in his throat. "I- I don't know anything!"

The woman swung her knee into his gut and he doubled over. He heaved for air, clutching his stomach with his good hand. Another kick landed on his ribs, causing him to clutch the wall for stability.

"You're lying!" she screamed. "You're protecting her! Why are you protecting her?"

He coughed, the metallic taste of blood lingering in his mouth. "Please, I don't know who you're talking about!"

The woman glared at him, baring angry teeth like a lion. Then, she released him. Tiesto fell to the floor, gasping for air. The cold floor pressed against his tear stained cheek.

"He's useless." Rasped the woman. "Let's dispose of him."

He would have screamed, but the paralyzation still held him hostage, not letting him move a finger.

The other cloaked figures nodded as one pulled a long knife from their pocket. He lent down to Tiesto, holding the blade to his throat. Terror released him, and all at once he started scrambling. He kicked at the man as a scream ripped across his throat. The cloaked figure barely moved, simply laying a strong hand on his chest and steadying his hold on the knife.

"Stop," the woman with straight hair commanded. "It's been a long day, I want to have some fun."

The man raised his knife from Tiesto's throat, tucking it away in his pocket. "What do you mean?"

"I *mean* I'm bored." Her innocent expression returned and she strode around the room, her hands clasped behind her back. "Let him up."

Tiesto felt the hand release him and he scrambled to his feet. "Come." The woman commanded, beckoning him to her side.

He quickly ran to her. She was quite a bit taller than him, and her posture definitely made her more intimidating. "Tell me," she had a crisp accent that he couldn't identify. "What's that?" she asked, pointing to the boiling pot of pure silver.

Terror once again had him in a choke hold. Even if he were to try to speak, nothing more than a squeak would come out.

"Well?" she asked, her angry rasp making its way back to her accent. "What?"

"Erm-" Tiesto stuttered, his lip wobbling. "It's a boiling pot of silver, supposed to show each metal's boiling points."

The woman nodded, looking intrigued. "Yes, very interesting." She said, the calm, innocent voice once again woven into her accent. "And what would happen, if we were to pour it on someone?"

Tiesto felt his heart start pounding. He couldn't breathe, all the air had left his lungs. Cold sweat beaded his forehead as a chill ruffled through him. The only thing he could do was run.

He started sprinting towards the exit, all his energy being directed to his legs. But it was no use, something grabbed his jacket. One of the cloaked figures slammed him to his knees as the others held his hands behind his back.

"Lamia, love?" rasped the woman, "Could you get me the boiling silver, as he called it?"

One of the figures stammered, "Cercel-"

"Do it!" the woman's cold accent had reached a new, high tone.

Lamia nodded as she walked over to the boiling metal, hesitation present with every step.

Cercel's lips curved into a malicious smile. She balanced a small throwing star on her fingertip. "Now," her grin faded. "Pour it on him."

Silence filled the room; only for a split second. Then, a scream ripped from Tiesto's throat. "*Please*!" he begged. "I'm a good person! I've done *nothing*!"

Cercel smiled. "We were all good people once." She clasped her hands behind her back, as if waiting for a show to start. "But the world *always* rips that from us."

With that, Lamia tilted the pot of silver. The shimmering liquid dripped onto his skull. Searing pain surrounded him as the hot liquid emptied. He tried to scream, only to have the hot metal enter his mouth. It was the most pain he had felt, but only for a second.

Then, everything went black.

Chapter One
Lilith

Three rugged-looking teenagers strode down the wet, dirty streets of the old city. Each had bows strung to their backs and a mischievous grin painting their face.

"Sometimes it's hard to believe she's human." Levi chimed as he, Lilith, and Ily strode down the frigid streets of Hanslack. "I would bet a lot of money that she's a hellspawn." Levi was one of the messy types of criminals that lurked in the wretched city. His greasy, long hair looked as though it hadn't been washed in years. The only clean thing about him was the bow and arrows that gleamed along his back.

Ily laughed, her blue eyes gazing at the midnight sky. "Fifty kangue says she's the one and only daughter of Satan." This archer looked more presentable than her brother. Her short, bleached hair was messy, but still well-cleaned along with the colorful clothes that stuck to her back. "By the time she's in her twenties, the world will be in a fiery blaze that she created."

Lilith gave a small chuckle. These were the many rumors that spread about Quilla Thorne. She was a mystery to most, very few people knew her face. There were no paintings, no photographs, no knowledge about the criminal prodigy at all. All the authorities knew was her name and the broken, scattered roses she left at the scene of her crimes.

"What do you think, Lilith?" Levi asked. Lilith's bright green eyes flashed as she heard his voice. "You're closer to the queen of con than any of us could ever dream of getting. So where do you think Quilla Thorne came from?"

Lilith's lips spread into a grin. Her skin was tanner than most of the people who dwelled in this city, and her light brown hair was strung into a tight braid. The vibrant red strand that was woven into her hair matched the deadly red arrows that were strapped to her back. "I honestly have no idea." She shrugged. "Quilla may have taught me how to shoot a bow, but she's never said a word of where she's gotten all *her* skill."

Ily let out an exasperated sigh. "It doesn't surprise me. She's always been annoyingly vague. I don't even know why we're here."

Lilith's smile widened. She was in charge of this mission, along with many others. Her rank in the criminal gang known as the Serpents had grown substantially throughout the two years she had been in the city. "I do."

The two archers gave an annoyed breath. "Like master, like apprentice, I guess." Levi groaned. "Care to tell us why the hell we have to walk across the city at midnight."

Lilith gave a small laugh. To others, it may not be a compliment to be compared to the seventeen-year-old criminal prodigy she called her teacher, but to the criminals and thugs of Hanslack, it was quite an honor. "Quilla's meeting the Stripes tonight to exchange a trade. Us archers are the insurance if Olan's scrawny ass tries to pull something."

Ily let out an exasperated sigh. "So we might not even be used?"

Lilith gave a small laugh. "Oh come now, you know Olan. Of course, he's going to pull something. Having a peaceful trade isn't possible in Hanslack. The climate simply doesn't agree with it."

Levi flashed a grin. "So there's going to be a fight?"

"Fifty kangue says there will be."

The three of them grinned at each other ambitiously. The excitement of a new job tingled inside them as they strode faster through the wet streets.

The Stripe's base was infuriatingly more spectacular than the small gambling den that Lilith had learned to call home. The tall, golden building was at least several stories high. The entire thing looked like a sports arena, and perhaps it was of sorts. But tonight it was eerily empty.

The three archers strode into the large building, watching every step for traps. Inside was abnormally dark. The gambling den, which was usually filled with flashing lights and drunk gamblers, was empty and quiet. The only sound was the gentle squeak of the floorboards as Lilith padded cautiously through the vast room.

"Quilla wants us to split up." Her voice felt out of place as it broke the eerie silence. "Make sure all the ground is covered, and get high up where you can get a good shot into the ring."

The siblings nodded, then ran into the darkness. Lilith started sprinting in the opposite direction, heading up a flight of stairs until she got to a high window that overlooked the arena down below.

The Stripes were notorious for their fighting games. Every night, they would put two poor captives in the sandy fighting ring several feet below her and have them fight to the death. Typically, the people watching from up above had placed money on the fight and were cheering for their bets more than the captive.

Lilith felt a shiver run down her spine. She hoped that she would never end up in that wretched ring, or have money placed on her just like a common bull.

But tonight, the ring wasn't filled with captives or fighters, but instead with cloaked figures that looked better suited in an orgy. They waited patiently for their prey to arrive, knives at their waists and bows on their backs. Lilith had to fight the urge to shoot them all dead right there. Her aim was good enough, and she could do it with very few arrows. But Quilla Thorne's pride was too strong to let that happen. The con queen had given her direct orders to wait until she showed up with the material to be traded.

Lilith's head flung around as she heard the large doors barge open. The crisp echo of heels clicked against the ground as a tall woman strode in. Her long, black trench coat fell at her knees as she stopped her stride. Long, pale fingers were run through her curly, coffee-colored hair as her black eyes sized up the competition. Compared to the men she was faced with, her young age was prominent. Though sometimes it was hard to believe that the wrath of Hanslack was only seventeen; it always became much more apparent when she was faced with an older opponent.

"Miss Thorne." One of the hooded men tipped his hood back to reveal an old, wrinkled face. His hair was gray and quickly retreating up his forehead. The scrawniness of his body was pitiful, not an inch of muscle lingered on his bone.

"Olan." Quilla's crisp accent rasped. She had a voice like no other. Lilith had known her for two years, and still couldn't pinpoint her country of origin. Of course, she didn't dare ask. "I would say it's a pleasure to see you, but it really isn't."

Olan's tired eyes remained squarely on the Quilla. "Trust me, the feeling is mutual." The old man pressed his frail hands together, "Well, let's get this over with. Miss Thorne, if you may?"

Quilla gave a small nod and held up a small, gold tiger. The trinket was covered in jewels of all kinds, just one of them would be worth a fortune. It was the Stripe's prized possession. Quilla and Lilith had stolen it from the gang after Olan and some of his men had stolen the Olearian, a small painting that the two seventeen-year-olds had swiped from the Hanslack Museum of Fine Art a couple of days before.

"Your turn Olan." Quilla rasped, her glare remaining planted on the old man.

Olan gestured to one of his colleagues. The man reached into his coat and pulled out a small painting, no larger than the palm of his hand. The piece of art was widely known, and tremendously valuable on the black market.

Quilla and Olan strode to meet each other in the middle of the room. Lilith loaded her bow, anxious to find out when the Stripe's surprise was going to reveal itself. Her eyes never left the con queen. She watched as Quilla and Olan exchanged trinkets, their hands not daring to touch each other's. Then she saw Quilla clasp her hands behind her back and twitch her long fingers rapidly.

The signal! Lilith pulled back her bowstring, searching the ring for any upcoming opponent. Right on time, several men came rushing into the sandy pit; swords out, daggers pointed.

Lilith released her bowstring swiftly, watching as the arrow soared into the ring and into an attacker's chest. A crimson-red liquid spilled from his flesh and flooded onto the sandy floor.

Quilla's knives flung out like claws. The criminal prodigy fired them half a second apart, each deadly weapon landing directly in the Stripe's forehead. Watching her master's fighting style was mesmerizing. Not a single mistake was made; not a single time did her hand slip when throwing the sharp blade.

Lilith loaded another arrow, breathing in as she pulled the bowstring back, and exhaling while the arrow fired through the air. As soon as it was gone, another was reloaded. She did her routine unconsciously, only paying attention to her targets down below and the light tingle on her fingertips as the bowstring snapped into place.

Arrows fired down from the different windows of the stadium-like place. They came down like rain, but each drop was deadly and precise, hitting its target with ease.

Lilith's eyes flashed as she saw Quilla's hand beckoning her into the ring. She pulled her bow behind her back and lunged over the window, plummeting into the sandy pit. Ily and Levi were close behind her, firing arrows as they stepped into the ring.

The perfumy smell of roses tinted the air as Lilith moved next to Quilla. They fought back to back, weapons firing with every breath.

"Quilla?" Lilith's voice was slightly panicked. "What are we doing down here?"

"Be patient!" Quilla's crisp accent rang through the fight in an agitated tone. "Just a few seconds and we'll be out of this hellhole." She reached into her coat, grabbed a handful of roses, and bit off the flower with her fanged teeth. She let the thorny stems fall to the ground as she broke into a run, her knives by her sides and eyes filled with cruel ambition. Lilith rolled her eyes. Her partner always had a flare for the dramatics, and that meant leaving her signature *everywhere*.

The three archers watched as the criminal prodigy engaged the entire mob of attackers. The Stripes surrounded her, weapons slashing as Quilla dodged every swing. Her knives fired mere seconds apart, and through the mob, Lilith could see blood flying like spilled milk.

Suddenly Quilla burst out of the crowd. "Time to go!" Levi, Ily, and Lilith ran with her, barely able to keep up with her long strides. Quilla pushed the large door open easily, letting it slam behind her as she sprinted into the dark streets.

The cold bit Lilith's fingers as soon as she left the stadium. It had started raining, the large droplets splashed into the mucky puddles that had formed on the road. Quilla's boot splashed in the dirty water as she sprinted down the concrete, knives still in hand.

Yells and screams sounded behind them, and Lilith could hear the Stripe's angry footsteps pounding behind them. She sprinted faster, fear creeping into her bones and pushing her legs to run faster. There was no way in hell that she would be put in that awful death ring of theirs.

In front of her, Quilla turned a sharp corner, heading down a small alleyway. Lilith, Ily, and Levi followed, their feet pounding against the wet cement.

As soon as Lilith turned the corner, her eyes met Quilla's. They were pitch black and glittered with a light that only emerged when they were in danger. The criminal prodigy was perched on a large wall. Her long hair blew in the wind along with her black coat.

"Get up!" she rasped, gazing at the mob that ran behind them.

Levi and Ily looked at each other skeptically, not having a clue how anyone could make their way up that large wall, but Lilith had trained for this.

She grabbed an arrow from her quiver and sprinted full speed at the wall. She stuck the arrow into the wood of the barrier and launched herself into the air. Her feet barely made a sound as they landed. Pride glimmered off her as she stood next to Quilla.

Ily and Levi sprinted to the wall next. With the same technique that Lilith used, they scrambled up the wood. The siblings landed with far less grace than she did, but at least they were on top of the wall. Safe.

Quilla gestured for them to run as the mob of Stripes emerged from the corner. The four of them sprinted along the roof at a speed that none of them except the criminal prodigy could keep comfortably.

"Why are we running?" Ily gasped once they had been sprinting for a solid ten minutes. "The Stripes are far behind us."

Quilla slowed to a walk, not even out of breath. "We're behind schedule, Gillen wanted us back thirty minutes ago."

Lilith furrowed her brow. "He's not going to be happy with you being this late."

The criminal prodigy scoffed. "I honestly don't much care what he thinks. It was an unreasonable expectation to be back within an hour, he knows that as well as I do." The frustration in her tone was prominent. "Besides, if he is mad, I think this will lighten his mood."

Quilla held up the Olearian in one hand, the small painting didn't even have a scratch on it. In her other hand, gleamed a small, jeweled tiger.

Lilith's mouth dropped as the trinket gleamed in the moonlight. "How did you-"

Quilla simply smiled, showing vicious, fanged teeth. "Just something I picked up on my way out."

With that she sprinted along the roofs, disappearing into the dark night of Hanslack.

Chapter Two
Nikolai

The vast sea was laid ahead of Nikolai's ship like a cornfield. Waves lapped against the polished, shiny wood and salty, cold air stung his nose. He felt the damp drops of dew rest on his wrist, signaling that a heavy amount of rain was about to pour down on them.

The promise of a storm did not seem to upset his crew. They leaped and swung from the sails, doing their shiply chores with a wide grin on their faces. The happy chatter was almost unfitting for a day like this, but any day outside of Shina was a good one.

He felt a hand rest on his shoulder. Rex was grinning next to him, his neat uniform polished and refined. "How was the meeting?" he was an older man, maybe in his mid-fifties, but his muscular figure and several tattoos made up for his old and frail bones.

Nikolai groaned, running a hand through his ungroomed hair. He was a man of straight posture and gold laces. His clothes were white as snow and hung on him in tailored creases. "Don't remind me." Every time he had to enter the wretched assembly hall, he felt a tiny part of him die. He didn't know what he hated more, the rebellion he was raised to fight for, or the Empire he was raised to fight against.

"That bad, huh?" Rex's grin faded, replaced with a grim feeling of worry. "Did you at least get your point through?"

Nikolai shrugged. "I'm here aren't I?" he laughed, trying to shake the rising fear in his throat. "Most of the councilmen were cautious, but they came around and realized that this is our only choice."

Rex sighed. "I don't know how sure I am that this will work myself." He looked at him, holding Nikolai's gaze with persistent, blue eyes. "We've never worked with these kinds of people before."

He was right. The main reason the councilmen of the League of Red Doves were worried about his proposal was the risk. It just so happened that the only people that could do this job were agents of chaos.

The League was always impeccably organized. They had to be if they were going to go against a dictatorship that had made its way to ruling the known world. Although they were losing terribly; it was part of the reason that he was on this mission in the first place.

"You know," Nikolai started, smiling at the ocean. "Some would say that we're just like them."

This sent Rex into a spurt of laughter. "You can't be serious." He looked at Nikolai, realizing he wasn't smiling. "Oh. Well, I think the first difference is that we fight for something moral, whereas they fight for money."

Nikolai shrugged. "Well, they have to survive somehow." He inquired. "We don't ever see them working for the Empire, do we?"

Rex sighed, rubbing his temples. "Nearly everyone has beef with the Empire, but that doesn't necessarily mean they're on our side." He smiled gently at Nikolai. "In my opinion, it's not what someone stands against that determines their value, but what they stand *for*."

"Wise words." Nikolai smiled back. "But value is not equivalent to skill, and right now, that's what we need."

"Really?" Rex raised an eyebrow. "I think Alohi would disagree."

Nikolai clenched his fists at the mention of her name. He tried to block any thoughts of his childhood best friend. The guilt he felt whenever someone spoke about her was immeasurable. Everyone kept telling him that it wasn't his fault that she was captured, but he never believed it. The only way the guilt would go away was if Alohi was home and safe. He would do everything to make sure that happened, even if it meant putting his trust, and a hefty amount of money, into the hands of two bloodthirsty criminals.

Nikolai rubbed his temple. "*Don't* say her name." He felt his blood pressure rising and his self-control depleting.

Rex just sighed. "My apologies, Nikolai." He strode away, leaving him wallowing in his own, terrible thoughts.

Now, his guilt was even more potent. Rex and the rest of his crew were like family to him, and they had volunteered to come on this mission for the sake of Alohi. He never wanted to be rude to them, they had given him something that no one else had; love.

But right now, he could barely think about Alohi without throwing up. It was his fault that she was enduring what she was. He should have done something to stop it, but instead he stood helpless, watching as it happened.

People kept telling him that it wasn't his fault, but that didn't help the guilt. He could have done something! He could have at least tried. But instead, he stood there, beating himself up from the inside out.

In the distance, he saw the dark shore of Hanslack. Its buildings looked as though they were about to fall over. Dim, yellow lights showed through the stormy mist, and as they got closer, he could almost swear he smelled oil.

In his studies, he had learned that this city housed the puppies who had been kicked so many times they turned into wolves. He was warned that if he failed, he would be cast into the slums of this city, where the wolves with the sharpest teeth and dimmest morals prowled.

He assumed that the two wolves that he was about to ask for assistance had the sharpest teeth of them all. Although, maybe that was a good thing.

For a rebellion that was supposed to oppose tyranny, the League of Red Doves had an unusual amount of dictatorship built into it. As far as he was concerned, Emperor Ghan, the dictator and mass murderer who he was supposed to take the place of once the League had achieved so-called victory, was no different from his own father.

Though he may be called the White King back at their base on the island of Shina, he knew that if they did win this war, which was highly improbable, he wouldn't actually be in control. Oh no, his father would be whispering every command, every order, every proclamation in his ear. He had been grooming him to take the throne right as Nikolai popped out of the womb. That is after he was done grieving for his wife who died in childbirth.

Sometimes he wondered what his father was like before his mom died. Maybe at one point, he was sweet. Maybe he brought her flowers and whispered his hopes and dreams of a better future in her ear. Or maybe he was the same power-hungry war criminal that raised Nikolai, wanting nothing more from him than power and skill.

His father had shown love to him occasionally, and Nikolai craved it like a drug. It was typically exhibited when he won a rather challenging sword-fighting match or brought home an almost impossible victory. His father would rush to him and embrace him in a warm hug. He would grasp his shoulders and chant positive phrases so loud that everyone could hear them. After that, he would make him spicy fish with sweet rice, and they would eat every bit, talking about what he had achieved.

That was why he worked so hard. Every morning, every night, and all through the day, he was either studying or fighting. Because if he was good enough, he would earn his father's love.

But some people would love him no matter how good of a swordsman he was. His crew had been with him from his very first mission. All they had shown was respect and love towards him. They were his brothers, his family that he could retreat to on the sea. And he wouldn't trade anything for them.

And of course, there was Alohi. They had met when they were only twelve and immediately bonded. She was there for him when no one else was, and he would hold her when she was going through a rough time. They didn't have much in common, but one thing held them together like concrete, unreasonable expectations.

"Nikolai?" a friendly voice interrupted his thoughts. "We're almost ready to dock, are you ready?"

He turned to see Nia standing beside him. She was a young woman who radiated sweetness. Her soft lips curved into a kind smile, "Is everything okay?"

Nikolai swallowed the sorrow and guilt. He had no time for such feelings. There was a job to be done, and it needed to be done swiftly, without setbacks. He plastered a confident smile on his face and straightened his posture. "I'm fine." He could almost sense the doubt in Nia's gaze. "Get my swords ready, I need to send a message to Quilla Thorne and Lilith Cole."

Chapter Three
Quilla

When Quilla, Lilith, and the siblings entered the Link, she was disgusted to find it had erupted with laughter.

The usual depressing gambling den was unfortunately frolicking with joy. Someone had decided it was a good idea to host a party, and Quilla was not in the mood.

"Ily, put these somewhere no one else is going to find them." She handed her the Olearian and the tiger. "Lilith, come with me."

Quilla strode through the mess of the party, narrowly dodging a mouthful of alcohol-tainted vomit that came her way. The room was small, the ceiling was low and the carpet stained. Typically, it was quiet in the Link, the lazy Serpents were too focused on the gambling match they were desperately losing to make any noise. But today, someone had sparked excitement, and it was exhausting.

Quilla finally made her way to the second story. It was quieter up here, the noise below was reduced to just a gentle hum. Her heels clicked against the hardwood as she made her way to her room, Lilith behind her.

She stopped at the door to her bedroom, unlocking it and turning the knob. As soon as Quilla could see inside the room, she hurled a knife at the man inside.

He dodged as Quilla reached inside her coat for more knives. Lilith's bow was already loaded and firing.

"Wait!" the man's accent was distinctly Salenian. "I haven't come to fight."

Quilla threw another knife at him, pinning his shirt to the wall. "Then you better have come to die!"

The two girls advanced on him, arrows and daggers in hand. The man looked around the same age as them, seventeen. His black hair was slicked back, and his poised expression matched his formal clothes. "I've come to ask about a job!"

Quilla pressed her knife to his throat. "And I am here to ask how the hell you got into my room."

The man swallowed. "Let me speak my mind and I'll answer your questions."

Quilla released him, but still kept her black eyes trained on his every move. "My name is Nikolai Lone." The man paused, as if expecting something to happen.

"We're not going to bow to you if that's what you're waiting for." Lilith's annoyed voice broke the air. Nikolai Lone, the name was familiar. He was the League of Black Dove's prized possession. Their future heir. The League was a pathetic organization that was supposedly the Empire's rival. They had done next to nothing in taking down the tyrannical emperor that ruled Thine and most of the world. They were more of a slight annoyance to the Empire than an actual threat.

"Very well." Lone straightened his coat. "You are Quilla Thorne and Lilith Cole, correct?"

The two criminals looked at each other. "Who the hell else would we be?"

Lone nodded, looking just as nervous as before. "Well, it seems that me and my organization have a problem that we can't solve." Quilla furrowed her brow. It was rare that a politician, especially one from a family as cocky and arrogant as the Lones, asked for the help of criminals. "But I believe you can."

Quilla crossed her arms, still very skeptical. "Please, indulge me."

"As you know, our League operates with four council members. One from each country. Unfortunately, our council member from Woodran has been taken by the Empire, and we don't know where she is or how to get her out."

A curiosity sparked in Quilla. As dangerous as an Empire heist could be, war crimes intrigued her. Her anger towards Emperor Ghan was intense and persistent. She had been looking for a way to hurt him since she was twelve. This could be her chance.

"A job this hard doesn't come without a steep price." Lilith chimed, her green eyes still glaring at the politician. "I hope you and your other comrades are willing to pay generously."

Lone smiled. "Name your price."

Quilla had to think about this. Though Lone was confident about his financial security, she wasn't sure that his pathetic rebellion could fulfill the request she and Lilith had in mind.

The archer, however, didn't hesitate. "A million."

This sent Lone into a fit of laughter. "We are willing to pay generously, but don't you think a million is a bit much?"

"Hardly." Quilla had reached into her coat and grabbed one of her long daggers. She was now fiddling menacingly with the sharp blade. "This heist could cost us our lives, and I will not be going head to head with Emperor Ghan for cheap."

Lone sighed. "I think I should explain what will be asked of you first." He gestured to Quilla's neatly made bed. "May I sit down?"

She gave a small nod. "Be my guest."

Lone sat on the bed and clasped his hands together. "First, a million is not cheap." Quilla and Lilith looked at each other skeptically. "And second, you will not be going head to head with Emperor Ghan himself. All that we are asking you to do is break into the Archives, find out where she is, get out, and free... Alohi from wherever she is being held." Quilla watched as his eyes flashed when he said the name *Alohi*. Something told her that Lone's relationship with the council member was more than just political.

"What's the Archives?" Lilith asked.

Lone opened his mouth to answer but closed it as Quilla started talking. "It's a facility that holds all of the Empire's information. It's located on a small island in the middle of the sea. Anyone alive or lived in the last two hundred years has a file in that place. Alohi's file will surely tell us where she is held." Her black gaze turned to Lone. "Speaking of which, how do you even know how to price us? She could be in the most secure prison in the world or a common community jail. For all we know we could be signing ourselves up to rob the Golden Palace."

Lone just shook his head. "We may not know much about the Empire's prisons, but I do know that one is quite remarkable." Remarkable was an understatement. A more accurate word for the great structure would be prestigious, or unreal. "And the Empire doesn't quite know who Alohi is, just that she is associated with the League."

Quilla pressed her lips together. "Then she's most likely in one of the medium-security prisons, that's typically where the Empire keeps low-profile war criminals." The look of disgust and shame on his face was enjoyable. "For a million kangue? I'll do it."

"Me too." Lilith grinned, excited ambition sparkling in her brilliant green eyes.

"Wait." Lone's face was painted with irritation. "I never agreed on a million. I'll do half that, final offer."

Quilla furrowed her brow, "A penny less than a million and you're not getting your politician back."

Lilith crossed her arms. "We're the best of the best. If you're looking for someone cheaper, I would recommend you look on the other side of Hanslack."

Lone growled. Based on the look on his face, he knew damn well that they were the only people who could pull off this heist. "Fine, a million. Nothing more, nothing less." He got off the bed and strode over to Quilla's window. "Meet me at noon tomorrow at the docks. I'll have a ship waiting to pick you up." He opened the window and stepped out onto the roof. "Oh, and don't be late." With those words he ran into the dark city, disappearing into the night.

As soon as he was gone, Quilla moved to close the window. Lone must have picked the lock, and that's how he got in.

"Well, that was interesting." Lilith yawned, stretching her arms out.

"Certainly." Quilla agreed. A million kangue was big money, and although she hated to admit it, the Serpents needed it. Bad. Ever since the freezing hands of winter had touched their side of the city, the amount of clueless tourists had decreased. Therefore less clueless people to rob.

"I'm going to bed." Lilith headed out of Quilla's room. "Oh, and Quilla?"

"Yes?" Quilla answered without turning her head.

"Thank you for letting me lead missions, it's a big honor."

Quilla turned to look at her, black eyes locking with her green ones. "Lilith, you're skilled. Of course, you get to lead missions." She turned back, looking out her window and at the buildings of Hanslack. "Just don't die. It would be hard to train another archer with as much talent as you."

Chapter Four
Alohi

Alohi lay on the cold floor of the cell, letting the cool concrete sink into her aching bones. She had been staring at the same ceiling for days. At least she thought it had been days. There was no sense of time in the dark cell, no change of light to tell her whether it was day or night.

She curled into a small ball, hugging her legs close to her chest. Her hair, which was usually pulled into a tight bun, was now let loose. The brown strands hung over her face in curls.

She was so far from what she once was. At the League of Red Doves, she was considered prestigious. The youngest of the four council members. The political prodigy. She typically wore delicate silks and beads in her hair, but now she was wrapped in a disgusting prison uniform. It smelled of sweat from the moment she got it, and the stains that painted the orange clothing were either blood or vomit.

Alohi painfully remembered the day she had been captured by the Empire soldiers. She remembered the hot sun beaming down on her bare skin. She remembered the way the train tracks glittered in the light, and she remembered her excitement when she heard the whistle, telling her a train was approaching.

"This one's mine!" she told Nikolai, who was standing next to her.

He looked at her skeptically. "No offense Alohi, but you couldn't kill a duck if it sat on your feet."

Alohi glared at him. "Rude." She scoffed. "And besides, I won't be doing the killing, just ordering it."

Nikolai sighed. "I still don't think it's a good idea." He rubbed his temple. "I mean, what if someone sneaks up on you from behind?"

Alohi shrugged the thought off. "They won't." She put a hand on her friend's shoulder. "You've robbed the last five trains and barely got a scratch. Your swords don't have a drop of blood on them and the League has enough supplies to last them weeks." She glanced at the track to see the train was rapidly approaching. "Let me have this one!"

Nikolai's lips curled into a soft smile. "Fine. But I swear to god, Alohi, if you die I will bury your corpse where god can't find it."

"Yes!" Alohi pumped her fist in the air with triumph. She turned to the rest of her crew. "Come on! We're doing this." She saw the smoke of the train poking out behind the sandy dune, signaling it was quickly approaching. Her legs bent, excitement racing through her veins.

The metal thing was coming at them at full speed. Its silver metal glimmered in the hot sun. Dark smoke puffed out of its smokestack, a blurry haze surrounding the polluted air.

Alohi and the rest of her crew stood confidently at the tracks, letting the wind of the train blow their clothes. As soon as the metal machine sped by them, Alohi leaped onto it.

Her fingers curled around the steel holds. They were pleasantly warm because of the beaming sun. When she looked back, her crew was grasping the train's side, patiently awaiting her orders. Nikolai, on the other hand, was holding onto the train with a smug look on his face, as if he didn't think she could do it.

A competitive rush overcame her as she climbed the side of the car, her crew following her. The wind blew her curly hair like a ripped flag as she reached the top of the train.

She gestured to a small hatch on the metal roof, and one of her men reached to open it. Without saying a word, they slipped inside.

The smell of fresh fabric and perfume tainted the air as she entered the room. But instead of the boxes of supplies that usually packed the cars, there was barely anything. Soldiers stood around them, swords and bows pointed directly at their throats. Their uniforms, which were typically a dark blue, were now a terrible silver.

A scream ripped from her throat as weapons started firing. Blood sprayed from the open wounds of her soldiers, but the Empire men were untouched. Tears rolled down her face as her men's heads were smashed against the wall, turning into a wine-colored mush.

She watched as arrows and swords slashed through the flesh of men she was supposed to be in charge of. All she could do was stare as life drained from their eyes along with their blood from the open wounds.

Alohi didn't try to fight it when she felt thick ropes tying her hands together. She didn't try to fight it when her body was lowered to the blood-soaked floor, or when her head was pushed against the warm liquid.

~~~

"Time to go." The ice-cold rasp broke her memory. "Quarantine's over."

She turned to see two Empire soldiers dressed in blue. They loomed over her with tired, angry eyes. Like it was nearing the end of their shift and they were just anxious to get home.

She stood and let them lead her out the door and into the cold hall. Pipes and switches decorated the bright room. It was a miserable gray, and a giant change from the bright white halls of the League's base on Shina.

"Where am I going?" Alohi asked, her voice smaller than she meant it.

"Breakfast." The soldier to her right answered in a deep tone.

Her cloth shoes padded against the metal floor as they strode around the prison. Other than the fact that she was in captivity, she had no idea where she was. But the icy feeling of the metal that surrounded her told her that it was somewhere cold.
~~~

"In here." The guards stopped at a small, metal door. The soldiers opened it and pushed her inside, slamming it behind her.

The bustling of the cafeteria was a big change compared to her small, quiet cell. Prisoners who were all much bigger than her roamed the bright room. They were all either chewing large amounts of food, laughing hysterically, or in the middle of punching someone.

Alohi padded through the room quietly, eager to draw as little attention to herself as possible. Her eyes scanned the room for any kind of food, her stomach growling with unbearable hunger.

On the far side of the cafeteria, was what looked like a line. Prisoners who looked strong enough to snap her like a twig waited for what looked like dog food. She walked to the back of the line, making an obvious effort not to brush shoulders with anyone.

"Um, excuse me?" she asked the muscular man in front of her. "Is this the food line?"

He turned to look at her with slits as eyes. Fresh tattoos painted his face and seemed to accentuate the muscles that bulged under every piece of skin. "What else would it be?"

Alohi recoiled, fear taking over her senses. "Sorry, it was a stupid question."

The man gave a hard laugh, coming directly from the stomach. "It certainly was." He then squinted, looking at her innocent face with terrifying eyes. "What are you here for?"

Alohi froze, not sure if she should answer the question honestly. "I- I'm a politician." Once again, her inability to lie failed her.

The man squinted at her, disbelief tinting his gaze. Then, he laughed. Deep, horrific belts coming from his chest. "You're what?"

"A politician..." Her voice felt small and she could feel her feet stepping backward without permission.

The man's eyes filled with joyous tears. He laid a rough hand on her chest, pushing her backward. "I never thought I would ever see one of you in here! Must be a big change from the usual fluffy pillows and fancy desserts."

Alohi felt anger rise in her. She may have had a traditionally privileged profession, but that didn't mean her life was without challenges. "It- it's not like that."

It was too late, a fist was already flying at her face. She was flung backward, landing on the cold hard floor.

Heads didn't even turn as she clutched her bruised cheek. Tears lingered in her eyes, pain rising in her face like a wildfire. *Don't cry.* She told herself. *Don't you dare cry!*

"Your kind is why I'm in this place in the first place." The man turned away from her, anger still radiating off his tattooed body. "I would kill you if there weren't so many guards around."

Alohi barely heard the last of his sentence. Her fear had motivated her legs to run. Far, *far*, away from anyone who could hurt her.

She finally collapsed in a corner. Her long, brown hands covered her terrified face. Her stomach growled with hunger, but there was no way that she was going anywhere near that line again.

Chapter Five
Lilith

Lilith stuffed a bunch of clothes into her bag. The anger inside her bubbled. What was it Quilla said? *It would be hard to train another archer.* She didn't know why she expected the queen of crime herself to care for someone. Quilla would have laughed at her troubles. Would have said something along the lines of, "Maybe you should focus on learning how to swim instead of why you're valuable."

What was weird is even though she was cruel, Lilith felt something for her. It was a bad idea. Quilla Thorne cared about no one but success. But even though she was narcissistic, she had saved Lilith's life. It was hard not to care about someone if they did that for you. Multiple times.

She looked down at her suitcase. Her whole life was in there. That was all she was. All her belongings fit into a small suitcase. And most of it was clothes. Just a few trinkets her dad gave her, and of course her bow and quiver. That was all.

She was rather excited about the new job. Half a million kangue was enough to get out of Hanslack. And to get away from Quilla. The idea of fighting Ghan was also quite appealing. He was the reason she had ended up in Grave Desert, mining for gold. That gold was supposed to go to the Empire. He was the reason she had been ripped from her home. He was the reason her dad had died a gruesome death. And he was the reason she had become the terrible monster that she was. Coming to Quilla Thorne's call like a dog to its owner.

~~~

All of a sudden, she was no longer in her small room in Hanslack. Instead, her bare feet brushed against the burning sand of the Grave Desert. Pain lingered in her bones like an old, unpleasant friend. The sun burned brightly in the sky, turning her bare shoulders a painful red. The shovel she was holding felt like it weighed tons, and the only reason she didn't drop it was because she knew what happened if she did. She had whipping scars to prove it.

Lilith wasn't the only slave in the desert. Around her, others wore tattered clothes and their ribs stuck out like branches, but none of them were as young as she was. Her slim, fifteen year old body looked weak next to theirs.

Deep holes and trenches littered the sandy dunes. Lilith slid down one of the small cliffs, getting ready to continue her long day of digging. She shoved the shovel into the crumbling sand wall. The little grains fell like flour, and for a moment, her brain thought that's what they were.

The slavers never fed them more than a small meal in the morning, just enough to keep them going for another day. She cradled her stomach as it growled in disappointment. There was no food out here, only sand.

She pushed her shovel into the little pebbles again, watching as they fell. It was hopelessly hard to make any dent in the massive sandy plains. Every time a small hole was made, more sand rushed to cover it.

But this time was different, sand still rushed to cover the dent she had made, but with it slid a small dart. Its rusty surface gave it a dark red tint. The old metal was chipped and scarred, but the blade was sharper than ever.

Lilith picked it up, examining the weapon. This thing could kill someone. And if thrown the right way, it *would* kill someone. She felt a smile spread across her lips, something that hadn't been shown on her face in years. The dart had power, and she held it.
~~~

She strode out of the hole with her hands clasped behind her back. Anger flared in her eyes, a feeling that was all too familiar. The hunger that bubbled in her stomach still ached relentlessly, but the hope that she could get out there kept her walking.

Lilith's vengeful eyes landed on the head slaver. His giant potbelly stuck out like a shark amongst small fish. Everything about him screamed fortunate; from his white hat to his flashy gold necklace.

He was talking to a young, brunette girl. Her long hair stuck out in random strands, and she had cuts and bruises that littered every inch of her skin. She wore tattered clothes, and looked like she hadn't eaten in days. But she wasn't a slave, that was for sure. Slaves didn't radiate confidence and power.

Lilith didn't know why she aimed at the girl. She didn't hate her, she didn't even know her. She wanted to hit the slaver, but for some reason she aimed for the girl.

Regret flashed through her head as soon as the dart left her hand. It was a pure, true form, heading right for the brunette's head.

The girl didn't flinch. Instead, she held up a small knife. The dart collided with it, making a small *clink*, then landed in the soft ground.

Lilith just stood there, stunned. The girl's black eyes gazed into her green ones, a blank expression on her face.

"Stupid, *stupid*, girl!" Lilith started to run as she heard the slaver's rock hard voice boom around the doons. His whip was raised above his head, and pure fury wrinkled his facial features.

She tripped over her own feet. The sand burned her as her back met the hot grains. The slaver held the whip and raised it, but before he could strike her a slim hand grabbed the whip.

"*Stop.*" That was the first word Lilith had heard Quilla speak, her accent rang out through the barren desert. "Stop, the girl has good aim. I could use her. How much?"

The slaver picked up Lilith by the collar and tossed her in the sand next to Quilla's feet. "She's yours." He growled. "I don't understand the brain of someone who wants something that is this useless and disobedient." With that he turned, leaving Quilla and Lilith alone.

Lilith dreaded what Quilla meant by "I could use her," she imagined more backbreaking work. Even though Quilla looked beaten, she still looked as though she could take anyone in a fight, and win.

She extended her slim hand. In it, was the dart, still holding as much power as before.

"That was quite a throw." Quilla looked around the desert, as if searching for any other possible threats. "You aren't forced to come with me." She told Lilith. "But it's the only way you will survive. There's desert for miles. No water, food, or shelter. Just the burning sand. Trust me, I've been here for three days." Lilith looked at her with prying eyes. "Going with me isn't going to be easy. But I do guarantee you shelter, food, and water. With that comes a life of con, danger, and blood. You will work for me, in return I'll teach you how to survive, shoot, and kill." Her black eyes met hers again, ambition giving them a terrifying tint. "Well? Are you in?"

She took the dart and stood up. Her hunger burned in her stomach as she nodded. Quilla smiled. It wasn't a kind one, but one filled with vengeance.

"What's your name?"

"Lilith." She mumbled, she wasn't even sure Quilla could hear her.

"Well, Lilith." Quilla offered her a piece of bread. She took it and buried her teeth in its crust. Quilla's dark eyes met hers. "I think we are going to do great things together."

<p style="text-align:center">~~~</p>

Lilith came out of her flashback to find Quilla at the door. She was leaning against its frame with pierced lips. "Quite a trance."

"Sorry." She picked up her small suitcase.

"May I ask what about?" Quilla asked. For once her eyes were caring, almost like a friend. *Almost.*

Lilith was taken aback. Quilla was never this considerate. She never asked about anyone's needs unless it benefited her.

"Why did you do it?" she asked, anger radiating in her voice. "I threw a dart at your head! Knowing you, it would have been a smarter decision to just leave me. Or to at least let the slaver have the pleasure of whipping me!"

This time Quilla was the one taken aback. She took a breath. "Is that what you think of me?" she almost sounded surprised.

"Should I think differently?" Lilith's response was colder than she meant it.

"I don't know why I did it." Their eyes locked. "I guess I felt empathy for you, knowing that at some point Ghan had gotten his hands on you. I saw myself." Her eyes darted back in front of her. "I can also sense talent when I see it, Lilith. And you had it."

Of course. The talent. She saw potential. But Lilith was not going to turn into another con lord. This was temporary. *Quilla* was temporary. And if she did Nikolai's job correctly, Quilla and these last three years would be erased from Lilith's memory *very* soon.

"Time to go." Quilla strode down the hallway. The quiet rooms of the Link looked similar to an old motel. Stained carpet laced the corridor, along with plants and vases. Lilith liked the second story of their criminal base best. Downstairs was where the chaos lived; up here, everything was calm.

She stopped at a door and opened it to reveal the real leader of the Serpents. He sat on his chair like a throne, then again, it did look like one. It was cemented into the floor, snakes were drawn onto its arms along with several green jewels.

Spencer Gillen sat there scribbling something onto a stack of papers. His hair was white and retreating up his forehead. Wrinkles littered his face, little canals of age. When you looked at him you would immediately notice his skinny body with the worst posture Lilith had ever seen.

"Quilla," he said, looking up from his work. "What a pleasant surprise!" though his tone was meant to be positive, the exhaustion was still very noticeable whenever the con queen entered the room.

"New job, Gillen." As usual, Quilla didn't make eye contact.

"How much?" it was like him and Quilla shared the same brain, short answers, dull faces. Lilith knew both of them were annoyed at every word spoken. Quilla despised Gillen. She would sometimes mention how it would be her on that throne soon.

"A million."

"You're kidding." Gillen tried to make eye contact but Quilla was gazing out the window.

"Do I look like I'm kidding?" Quilla kept her eyes on the birds passing by. "Money like that can get us out of our rut."

"How about Lilith?" Gillen gave up on eye contact. "I need her for a heist."

"There are other shooters." Lilith told him. "I'm Quilla's safety. If she doesn't come back alive, you don't get your cut of the money."

"And unless this heist of yours is worth more than a million kangue, I think I may need her more."

"Fine." He shifted his weight. "But in future, Quilla, don't make plans without my consent. The city may be giving you flattering nicknames, but I'm still head in command. You answer to me. Don't forget that."

"Don't worry." Quilla turned on her heel. "I remember." With that she walked out the door, Lilith followed.

The cold air of Hanslack was an immediate change to the warm comfort of the Link. As soon as they stepped onto the cold, wet concrete, a shiver ran down Lilith's spine. A light mist had dusted the streets, and the smell of thick oil made her nose wrinkle.

Quilla's anger was radiating off her. She looked like she did when anyone mentioned another gang that was more powerful, or anyone that held more power than she did. It got really bad when someone mentioned Ghan.

"What's the end goal?" she blurted out. As soon as Quilla looked at her with midnight eyes, she immediately wanted to take it back.

"You're going to have to be a little more specific." Quilla told her.

"All of it." She clarified. "Your relationship with Gillen, why not start your own gang? And what's up with Ghan? Why do you tense up whenever someone mentions his name?"

"Why do you associate with me?" Quilla lifted her chin. Lilith felt her eyes shift to the floor. She knew why. It was to reach *her* goal. Her life now was just a stepping stool. The thing she was trying to reach was a somewhat normal life. She wanted to recover from her past. She just wanted to forget about the last four years. And helping Quilla would get her there. Even if it meant becoming a coldblooded killer.

"As for Ghan." Lilith felt Quilla's tone shift. "He hurt me. My life isn't complete until I hurt him back. And as long as that's still on my agenda, his name still haunts me."

Lilith decided not to ask anymore questions. After that response she didn't think Quilla was very eager to answer either. What had Ghan done? Lilith wondered if Quilla had always been a monster. Maybe born to some gangsters that raised her to be a con queen. Or maybe she was a normal kid at some point. Going to school and eating candy. The thought of Quilla as an innocent child felt obscure.

They walked in silence until they saw Nikolai. His ship was huge. Sails that towered over buildings. The wood looked polished and shiny. Nikolai stood in his impossibly white outfit. He was bossing people around like a father and his children, although most people on the ship were older than him.

When he saw them he strode over. As he gazed down at their bags, his face shifted to one of curiosity and concern.

"Is that all?" he asked. They both glared at him. "Sorry, it's just that it's so small. You know it's going to be more than a few days, right?"

"Unfortunately," Lilith told him. "These are all of my belongings."

"And these are all of mine." Quilla held a bag smaller than Lilith's. She wondered what was in there. Anything from her childhood or just clothes and weapons. "Assuming you're going to feed us."

"Yes, food is included." Nikolai's face was almost sympathetic. "Now get on the ship. I want to get out of here as soon as possible." He flinched away as a drunk man tumbled and fell into the sea, bringing some crates along with him.

"Are you sure?" Quilla asked him. "I'd love to give you a tour." The look of disgust on his face made Lilith smile. She had been on these streets for years. Watching Nikolai try and survive a few hours would be the height of amusement.

They walked to the ship. The boards creaked as they moved. Each one held the danger of breaking, dropping you in the turbulent water. The ship was even more spectacular up close. The shiny boards didn't creak at all and the sails looked as though the cloth was as hard as iron. Though it looked strong, it flapped in the wind like a flag. She turned around, getting one last look at this terrible city. When she returned she would have enough money to buy a boat and live a life of dreams. She thought of the house she would own in the mountains. Her children would play in the snow when it fell and in the streams when it didn't. She would find a partner to live out the rest of her days, to help raise her kids, and to help reach her dreams. All the bloody, terrifying nights in Hanslack would slowly fade to the back of her mind, and all would be perfect. *Perfect.*

Her thoughts were interrupted with a piercing pain. It felt as though something was in her stomach; eating away at her flesh. She fell to her knees, clutching the wound. She lifted her shaking hand to see that it was soaked with her own blood. Her eyesight went blurry. A figure ran towards her and soon hands grasped her. A slight scream escaped her lips. She felt dizzy. The faint smell of roses tainted the air, with that she knew Quilla was holding her. Then the pain dulled, and her conscience drifted from her body.

Chapter Six
Nikolai

Nikolai heard someone scream.

He spun around to see Lilith in Thorne's arms. An arrow was firmly planted in her stomach and crimson blood flooded out. He immediately started yelling at the crew.

"Get her help!" he screamed as he ran to Thorne's side. "Who shot at her?"

Thorne turned, her eyes filled with panic. Nikolai was shocked that anything other than anger and cruel joy could paint her face.

"I don't know!" she yelled at him. The anger had returned. She lifted Lilith, whose eyes were closed in a state of unconsciousness.

"There's a bed just inside the cabin." He gestured to the ship. "Put her there then help me identify the attackers."

"No!" Thorne's voice was shrill. "She needs medical attention. I-"

"We have medics on board!" Nikolai hollered at her. "Now come help us or we'll all die!" authority rose in his voice. It was a nice feeling. He felt his back straighten with those words as confidence filled him.

Thorne hesitated, her eyes glowing with fury. Nikolai didn't know what at. Then she turned on her heel, sprinting towards the cabin.

He turned. There was nothing. Just the ugly buildings of Hanslack. He suddenly jumped back as an arrow flew directly at him, sticking to the wooden boards of the dock. Another hit one of his men directly in the chest. He felt his heart pound as the fear that an arrow might strike him as well curled through his body. He ran to his crew member when he heard another scream. He looked to see another one of his men down. Instinctively, he started shouting orders. Getting the wounded inside and figuring out who the attacker was. But that job was already done.

"It's the Stripes." Thorne had appeared behind him. "Lilith and I may have had a small disagreement with them before we met you." Her knives were drawn and her eyes had a new fiery essence.

"Big enough of a disagreement for them to take down two of my men?" Nikolai asked, this time he was the one with anger in his eyes.

"Bloodshed isn't exactly rare here." She spun her knife in her hands. Within a second her eyes became very alert. She lunged at him, knocking him to the ground. An arrow hit and broke the wood where he was standing.

"Huh," Thorne said. "Their aim has improved."

Nikolai stood up. "Everyone inside the ship!" he yelled. The men ran inside the cabin, grabbing the wounded with them.

"I'll hold them off!" Thorne was already running. "Get the boat ready. We leave in five." Nikolai didn't like taking orders from her, but she knew what needed to happen. And her voice was filled with such authority that Nikolai was afraid to refuse.

Nikolai ran as rain started to fall. Strong winds came with it. Good, he thought. It's easier to get out. There was no way he could ask the crew to help him, not when they had been shot at. He grabbed the rope and frantically untied the knot, his fingers slipping with the cold weather. He finally got the rope undone, it fell and the sail unraveled. The cloth immediately caught the wind and the ship jolted forward, only to be pulled back by the anchor.

A scream made him turn his head. Nearby he saw a man fall out of a window. I may not like you, Thorne. He thought bitterly. But you can get the job done without being asked.

He swiftly moved to the next sail. His hands were numb and wet, which made it harder to untie the tight knot. Its thread was soaked along with his clothes and hair. He finally got it untied. The rope fell, rubbing against his fingers. He yelped as he looked down to see a nasty, red rope burn. *Suck it up, Nikolai!* He told himself. *If Thorne can do her job, you can do yours!* He headed to the last rope. His hand burned with the open flesh. His fingers slipped between the rope and loosened it. Then, with all his strength, he pulled it apart and the sails unraveled.

The anchor. He thought to himself as he rushed to raise it. The boat was soaked, raindrops pattered on the puddles. The sails shook violently, just waiting to take off. The cold metal of the anker chain eased his rope burn. But pulling the anchor up was not so easy. His arms were tired, and the last few nights were sleepless. His dreams were haunted by Alohi's scarred, lifeless body.

As soon as he realized that she wasn't coming back, he fell to the ground. He had waited by those tracks, just waiting to see her silhouette running towards him. He would have stayed on that ground for days if Rex hadn't coaxed him into getting up. His entire crew had been devastated by Alohi's loss, and none of them wasted any time trying to figure out how to get her back.

No matter how many times Rex and the rest of his seafound family told him that it wasn't his fault, there was no convincing him. Guilt was constantly haunting his thoughts. There wasn't a time when the wretched emotion wasn't at the back of his head.

Tears streamed down his face thinking of her. All this pain, all the men he lost, it was to get her back, safe. She would not die. Not while he was there. She was not allowed to die. He heaved the anchor up and the sails caught the wind, propelling them forward.

He saw Thorne running towards them, but the boat had already taken off. The water was choppy, and the ship carved through it like a sharp knife. The con queen didn't hesitate. She dived into the ocean, her form perfect. Nikolai was surprised at the speed she could swim. It was like she was in a trance, focused only on the moment; the goal at hand. Thorne got to the edge of the boat within seconds and Nikolai threw her a rope. The speed she climbed the boat was almost faster than the speed she swam at.

Thorne was dressed in a long coat laced with knives on the inside. She had a cut across her cheek which looked like it came from a knife. Nikolai knew she was only seventeen, but the stress lines on her face made her seem older. Not in a bad way. No one would take orders from a seventeen-year-old, but no one would refuse them when they came from Thorne. Then again, at first glance, no one would take orders from him, and yet he had a whole crew of very experienced men who obeyed his every command.

"Maybe you could have done me the courtesy of waiting?" she told him in her sarcastic accent. Her lips spread into a cruel smile as she saw his face. "Well, if I knew getting the boat ready would be such an emotional task, I would have had someone else do it." She brushed past him, heading to the cabin. Nikolai followed, wiping his tears self-consciously.

Chapter Seven
Quilla

"What are you doing?" Quilla screeched as soon as she entered the cabin. Lilith lay in a bed, blood gushing from her stomach while medics gathered among the other wounded soldiers. "She's bleeding out! This guy barely has a scratch!" she gestured to a man with black hair and a tiny wound on his shoulder. It looked like the arrow had grazed him, not landed in the center of a vital organ!

"Ma'am, our first priority is always our men." One of the medics explained.

Her eyes narrowed, no one needed medical attention more than Lilith. Lone had done a horrible job with training his crew.

"Really?" Quilla glared at the medic. "Based on the way Lone cries, I could have sworn it to be Alohi Windlem." This took them by surprise. The girl that was captured meant something to all of them. "In case you imbeciles are not in the know, I'm the one that's supposed to retrieve her, and I'm not doing anything if she dies!" Quilla gestured to Lilith. Their faces were stunned, a moment of silence. Then several medics rushed to Lilith's side.

She left the cabin swiftly, her heeled boots clicking against the drenched ship deck. The rain poured on her head and she looked up to see the cloudy sky.

Her heart pounded in her chest with a furious rage. Her breathing had quickened and her lungs felt as if they were about to burst out of her chest.

But anger wasn't the only wretched emotion that lingered in her heart. There was another, one that had nearly gotten her killed, many times. And she was not about to fall to an easily righted mistake.

Quilla reached into her cloak and hurled a knife at the mast. It was a clean stick. She strode over and pulled it out of the wood with a frustrated yank. The fury was still pushing on her skin, begging to come out in some shape or form.

But the second blasted emotion still stung her with its presence. It was warm, wholesome, and vulnerable. It may have been gentle, but the feeling was strong and obnoxious, making it impossible to ignore.

No! The familiar, rash voice that lived in her head said. *Caring about people is how you got into this mess! Don't repeat past mistakes, Thorne!*

This threat seemed to make her heart shut up. She climbed the mast, her grip loosened around the ladder as her hands numbed. The droplets hanging on the wood were little tiny people. At least that was what Quilla believed when she made them fall off her hand and splatter on the ground. They were insignificant, one among thousands of tiny raindrops.

The rain hit her harder as she reached the crow's nest. She looked up at the sky, nothing but dark gray for miles. This made her smile. She sat on the fence of the high balcony, swinging both legs over the edge.

Her hand reached into her jacket and pulled out a knife. It was the one that had been hit with Lilith's dart the first time they had met. The dart must have been cheap, because it barely made a dent in her blade. The knife was still very usable. She held it for a while, admiring its shiny surface. The cold touch of the metal left her hands as she flung it at the sail in front of her.

It landed in the middle of the mast. She jumped off the crow's nest and grabbed the blade. Her feet slipped on the wet wood but her hands held steady. It was a clean stick. The knife was wedged in there like a nail to a wall.

She stopped for a second. The ocean was turbulent, the waves crashing against each other. She let her left foot and arm dangle above the deck while her right arm and foot held tightly to the knife and mast.

The rough ocean crashed in front of her. It was endless, going on forever without stopping. She had come to admire the gray body of water, relentless in its pursuit. She knew that it had once covered the planet, and would cover it again long after she was buried underground. What would the world be if humans were this persistent?

Quilla tugged the blade out of the wood and landed on her feet. The knife was as good as new, except for the previous small dent and a couple of small splinters. Quilla brushed them off. This was high quality; she would strive to keep this one.

"Impressive." Lone appeared behind her.

Quilla turned to glare at him. "I know."

"Don't get too cocky, the knife did most of the work."

Quilla held his hard gaze, not sure how to retort.

"Tell me the plan." She wasn't in the mood for small talk anyway. She wanted to take her mind off Lilith, and this job was a hard one. All lines that were severed needed to be tied together.

"The first step is to find out where they're holding her." He told her. "Which means we have to break into the Archives." Ah, the Archives. A giant library with all the blackmail Quilla could ever ask for.

"I figured." She looked down at her feet, the Archives might be more secure than the Golden Palace itself. No matter, she was always up for a challenge. "I'm assuming you do not have a map or anything that may help us."

"Don't give up on me so fast, Thorne." Lone beckoned her to a hatch embedded in the shiny boards of the ship. He opened it and gestured with his hand. "Ladies first."

Quilla walked forward, a smile curling along her face. Her eyes locked with his. "That," she told him, "Was pathetic." They glared at each other for a second, and then she jumped down, not bothering with the ladder and landing below deck.

"I would prefer if you paid a little more respect for the vessel that is keeping us above water," Lone told her. She didn't try to hide the disgusted look on her face.

"Oh please," it was almost impossible to comprehend how annoying this man was. Quilla drummed her fingers against a table. The room was eerily dark. Lone flicked a switch and it lit up. The table her fingers tapped against had a large map laid against it. "Judging by this room, you have more than enough money to maintain this ship."

She moved around to get a better view of the map. Her boots clicked against the wood as she dragged her fingers along the smooth surface of the table. The map was more of a blueprint. There were countless labels. Each tiny room had a detailed explanation. It was undoubtedly a map of the Archives.

"How did you get this?" she asked him. "It would be worth millions on the black market. That's a hefty amount of kangue even for you."

"You're not the only person that can pull off a heist, Thorne." He told her. Quilla was shocked that someone as pure as him could do something that was so... *her*.

"Impressive," she relented.

"The goal is to get to the file room. I would recommend we enter here." He pointed to what looked like the main entrance.

"How do you suppose we do that?" Quilla asked.

"A diversion." Lone looked very proud of himself. "We start a fight at the gates with my men while you and Lilith slip past."

"It won't work." She somewhat enjoyed his prideful expression fade with those words. "The base has explosives that can blow up your men in seconds. No one would survive. And even if, magically, me and Lilith were to get by unnoticed, they have heavy patrol that would detect us and immediately blow us into oblivion."

Lone crossed his arms. "If you know so much, how would you do it?"

"Easy," Quilla told him. "All areas of the Archives are heavily guarded, but what's the least protected?"

"The back." Lone still looked confused. "But there's no entrance, the only thing that's back there is…" he trailed off, revelation slowly lighting up his face.

"Air vents." Quilla looked at the map. She traced her finger along an air vent that landed in a corridor. "The real challenge is getting from here," she dragged her finger along the corridor, "To here." It landed in the files room.

"I'm assuming there's patrol there too?" Lone asked her, staring down at the map.

"Actually," Quilla's tone lifted. "This is where Ghan starts to get lazy. There is a patrol, but it only happens every two minutes and no stationed guards. But that's what we need to look out for. If we kill one soldier the rest are notified, not to mention they're on the more skilled side of Ghan's troops. If we were to attempt to get inside we would have to time it right." She leaned over the map, staring directly at the files room.

"It doesn't say this stuff on the map." Lone looked at her suspiciously. "How do you know all of this?"

Quilla shifted her gaze. "I just do… okay?" the confidence left her tone, the only thing left behind was raspy anger. "It doesn't matter where I get the information, just that I have it."

Lone nodded, as though he understood her reluctance to share. This information was tainted with her past. As helpful as it was in these kinds of situations, it was a scar that would never heal.

Lone walked around the table but jolted back as a scream rang through the air. Quilla instinctively felt her hands rush to the inside of her coat. They curled around the hilt of the closest knife. She bent her legs, ready to fling them at any intruder that may come down the ladder.

Lilith! She hated that she was the first thing that her mind thought of. But every time she tried to get it to shift to something more productive, it darted back to her partner.

Quilla felt anxiety slither up her legs. It grabbed her organs, squeezing tightly as its nails dug into them. Nausea bubbled in her stomach. Her legs felt wobbly, as if they would collapse at any minute. *Get it together, Thorne!* She took a breath. Whatever happened to Lilith, it wasn't something she could control.

She looked to see the two long blades that Lone drew from the hilts on his back. His legs were bent and the weapons were in his hands, it looked as though if a fly was to come close it would be cut in half.

They exchanged a look, then quietly proceeded up the ladder, ready and waiting to fight whatever was on deck.

Chapter Eight
Alohi

Alohi's stomach still growled with hunger when the soldiers rushed to escort them out. Their shiny, blue uniforms gleamed in the light of the cafeteria and their yells and orders echoed off the gray walls.

"Time to go!" the soldiers hollered as they bustled the prisoners out of the cafeteria. Each was heavily armed, swords and bows waiting at their hilts. The strong, terrifying men that seemed untouchable before now looked scared and small. Obedience tainted the room like a foul smell.

The prisoners were led into the depressing halls. Gray colors seemed to match the aura of depression that came off each of the inmates. Sadness crept into her brain like a disease, draining her energy and hope.

Of course, hope was slim here, whether or not you had a mind free of misery. Alohi found that even the most positive personalities were soon drained. Just the colors of this wretched place soaked up all happiness, not to mention the terrifying convicts and even more terrifying prison guards.

The line of prisoners finally halted as they approached a door. It swung open only to reveal an oblivion of darkness. The inmates headed inside, being handed a bucket, a pickaxe, and a flashlight.

Alohi studied her tools thoroughly. The cold of the metal was soothing against her swollen, dry hands. Clicking the flashlight on, she headed inside the room.

Her cloth shoes padded against something that felt like sand. The light of the flashlight shone on the walls to reveal moss and rock. The gentle sound of dripping played over and over like a melody.

She followed the line of prisoners cautiously, fully aware of how the darkness had limited her vision. Her eyes widened with awe as her gaze landed on the cliff.

The drop-off was sudden. A rope ladder ran down from the ceiling and onto the sandy floor. Several pools of black water glimmered below, little drops of water breaking their surface and entering their black void.

Alohi made her way down the ladder cautiously. Its ropes looked thin and worn, she wouldn't be surprised if they would snap at any given moment. But they had held the other prisoners that most likely weighed twice as much as she did, so they could withstand her scrawny size.

As her fellow inmates reached the ground, they started swinging their pickaxe into the hard wall of the cave. The rock crumbled away, landing on the soft sand with a poof.

Alohi looked at her own pickaxe. It was heavy, she barely managed to carry it down the ladder. It was hard to imagine her muscleless arms slamming it into the hard cave wall. It was even harder to imagine that she could even make a crack in the wall.

The other inmates were strong, their muscles as large as their brains were small, but Alohi's strengths came with mind. No political prodigy was ever expected to work in the coal mines or wield a sharp weapon. She made that choice when she was seven, and hadn't ever regretted it.

~~~

The memory burned bright in her mind like it had only happened yesterday. Flames seemed to surround her thoughts, matching the intensity and pain of the past. She was back in her childhood home, sitting on a high chair and watching the life-changing event that was about to happen before her.
~~~

"Father please!" Ranine, her older sister, was wailing on the wood floor. She was around ten at the time, which would make Alohi seven. Tears had soaked her pink cheeks as she begged her father. "I don't want to kill it!"

Alohi's father held a baby pig. His eyes were blank, unreadable. His face was hard as stone and cold as ice. The brown, straight hair hung in front of his black eyes like a madman's locks. Perhaps her father was half insane, Alohi hadn't quite figured that out yet.

"*Please*!" the knife was held loosely in Ranine's hand. "Don't make me do it!"

Her father's calm voice was infuriating. "All I'm giving you is a choice, Ranine." He cocked his head to the side. "Your family, or the blasted pig."

"*Dad*!" her voice was shrill, it was the last time Alohi would ever hear her powerful sister beg. "The pig's done nothing wrong!"

Her father's black eyes squinted, narrowing in on his eldest daughter. "Is that the same excuse you would use when Empire soldiers break down our doors? Are they worth more than your family, Ranine?"

"*No*!" Alohi recoiled at the intensity of the scream. "But the pig has done nothing wrong. He doesn't deserve to die! *Please*, Dad!"

Her father gave a small laugh. "Oh, but what if I say he deserves to die?" Ranine's tear-flooded eyes looked up at him with horror. "I've given you everything. A roof over your head, warm food on your plate, never-ending *love*. The least you could do for me is do what I ask." He jutted out his jaw. "And I ask you to kill the goddamned pig!"

Ranine wiped her tears and got to her feet, every inch of her trembling. Alohi's eyes widened as she saw the knife gleaming in her sister's hand. It was clean, not a spot on the stainless metal.

Her father leaned down and released the pig. The animal looked at Ranine with pleading eyes, the poor thing's last attempt at life. But her sister's eyes were as cold as her father's. She didn't even blink as she plunged the knife deep into the animal's back.

Blood sprayed the room like an erupting volcano. The pig fell to the ground with one last ear-splitting squeal. It lay there, motionless and pitiful as the wine-colored blood spilled from the open wound.

"Well done!" emotion finally tinted her father's voice. "Very impressive, Ranine! You will do quite well in this world."

Ranine's face was still expressionless. An unreadable daze ran over her eyes as she watched the rest of the pig's life leave its body. "If this is the world you're training me to live in," she met her father's eyes, taking a sharp breath. "Then I wish I was the pig."

The memory burned. Its borders went up in flames like a picture that was aflame. Instead of Ranine, it was Alohi standing with the knife. Tears ran down her cheeks as she stared into the pleading eyes of a baby goat.

"Father, *please*!" The same words that had left her sister's lips three years ago had now left hers. "I don't want to do it!"

Her father tilted his head. His jawline had gotten sharper and his eyes had tightened into angrier slits. Stress lines wrinkled his skin, making him look much older than forty. "Life is full of things you don't want to do, Alohi." The kindness in his voice betrayed his actions. "The way to survive is to do it anyway."

"No." Alohi felt her chest rise and fall rapidly. Her heart was beating so fast she thought it might bounce out of her chest. "No, there has to be another way. It's not kill or be killed. There's *always* a middle ground. There *has* to be a middle ground!"

All her father did was laugh. "Not this time, dear daughter." He crossed his arms, an expecting look spreading across his face. "Not this time."

Alohi's hands shook. Tears slid down her cheeks as she raised the knife to the goat's neck. The flesh was soft and the fur silky. The animal's eyes looked up at her with a pleading look, tears starting to well in them too. The rise and fall of the animal's throat was steady and gentle. The breathing couldn't stop. It *wouldn't*.

She let the blade slip out of her hand, watching as it clattered against the tile floor. "No." Her voice may have been small, but she did not doubt that everyone in the room heard it. "No, this isn't right. I will not be a pawn in this horrible game. I won't just be another soldier in this terrible war!"

The silence was all that remained after the words left her mouth. Just for a second, then chaos erupted.

Her father's hard, calloused fist came rushing towards her. She was propelled backward as his hard knuckles slammed into her face.

She landed on the cold, tile floor, just below her sister's feet. Pure sympathy wallowed in her gaze, but her limbs were unmoving. There was *nothing* she could do to help. "Oh, Alohi." her voice was barely over a whisper. "What have you done?"

The goat had started running, its little legs carrying it as far as it could go. An ear-splitting wail ended its flee to safety as a knife landed in its back. Red liquid leaked out of the wound as it fell to the ground.

Alohi screamed, tears running from her eyes as sympathy for the poor animal flooded her head.

"Cook this, Lindsay." Her father told his wife, who was cowering in the corner. He turned back to Alohi, his voice cold and emotionless. "Failures don't eat."

"Gael-" Alohi's mother began, still holding the dead goat.

All her father did was shoot his wife a look, and her mouth shut closed as fear glazed over her eyes. "And you," he turned to Alohi. "Go to your room. Don't come out until you're worth something."

She could feel her heart bulging in her chest as she scrambled to her feet. Alohi didn't think she had ever run so fast. There was no stronger motivator than getting away from her raging father.

As soon as she slammed the door behind her, she fell onto her bed. The soft covers swallowed her in an exhausted oblivion. She let her tears sink into her pillow as she cried. Insults and swears rung in her head, all in her father's distinct tone. They called her weak, incompetent, and a *failure*.

Time seemed to blur, becoming an illusion as the emotions that cursed her head became very real. She didn't notice the dark sky looming outside her window. She didn't notice the growl of her empty stomach. She didn't notice how the air around her was getting progressively hotter.

The only time her head lifted off her tear-soaked pillow was when she saw the orange light flickering outside her room. Cautiously, she got up from her bed and headed to the door.

Her hand immediately recoiled as she touched the metal door knob. A small scream escaped her mouth as she saw the terrible burns blistering her dark skin.

Just then, the door went up in bright orange flames. Smoke filled the room with its putrid scent as the firewall got larger, blocking Alohi's only escape.

Her eyes watered as the sting of ash entered her iris. A waiting coughing spree rumbled in her throat as she breathed the tainted air. She took strained, panicked gasps as the fire got closer.

A million thoughts fluttered in her head, but one screamed louder than the rest. *You need to get out of here.*

Alohi ran to her window, sweat beading on her forehead. Through the glass, she could see the thick woods of Woodran, her childhood home. Unlike her house, the trees were not on fire. Instead, they shone with drops of water from the night rain.

Survival instincts took over her. There was no way she could break her window, and even if she did the metal bars would keep her from escaping.

She turned to the flaming wall in front of her. The flame was growing stronger, its overwhelming heat making her nauseous. She took a breath, gagging as all that filled her nose was black ash, then sprinted into the fire.

The heat was nothing she had ever felt. All sense of direction left her vision as she fell to her hands and knees. She could feel her flesh bubble and blister as the light touch of the flame stroked her brown skin.

All of a sudden, the fever relented. The blackness that surrounded her vision dulled, and the roar of the fire faded into the distance as she crawled from the flaming wall.

Alohi was still on her hands and knees, her legs barely able to support her weight. Out of the corner of her eye, she saw her father running from the room and out into the hall. Sweat beaded along his own forehead, his straight hair blowing in the wind of the flame. An unconscious Ranine hung over his shoulder, her curly hair drifting in the wind.

They locked gazes for a second, her father's eyes harder than rock. Silent understanding flashed both of their gazes. *Failures don't get saved, failures are on their own.*

Alohi didn't try to plead for her father to come back, instead, she just looked after him. She let her arms and legs collapse beneath her, her droopy eyes aching to close. She wanted to give up, she wanted to just lay there and die, but she couldn't. Right now, she had something to prove, and she was going to prove it.

One at a time, Alohi told herself as she started clawing her way to the door. *One at a time.* The heat behind her was getting more intense. *Just a couple more.* Through her blurry vision, she could see the open door. She could see the wet trees, the wet grass, her *escape*.

The wood floor was getting hotter and her feet felt as if they might catch fire. The burns on her back had started stinging as thick smoke entered her flesh. She clenched her jaw. *Just a couple more.*

She extended her hand one last time, it shook from exhaustion. Instead of the hardwood she expected to find, her fingers landed on soft, wet grass.

A sense of life refueled her. Alohi lifted her shaky head to see her family standing in front of her. She met her father's gaze, but instead of the rock-hard expression, a friendly smile spread across his lips.

"Well, what do you know?" his cool tone broke the silence. "Maybe you are worth something."

Chapter Nine
Lilith

Lilith had always had anger issues. It wasn't something that she had developed along the way like her ability to kill without a second thought. They had always been there, but nevertheless, they had always been a problem.

It might have been her third night in Hanslack. She had already hated the wretched city, and Quilla wasn't usually around. She was always on some job, pissing some unlucky person off. Lilith just stayed in the small room she was offered. She never spoke to anyone and no one ever spoke to her. She didn't know if it was Quilla's doing or just miraculous luck that no one bothered her until her third day. Back then she had no reputation. She was just the random, beat-up girl who wandered the bar and gambling hall occasionally.

She remembered the first time Hannslack had gotten interesting. It was about seven in the evening when it happened. She cautiously headed down one of the many staircases. The room was very dark. In an average gambling den, drunks are howling with laughter. But not the Link. Serpents lurked here, and they were all beaten-down men who had no choice but to become thieves and murderers. Lilith found herself repulsed by them, but once in a while, it crossed her mind that this was what she would be. What she was.

If you could imagine the most depressing room on earth, then multiply it by ten, and you'll have the Link. Most of the floor is a dark green with thin carpet. Vomit and blood stains scattered around. The room was fairly big, but the walls were seven feet tall at max. It gives you the feeling of being compacted into a prison of death and misery, never to escape. The wretched smell of alcohol and smoke filled the dim room. Lilith would bet a lot of money that Quilla had designed it.

As soon as you entered the room, the wretched smell of oil and secondhand smoke stung your nose. Heavy-eyed hoods lurked in the depths of the dark room. Most wore nothing but rags; evidence of the poverty-ridden city. But some looked rather poised. Their skin was still oily, and their eyes were still exhausted, but they wore suits and dress coats. If she didn't know better, she would have figured they were businessmen.

Lilith wrinkled her nose. It was in and out. Just get a drink to empty her thoughts from her mind, and retreat back to her small room.

She had been in her bedroom the size of a closet alone with her thoughts, and her thoughts were not kind. They kept telling her that all of this was her fault and that she could have done something to stop it. If Lilith had done something her father would still be alive. But instead, she just stood still, and look where that ended up. She hated herself for being helpless, for being weak. She blamed herself.

Her footsteps were light, trying not to make a sound. A small bow and full quiver were strapped behind her back. She slowly approached the bar and sat on a stool.

Her fingers moved restlessly as she waited, anxiety creeping up her bones. The waiter was delivering drinks on the other side of the bar. He was a tall man with golden sideburns. He wasn't nearly the scariest one there, but nonetheless, Lilith didn't dare bother him. She just sat there with anxiety and caution wracking her bones.

"You 'eed somethin', sweet?" the bartender was leaning against the counter, and Lilith nearly jumped. "You keep watching me with those green eyes of yours."

Lilith didn't dare look up. She barely made a sound. "A drink," she swallowed, trying to calm her nerves. "Please."

She wasn't even sure he had heard her until he said. "There's more than one 'ind of drink, hun." He smiled, revealing his crooked teeth. "What ya want? Shots, martini, 'argarita, or just a plain beer." His voice was kind, she felt bad about how afraid she was at that moment.

"A shot." She didn't come here to enjoy a drink with friends, she came here to silence her brain with alcohol.

"A'right then!" the bartender exclaimed. He left and Lilith found herself frantically fiddling with her hands. She gazed around the room. At a nearby gambling table was a group of boys in their twenties glaring at one another. Each looked competitive enough to kill the next.

Beside them was a group of older men. One of them balanced a knife on his pointer finger. He had long, black hair and he wore a ripped leather jacket. His mouth released a puff of smoke as he took the burning cigarette from his lips.

She realized she had been staring a second too late. The man looked at her, then smiled and turned to his friends to laugh. Lilith didn't think she had ever been so scared.

"Here ya go!" the bartender said. He placed a small glass on the counter. Lilith reached into her pocket to grab the small amount of change Quilla had given her, but the bartender stopped her. "On the house!" he told her in a joyous tone. "I can tell when someone 'eeds a drink, and you, my friend," he smiled at her. "Definitely 'eed a drink."

That was the first drop of kindness anyone had given her in over a year. For a second her heart lit up. She nodded in thank you, then reached for the brown liquid.

A giant hand closed around the cup before hers had a chance to. The air smelled of leather and strong alcohol. Lilith looked up to see the man with the knife and cigarette. She felt her breath leave her. The man was standing over her; and he was close enough that she could feel his hot breath. A vicious smile curled around his lips and he showed his yellow, crooked teeth.

"Hey, little girl." He tipped his head back and drained her shot. "You were staring at me and my friends. Thought I might come over and have a... *chat*." With the last word his smile got bigger and his oily face closer.

"I- I'm good." Lilith stuttered. She felt fear climb up her bones as one thought flooded her head; *get back to your room*. She got up from her stool and tried to weave around the man.

He stepped in front of her. "You seem nervous," he told her. His friends were howling by the door. "I can help with that." Lilith winced as his hot breath hit her face. She stepped around him but he grasped her arm.

The feeling of rage was familiar. She tried to breathe. *No, not here, not now*! The last thing she wanted to do was cause a scene. *In and out*. She told herself, remembering the breathing technique her father had taught her. *In and out*. But the firm grasp of the man sent her brain into a spiral. She grit her teeth and lunged at the man.

Her fist hit his face and he doubled back. The flirty look changed into something similar to the look Lilith had on her face. "Oh." He looked more dangerous now. "Looks like we have a fighter."

The entire Link had turned to look at them. Fights were common, but this one seemed to grab some extra attention. *No*! Lilith thought. *No, this can't be happening*! But her mind had started spiraling. Anger crawled up her legs and entered her head. And once it was there, the emotion had control. Without thinking, she drew an arrow from her quiver. The weapon felt heavy in her hand; powerful. And that power was being controlled by pure, unfiltered rage.

She lunged at him. The man didn't even move. Just as the arrow was about to puncture his forehead, he grabbed her arm.

His grip was tight, cutting off her circulation. The air seemed too still and Lilith's eyes widened with fear. Then, she was slammed onto the ground.

Her face hit the floor with a crack. The arrow rolled out of her limp hand as she felt a weight on her neck. The man had placed his knee on her throat. She felt the air depleting from her lungs as she struggled the breathe. Cold sweat leaked from her pores, making her panic swell.

The Link erupted with laughter, while embarrassment erupted in Lilith. The anger had left her with nothing but useless shame.

The knee pressed deeper into her neck. Lilith gagged, her nails clawing at the ground. She needed air. She needed to sprint back to her room and hide. She needed to escape.

"*Stop!*" the cheering vanished as a crisp accent rang through the air. "She's mine."

The man stepped aside. "I'm so sorry." Fear quivered in his voice. Even though he was about a foot taller and at least twenty years older, the girl looked far more intimidating.

Quilla had a small black bag at her side. She was dressed in a cloak that almost made her invisible. But she was not invisible at this moment. She was very much seen.

She strode up to Lilith and grabbed her by the wrist. "Let's go!" her voice was fierce and laced with anger. Lilith gulped. She had saved her from the man, but whatever Quilla meant by "she's mine" couldn't be good.

Quilla led Lilith to her room. It was slightly bigger than her own, with a bed, desk, and window. It was one of the most tidy places Lilith had ever seen. The bedspread was black and the walls were plain gray.

Quilla took off her cloak and gave it to Lilith. "Hold this." She told her. Then she unstrapped the bag and pulled out a small safe. It was a stiff metal that Lilith could not identify. Quilla tried the lock a couple of times, punched the safe in frustration, and then proceeded to jam a knife into it. The safe clicked and swung open. Inside was a small golden cat. It looked old, but old enough to be valuable. Quilla grabbed the trinket with her long fingers and placed it in her own safe.

Lilith watched as she did this. Her legs shook with fear and embarrassment. She didn't know what was going to happen to her after Quilla was done with whatever she was doing, but in the meantime, she was perfectly content being Quilla's coat hanger for as long as possible.

"What was the end goal?" it took Lilith a second to realize Quilla was talking to her. "Hm?"

"What do you mean?" Lilith asked.

"I mean," Quilla took her coat from her and hung it on her desk chair. "What were you trying to accomplish by attacking him?"

Lilith opened her mouth to speak, then realized she didn't have the words. Why had she done that? "I guess I wanted to show him I wasn't weak."

"That would make sense." Quilla leaned against the desk. "But you are barely a fighter. You haven't practiced and most likely couldn't kill a duck if it sat on your feet. And on the off chance you did slam that arrow into his forehead, what would happen?" Quilla's black eyes bore into hers. She stared at her relentlessly, waiting for an answer.

"I don't know," Lilith told her. Shame was a blanket that covered her from head to toe. She kept her head down, trying to keep herself from crying.

"I think I might." Quilla strode around her. Her heels clicked against the ground. "You would be wrestled to the ground and pounded by his friends. If you were lucky, you would die quickly. If you weren't, well... you would be beaten, and some part of you would die. The last bit of morality. The side that lived; consumed with vengeance beyond caring about anyone or anything else other than taking down whoever hurt you."

Quilla lifted Lilith's chin with her long fingers. They saw eye to eye, but somehow Quilla felt so much taller than her. The smell of roses tinted the air. "The man's name is Polar Zinglor. He lives on the rich side of Hanslack, he and his friends come here every Friday evening to have a good time." Lilith clenched her teeth. Polar had hurt her, embarrassed her, scared her. That night she made a promise to herself. It didn't matter how much she hurt or how exhausted she was. Polar Zinglor would fall to his knees. She would be responsible, she would shoot him in the neck. And this time she would not *fail*.

"I'm going to kill him," Lilith told her. It was quiet. *Weak*! "I'm going to kill him!" she nearly yelled it. She was weak, but not for long.

Quilla smiled at her. It was cruel, her teeth like bloody fangs. "Never fight a fight you can't win, Lilith. Always challenge yourself, but never not win. Because if you don't survive, then you go down a failure! Your grudges go unresolved, they get away with hurting you." Quilla's eyes had narrowed as if remembering her own anger. "Grudges are a useful tool. Hate will fuel you, and a wounded ego will push you to achieve wonderful things!"

~~~

Lilith awoke with the sound of a blood-curdling scream, Quilla's past words still ringing in her ear. She was in a white bed that looked like it was more fitting in a hospital than a boat. The room's walls were decorated with several different types of wood Lilith could not name. The ceiling was high and blinding lights hung down from it. Her eyesight was slightly blurry, but it didn't matter. The sound of any potential danger had awoken her more than enough.

She sat up and immediately regretted it. A piercing pain rattled her as her hands sprang to the area in her stomach that had been wounded. She had her regular pants on but her shirt had been taken off. Bandages were tightly wrapped around her stomach.

Gritting her teeth, she stood. The pain felt as though something was eating her from the inside out. Her blurry gaze scanned the room, searching for her bow. Her eyes landed on a small dresser by the door. She ran over and swung open the doors.

There, on top of a set of pillows, was her bow and arrows. They were black with colored stripes that caressed the sides. Lilith laid her hands on the soft wood and slowly lifted the weapon. She was no longer weak. She was dangerous.
~~~

Lilith hurried out the door, arrows ready and loaded for whatever danger may be waiting. The rain hammered down on the wood deck, the cold droplets felt like little needles piercing her skin. Through the gray skies, she saw the familiar posture of the Stripes. She hadn't a clue how they got on the ship or avoided Quilla enough to stay a secret for so long, but they were dead now.

Nikolai and Quilla had emerged from a polished trap door. Lilith and her partner made eye contact, then, through silent understanding, ran towards each other.

Lilith bent down on one knee and held out both hands. Quilla's shoe planted in her palms and Lilith launched her into the air. Quilla's knives were drawn like claws. She sprang a few feet in the air then fell in the center of chaos. Her knives cut through the enemy's skin like bread as wine-colored blood sprayed from the opening. Lilith watched from afar. Quilla's eyes were focused but fired with anger. Her hands moved in precise, powerful swings.

Lilith stood in a daze until she saw a man holding a knife running towards her. She quickly drew back her bowstring, letting go just in time. The arrow landed in his chest and the cherry-red liquid poured out of his lifeless body. Before, Lilith would have flinched or screamed at something like that. Now, it filled her with ugly pride.

With blood on her face and bow in hand, she rushed to join Quilla. Her arms moved without command, fingers squeezing the weapon, eyes trained on the target.

"Duck!" Quilla shouted at her. She did as was told and one of Quilla's knives came whizzing towards her. It passed over her and landed in the throat of a small, mouse-like Stripe. "You should be resting." Quilla rasped, suddenly a lot closer than before.

Lilith turned to look at her. There was that look in her eyes, the dangerous one. It was the same one that crossed her face when they had first met and she told Quilla her name. The same one glittered when Lilith showed anger. It was familiar, yet, it never seemed to get less scary. "Kinda hard when there's a gang fight outside my door."

Several Stripes came charging towards them. Quilla slid between one's legs, her body low and spread like a spider. Once on the other side she stood and stabbed each one between the shoulder blades.

Lilith, on the other hand, twirled around the boat, stopping only for a split second to fire. Her aim was flawless, puncturing the skin wherever she had intended. She found the mast and used it as a shield for any incoming arrows. A few hit the polished wood, but she wasn't hurt yet.

Quilla slid down the mast. Lilith had no idea how she had gotten up there, but she was a master at doing things unnoticed. The fire in her black eyes burned bright. "Go long and short."

Quilla charged into the battlefield. Her knives slashed as many enemies as she could. Lilith hit the remaining from a distance. She climbed the ladder to get a better view. People were fighting left and right. Near the cabin, a group of Nikolai's men were fighting the mouse-like Stripes. The Stripes fought aggressively, but their technique was flawed and the many mistakes and holes in their craft left many windows for Nikolai's men to attack. But they didn't. In fact, they looked as though they were trying to stay on defense. It was as if to them, the goal of the fight was to get everyone out alive. She turned to look at Nikolai.

He had his long blades drawn but was only using them to block. He was fighting with the same style as his crew. His moves? Flawless. Technique? Genius. But it looked as though he was holding back his potential. Then it hit her. Nikolai Lone had the same problem she once had. He was afraid to kill.

Lilith decided to do him a favor. She pulled back her bowstring and shot at a man trying to stab him. The arrow hit him in the chest and cherry blood flooded from the wound. Nikolai looked up. His fists clenched in anger, but sorrow quickly replaced it as he gazed at the man.

Lilith turned away. The way his eyes sank reminded her of herself, alone in the Link. She would flinch every time someone was punched, let alone killed. But she had gotten used to it. In the moment she could kill without hesitation. But once the adrenaline was gone she would remember all the blood on her hands and her guilt would catch up to her. She would sometimes lose her appetite, start bawling at random times, or when it got really bad she would throw up, remembering the warm blood on her fingers. It was something she would never forget.

She turned to look at Quilla. Her knives were out, hands flying like birds, eyes focused. She looked dangerous. If someone were to disturb her, they would either be ignored or stabbed. Lilith marveled at her skill. The dedication that she put into her craft and her vengeance was either remarkable or disturbing. Nothing would phase her in battle or just in life. She would not be knocked off track. No force, no matter how big or how powerful, would distract her from her mission.

Quilla suddenly broke from her mesmerizing trance. Her knives rested in her hands and her hair blew over her eyes, like a flag that had been cut into a thousand little strands. Her eyes set on one man.

He was skinny, and the cloak he wore was loose on his body. His eyes were tired and deprived of hope. Wrinkled joints bent in unusual ways. He was old. Too old to be playing this wretched game. Yet here he was. A reminder of what happens to them when they fail. When they don't escape from Hanslack's prison of crime, they end up old, hopeless, a failure.

Lilith slid down from the ladder. Her bow was ready with an arrow. Her legs took long strides. Her green eyes locked with the man's gray ones, glares focusing on each of their gazes. He pulled down his hood to give them a better look at his exhausted face. "Afternoon, Thorne, Cole."

Despite his friendly tone, this man was no friend. Lilith lifted her chin. "Afternoon, Olan."

Chapter Ten
Nikolai

Nikolai was good at fighting. He could handle his two small swords better than anyone. His feet moved entirely on instinct and his hands struck in the right places at the right time.

But being good at something is so much different than liking it. If it was up to him, he would be a writer. But he wasn't one. He could never be one. The rebellion didn't need a writer. They needed a fighter. A person who would lead them to an almost impossible victory. And unfortunately, he was born into that role.

They were all relying on him. He was the one that would lead them to victory. The White King. That was his nickname. He was destined to rule, destined to overthrow and kill Ghan. The prodigy trained hard from birth. You've heard about the chosen one in books. But Nikolai wasn't like that. The chosen one had fun as a child. There was a point where they were happy and innocent before everything went wrong. But him? He was born with unreasonable expectations on his shoulders.

Of course, there was competition. Her name was Tnil; she was incredibly skilled and wanted to be good. She wanted the leadership position. Not her parents, just her. And Nikolai would have given it to her if it wasn't for his father. He wanted Nikolai to bring honor and fame to their name. If he didn't succeed, if he didn't become the best, then he wouldn't get his father's approval, his father's *love*.

So that was what he craved most in life, his father's very conditional love. He made sure he was practicing before and after Tnil, which turned out to be a very difficult task. Sometimes they would be in the training facility until midnight, just waiting for the other to leave. Nikolai's young eight-year-old self had learned how to run on four hours of sleep, and still pull off things any grown man couldn't do with a full night's rest.

He remembered when he and Tnil had become so good that the League hired arguably the best trainer on the planet. Nikolai was fifteen at the time. He remembered every detail about the day. It was raining outside, he had slightly undercooked eggs for breakfast and his father spent the entire morning staring at him with angry, expectant eyes. He got to the training facility at about six in the morning. Tnil arrived at about the same time.

Her white hair was pulled into a high ponytail, and she wore tight, black clothes that highlighted her muscled body. They glanced at each other as they walked into the training ring, competition buzzing inside them.

The training ring was a circle, its high walls littered with climbing holes and unusual tools such as a coil of string or a paintbrush. Nikolai felt his hands stiffen, he was not ready to do any climbing.

Tnil stood in the light, her eyes like daggers. She knew. He knew. This was it. The final fight. The deciding moment. Nikolai clenched his fists. It was her or him, their lives would never be the same. The trainer came to the middle of the ring. He stepped between him and Tnil.

Nikolai expected the greatest trainer in Thine to be terrifying. Or, at least he expected him to be collected and poised. Instead, he found himself gazing at a man who would have been more fitted for a nightclub than a fighting match.

The man smelled of strong perfume. His manicured hands were as perfect as could be, not even the smallest chip in the polish. The long robes that hung off him swayed when his tall heels clicked against hard concrete.

"Morning." His Salenian accent was thick and crisp. "My name is Killen Sealock. I suppose you two are eager to fight, given the way you are looking at each other." He was right, he and Tnil had locked glares a while ago. "So I'll go through the rules quickly. Don't go outside the training ring, don't bring any tools or weapons from outside the ring into the ring, and please don't kill each other." The master gazed at his manicured nails. "That's a lot of paperwork that I *don't* want to deal with."

Nikolai looked at him with curious eyes. Killen was certainly out of the ordinary. The master raised his hand, and both of the opponents dropped into a fighting stance. With one smooth motion, Killen swung his hand down. The fight had begun.

All the nervousness faded. Nikolai's legs raced to the nearest piece of string. Tnil raced along the other side. He hoisted himself along the wall, even the nearest coil of string was placed in a ridiculously obscure location. It was obvious this course was made for the best of the best.

Nikolai scaled the wall with his athletic body, but in these types of training situations he had used chalk, but there was none here. He now understood Tnil's idea of limiting her resources, she was better prepared. It just hit him now that Tnil had trained for this. She had the advantage.

Tnil had retrieved a piece of string and was heading for him. There was a paintbrush in her other hand. Nikolai had planned to strangle her until it was either tap out or die, he couldn't imagine what terrible plan she had for him with those materials.

Tnil jumped and grabbed Nikolai by the waist. He felt his hand slip off the tiny hold he had on the wall as he fell to the ground, landing with a thump. His head hurt and his heart was pounding. His vision went blurry and for a half second, he was completely disabled. Half a second too long. Tnil and pounced on top of him. She quickly turned him onto his back and held the string around his neck. *So what's the brush for?* He could handle being choked, but Tnil was smart. She had something bigger up her sleeve.

He knew exactly what she was planning when he felt a sharp pain between his shoulder blades. A pressure point! He felt his legs go numb. The pain was unbearable. A screech ripped from his throat. It took all of his willpower to stop himself from tapping out, and when he didn't, Tnil pressed harder.

She leaned over and whispered in his ear, "It's been a pleasure, Nikolai. Really, I'm always up for a challenge." She pressed the paintbrush harder into his back. "Just remember, I work harder, train harder. I am better!"

And at that moment he knew she was right. Tnil wanted to be a leader, she wanted the crown. It wasn't Nikolai who wanted to rule, but his father. At that moment, he knew she was right. Tnil had the motivation. She had the drive. He only had the threat of his father not loving him back.

Then he saw him. His father was giving him probably the most intense stare he had ever been given. And at that moment he knew his father's heart was water in freezing temperatures. If he failed, it would be frozen and would never thaw. It was up to him to warm the temperatures, and he knew there was only one way to do that. He then recognized there was something more powerful than drive. A father's love, and the threat of it being pulled away.

With all his strength he lunged and grabbed a tuft of white Tnil's hair.

~~~

A seventeen-year-old Nikolai grabbed the attacking criminal's hair. It was greasy and he hollered as his head was yanked. Nikolai jammed his blade into his shoulder. The hood hollered and crumpled to the ground. *He'll be fine.* Nikolai told himself. He had to believe it.

Two more men came rushing at him, their tiny blades clutched in their hands. Nikolai swung his sword at them. The first one ducked and the blade flew right over him. The other one wasn't as lucky. The tip of his sword sliced his throat open like a fruit. Hot, sticky blood sprayed Nikolai in the face as he fought back a wave of nausea. While he was in this state of panic the first hood pounced on him. He felt his hot breath in his ear. Even though he couldn't see, he could tell a knife was about to be impaled in his back.
~~~

He quickly turned and stabbed the hood in the heart. Just then, three more men came rushing at him. It was like they would never stop coming. He felt his sword brim flesh and he silently prayed that it wasn't lethal.

The mix of rain and blood had caused him to go nearly blind. He could sense their movements, and that's how he fought off two of three criminals. The sudden presence of tar-smelling air told him to swing his blade. As soon as he felt the sticky flesh he knew he aimed right.

The third hood came rushing at him, but this one was smarter. He knew how to move without being traced, and that was the reason he had pounced on Nikolai. He didn't seem too heavy, or strong. He felt old, scrawny, weak. But the hood knocked the hilt of his knife against Nikolai's head. Blackness creeped along the edges of his vision but he willed it back. Something sharp scraped his arm and he felt his own hot blood pouring out.

Cold fear rushed over him as the hood dug the knife deeper into his skin. Death was a dear friend, but he wasn't ready for a formal greeting yet.

Suddenly the weight of the thief was lifted from his body. His vision cleared as he saw Rex battling the man. His moves were swift and precise, a determined gaze layered his eyes. Nikolai didn't think he had ever seen his friend so eager to kill someone.

Rex's knife penetrated the hood's torso rather quickly. Shiny, thick blood came gushing out as he twisted the knife farther into the flesh. The criminal let out a spurt of coughs, and blood flew out of his mouth. Then he crumpled to the ground, all the life and anger leaving his eyes.

Nikolai stood, looking at Rex. The two made eye contact, just for a split second. Then he flashed a smile to his crewmate. A silent thank you.

His hand brushed away the blood and water limiting his vision. He scanned the area. Bodies lay everywhere, blood and water had mixed and covered the ship with a deluded red liquid. The rain came down hard and the sea was choppy.

He turned his gaze to the cabin. There, he saw Thorne facing a lean man who looked like he was in his seventies, he was wrapped in a cloak that almost consumed his bony body. His long gray hair flapped in the wind and his empty eyes were highlighted with the rain.

Lilith ran towards them, her messy braid flying behind her. The rain pounded on both of the girl's heads but their faces were straight as the horizon.

Nikolai ran to them. The rain was soft pebbles pounding on his face. He felt his hand tighten around the hilt of his sword. "Who is he?" Nikolai asked through panting breaths. Lilith and Thorne didn't shift their gaze from the man.

"What do you want, Olan?" Thorne spoke with confidence, not a quiver in her voice. Nikolai's head swarmed with thoughts. Somehow he had forgotten Thorne had enemies, and that man was one of them. He didn't seem very dangerous. He was slim, wrinkly, and old. He seemed like he belonged on a porch, watching people walk by as he gently swayed in a rocking chair.

"What do I want?" Olan spat. Then he started to giggle. At first, Nikolai could hardly hear the small laugh. But then it escalated. Louder and louder until Nikolai felt the urge to step and run. "What do I want? I'll tell you what I want, Miss Thorne! I want to see the fear in you and your partner's eyes as my knife digs through your sinner face! This charade has gone on long enough, and I will not be bested by a couple of overconfident, cruel bastards!"

Nikolai expected some sort of reaction from the two criminals. But instead, they kept their gaze steady, arms by their side, weapons resting in their palms. Only the hint of a smile curled on Lilith's lips as she spoke in an unbelievably tranquil tone.

"Oh, Olan." She said, "You have no idea who overconfident, cruel bastards have bested." With those words, the two lunged. Their movements were synchronized, it looked as if even their hearts beat in sink. Olan's men charged at them. Thorne killed silently whereas Lilith's bow made a surprising amount of noise.

Suddenly, Lilith got down on a knee, stretching her hands to make a step. Thorne's slightly heeled boot landed on her hands, and with one swift motion, Lilith flung her in the air. Thorne looked like a bird taking flight. Her knives clicked out like claws. Thorne landed in the center of the crowd without a sound. Her knives slashed, killing with one motion. Lilith was running back and forth, shooting from the outskirts. She never missed. It was like dancing, beautiful. Nikolai had never wanted to vomit more.

Lilith progressed further and further towards the madness. Arrows were flying, and though Nikolai couldn't see her entire face, something about the energy she was displaying told him she was smiling.

Through the thicket of madness, Lilith somehow got hurled back, smashing into Nikolai. She quickly recovered. Her braid was messy, and the red strand that was woven into her hair seemed to match the blood that was splattered on her face. Her green eyes glittered with excitement. Nikolai guessed she healed quickly because he had almost forgotten she had been shot before. And from the looks of it, she had forgotten too.

"Whenever you want to join in, feel free!" she said in a somewhat spiteful tone, then bounded back to join Thorne in the fight. Nikolai hadn't realized he had been completely stunned. His father's voice boomed in his head, scolding him for his mistake. He shook his hands, trying to cut loose the criticism. His hand tightened around the hilt of his long blade as his legs ran towards the chaos.

The fight was messy, men lay wounded, getting trampled by incoming traffic. Nikolai hated every second of it. But he supposed he better get used to it. After all, he was about to become very close business partners with the queen of con and possibly the best archer in Thine.

Through the mess of sweaty street fighters, he saw Olan. The old man was surprisingly graceful when it came to fighting. His movements were all voluntary, steady, but quick. He saw the crowd lighten as more of the men turned to fight Lilith. For a moment he watched Thorne. She was fighting three people at once, and yet, she still looked bored. Her knives swung in various movements. Sometimes, she would throw one of her silver blades. Her aim was as close to perfect as it got, splattering blood around deadly areas.

Nikolai was very sidetracked today. So much so that he didn't see two hoods with very heavy footsteps charging at him. He righted himself quickly, stepping aside just as a switchblade was jabbed in his general direction. He swung his blade along one of the hood's legs. The criminal screamed and fell to his knees.

The second one lunged for Nikolai, but this time he was ready. He stepped out of the way in a graceful stride. He gently put his two swords in their hilts and clasped his hands behind his back. The hood pounced, but Nikolai dodged. A playful smile spread across his lips as the criminal charged again, all his weight going in one direction. All Nikolai had to do was step aside, and the man went flying past him. Laughter bubbled in his throat. It was cruel, but somehow it felt so good. He decided he had enough as he drew his swords and slashed across the man's chest. Blood splattered against his face and the nauseating guilt returned.

Nikolai turned to see Thorne and Olan engaged in a duel. Thorne's hair clip had come out and her long, wild hair whipped in the wind. She spun around Olan while he barely dodged her attacks. The old man was backing away as she slashed her many blades. His feet stumbled over each other as he covered his eyes with his arms. The heavy rainfall must have been taking a toll on him as well. The fighter that Nikolai saw in the old man was gone, instead, he looked terrified in the presence of Thorne, shrunken.

Olan kept stepping back until he ran into the mast. He stuttered and tried to turn, but Thorne saw her opportunity. Her knife flew and caught his white shirt in the wood. Olan's other arm reached to set his sleeve loose, but before that another knife pinned him to the mast. Two more were thrown at his ankles, making him completely stuck.

Thorne flipped her loose hair back, straightened her coat, and beamed. "Well," she chimed. "Are we having fun yet?"

Chapter Eleven
Quilla

Quilla's boots clicked as she approached Olan. His face strained as he tried to free himself from her knives. As his eyes fixed on her, his expression changed from confused to angry.

"You!" he spat. "I'll kill you and everyone you love!"

Quilla simply laughed. She leaned closer to him, feeling his hot, panicked breath on her cheek. "That's the thing," she told him. "I don't love anyone." The words rolled off her tongue so easily, like she was only stating a fact.

"You make terrible, terrible threats. Try to be 'oh so scary.'" Quilla felt anger rising. Olan was a man she had been quarreling with quite often. Over the years he had become less a threat and more an obstacle. She was quite eager to be rid of him.

"Well, you should rethink your goals." She said calmly, trying to keep the anger and grief down. "Everyone I love is already dead." The words came out of her mouth emotionless, her accent adding a crisp to their tone.

For the smallest moment, Quilla felt like collapsing into a ball of tears. *Compose yourself, Thorne!* These angry words seemed to bring her calm, emotionless aroma back to her. Quilla straightened her back and ran a couple of fingers through her messy hair. "As for killing me. There have been countless people who have made that promise. Screamed it in my face, sent a letter, or even whispered it. Do you know how many succeeded?" Quilla held up a fist. "None."

Olan's teeth were tightly pressed together. His eyes were slits of flame. "You're angry," Quilla observed. "Usually, that's my favorite quality in people. But I've had a very long day of fighting you ignoramuses and I'm extremely tired." She yawned, then pulled a serrated knife from her black trenchcoat, balancing it on her finger. Olan's expression shifted and fear clouded his eyes. "Today, I just find that kind of rage quite aggravating. So, for the time being, I'm going to be doing the talking."

Quilla drew in a deep breath, then grabbed Olan by the collar. "I'm going to ask once. Why did you attack our ship?"

Olan's lips quivered but never opened. Quilla let out a sigh, she wasn't in the mood for this kind of thing at the moment. She tightened her grip on the blade, tracing it along Olan's shoulders.

"Stop!" Lone's voice boomed through the air. "You don't torture on *my* ship."

Quilla turned to look at him. His posture was straight, eyes focused. "Would you rather be oblivious and vulnerable to another potential attack?"

"I would rather we don't resort to cruel tactics just to extract information."

"In that case, you shouldn't have hired me."

Quilla and Lone stood there glaring for a while. Then she grit her teeth, and turned to Olan. "Why were we attacked?"

With Olan's silence, she snapped. She picked him up by the collar. The knives that held him to the mast clattered to the ground. Quilla threw him to the floor of the ship, planting her boot on his chest. Next to her was a cinder block. She picked it up and hurled it onto Olan's arm. An ear-splitting *crack* told her the bone had shattered.

The old man screamed in pain. But Quilla was far from done. She lifted the stunned Olan and held him over the railing. "Last chance! Why did you attack our ship?"

The anger had completely drained from Olan's face. He looked scared. Quilla was holding his life in her hands, and she liked it. His white hair blew in the wind as well as his tears. The rough ocean sent waves to splash his feet. His chin wobbled with the fear of Quilla dropping him into the cruel ocean.

"It was the authorities!" he sobbed. "The ones dedicated to finding you! They took my son! Please, Quilla! I had no choice!" he had never called her *Quilla* before. Or begged. But she had waited for this day for a long time.

Quilla shrugged and started to set him on the deck until he started to speak again.

"I can get you a slave! The Grave Desert has tons. I'll pay for it! It can help with your bidding. Do your dirty work!" a shaky smile spread across Olan's face. But Quilla was nowhere near smiling. Anger burned with every word he spoke. She narrowed her eyes and swung him over the side of the boat.

Olan realized his mistake quickly. "No no no! Quilla, please! I-"

Quilla turned away, eyes on the floor. "Your son is better off without a cruel father like you." Her hand released his shirt and he fell with a splash and a scream.

Quilla walked towards the others. Lone's mouth was wide open in shock, as were his crews. They looked as though their jaws would break free from the rest of their faces and clatter to the floor. But it was Lilith who had Quilla's attention. Lilith's eyes bore into hers with an unreadable expression. Disbelief, maybe? Her loose braid flapped in the wind, the red streak matching the dried blood that was splattered on her face. Their gazes locked for a split second. Then they both turned to look at the floor.

Quilla thought that if she had to stare at Lone's useless crew gaping at her any longer she might hurl. "Well?" she asked. "Are you fatuous imbeciles going to just stand there or are you going to clean this mess?" this time, they didn't hesitate to follow orders. Scrambling to grab a broom, towel, or any other thing that could wipe up blood. Some just took off their fancy shirts and started mopping with that.

Lone ran to join them but Quilla stopped him. "We need to explain what needs to be done when we reach land." Lone nodded, but his glare was fierce, and obviously meant for her. Quilla didn't mind though. Many people had shot her glares throughout her life. That was how she knew she was doing her job right.

"Lilith, we need to show you some maps," Quilla told her. Lilith strode towards her, and that was when Quilla noticed she was only wearing a bra. Her stomach was strong, but she couldn't help but notice the scars that ran across her back. The area where she had been shot was heavily wrapped in bandages.

Lone held open the trapdoor for them. He looked like a waiter at one of the fancy restaurants they had in Hanslack.

"You look pathetic," Quilla told him flatly.

"You just hurled a man off a ship. I think 'pathetic' in your eyes might be a good thing."

"Well, in that case let me reword my sentence," Quilla retorted. "You look as though you're bowing to a helpless princess. I don't know what you usually do with Windlem, but I just threw a man off a ship. So I find it hard to believe that Prince Charming is the way to act around me."

Lone laughed, sensing her annoyance. Then he deepened his voice and sang, "Beautiful young ladies, may I?" he bent over, trying to hold Lilith's hand to kiss it. She moved it with a jolt and slapped his face.

"So charming!" she had a light, delicate laugh that was unfortunately contagious. Soon Lone was laughing, and to her disgust, so was she.

"Thorne! You can laugh?" Lone asked in disbelief.

Quilla shoved him, sending Lilith into another cackling spree. She quickly slid down the ladder. The others followed shortly, still overcome with giggles.

Lilith came to the map and started to trace her hand along the possible exits and entrances. Her eyes were strained with focus, and Quilla didn't dare disturb her. She had trained the archer herself to read maps and form escape plans.

The key to a successful plan is to be cautious. Never run into one of these situations without a way out. Because if you are sloppy, you won't come out breathing. That was Quilla's advice to the archer, and from what it looked like, it was working. Lilith's green eyes were concentrated on the map, boring into every possibility.

She suddenly looked up. "Vents."

Lone's mouth dropped, but Quilla simply nodded. "You and I have two minutes in the corridor to get the information we need and get out. Guards come on the dot, so we need to be swift."

Lilith started to walk to the files room on the map, then collapsed to her knees, clutching her stomach. "Ah! That was sudden."

Quilla hated herself for rushing over to help her. She wasn't supposed to care. Instead, she felt her hand grasp Lilith's arm and her second hand land on her chest to stabilize.

"You aren't completely healed," Lone told her. "You need to rest, we can do this another time."

"I'm fine," Lilith told him, then removed her hand from her stomach.

Quilla drew in a sharp breath and her hand immediately flew to Lilith's stomach. Red, thick blood had soaked through the bandages. "We need to wrap this up. Now!"

She and Lone helped Lilith get to her feet. She consistently insisted that she could walk on her own, but thankfully, Lone kept threatening to order her to bed rest until there was barely a scar. Quilla had her hands around Lilith's warm body. They each took sharp breaths and Quilla held out her shaky hands for Lilith to lean on. They walked in silence, hearts in sync, not daring to talk about the events of the day and the later events to come.

Chapter Twelve
Alohi

With all her strength, which wasn't much, Alohi swung her pickaxe into the hard wall of the cave. Sweat beaded on her skin and she was panting. It felt like she had been mining for hours, but common sense told her it had barely been ten minutes. Even if she did do anything more than chip the rocks, she wouldn't know what to do after.

She would have asked the other inmates, but they were eerily unresponsive. The once loud, obnoxious prisoners were now quiet and submissive. It was as though someone had flicked a switch, and now these men were completely different people.

She slammed her pickaxe into the hard cave wall. A tiny piece of rock chipped away and fell to the ground. Behind it, was a small piece of red, translucent stone.

Alohi squinted at the rock. It was something that she had never seen before. The redness was enchanting, its sparkle shone in the dim light of the cave. She ran her fingers along the transparent stone, the soft touch felt relieving against her rough skin.

"You should hide that." Alohi nearly jumped when the rasp sounded behind her. "People around here are willing to kill to get that kind of stone." She turned around to see an old man leaning against the stone next to her. His skin hung off his bones like a piece of wrinkly cloth, and the blue tint it gave told her that he was not healthy.

"Who are you?" her voice was smaller than she meant it.

"Nathaniel." He whispered as he stroked his long, snow-white beard. "And you?"

Skepticism ran over her like a cold shiver. The people in here were far from nice to her, and it wouldn't surprise her if this man had an ulterior motive. Then again, he was old and frail. It didn't look like he could pack a punch if he tried.

"Alohi." Her voice had gotten louder, just above a whisper.

Nathaniel's eyes widened as she said the name. "Quiet!" the whisper was rushed and panicked, but still silent. "If they hear us talking we'll get beaten."

Alohi clasped a hand over her mouth, afraid to speak again.

Nathaniel ran his deathly thin finger along the red rock. "This is what the Empire uses to power their trains. The amount of raw energy in a grain of sand alone is worth at least a thousand kangue, but this..." He peered at the transparent rock. "Is worth about a small fortune."

"So what do I do with it?"

Nathaniel's blank eyes drifted to small train tracks on the far side of the cave. "Minecarts come every few minutes, anything you find that seems useful is put in there."

Alohi looked at the tracks. "Where do they go?"

Nathaniel shrugged. "Outside, I'd assume. I don't know the specifics."

She furrowed her brow. "Hypothetically, could a human fit in these carts?"

A small gasp came from Nathaniel's chapped lips. "You can't possibly be considering..."

"Look," her voice was surprisingly confident. "You've clearly been here for a long time, no offense. Don't you want to get out? This may have become your reality, but it doesn't have to be!" the power of words had risen with her. Since she was a kid, she had learned that knives could kill, but phrases were more effective. The power of persuasion was one that she used often in the League of Red Doves. She didn't see why she couldn't use it here. "I don't want to spend the rest of my days in this hellhole, and I don't see why you have to."

Nathaniel fiddled with his beard. "There's a lot you don't know."

"So tell me!" the words were louder than she wanted them to be.

The old man sighed, and Alohi thought she might have seen pain touch his face. "It's not like people haven't tried." He rasped. "You're right, I have been here for a long time, which means I've seen a lot. There were tons of people like you that came in here. As soon as they landed in this sand pit they wanted out. And trust me, Alohi, the fate they received for trying isn't worth it."

Alohi looked at the sand. When she squinted, she could see blood-red taint that colored the little grains. "So they got caught."

"Caught," he lifted his frail hands, as though weighing a scale. "Killed. It depends on the scenario."

Alohi's eyes were still trained on the tracks. They looked shiny and new, with no evidence that any deaths had taken place on them. "Has anyone ever tried to get out using the rails?"

Nathaniel took a breath. "Not that I am aware of." His gaze then shifted to the other prisoners. "But then again, most of these people wouldn't fit."

"But we can!" Alohi pleaded. "If no one has ever tried this way before, that means no one would expect it. They would think prisoners wouldn't fit in the minecarts, but we're small enough."

"I'm not." The deep voice rang somewhere behind them. Alohi's head whipped around to see the prisoner who punched her in the cafeteria.

Without her permission, her arms swung the pickaxe over her shoulder, ready to attack if he got any closer.

The inmate just laughed at her. "Really?" he raised an eyebrow. "I've been watching you swing that thing into the wall. Even on the off chance you hit me, I doubt you would leave more than a scratch."

Alohi kept the pickaxe above her shoulder, not moving a muscle.

"Besides," the prisoner started again. "I'm not interested in hurting you. All I want is to be included in your little escape plan."

"There's no plan to be included in," Nathaniel told him.

"Yeah," Alohi joined, surprised at how calm she sounded. "You heard wrong."

The inmate raised his dark eyebrows again. "I'll let the prison guards figure that out while torturing you." Alohi tightened her grip on the pickaxe. "I've seen it before, and so have you. Haven't you, old man?"

Nathaniel's tired eyes lit up with flames. "What's your name?"

"Joshua."

Alohi looked at him. Although he had been a filthy excuse for a human being before, there was nothing but honesty in his gaze. For a second, she figured the sparkle in his eyes was pleading. He wanted to get out of this hellhole as much as she did. Even though he was morally twisted, who wasn't in this world?

"Fine." She told him. "But you don't talk about this to anyone, understand?"

Joshua's face turned to stone, a cold gaze drifting over his eyes. "I don't take orders from a politician."

Alohi cocked her head. "Really?" she could feel her tone growing more agitated by the second. "Then I may have overestimated your intelligence."

Joshua kept his glare centered on her. "What did you say?"

Alohi crossed her arms. She felt the power rising in her throat as the words formed on her tongue. It was a power she had become accustomed to, one that had saved her countless times. "Well at first I thought your brain was the size of a piece of gravel. But now I imagine it as a pebble found at the bottom of a river. Small and smooth." A cruel smile spread across her lips. "Just like you."

Anger flared on Joshua's face as his single brain cell put together that her metaphor was referring to his noticeably bald head. "You politicians are all the same."

Alohi sighed. "I'm not going to argue about the morality of my profession, for that's a battle I cannot win. But I can say that if you tell a soul, I will run crying to the guards about a big, tall man who's planning an escape attempt."

Nathaniel and Joshua looked at her in disbelief. They both knew that if she told the guards *anything*, they would believe her because of her small size and stature. However, Joshua starting an escape plan would be highly believable.

The muscular inmate took a breath. "You wouldn't."

Alohi leaned against her pickaxe. "Are you really willing to take that chance?"

There were blank stares for a second, then she broke the silence. "We meet at dinner to discuss our plans. I'll find you. Don't be late."

Chapter Thirteen
Lilith

Lilith had never felt so awkward.

She felt like every breath she took could lead to the entire ship blowing up. She didn't dare speak; she might say something to make Quilla feel uncomfortable, when she already looked as though she would burst out of the room in embarrassment.

Quilla was standing by the door, fiddling with her hands. She was glaring, but she was always doing that. Her jaw looked tense, as if she was trying to launch it out of its socket. She kept pacing, sometimes coming closer to the bed Lilith was sitting on, then retreating back to the door. It was like a threshold she didn't want to cross. One second she looked like a kindhearted nurse helping a patient, the next she angled herself toward the waiting door.

Lilith was perched on the bed with a roll of bandages. She kept meeting Quilla's gaze, just a split second. Then both their eyes shot to the floor. She felt delirious, like this was a dream. Then again, the massive wound probably wasn't helping.

"I like Nikolai." She finally said to break the silence.

"I don't."

Lilith laughed awkwardly, "He made you laugh! I've never seen you laugh like that!"

Quilla spun and looked her right in the eyes. "*You* made me laugh." Her voice was serious, direct, and scary.

Lilith's eyes were wide. "Okay." She took her focus back to stopping the blood. "Thanks, I guess."

Quilla nodded and turned away, retreating to her distant demeanor.

They heard a yell coming from the front of the ship. Panic and possible scenarios rushed through her head. She tried to get up, but Quilla placed a heavy hand on her shoulder, keeping her from moving any further. Their faces were so close. Quilla's lips opened in a little split. Her eyes were wide with emotion that Lilith couldn't identify. They both took slow breaths and the air became still. For a moment they were left staring into each other, then Quilla's face hardened. She turned away. "Stay here."

Lilith sunk back into the bed. Quilla turned and ran in the direction of the scream. She rested her head on the crinkly pillow and exhaled, staring up at the ceiling. It seemed to swirl.

There was a bang and Lilith sat up. Nikolai was standing in the doorway, his eyes bright with anticipation.

"We're almost there!" he exclaimed. "You can see it!"

Lilith leaped out of bed and ran onto the deck. The rain still poured hard, and the wind blew her hair in front of her. Quilla was standing on the opposite side of the ship. Her curly, long hair blew to one side as she gazed at the oncoming land. It was an island. Rocks that seemed to fall from its high cliffs that lined the shore. Waves crashed, making a splash and sometimes a large boom.

"You... grew up here?" Lilith asked Nikolai, who was buzzing nearby.

"Yep!" he said, trying to untie a rope that was laced to the mast. His fingers struggled to creep under the tight knot. Lilith sighed and pulled the rope to loosen it.

Nikolai walked to the taffrail. "Home sweet home." He sighed. His eyes, that just a second ago were full of hope, had now dimmed and seemed to be dreading their arrival. Lilith guessed he had some unresolved conflicts at his rocky home.

"What's it like?" she asked.

"Big, white, bright, filled with perfectionists." He turned his gaze to the water.

"Huh," Lilith looked at him. His white shirt, which was once so clean and perfect, was now stained with blood and ripped. His hair, which was once combed to make you think a strand could never fall out of place, was messy and ragged. "So, if it's so bright and white, why the Red Doves?"

Nikolai chuckled. "Thorne wasn't the only one who did her research." He looked at her. "The dove symbolizes hope, and the red is the horror that we will go through to bring it. It's supposed to say that we will bring down Emperor Ghan, whatever the cost."

"Her name is Quilla." Lilith had turned away. She didn't know why she cared. Quilla probably didn't care. But for some reason, first name basis was very important to her.

"I don't think she would find it so enjoyable if I started calling her that." He said with a laugh.

"Would you call me Cole?"

"No, I'll call you Lilith, but somehow, Thorne seems more..." He paused, thinking of the word, "Prickly."

Lilith burst out laughing. "Prickly?" she managed through breaths. "Why is that so perfect?"

Nikolai was cackling now. "She's like a cactus!" joy spread all over his face. "You touch her once and there's thorns in your finger for weeks!"

Lilith was leaning on a barrel for support now. "I wonder if beyond those thorns is a sweet, soft, fruity inside?"

Nikolai had stopped giggling, but a new laugh had taken his place. It was crude, dry, and unsettlingly familiar.

Quilla stood in front of them, holding an orange, and a knife. Her laugh stopped with a jolt. "Unlike a cactus, my thorns can attack without hesitation. A cactus remains still, waiting for its prey to become vacuous enough to land on its thorns. I don't wait for my prey to land on my knives, my knives slice into the quickest, smartest, most skilled prey. Because also unlike a cactus, there is no one as skilled, cunning, or ambitious as me. I am one of a kind!" Quilla tossed the orange in the air, then threw the knife. It sliced the orange mid-air and stuck clean into the barrel. The slices rolled at Lilith's feet. Quilla retrieved the knife and put it back in her jacket. Quilla then loomed over her partner. Lilith could smell roses. Quilla's long, brown, curly hair brushed her face. Her black eyes bored into her green ones. "Oh, and don't worry about the sweet, soft inside, because that was burned a long, long time ago."

Quilla's words pierced into her. Even as she turned and left, every thought that lingered in her mind wondered who had set fire to whatever soft side the criminal prodigy once had.

Chapter Fourteen
Nikolai

Nikolai was in the flashback again.

Tnil hollered as fifteen-year-old him yanked her snow-white hair. He pulled her back and she landed on the training mat, panting.

Nikolai didn't waste any time. He grabbed the string Tnil had retrieved from the wall and turned, but his opponent had vanished. Panic rushed over him. He felt his heart speed up, his fingers curled around each other as he anxiously scanned the room.

His head snapped around as he heard a cackle. Tnil's rash voice rang through the air. "You can't do anything with that string if you can't see your target." The voice came from somewhere high. She had the high ground, the advantage.

He suddenly felt a sharp pain in his right arm. He turned just in time to catch Tnil's punch. With her own momentum, he flung her past him. She stumbled but caught her balance before she fell. Sweat beaded her forehead, her white hair fell in front of her eyes. A smile crept upon her lips. Her breaths were quick and raspy. She cackled demonically and swung at Nikolai.

He spun around her, his face brushing her incoming fist. Once he was behind her, he tried to punch her with his right hand, but it didn't follow his command. Instead, it lay motionless at his side.

Nikolai gasped, "No." Shock brimmed his voice. His arm was *paralyzed*. Tnil could *paralyze* limbs!

Tnil laughed. Her white hair dangled in separate strands. "Yes!" she suddenly spun herself on the ground, sweeping her legs under his. Nikolai barely jumped in time, and his ankle rolled when he hit the ground. Tnil spotted it and quickly punched his left arm. Pain shot through it and he realized it was unmoving too.

"What did you just do to me?" panic filled his screech. Tnil swung again and Nikolai barely spun around it.

"I blocked your nerves," Tnil replied as she kicked Nikolai from behind.

"*Agh*!" he cried as he rolled on the ground. He didn't get up. Even though he could already feel his father's hot breath as he chewed him out for being weak, he lay there, cradling his arms.

"Relax, Nikolai, it'll go away in about an hour." He could feel Tnil getting closer. "I could teach you, but I don't know if I'll still be practicing here." *A little closer,* he edged. "You know, once *I'm* Killen's prodigy."

Now! Tnil was leaning over him. He kicked his legs into her stomach. Tnil flipped into the air. She landed on her stomach and gasped for air, as if it had been taken from her lungs. Nikolai stood, he walked over and placed his foot on Tnil's head. "It's over."

Tnil wailed as she tried to free herself, ugly sobs choking her screams, but Nikolai's foot kept her pinned to the ground. Tnil cried, screamed, and pounded her fists against the floor. Horrific sounds, but Nikolai savored every one. Then, she went still, the noise stopped. The room was silent aside from a light tapping. Tnil's limp hand tapped twice against the floor.

She tapped out. Tnil tapped out. The fight was over. He won. He lifted his foot off of her. She got up and ran, sobbing.

He walked towards the master. Nikolai extended his hand. But the master just turned his back to him. "Training at seven. Don't be late." And with that he walked away, disappearing out the doors.

Nikolai just stared. Disbelief and confusion lingered in his mind. Around him, the gym was completely silent. Then footsteps, heavy. His head whipped around to face a tall man. He had black hair that was highlighted with grays. His mustache was sleek, not a hair astray. The man opened his arms, a smile crossed his lips and pride twinkled in his eyes.

Nikolai ran to his father. Tears welled in his eyes. His hands wrapped tightly around his dad's waist. They were still numb and weak with whatever Tnil had done to disable them, but he held his father tight. He felt a rough hand hold his head. A feeling of joy exploded in his heart. The feeling spread to his body like warm water. But it wasn't just joy, he felt relieved. A relief that he had never felt, ever.

"I am so proud of you, Nikolai." The two pulled apart. His father's eyes sparkled.

"You are?" he asked, disbelief flooding him. Had he gained his father's love? Had he finally done it?

"Of course!" ambition laced his father's words, and Nikolai's heart sank deeper than it had ever sunk before. "You will lead and become the best this world will ever see, and it all starts with this one win." Nikolai felt as though he would burst out of the room at any given second. Only his eyes, locked on his father, kept him poised. "After many early mornings, after many late nights, after many wins, you will be king. And we will rule side by side. Together!"

Nikolai gulped, swallowing his sorrows. "Together."

~~~

Nikolai came out of his memory to find that the heavy rain had ceased and they were almost at the dock. The wind blew his black hair rapidly. The sudden cold gushes turned his cheeks red. The trees on the island swayed back and forth and the waves crashed on the rocky floor. He saw the huge, thunderous waterfall that told them they were approaching rapidly.

"Everyone inside!" he commanded. "Raise the sails, we cross in five." The crew rushed to put the sails up, having the boat sailing only on the current. The waterfall was wide and full. He could feel the splash from there.
~~~

"We can't possibly be sailing through that." Lilith approached him, eyeing the massive spray. Nikolai simply smiled.

"Trust me, you'll be pleasantly surprised."

Lilith let out a dry laugh. "I hate you already." She turned on her heel and headed to the cabin. Nikolai took one last look at the vast waterfall and headed in after her.

The cabin was crowded and buzzed with the usual excitement of the crossing. Thorne and Lilith leaned against the wall in a corner, flashing confused looks to him.

A rushing sound suddenly hit the cabin. The room was silent as the pounding water hit the roof. It was loud, thunderous, but only for a second, then it was gone. Nikolai felt a smile spread across his face. He strode to the door, Thorne and Lilith at his heels.

The door burst open to reveal a giant cave. The intense weather seemed to disappear here. Lights of many colors lit the docks and hundreds of ships lined the shore. The water was crystal clear and fish raced along the side of the boat.

The ceiling was rock and laced with vines. Birds fluttered around freely and the docks buzzed with the sound of rapid chatter.

Nikolai clasped his hands behind his back. "Miss Cole, Miss Thorne," he smiled. "Welcome to the League of Red Doves."

Chapter Fifteen
Quilla

Woah...

That was the first thing Quilla thought as she saw the docks. Crystal lights filled the room with an eerie glow. The water was so clear you could see the wavy bottom.

Lone strode toward the bow of the ship. His posture seemed to straighten. He stroked his hair back, confidence brimming his presence. Lilith and Quilla followed, more confused than confident.

"So... you live here?" Lilith chimed, a pathetic attempt at small talk.

"Born and raised!" he replied proudly, then sighed. "I have to warn you. These people, they're not going to be comfortable with you and your kind right away, if at all."

"Our kind?" Quilla leaned against the taffrail, she sharpened her glare and raised an eyebrow. "You mean killers and thieves."

"Look," Lone replied, looking down at the water. "I grew up here, and putting it simply, we're pretty stuck up and arrogant. Seeing that a couple of teenagers from Hanslack are more fit to pull off a job than anyone from the League of Red Doves, well, that's a pretty big blow to the ego."

"Call us what we are." Lilith joined Lone's sad aura and stared at the water. "Murderers and criminals."

Quilla rolled her eyes to the sky. "If you two want to dwell on unpleasant realities, so be it. I'm getting my things together before we dock." She turned and headed in the opposite direction.

The rest of the crew was readying for departure, so Quilla was alone in the cabin. The wood smelled of old glaze and it was making her nauseous. She sat on one of the many beds, then collapsed, resting her head on the pillow.

Curiosity wracked in her brain. The thrill of adventure left anxiety and fear slithering up her body and into her worrying mind. She wondered if they would leave right away, or if they would wait. Was this a bide-your-time mission, or could they go right away? She assumed Lone felt the need to explain everything on the way there for a reason. He was too eager not to be in a rush, unless breaking and entering was a passion of his.

Even though the probability was against it, Quilla felt as though she wanted to stay for a bit. The thought of a rebellion intrigued her, and her thirst for revenge, especially towards Ghan, had not dulled. After all, he was the reason she was in this mess in the first place. If he had not interfered, her life would have been no different from a normal teenager, even though that thought perplexed her mind.

It had been so long, so long since she had felt free, had been free. The stress of simply surviving, and keeping her survival a secret, weighed her down like chains and weights. She had done a good job, for two years at least. No one had found her, or even come looking for her. Staying hidden, a strong alibi; that was what was keeping her alive.

But she hated it. Every second, she was alive, but she hated it. Because staying alive was her only purpose, her only choice. Death wasn't an option. If she died, no one would pay, the only way she would win is if they all paid. If she lost, death would be much too merciful a punishment for her. They would break her physical body down so many times it would self-destruct itself.

But this was an opportunity to win. To beat them. To relieve herself of the weight she had been carrying for five long years. This was why the money had almost lost meaning now. Her head was set; if she was given the opportunity, she would hurt Ghan in any way she could.

That was her oath, an oath she had said to herself when she was young and scared. An oath she would repeat every night before she fell asleep. An oath before every battle, every job, every heist. Because everything she did, everything she lived for was to complete that very oath.

The boat lurched and Quilla flew forward. She jumped out of bed, grabbed her things, and strode out of the cabin. When she swung the door open, her eyes landed on an old, stubby man. His white hair was brushed back in a similar style to Lones. His eyes were tired and eye bags lingered under them. He was wearing a tailored suit that seemed to accentuate his circular stature. His black shoes clicked against the deck as he approached her.

"Miss Thorne." He said joyfully, his hands clasped behind his back.

"Mister Lone." She replied, sticking out a hand to shake. Grandez Lone hesitated, keeping his hands tightly held behind his back. Quilla rolled her eyes. "Shake it, for god's sake, it's not poisoned."

Mister Lone took her hand and gave it a timid squeeze. As he was about to pull it away, Quilla grabbed it, looked him right in the eyes, and shook it rapidly.

He looked taken aback, but she smiled, still holding eye contact. Nikolai's father shook off the flustered look and cleared his throat. "Shall we head inside, then? We want you to leave to retrieve Miss Windlem as soon as possible."

He turned and headed off the ship, brushing past the soldiers without a second thought. He brushed shoulders with his son and Lone looked at his father with hopeful eyes, but he didn't even turn to look at him. Instead, he walked right past, and everyone followed.

Quilla glanced at Lilith, who looked just as confused as her. She then shrugged, Grandez Lone was a powerful man, it couldn't do them any harm to get on his good side, even if it meant kissing his old, boney ass for a couple of days.

The docks were busy with shipments, soldiers boarded ships carrying large boxes. Their uniforms were black as night. Right on their heavily padded shoulders, was a red dove. The bird was turned to the side, its wings were extended behind it, and the tail was long and majestic.

A few ships over was a much more tragic sight. Men and women were unloading with bandages and crutches. Some carried stretchers, and the people laying on them were either groaning in pain or not moving a muscle. Each and every one of them looked gaunt and exhausted. They didn't wear uniforms, instead, they looked like humble farmers caught in a ruthless bloodbath.

"Where did you send them?" Lilith asked Lone, her tone concerned.

"Brighan." He said. "We were low on supplies here on Shina. We sent them there to get food and medicine. The Empire found out they were connected to us... and well... they attacked."

Lilith looked horrified, but Quilla knew Emperor Ghan followed no moral code. "Oh don't look so surprised. You had to see this coming, I mean you sent them to the capital of Thine. Ghan's not daft, he'll sniff out rebellion a million miles away, not to mention right under his nose. I'm honestly surprised this magnificent base of yours hasn't already been found and burnt to the ground."

"That's why we chose Shina. It's almost impossible to find, and even if you do, it's one of thousands of islands. And a small one at that. You would have to know it to find the League of Red Doves." Replied Lone, Quilla could feel the pride in his voice.

"That I applaud." She relented. "It takes time and skill to develop and build a base so secret, and yet, so massive. It is something to be proud of."

Lone nodded, almost unsure how to take a compliment. But Quilla's eyes had turned to Lilith. Her gaze was wide, but filled with sorrow. "How could Ghan do something like this?" she asked, disbelief brimming her voice. "They were unarmed, there for supplies, peacefully!"

Lone looked at his feet. "It's not like he hasn't done this before."

"What do you mean?" Lilith looked at him with curiosity burning in those brilliant green eyes.

"There was a country, Lunan Renel. It was small, and relatively new, but growing fast. When Ghan became emperor he found every country had a resource that could be shared with the world, and, more importantly, no country could live on its own, except Lunan Renel. It was called the breadbasket of the planet. Ghan knew that as long as it was still there, he wouldn't control anything. It was the center of rebellion for a while. It saw Ghan's dictatorship and acted. It sent troops right to Brighan, and the rebellion troops were obliterated. The rebellion calls it the First Battle of Sorrow. But it was a spark, and Ghan needed to put it out." Lone took a breath. "So he decided to explode the entire country. He set five nukes underground. Spread throughout the land. And, at midnight exactly, he blew the entire civilization to bits. No survivors were recorded. Now, all that remains of the League are tiny bases on remote islands like these. I was five. Twelve years ago."

Lilith looked as though she was about to throw up. Her mouth opened, and it seemed like nothing could come out. "No survivors?" she finally managed.

"Lunan Renel had the smartest and most athletic kids in the world. There are rumors that Ghan took some, five to be exact, and made them into something he called the Golden Class." He sighed, "It's just a rumor, though. Probably fake. But the story of Lunan Renel stands as a warning. If you cross the Empire, the Empire will make sure you don't live to see the other side."

Chapter Sixteen
Alohi

Alohi stood at the minecart tracks, watching the little holes they came out of for a little, metal cart. She still held her pickaxe beside her, just in case there was another attacker who decided to come at her from behind.

Joshua and Nathaniel stood beside her. The three of them had met in the cafeteria just an hour before and discussed their plan. She and the old man were to squeeze into the same, small cart while the more muscular inmate held onto the back and prayed not to fall off.

The thought of Joshua clinging onto dear life made her laugh. The man liked to project himself as strong and invincible, but Alohi saw right through it. He may have been notorious for *something* outside of this hellhole, but in here, no one was strong. Here they were all equal in brains and brawn.

Alohi, however, still felt her pride gleaming. Unlike skill with a knife or hard fists, words were a weapon that could be used no matter the situation.

She could sense Joshua bristling next to her. The inmate still held a grudge against her for her occupation, and for all she knew, it was well deserved. In some ways, politicians had fewer morals than dirty criminals, and she was used to the angry stares she got when she strode around.

Alohi couldn't say she disagreed with Joshua's point of view, not that it mattered. She knew perfectly well that her profession wasn't for the good of mankind. But just like a life of con extended its hand to criminals when they needed it, politics extended a hand to her. It had given her a purpose, a worth, and most importantly, her father's love and approval.

"Look!" Nathaniel pointed eagerly at the tracks. The cold steel had begun to shake, a gentle shiver in the metal. "Get ready."

Right on cue, a small minecart came rushing out of the small black hole. It was dusty and old, the red tint of rust dusting its joints. To her dismay, it was smaller than she imagined.

The tiny thing came to a halt in front of them, squeaking on its cracked wheels. The three of them looked at each other, unsure of what to do next.

"It's now or never, I guess," Alohi said, shrugging. She then lifted herself into the small minecart, wincing as the ice-cold metal touched her bare skin. Wherever this thing had come from, it was cold.

"Nathaniel?" Alohi beckoned. "Your next."

The old man walked cautiously to the cart, almost afraid of the steel. "I'm still unsure. What if we get caught?"

Alohi sighed. "Look, it's either we try this now, or we spend the rest of our lives in this hellhole. I would rather die knowing I tried everything I could than knowing I didn't try at all."

"And let's be honest, old man." Joshua's ugly voice chimed in. "You don't have many years left."

Alohi shot him a scowl, but all Nathaniel did was nod. Still looking unsure, he got into the cart, sitting right on Alohi's lap. She had to fight the urge to wrinkle her nose at the smell, but common sense told her she didn't smell much better.

"Well?" Alohi asked Joshua expectantly. "Your turn."

The prisoner looked at her with disgust but still obeyed. Though the two of them didn't like each other, Joshua followed her orders without a complaint and Alohi had to admit that he was a valuable asset. Even if he was a pain to be around.

Joshua pushed the minecart, and they started sliding down the rails. At first, it was painfully slow, and the fear of getting caught started to grow within her. Then, as soon as they entered the cold, dark rock, the cart dropped.

The wind howled in her ears as the cart sped faster and faster, turning suddenly. It was pitch dark in the tunnel, the only sound being the minecart's wheels on the steel track. Alohi felt her hair blow behind her as they sped through the tunnels.

All of a sudden, the minecart slowed. Her hair returned to her shoulders and a terrible feeling of nausea drifted over her. She supposed she had left her stomach back at the cave.

"Joshua?" Nathaniel called, his voice more wobbly than usual. "Are you still there?"

A frightened grunt told them that the muscular man still clung to the back of the cart. Alohi had to battle the urge to groan and push him off right then and there.

Her eyes flashed as she saw a light. It was coming from what looked like the end of the tunnel. It was faint and gloomy, the tiniest bit of blue lacing its glow, but all the same, it was a light.

"What's that?" Joshua's small voice rang behind them.

Alohi squinted her light blue eyes. "Our way out, hopefully."

The minecart swerved around the corner to reveal a large cave. Water dripped from rocks on the ceiling into small pools that were dug into the sand. On the side of the cave, was a large, metal door.

Alohi pushed Nathaniel off her eagerly. The old man was surprisingly light and fell to the ground with little effort on her part. She jumped out of the cart and headed to the door, trying the handle with far too much enthusiasm. It didn't budge.

"You really thought it would work?" Joshua's agitating voice rang behind her.

Alohi turned to him, a glare already painting her expression. He was kneeling on the sand, his arms wobbly. Just below him, was a pool of vomit that dripped from his mouth much like the water in the cave.

She wrinkled her nose. "You're disgusting."

Joshua wiped his vomit-covered mouth. "You're delusional."

"Alohi?" Nathaniel chipped into their conversation. His eyes were covered with a sparkling fear. "Look behind you."

Alohi whipped her head around and an equal, gut-wrenching fear filled her head. Behind her, was a large, pale lion. Its teeth were sharper than any she had ever seen. A bubbly saliva dripped from its mouth along with what looked like hints of blood.

The cat lunged at her, claws out like daggers. Alohi barely swerved out of the way as the lion crashed into the cart.

Nathaniel and Joshua scrambled to the far side of the cave, Alohi quickly joining them. The beast had squared up a second time, growling more fiercely as it lunged at them.

They dodged, but Alohi felt the lion's sharp claws grazing her skin. Warm blood leaked from where the wound stung. The cave shook as the cat tumbled into the rock, making a loud clang.

The three of them looked at each other. A silent understanding flew over each of their faces. *This was not the way out.*

Just then the door beside her swung open. A battalion of Empire guards ran out, their blue uniforms shining in the blue cave light. A chorus of shouts and orders rang around the rock as a dozen men charged at Alohi.

There was no way she could dodge them. All she did was stand there as she was brought to her knees, the cold blade of a sword touching her throat. She watched helplessly as Joshua and Nathaniel were thrown to the ground and restrained. There was nothing she could do. She was paralyzed, helpless, weak.

A loud bang was the last thing she heard, a giant pain in her head was the last thing she felt. Then her vision darkened and she drifted into her dreams.

Chapter Seventeen
Lilith

When Quilla and Lilith had walked into the vast assembly hall, it felt like the entire room's eyes were solely on them. Two men who looked as though they were in their forties had shown them to their rooms just minutes before, where they had unpacked, and were told to meet in the assembly hall in thirty minutes.

"You're late," rasped Nikolai's father. He was sitting on a small balcony that towered at least ten feet above them. He, Nikolai, and four other well-dressed people sat in decorated thrones. Around them was what looked like a theater. Several hundred people sat anxiously, as if awaiting some kind of circus show.

"Obviously," Quilla responded hastily as she went to take a seat in one of the old, chipped chairs that she and Lilith were given. "You led us to a random dorm in your corn maze of a base, told us a room, a time, and good fucking luck."

Lilith wrinkled her nose as she sat in her splintering seat. The wood was rickety, and it seemed like it would break into a pile of lumber at any second.

"Shouldn't a real spy be able to navigate any building?" a man yelled from his throne on the balcony. He looked young, maybe thirty, and his blonde hair was wild and messy. "Maybe you aren't as cut out for this mission as we expected."

Nikolai cleared his throat. "Let me introduce you to our representatives from our five nations. This is Nathaniel Bolian, leader of our forces in Salenian." He gestured to the man with messy hair. He wore a t-shirt and looked far less dressed up than the other councilmen on the balcony. "This is Raya Spin of Courna," he pointed to an elderly woman in a fluffy jacket that looked as though it was meant for negative temperatures. "Coriolanus Dacnoff of Thine." A well-dressed man in his mid-thirties gave them a small wave. "And Ranine Windlem of Woodran." A young woman was staring intently at Quilla, her fingers pressed together and her gaze unwavering. "Miss Windlem is unfortunately taking the place of her sister, who for reasons already known, could not attend this meeting." The way Nikolai's voice wavered when he said the last sentence told her he was barely holding it together. "The rest are war generals, or honorary guests who we think this matter concerns." Once he was done, Nikolai nodded to his father, signaling he was done.

Grandez Lone nodded back at his son. "How much of the plan do they already know?"

"I've already told them most of the beginning." Nikolai chimed. "Sneak into the Archives, find where she is, and get out without getting noticed. We've decided to go through the vents near the back of the building. They will have two-minute intervals to get to and from the center room without getting caught." Nikolai turned to them. "It's crucial you don't get caught, or they'll know we're coming."

"We won't." Responded Quilla. "Two minutes is more than enough time."

"Another thing." The elderly woman called Raya added. "We don't know much about Empire prisons, but we do know they check who was viewed in the Archives every twenty-four hours, so it's best you go from there to wherever she is being held as quickly as possible."

"Don't get seen!" a young woman from the bleachers told them harshly.

"And don't explode anything!" another felt the need to add.

Lilith looked at Quilla. She looked as though she was waiting for a boring scene in a book to end. Nikolai was right, these people were perfectionists. She was losing her patience as the ramble of different reminders kept going.

"We get it." Quilla finally rasped. "Don't draw attention, and don't blow something up." She rolled her eyes. "And in case it makes you feel better, I don't plan on releasing a herd of half-bred geese-rhinos, either."

"We just want to make sure you're prepared for this mission," Grandez Lone inquired, a forced calm tainting his growl.

"I'm perfectly prepared," Lilith shot back, frustration beginning to linger in her head. "Get into the archives, find where the girl is, get out. Get into prison to get said girl, get out. No noises, no explosions, no rhino-geese. Can I go now?"

Ranine wrinkled her nose. "You seem awfully rushed to get out of here. How do we know that you're not going to turn us in and get a hefty amount of money from the Empire?"

Quilla rolled her eyes. "Because the Empire isn't exactly fond of us, in case you forgot."

Lilith matched her partner's sarcastic expression. "Honestly, I think they might pay more for us than they would for the entire League of Red Doves."

With that line, the entire assembly hall looked at them with intense hate. Lilith and Quilla only smiled, enjoying the familiar looks of resentment.

"I would watch your tone." Rasped the councilwoman from Courna. "We could have you locked away for as long as we like."

Quilla huffed a small laugh. "I would like to see you try." The cruel, ambitious expression had returned to the con queen's face. Lilith had noticed that Quilla always looked alive when chaos tinted the air.

A cruel expression identical to her partner's painted Lilith's face. It had become more and more of a regular emotion since she had met Quilla. "Careful," her voice was laced with poised savagery. "If you lock us up, who would retrieve your dear Alohi Windlem?" the crowd flinched as she said the name. "Not anyone from this pathetic organization, that's for sure."

Angry shouts erupted in the hall. People were standing, spitting insults in their directions. The words *heathen*, *hood*, and *lowlife* echoed off the walls.

Quilla just sat there, a pleasant expression lingering on her face. But Lilith could feel her blood pressure rising. Her heart beat faster and her head swam with the offensive words. Familiar rage formed a lump in her throat, begging to come out.

"Of course." Nathaniel Bolian scoffed from his high throne. "I wouldn't expect anything less from a couple of *criminals*. Do you even know they're qualified? To me, they just seem like a couple of rebellious, narcissistic kids."

Lilith stood abruptly, the chair squeaked against the white floor. "Step outside with me and I'll show you just how qualified I am!" she glared at the man, her teeth grit and fists clenched. The lump of anger had come out, and it was ready to fight.

A pair of hands grasped her shoulders, gently pushing her down into the chair. The scent of roses tainted the air. "*Sit down.*" Quilla whispered in her crisp accent. Her long, curly hair brushing Lilith's cheek as she leaned next to her ear.

The criminal prodigy's eyes narrowed into focused slits and she ran her hand through her wild hair. "We're done here." She told them, looking more authoritative than anyone in the assembly hall. "The ship to the Archives leaves in an hour. Nikolai, you will captain it because you're the only one in this room I can tolerate for more than five minutes. We will be there with our weapons and tools." She grabbed Lilith by the wrist and headed towards the door, stopping only for a second to look over her shoulder and say, "Oh, and we're doing this our way."

Chapter Eighteen
Nikolai

As soon as Thorne pulled Lilith out of the room, Nikolai stood to leave. He clasped his hands behind his back, turned to his father, and took a small bow. The assembly hall was left in shock after that alarming meeting, and he knew he had to clear things up with Thorne or get a ship ready quicker than he ever had. He pushed in his chair and scrambled out the door.

The two girls were walking quickly. Or, more accurately, Thorne was dragging Lilith with her as she strode through the halls. Nikolai ran to them.

"Well congratulations," he said, frustration brimming his voice. "I barely managed to hire you in the first place, and now the few allies you had in that room you lost."

"Not a problem," Thorne told him, still not slowing her pace. "Once we get paid, we won't be available for hiring."

"Doubtful if you will get paid after that performance." Nikolai retorted. Thorne stopped abruptly, turning to face him.

"If we don't get paid, we don't do the job," Thorne said frankly, looking him straight in the eye.

"Then maybe you should pay a little more respect to the people who are paying you." He took a step closer, glaring down at her. "Don't forget, we could lock you up any time, anywhere, without warning."

"Oh please." Thorne rolled her eyes. "You know no prison can hold us." Nikolai's fists curled in frustration. He could barely hold back his tightened knuckles, and it looked like Thorne was struggling to do the same.

"Okay, enough." Lilith stepped between them. She turned to Thorne, annoyance gripping her tone. "Stop dragging me around like a disobedient child, and you..." She turned to Nikolai. "Stop making empty threats. Let's just focus on getting the mission done."

They just glared at each other for a while, then Thorne extended a hand, still staring at Nikolai, but with expecting eyes. "Truce?"

"Truce," Nikolai replied, shaking her hand. It was more calloused than he expected, and her handshake was rough and quick. Once it was over, she turned and headed in the opposite direction. Lilith walked by her side, skeptically. "Where do you think you're going?" Nikolai asked.

"Oh, she has no idea." Lilith turned and backpedaled alongside her. "We're definitely going to get lost. I'm going with her because if we do get lost, at least we'll get lost together."

Thorne stopped and turned, giving her a friendly nudge, Lilith nudged back. "And because she's my partner." She added, smiling. They reminded him of the sun and the moon. Lilith, always so sunny and bright, and Thorne, serious and sarcastic. But somehow, they worked so well together, fitting together like puzzle pieces. He smiled, and he thought he saw the corner of Thorne's lips curl.

"I can show you to the training center, unless you need to go back to your room?" he offered.

Lilith checked her things. "I think we're good." She said brightly. "I want to see this training center!" she ran to Nikolai's side, this time dragging Thorne with him.

Painfully, the first thought that crept into his mind was; *Alohi would love her.* Lilith's energy was bright and positive, but she also diffused pointless fights and arguments. She was a daily reminder to Nikolai about what was missing, and what he was in danger of losing, maybe forever. Alohi would also get along with the criminal prodigy. Taking her rough, dismissive aura as a challenge, and eventually cracking her like a safe.

Nikolai led them through the corridors he had memorized, the ones he had to navigate to make it home at midnight when he could barely move from exhaustion. He remembered being half asleep, stumbling through the halls at four in the morning, the light blinding him as he craved the blackness of sleep. His legs would ache every morning, and his muscles would scream at him to take a break, to sleep in, just once. But every time the thought crossed his mind, guilt and fear of failure would storm his head and keep him going. Keep him fighting, because that was what he would do, he would fight until he won. It didn't matter how tired he was, he would keep fighting until his dying breath.

"Here we are," he told them as he stood in front of the giant doors of the training center. "The pride and joy of the League."

Thorne crossed her arms, staring at the doors. "Why would you spend so much time on the entrance when that energy could have been spent on what lies behind those doors?"

Nikolai cocked his head. "Actually, we spend a lot of money on the training center in particular. Half of our funding, to be exact."

"So you would rather develop troops than the equipment they use?" Thorne replied accusingly. "Technology is just, if not more important than skills these days. Skilled men are only so much without their weapons. I think about it as bringing a sword to a long-range battle. Useful in some situations, but not others."

Nikolai opened his mouth to retort something but closed it when Lilith chimed. "I wouldn't say anything." She smiled, resting her elbow on Thorne's shoulder. "You're just going to dig yourself into a deeper hole."

He sighed, realizing they were both smiling now, and they were just going to have more fun messing with him if he stayed longer. "I'll come get you when the ship's ready." He turned but stopped abruptly. "And stay here." He didn't need them causing any more trouble. After they were gone and all of this was over, Nikolai would be taking the fall for anything that went wrong during the mission.

He walked quickly to the dock, taking wide strides and avoiding anyone who passed him in the halls. Even though this was where he grew up, he wanted to leave as soon as possible. Everyone here seemed to be looking at him with judging, expecting eyes. He would never be good enough, not in their eyes at least. He would be worth nothing as long as Ghan still ruled. He was the one that was supposed to take his place. He was the heir to the throne, even though he had no birthright, and no will to take the throne.

The lights of the halls still blinded him. The bright white was slowly driving him mad with boredom. That's why, once he was old enough, Nikolai would spend most of his time doing missions for the League. Every time something popped up, Nikolai would be the first to volunteer, just waiting to get out of the bland base and into the dangerous, exciting world.

That is aside from his lessons with Master Killen. The swordsmen always made things interesting. He would give Nikolai a task that seemed so bizarre and pointless that his motivation would decrease from pure disbelief. But he knew that once the task was done it would make him better in one way or another.

The most peculiar was on a hot summer day. Master Killen had called him to a beach on a rare day when the fog had not swallowed the island whole. It was eight in the morning, another rare day when Killen let him sleep in. He remembered his master looking very out of place on the sandy beach. His long, flowing, red robes blew around him, his manicured fingers clasped tightly behind his back. His strawberry blonde hair flowed like water, waving ever so slightly in the small breeze.

"Good morning, Nikolai," Killen said in his smooth, deep voice.

"Good morning, Master Killen." Nikolai replied, taking a small customary bow.

"Your swords." Killen extended his hands. Nikolai reached behind him to the two swords strung behind his back. He lifted them gently, holding them by the tip for Killen to grab. He had forged them himself only at the age of ten. They were crafted from obsidian; the gold that striped them had taken him weeks to mine out of the island. Every time the swords left his hands, he felt a tiny pang. He felt like a piece of his identity was stolen from him, but still, he held them out to Killen.

The master took them, spearing them into the sand. Nikolai almost flinched, he was not about to spend another week looking for gold, and another month building up the courage to ask his father for more obsidian.

"I have quite a daunting ordeal for you today, Nikolai," Killen told him.

Don't you always, he thought. He never let the thought dictate his appearance, careful to keep a positive, excited expression on his face.

With that same expression, and a delightful, ever-so-fake tone, he asked. "What is it?"

Killen smiled. "There is a fruit tree at the top of the island; Sand Mangos, I believe they're called. Could you be so kind as to retrieve one for me?"

Ugh! Nikolai had hiked to the top of the mountain once before, a daunting task that he was not eager to complete again. There were no trails, mostly because no one bothered to hike up there. After all, there was nothing up there besides Killen's "Sand Mangos."

Nikolai nodded, clasping his hands behind his back and dipping into a traditional bow. He turned, sizing up the island he was about to climb for a stupid fruit. He tripped through vines, almost drowned in overflowing rivers, and got lost at least seven times before he finally found the fruit.

Probably the most painful part of the journey was when he realized that to retrieve the fruit, he needed to scale an extremely tall tree. He let his eyes roll back into his head and he let out a soft growl, then ran towards the tree.

He planted his foot in a small dent in the bark, just enough for him to launch himself to the nearest branch. His hands gripped the rough surface of the wood and he felt his skin tear and blister as he dangled from the branch. With every inch of him howled from pain and exhaustion, he hauled himself up to the limb, standing on it with full confidence.

Suddenly, he heard a heart-stopping crack. Instinct took over his body and he leaped from the breaking wood. His hand found a nearby branch, and he gripped it tighter than he had ever held onto anything. An angry scream burst from his lungs as he dangled from the bark.

He hauled himself onto the branch, more carefully this time. For a while, he sat, giving his mind time to calm itself; to reset. Killen would not stand for this. If he exhibited this kind of behavior while his master was there, Nikolai would be running until he threw up. But Killen wasn't here. Killen was on the beach waiting for his stupid mango. Henceforth, Nikolai could get as frustrated as he wanted.

His eyes widened when he saw it. It was a light beige, taking the shape of a slightly dented oval. It was right there, just in front of him. He reached for the sand mango, not believing that he was touching its smooth skin. He twisted it slightly, and the fruit came loose. He gazed at it for a second, disbelief flooding his senses. Then another blood-curdling crack.

This time, his instincts did not save him. Nikolai fell to the ground, cradling the mango as though it was his child. His back hit the soft sand and he felt his gaze waver. But he had the mango. The mango was fine. That was all that mattered. At the moment all that mattered was the mango.

He gazed up at the blue sky. The sun stared back at him. It was about noon, he had plenty of time to get back. Maybe he would even get to bed before midnight.

The hike down wasn't nearly as treacherous as the journey up. This time he had memorized landmarks. He looked for a peculiar tree, a field of pebbles, anything that could help him find the beach. He followed the path of grass that he had trampled on the way in, looking for any possible sign that could lead him to the beach.

He was wacking a familiar vine out of the way when he saw it. The blue water of the ocean. And right there, just in front of him, was Killen, beaming at him.

Nikolai broke into a sprint. Sand kicked up as he ran towards his master, holding onto the mango tighter than he had ever held onto something before. He scurried to a stop right in front of Killen. Then held out the mango like a piece of gold, the most valuable gift that could ever be given.

Killens manicured hand reached for the mango, grabbing it from Nikolai's palm. His face was emotionless as he examined it, tilting it side to side, turning it to make sure it was in perfect condition.

Eat the damn fruit! Nikolai thought, barely able to keep himself from jamming it in Killens mouth himself. But Killen just examined the mango, tilting in, running his hand along its smooth side. Nikolai just watched, unsure what was happening.

Then, Killen cracked a smile. He lowered the mango to his side. Nikolai almost jumped as his sharp, long, painted nails dug into the fruit. Juice leaked from where Killen had punctured the mango; it slithered down the fruit in tiny rivers, dripping into the sand. Killen squeezed harder, squishing through the skin and separating the mango into different pieces. Then, without warning, he let go, letting the fruit fall into the sand.

"Why would you do that?" Nikolai screamed angrily, regretting it immediately. Why had he let down his guard? He closed his eyes, waiting for whatever punishment awaited him.

But instead, Killen simply laughed. Nikolai opened his eyes to find him beaming. "I've been waiting to see some kind of reaction from you." He told him, patting his head kindly. "I usually try to develop a friendship, as well as a work relationship with my students."

Nikolai just stood there, stunned. "W-what?"

"I crushed the mango because I wanted to show you that once you go through something with someone, you care for them." He gave a gentle smile. "Caring for people is important in life, Nikolai, remember that. But also remember this, if anything happens to someone you care for, it could destroy you."

Chapter Nineteen
Quilla

"We are definitely not staying here."

That was the first thing Quilla said after the giant doors of the training center closed behind them.

"Figured," Lilith responded. "I've never known you to follow rules, especially rules put in place by someone you're not fond of." She ran her fingers through her chestnut hair and reached for her bow that was strung around her back. Her green eyes glittered, the excitement of adventure filling her face. A smile spread across her lips and her dimples started to show. She gently tilted her head to the right, and their eyes locked, just for a second.

Caution drifted over Quilla and her gaze flew to the ground. Out of the corner of her eye, she saw Lilith's smile fade. Her heart dropped a little. She wanted to make her smile so badly, but she couldn't; she wouldn't make that mistake again.

"Where are we going?" she asked in a voice that was deprived of the previous lively energy. Quilla felt a pang of guilt, but quickly shook it off.

"You saw how big the assembly hall was." She turned to Lilith, eyes stern. "No one would notice if we slipped into the crowd to eavesdrop. We're gonna find out if there is an alternate plan for hiring us, and if there's anything more we can squeeze out of this job."

"Okay…" Lilith started, looking skeptical. "So how are you going to find it again? These halls are designed to get anyone lost who doesn't know their way around."

Quilla gave a frustrated exhale. "While you were busy buzzing about this training center, I was memorizing the way there." She turned and started walking towards the meeting room, not looking back.

They walked in awkward silence. Quilla was repeating the directions in her head, making sure they wouldn't get lost. Lilith seemed to be walking a couple of steps behind her, not making a sound. She was so quiet Quilla had to look back to make sure she was still there. The white halls were blinding, bright lights littering every corner.

"I don't get it." Lilith grumbled after a while. Quilla turned to look at her, a skeptical look painting her face.

"You're going to have to be a little more specific." Her crisp accent rasped.

Lilith huffed. The brilliant light that once filled her green eyes was replaced with frustration. "You hate Ghan for some unknown reason, but when you meet the very organization trying to overthrow him it's like you have something against them too? I don't have any reason to be nice to them, but you… you make no sense-"

Quilla grabbed her and pulled her into a dark corner, covering her mouth with her hand. She struggled, then saw the poised, well-dressed man walking past them. His mustache was combed to perfection, not a strand out of place.

They looked at each other, not daring to make a sound. If Grandez Lone found them sneaking around the League, then any hopes of getting on his good side would be gone. As much as she hated to admit it, the filthy rich politician did have quite a bit of sway over what happened to them.

Lilith pushed herself away, knocking Quilla into the wall. It made a much louder sound than comfortable. Quilla glared for a second, and lunged at Lilith, knocking her to the ground. Lilith rolled, now on top of Quilla as she brought her knee up, knocking Lilith off of her and onto the ground.

"What's wrong with you?" Quilla asked furiously.

"What's wrong with *me*?" Lilith responded, spitting blood onto the ground. "You're the one that's about to get us caught and lose this job!"

"Oh," Quilla let out a shrill laugh. "You wanna talk about losing the job? You're the one who tried to get in a fight in the assembly hall. You're the one that can't control your temper."

"Oh really?" she stood, standing face to face with Quilla. "Didn't you throw a man off a boat earlier today? Was that temper? Or was that your sick idea of mercy?"

"Would you rather he was still here?" she retorted. "I do what I have to do to survive, it has nothing to do with temper!"

"Keep telling yourself that." Lilith's shrill voice caught on Quilla's last nerve.

She opened her mouth, about to say something vile when the sound of clapping rang behind them.

She turned her head and horror filled her eyes as she gazed at Grandez Lone. His manicured hands were clasped behind his back. His lips spread into a sick smile. "Miss Throne, Miss Cole, what's all the commotion about?"

The two of them scrambled to their feet, brushing off their clothes in an attempt to look somewhat presentable. "Mister Lone!" Quilla chimed. Her fake, cheerful tone was nauseating. "*Wonderful* to see you again."

Lilith kicked her shin, it was almost hard enough to make her double over. "We're very sorry about this, it won't happen again."

Quilla shot her a look. "You suck up."

All Nikolai's father did was shrug. "What more could I expect from a couple of criminals?"

Quilla's eyes tightened into a glare. "Everyone here is making a much bigger deal about our con-filled past than it needs to be."

Grandez Lone lifted an eyebrow. "Are we?" his voice was excruciatingly pleasant. "Dirty fighting is all you know. You can't be expected to act poised in an *organized* situation." Quilla could almost feel her blood pressure rising. There was false advertising, and there was organization. The League of Red Doves had false advertising.

"Besides," Quilla felt a growl rumble in her throat as the politician opened his sappy mouth. *Why is he still talking?* "It was probably your parents that got you on this *wretched* path in the first place. If I were to guess, I would assume they were ten times worse than you ever could be."

Lilith's face had caught fire and rage flickered in the hot flames. "How dare you!" she growled. "Me and my father were peaceful farmers in Salenian. I became a criminal because the Empire took *everything* from me." Her voice was sharp, anger tinting every syllable. "You have *no* right to accuse me of anything. Your privileged ass has no idea what any hint of a struggle means."

The Lone shrugged. The calmness in his face was nauseating. "Yes, I suppose I don't have a sob story. But it doesn't matter." His lips pinched into a pitiful expression. "I would have *never* sunk so low."

Quilla could sense Lilith was about to knock the sense out of the man. She laid a steady hand on her partner's shoulder; not so much holding her back, but bringing her back to reality.

"Well," Quilla started with a smile. "My father was a dirty piece of shit."

This seemed to catch the politician off guard. He quickly shook it off, returning to his poised demeanor. "Really?"

"Oh yes." Quilla clasped her hands behind her back, striding around the Lone. "He made me an impossible opponent. Chaotic, unpredictable, *unbeatable.*"

The Lone lifted his chin. "Ah, so he was a thief."

Quilla huffed a laugh. "*God* no!" her heels clicked against the hard floor. "He was much too prideful for that. But don't go thinking he was morally right. This man had less ethics than a starved mosquito."

The Lone looked at her with a skeptical expression. "Then who taught you how to steal?"

Quilla shrugged. "I like to say I'm self-taught." A stout cackle escaped her lips. "Father dearest would hate it."

Understanding once again flew across the politician's face. "So you do it in spite of your father?"

A smile spread across her lips. "Sure, if that's how you want to look at it." She knew exactly what this man's game was. Demoralize until there is no pride left to take. A familiar, ugly feeling filled her. Two could play in that game. "But no matter how it's said, vengeance gets me out of bed, anger fuels me when rest is limited, and deep, pure, hatred is what drives me to work harder than everyone else." She flashed an accusatory look, whether it was directed at Lilith or Grandez Lone, she did not know.

Either way, anger spurred in both of their eyes. Lilith's green gaze was fiery and just as directed at Quilla as it was directed at the Lone. The rage was just as familiar as it was powerful.

"Well." The politician straightened his suit, the poised, stuck-up demeanor returning to his frame. "I should get going. Lovely chat. But I do ask that you stay wherever my imbecile son has asked." Quilla made a silent note of the negative tone the Lone used towards his offspring. "We wouldn't want you getting into trouble, now would we."

Quilla dipped her head. "We sure wouldn't."

The two girls watched as the politician turned on his heel and strode in the other direction. As soon as he turned the corner, Lilith pinned her against the wall.

"You couldn't be any more stuck up, could you?" the archer had gripped Quilla's shirt by the collar. Her heels dangled in the air, a couple of inches from the ground. "You're disgusting, you know. A thirst for revenge isn't something to be proud of, and neither is putting down others to make yourself look good."

"Oh?" a slick smile spread across Quilla's face. "I didn't realize you wanted to be called a skillful con artist. You had that big speech about how *innocent* you were."

Lilith tightened her hold on Quilla's collar. "Just because becoming a cold-hearted criminal wasn't on my to-do list doesn't mean I'm not good at it." She grit her teeth. "Even though I didn't have a choice, I still worked hard to survive!"

A cold, dry crackle ripped from Quilla's throat. "Oh come now, Lilith, we all had a choice." Her fanged teeth glittered as her lips parted into a cruel smile. "My choice was either die a nobody on concrete or fight my way to revenge. Yours was to fight your way out of the Grave Desert alone, or become a notorious criminal's right hand." A fiery light burned in her black eyes as she paused. "Now tell me, Lilith Cole, do you regret it?"

Chapter Twenty
Alohi

Alohi dreamed of the past.

A thirteen-year-old girl ran through the white halls of the League of Red Doves. Her shoes slipped whenever she made a sharp turn and her arms jutted out to keep her balance. Her hair was in a slick bun her mother had put up, not a strand astray. That was until the girl had left their small complex, and pulled two strands free. They dangled in front of her face, slightly swaying when she walked like a flag waving in a light breeze.

Her little blue eyes were wide. Looking in every corner. They flew around as her legs carried her through the maze that was the Shina. She took rapid breaths, panting from the running.

"Nikolai?" her voice filled the empty corridor. Silence followed. "Nikolai? It's okay, it's just me."

She slowed her pace and walked around, scanning the empty corners. Then she stopped, and out of the corner of her eye, she saw messy strands of black hair peeking out from behind a box. Like a mouse hiding from predators. The girl smiled, sliding next to him.

He turned away, his messy hair, which was usually firmly tamed, was tangled and covered his eyes. His uniform was spattered with blood as well as tattered and torn. Crimson blood trickled from a gash on his wrist.

She tore a part of her shirt, wrapping it around the cut gingerly. Nikolai remained turned, his hand shaking as she bandaged it. His skin was colder than usual, its color had turned pale, almost a bluish tint. The girl ran a finger along his hand. "Nikolai..." She asked slowly. "What happened?"

He snatched his arm back, cradling it against his chest. "I failed, Alohi." His hair came over his forehead in strips, tears leaked from his eyes where anger shined bright. His teeth were clenched, pressing so hard it looked as though they would crumble.

"You failed," Alohi repeated. "Trust me, I get it. I get the fear that comes with every time you have to perform, I get the shame that comes when you don't meet that high standard. I get the glares, I get the disrespect, I get the laughs." She let out a shrill cackle of her own. "Believe me, Nikolai, I know it hurts. But when the pain and embarrassment fade, you are left with pure, beautiful anger. It drove me; those people that laughed, that told me I was nothing, will bow in due time!"

Nikolai turned, tears still staining his eyes. "But they won't forget. You know that." He placed his hand on the wall, pressing his fingernails into the paint. "I did everything right, I was out there every day, earlier and later than her. I had tougher competition. She beat me once, and now that's all anybody will remember."

The memory shifted, going up in flames that engulfed her best friend's tear-stained face. Instead, she was on the stage, her legs felt like glass, her hands sweaty despite the cool air that surrounded her. The curtains opened, and the speaker called her name. A fourteen-year-old Alohi swallowed, trying to drown her anxiety, and stepped onto the stage.

Her competition was called, and Alohi felt like crying as soon as the speaker echoed the name Tanor Unighast. The last of her confidence fell out of her body. Tanor's long, black hair was pulled back into one braid. His hands were laced with rings, a singular hoop earring hanging from his right ear. His grin was powerful, dangerous. She watched as his eyes scanned the audience, and drifted to her. They were midnight black, sparkling in the light. The grin turned from dangerous to evil. "Morning, Alohi."

She recentered her gaze. The audience was cheering below her, all but one. Her father sat in the front row, his fingertips pressed together, leaning back in his chair. His eyes were focused on her, only her. One wrong step and it was over. She needed to watch her breath, her eyes, her posture. One wrong move and his respect and love would vanish.

The host came onto the stage, standing between her and Tanor's podiums. He was a tall man, his hair in a high ponytail that fell to his shoulder blades. He reached a gloved finger into the jar, pulling out a small strip of paper. As he unfolded it, he read it allowed. "Tanor, you will be arguing for Emperor Ghan on the subject of destroying nations." There was a gasp from the crowd. The idea was obviously wrong, but Tanor just smiled. "Alohi, you will be arguing against the prohibition."

God, it was supposed to be easy. How could it go so wrong?

Tanor spoke first, his voice echoing around the room. "The shock and terror that rang around the room when I was given my prompt was appropriate, after all, destroying a city, killing millions, that's wrong, right?" Tanor shifted his stance, clasping his hands behind his back. "But in this world, there are toxins, and toxins have no use. Look at it from a different point of view. I ask all of you, if you were given a chance to blow Brighan and all of Ghan's forces to a billion pieces, would you hesitate even a second?" his voice echoed around the room in confident, smooth tones; each syllable capturing the audience like a net. "Burning flames, structures coming down, trapped." He advanced towards Alohi, smiling. Thoughts spun in her head like a hurricane. *Burning.* "But it's Ghan that's trapped." *Trapped. Coming down.* "Destroy anyone that's hurt you." *Destroyed. Everything.* "Make them feel the pain and failure that you did." *Failure. Pain. Failure. Pain.*

"Alohi."

You're a failure. You'll never be as good as your sister. Failures don't get protected. Failures are on their own!

"*Alohi*!" the host's voice rang through the air. "It's your turn. Please pay attention." He said, agitated.

"Sorry, sir." She replied, embarrassed. Her eyes gazed at the large crowd, it seemed to grow with each passing second. The clock ticked. Getting louder, and louder. *Tick, tick,* her lungs tightened. *Tick, tick.* Her eyes flew to a man in the audience. His fingernails scraped along the velvet seat. His black eyes looked back at her with respect fading every tick. *Tick, tick.*

"I-" she began, trying to remember something, anything! But she couldn't. Her mind was broken, tainted with words from her past. *Failure. Burn. Trapped. Failure.*

"I- I'm sorry." She didn't know who it was directed to, but that was all she could say. Her father, the audience, herself?

The tears leaked from her eyes before she could stop them. All she could do was turn and run, leaving the audience speechless, and the last bit of confidence she had demolished.

Chapter Twenty One
Lilith

Lilith pushed the doors of the training center open angrily. She strode in quickly, teeth grit, fists clenched. Anger raged through her blood. It was pushing on her skin, on her lips, begging to come out. She needed to punch something, preferably someone. Actually, preferably her partner, but for obvious reasons that wasn't an option.

She eyed the sparring ring, right in the middle of the training center, a red dove in flight was painted on the arena. A couple of people were training there, they looked around the same age as her.

She recognized a girl from the earlier meeting. Ranine? Her skin was dark amber, and her curly hair was pulled into a ponytail that ran down her back. She was in the middle of hand-in-hand combat with another girl. This one's hair was snow white, cut just above her shoulders. She wore tight black shorts and a black sports bra. She struck in ways similar to a cat. Her punches were quick and precise, but Ranine dodged everyone without difficulty. Neither seemed able to hit each other.

Lilith leaned against the entrance to the ring. They didn't seem to notice as she watched them throw countless unsuccessful punches. It was like watching someone run in circles, going nowhere but getting progressively more exhausted. These two girls were running in circles. The same mistakes were being made, and no effort to correct them

Eventually, Lilith had enough. "May I suggest something?" they stopped fighting, looking at her with skeptical eyes. She pushed off the wall and entered the ring, the eyes of the two girls following her. "Lilith Cole." She extended a hand, but no one took it. Rolling her eyes, she let her hand fall to her side. "Deception is key whenever you're fighting. A reaction that may be good in one situation is also a target in another."

The girl with white hair crossed her arms. "In what world would you be giving us advice?"

Lilith just let out a small giggle, "What's your name?" she asked sweetly, almost as though she was talking to a frightened child.

"Tnil Limpana."

"Well, Tnil, out of all the skilled assassins that live under this roof, Grandez Lone sent ships and bargained a hefty price for me to retrieve some girl from Emperor Ghan. So to answer your question, in this world, I am in a position to give you advice. Whether you take it or not, I couldn't care less."

Ranine gave her an intense glare. "She's not just some girl. She's my *sister*."

"Hmm." Lilith raised an eyebrow. "You were at the meeting right?"

"Yes, I was. Sitting in for Alohi Windlem, who I think you are ill-fitted to retrieve." Ranine's Woodran accent was dripping with disgust.

"If you think that the criminal prodigy of Hanslack is ill-fitted for a simple heist, then you seriously need to do more research." Lilith tried to make her tone just as insulting, hoping the girl would back down.

Instead, a cackle ripped from Ranine's throat. "Oh!" Lilith crossed her arms as she waited for Ranine to get over her giddy laughter. "I wasn't talking about Quilla Thorne. She seems quite competent." Her lips curled into a smug smile. "I was talking about her immature student with anger issues." She raised her eyebrows. "Speaking of which, where is your boss?"

Lilith felt her teeth press together in anger. "She's my *partner*. And I have no idea where she is. Quilla goes where she wants, she isn't the best at listening."

This resonated on the girls' faces for a second. Then they straightened their posture and curved their lips into grins.

"Okay, Lilith," Tnil mocked. "Why don't you show us how to be *deceptive*?"

Lilith felt a spark of petty joy. "It would be my pleasure." Ranine started walking towards the exit, but Lilith held up a hand. "Stay. It'll be more fun this way."

Lilith took slow steps, her hands ready to block any sudden swing. She kept her body low, her feet wide. Tnil was taller than she was and looked like she had a stronger core. Ranine, on the other hand, was the same height. Her stance made her look like she could accelerate fast and change direction quickly. But she stood high, off balance.

Tnil made the first move. Lunging at Lilith with her left wrist. But instead of moving away, Lilith moved towards her, spinning just around Tnil's body. Before Tnil could turn, Lilith jumped and stuck her foot into her back, causing her to topple over.

Ranine was charging at her a second later. She swung her fist forward, but Lilith ducked, just bending her knees. She struck again and again, each attempt faster than the last, but Lilith dodged everyone, her feet not even moving. Ranine's legs straightened after the last failed punch, and Lilith took advantage of the opportunity. She stood, turning away from Ranine, and kicked one of her legs back, nailing her in the stomach. She flew back, knocking against the side of the arena.

Lilith stood, sticking her hands in her pockets. She smiled, blowing the hair out of her eyes. "Huh, I thought you guys were supposed to be good at this."

A second later, Tnil got up, charging at her. Lilith moved towards her at the last second, bending her knees and torso. Tnil tripped over her, toppling to the ground. The stubbornness of the girl was unbelievable, because a second later she got up, swinging her legs under Lilith's. She simply stepped over them, hands still resting in her pockets.

Tnil suddenly collapsed, panting hard, fast breaths. Her chest rose and fell, anger spurred in her eyes, but it was also accompanied by a dazed, exhausted look. Lilith leaned down, her face directly over Tnil's. "And that-" She told her, beaming arrogantly, "-is why I can give you advice."

Her head whipped around to the sound of clapping. A tall girl was walking towards them, the two front strands of her hair hung over her eyes. She wore a black, cloth coat that went down to her knees. "Bravo! Truly, quite a performance!" Quilla smiled, stepping into the ring. "Mind if I go next?"

Lilith smiled, it looked like her anger had gotten its wish. Her partner walked around the ring, Tnil and Ranine got up and left, but lingered around, eager to watch.

Quilla took off her coat, throwing it a few feet away from her. She wore a white blouse, and leather gloves that covered no higher than her palm. A chain necklace was strung around her neck. Lilith copied, taking off her leather jacket, and dropping into a stance. She watched Quilla's movements like a tiger to its prey.

Quilla took slow steps around the ring, her posture perfectly straight, her strides dramatic, and a sadistic smile along her lips. "So, no weapons, just hand-to-hand combat?"

Lilith nodded. "Let's not get hurt before the mission." She smiled, and the two girls made eye contact for a split second, then Quilla hurled herself at her. Her balance was perfect, her torso perfectly in line with her legs, but she moved fast. Lilith barely moved out of the way in time, her hair brushing Quilla's shoulder. Quilla didn't hesitate after the first failed attempt. She lunged at Lilith, this time going for the legs. But Lilith was ready. She jumped vertically, bouncing off the ring wall. Her feet landed on the opposite side of Quilla.

Before Lilith could attack, Quilla moved out of the way. She had her legs bent and her hands outstretched. Lilith grinned, her opponent had shifted to defense. Taking advantage of the situation, she pounced, attacking Quilla at full speed. But instead of dodging, the criminal prodigy leaped toward the wall of the ring and started climbing, like a spider escaping a predator.

Lilith gazed up, the wall was tall, maybe twenty-five feet. It had various holds that made it easy to scale, but she still pondered climbing after Quilla. Falling would be catastrophic, with serious consequences for an unnecessary fight. But if Quilla could do it...

Lilith hurled herself at the wall, gripping the holds with all of her strength. She was climbing, but it wasn't as graceful as what her partner had done. The grips seemed slippery, her nerves fluctuated with every inch higher. It caused her to slip, she lost her footing. It almost stopped her heart, knowing that the ground was just waiting to take her life.

The floor kept getting farther away. Her anxiety coursed through her body, making the holds somehow increasingly more slippery. One at a time, she told herself. All that she was focusing on was the next one, not her burning muscles or the nerves, or the ground that awaited her fate. Just the next hold.

You're so close. She told herself. *Three more holds.* Her arm stretched for the small nob. *Two more.* Her legs ached. *One more.* Her thoughts pounded in her head as she made the final push, finally seeing over the climb.

It was dusty on top of the wall. Pipes scattered the floor, as well as switches and wheels. Quilla was leaning against a larger, blue pipe. She didn't look the least bit exhausted. Her head tilted and she flicked her finger. "Rusty?"

"You retreated!" retorted Lilith, trying to sound less winded than she was.

"Hm." Quilla gave a small laugh, then grabbed an overhanging pipe, and swung forward. Her heeled boots landed on Lilith's back, knocking her to the ground. Immediately, she felt Quilla making another attack. Lilith faked one way and rolled another, causing Quilla to misstep.

In the split second she had, Lilith scrambled to her feet and started running along the edge of the wall. Her partner corrected quickly and hurled herself in the direction of where Lilith was going to be. Her steps were quick and sure, but just when they were about to collide, Lilith stopped abruptly.

Quilla's top weight leaned over the edge, causing her to lose her balance. She started to fall, horror sparked in her eyes as she realized gravity had taken control. Lilith lunged for her partner, grabbing her chain necklace.

"Hold on!" Lilith pleaded. "I've got you!"

Horror sparked in her own eyes as she heard a click. Quilla held up a fist, a sharp blade had sprouted from her gloves. "No, you don't." She whispered, a faint smile spreading across her lips. Her hand made a rapid motion, and she cut the chain.

Lilith expected Quilla to fall to the ground, but instead, she stuck her glove blade into the wall. It made a screeching sound for a couple of seconds, then her fall stopped, and she remained on the wall, grinning up at Lilith.

Fine! Lilith grit her teeth. *You break the rules, I break the rules.* With that, she lunged over the edge of the cliff. The wind whistled in her ears as she plummeted to the ground. She quickly covered her head with her hands and positioned her legs to be slightly bent. The impact wasn't as hard as she projected, the sparring ring was padded and her falling position was good, the impact felt light.

She raced to her bow and arrows, they were sitting on the outside of the sparring ring. She shuffled through her quiver, the arrows inside were lined with colored stripes. Blue for dull, red for sharp, and yellow being somewhere in between. She paused, holding the arrows in a bunch; then, with a sigh, she grabbed the blue ones. They would barely leave a bruise.

She ran to the center of the ring, an arrow already loaded. She pulled back the string, aligning it with her target. Quilla was swinging from hold to hold on the wall, occasionally pulling out her gloved blades to catch her fall. She moved swiftly in unpredictable ways, never stopping or slowing down. Lilith had to constantly shift her aim, trying to predict where her target was going to move next. She inhaled, readjusting her aim quickly, and let go of the string, breathing out while she did it.

The arrow whistled up the wall, landing a foot above Quilla's head. Her opponent stopped, gazing at where the arrow was stuck to the wall. She raised her eyebrows and continued moving.

Lilith quickly reloaded, aiming with an inhale, and firing with an exhale. Her aim was on track, but Quilla saw it coming, and stopped suddenly, causing the arrow to miss just inches away from her stomach. Lilith saw the opportunity and quickly reloaded. She didn't have time to aim, so she fired, but her practice and repetition pulled through. Her aim was direct, on track to strike her right in the shoulder. But Quilla's head turned at the last second. She held up her hand and caught the arrow in a swift, effortless motion.

The criminal prodigy paused, examining the weapon with curiosity, then she threw it back down, a perfect spiral, right at Lilith's head. The archer rolled out of the way, watching the arrow puncture the pads at the bottom of the ring.

She looked up to see that Quilla had jumped down. The con queen stood straight, her hands clenched into fists and a grim smile on her face. Lilith got to her feet, grabbing two of her arrows from her quiver to wield like spears. Her legs bent, positioning the arrows at her side. She heard a familiar click and saw that Quilla's blades were out.

Her opponent charged, still smiling. Lilith twirled around her, attempting to use her arrows. Quilla turned and blocked it with one of her knives, with the other she made a jab at Lilith's stomach. Lilith backed up just in time, sliding her feet on the soft mat. She crouched, her arrows out, waiting for Quilla to make a move.

Quilla lunged, her blades out like claws, charging towards her like a cat. At the last second, Lilith twirled behind her, arrows out in front of her. They were meant to point at the back of her partner's neck, but instead, Quilla twirled at the last second, her throat just inches away from Lilith's arrows. When she stopped swirling, her arm was extended, her blade pointed at Lilith's throat.

They stood there for a second, panting hard breaths, neither letting down their weapon. Quilla's hair was messy, several strands hung down in front of her face. Her eyes were locked on Lilith's, not dropping her focus for a second.

Someone behind them cleared his throat. The two of them whipped their heads around to see Nikolai standing before them. His hand was over his eyes and his head was down in what looked like frustration. His clenched fists were turning white. He looked up only for a second, eyes burning with rage. When he spoke it felt like he was about to explode with rage, "Ship. *Now.*"

Chapter Twenty Two
Nikolai

Nikolai was pacing around his cabin. His fingers were pressed against his temples, his brain struggling to think through the anger and frustration. He kept glancing towards the two unruly girls that sat on the two seats at his desk, unsure that they would still be there when he looked again.

Lilith sat straight. Her hands were clasped on her lap, and she fiddled with her fingers nervously. Her green eyes were soaked with guilt, watching Nikolai as he paced.

Her partner, on the other hand, was slouched in her chair. Thorne's feet were resting on Nikolai's desk. Her arms were crossed and her glaring eyes followed Nikolai's every move.

"Feet. Off!" he told her sternly, slamming his fists on the table. Thorne raised her eyebrows and smiled. To his surprise, she lifted her feet off the table and gently set them on the ground.

Nikolai sighed, sitting in the chair on the opposite side of the desk. "Look," he rested his cheek in his palm. "I know you're new to the League, or maybe any kind of organization in general, but we don't make a mess of everything we touch here. I need you two to be somewhat responsible."

Thorne looked as though she was about to open her mouth, but Lilith nudged her. "Sorry, Nikolai."

"Ghan's forces are disciplined, organized, and trained from birth. If we even want a slim chance of winning this war we need to be better. More disciplined, more organized, more-"

Thorne held up a hand. Her lips were spread in a flat line, like she was bored. "You're going about it entirely the wrong way." Her crisp accent was infuriating. "You're trying to beat the best of the best with their own game. As impressive as it might be, you don't have the resources nor the knowledge to even come close. In my opinion, you should catch them off guard. If you take away their order, Empire soldiers are like headless chickens running in circles." Nikolai crossed his arms, unsure if the criminal prodigy was going to continue with the advice he didn't need nor want.

"What makes you think I want your opinion?" Nikolai asked accusingly.

"You're not the only one that's considered a strategist, Lone."

"I thought you were a criminal."

A fanged smile spread across Thorne's lips. "No reason I can't be both."

Nikolai sighed and pressed his finger against his temple. "Fine." He said looking up. "Since you're such an expert, how would you do it?"

"The Empire has several different classes, each trained from birth. Each class has around twenty members, or, if you're unlucky to come across one with less than ten members, that's a silver class. These classes have been trained in order and discipline from the moment they popped out of the womb, so naturally, they know nothing else. When you take that order away, they have nothing. Their entire life they've been fighting organized opponents. Skilled, disciplined, and oh so *predictable*." Thorne leaned forward in her chair. "Another thing, each class has a leader, and they can't operate without them. Cut off the head and the body will die."

Lilith turned to her partner. "What's the difference between a regular class and a silver one?"

Thorne frowned. "Regular classes, or bronze classes, train around four hours a day, whereas silver classes train closer to eight. Silvers are also trained by better instructors, not just for fighting but for leading as well. They are usually the leaders of the bronze. But once in a while, for a big mission, they'll go out as a class, and they're almost unstoppable."

Nikolai leaned forward. Something wasn't right, how did Thorne know more about the Empire than an organization that was dedicated to taking them down?

"What about the Golden Class?" he asked skeptically.

Thorne hesitated, something sparked in her eyes, but a second later it was gone. "To my knowledge, they're nothing more than a myth."

Nikolai looked skeptical. "How do you know more about the Empire than me, who, may I remind you, was trained from birth to take them down?"

"Maybe the League hasn't been telling you as much as you thought they were."

Nikolai sighed, pushing down the anxiety rising in his throat. "Show me your neck, Thorne." He said in the calmest voice he could manage.

"Nikolai she's not-" Lilith tried, but Thorne held up a hand. She stood, turned around, and brushed her long hair over her shoulder. The only tattoo on her neck was a black rose, no sign of an Empire symbol.

"See?" she said in a spiteful tone. "I'm not one of them." She turned and headed for the door, slamming it behind her.

Nikolai sighed, his head was beginning to hurt. "How can she be this difficult?"

Lilith huffed a laugh, "Years of practice, I guess." She smiled gently. "Quilla's hated Ghan for forever. She would sooner destroy her reputation than work for the Empire. I'm not saying I know her at all, but trust me on this. When it comes to hurting the Empire, she's trustworthy."

"Why does she hate him so much?" Nikolai asked.

Lilith sighed. "Dunno, it's a pretty sensitive topic. I try to stay clear of anything that mentions the Empire." She turned, looking out the door. Worry seemed to glimmer on her face. "What was Alohi like?"

Nikolai looked towards the ceiling. Warmth filled him as a smile spread across his lips. "Brilliant." He said softly. "She always knew the right thing to say, and she always knew where to find me when I was at my lowest. She knew how to keep the League of Red Dove's together, like when she was there, we suddenly felt like a family."

Lilith smiled, looking down, as if remembering a fond memory. "She sounds great. Warm."

Nikolai laughed. "She was!" he leaned against his desk with excitement and passion. "Once, when I was young, I lost a sparring match that should have been easily won. My father yelled at me. I remember him hitting me so hard, it felt like my whole world was falling apart." Nikolai flinched at the unpleasant memory. "I just locked myself in the training center after that. I didn't sleep, didn't eat, I just trained. Alohi found me one day, she had me sit down, and I put my head on her shoulder. Soon I was asleep. When I woke up, there was breakfast right in front of me. She told me that if I didn't go to the cafeteria to eat food, she would bring the food to me."

Lilith's eyes filled with compassion. "Oh, Nikolai, I'm so sorry."

Nikolai laughed. "It's okay, it was worse back then." He rested his cheek on his palm. "So, where are you from?"

Lilith sighed, her eyes downcast. "I was a slave in the Grave Desert."

Nikolai gaped. "I had no idea, I'm so sorry." Sorrow and empathy filled him. Lilith seemed so optimistic and bright, he would have never imagined she had a past that dark.

"That's okay," she told him, her tone still downcast. "It was a while ago. Quilla rescued me, actually." She ran her hand through her hair. "She was making some kind of deal with my owner, and looked pretty battered too. I threw an arrow at her, but she blocked it. Saved me from a beating and took me with her to Hanslack." She took out one of her arrows and ran her finger down its smooth side. "She taught me everything I know."

Nikolai examined the arrow, blue stripes ran down its sides like the ones of a tiger. "That explains why she threw Olan off my ship. She must really care about you."

That sentence sent Lilith into a spurt of laughter, she tilted her head back as happy tears formed in her eyes. "Quilla doesn't care about me. All she cares about is her list of revenge, and my talent plays a large role in that."

He looked at her skeptically. "She was about to spare Olan's life. Not until he started talking about the Grave Desert. It wouldn't affect your shooting if he was or wasn't alive, but it would affect you." He lifted his chin. "So I beg to differ, she cares about you."

Lilith sighed. "She never talks about her past. I'm about the closest one to her and I don't have a clue where she comes from."

He looked out his large, circular window into the blue, chaotic sea. "Maybe it's best we don't know what dark hole she crawled out of."

Chapter Twenty Three
Quilla

A young girl ran through the train. Several seats lined each car, they were a terrible, all too familiar dark blue. Tears streamed from the girl's eyes, her mind trying to block the event that happened just hours before.

The girl reached the end of the car quickly, crying large sobs. Her tiny hands lunged for the door handle, shaking it desperately. It wouldn't budge.

The girl's breath began to feel short. She collapsed to the floor, sobs overwhelmed her body as she shook.

Wake up! She thought. *This is a dream. When you wake up, you'll be home, and everything will be okay*! She yanked her hair vigorously, then dug her nails into her cheeks.

"WAKE UP!" the yell sprang from her throat like a rabid frog. She got up and banged her head against the locked door. The physical pain felt almost comforting, like a world that was robbed from her. A world that everyone else could dwell in, but the universe withheld her from.

Tears streamed down her face as she fell to the ground once again. The mental pain was unbearable, her hands covered her ears, attempting to block out her thoughts.

I'm home. She told herself, not believing it at all. *My dads are home, it's all still there. None of it is real!* She chanted it to herself, alone in the dark. "It's not real, it's not real, it's not... it's not..."

She sat up and screamed again, her pain ripping out in a horrid, loud sound. It seemed to go on for minutes, but when she closed her mouth, a scream was still going. She opened her teary eyes to see another girl.

They appeared to be the same age, five at the most. Her eyes were puffy and her face tear-stained. She was all sharp edges and straight hair. Her white, fanged teeth were pressed together in a world of pain.

"They're-" she started, sobs lining her voice. "They're really gone, aren't they? All of it is all gone." Her voice was quiet, barely a whisper.

The curly-haired child put her arms around the sobbing girl, holding her while they shook.

That was when the realization hit, it was all gone, and never coming back. She would never see any of it again. This caused her to shake more violently, sobs racking her voice. She hugged the girl harder, pressing her nose into her soft hair. 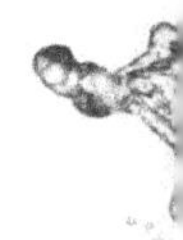

Eventually, the girl with straight hair sat up, tears still stained her face. Strands of hair fell in front like a small trickle of water. "What's your name?" she asked in a small voice.

The curly-haired girl wiped her eyes. "Rosalie." Her voice was small, barely a murmur, but the girl with straight hair nodded.

"Rosalie?" her face brightened. "That's a pretty name." She moved closer, resting her head on her shoulder. "But I'm gonna call you Rose."

Rose smiled. "I like that." She wrapped her arms around the girl. "What's your name?"

The girl kept her head buried in Rose's chest. "Cercel." She said softly. "But you can call me Cerce."

~~~

Quilla awoke with a jolt. Cold sweat covered her body. She grasped her chest, panting rapidly. "Shut up!" she told herself in a whisper. The name still echoed in her head. *Cerce, Cerce, Cerce.*

"*Shut up!*" she said, louder than she meant to. "You're dead! Now stop tormenting me!" she threw the knife on her nightstand across the room. It stuck in the door perfectly.

"Quilla?" she whipped her head to see Lilith sitting up. "Who are you talking to?"

Quilla growled. She got out of bed swiftly and pulled on her coat. Her long fingers curled around the knife as she strode out the door.

The night was icy. The wind of the ocean blew her hair behind her like a shredded flag. Tears slipped from her eyes, from the wind, or from emotions she could not tell. Her mind frantically tried to push back her thoughts.

Why now? She asked. *Why then?* She kept her eyes trained on the turbulent ocean. *Why me?*

Something touched her shoulder suddenly. Quilla whirled around, her knife landed right at the person's throat. Fear shook in her unsteady hands. She took rapid breaths, her chest rising and falling quickly.

Her vision focused, revealing Lilith standing in front of her. The archer grasped her hand, gently lowering the knife from her throat. Quilla turned away from her, resting her elbows on the taffrail. Lilith leaned next to her.

"Quilla," she started. "What's going on?"

She turned her head, narrowing her eyes with resentment. "It's none of your concern."

"I'm just worried." Lilith reached for her shoulder, but Quilla batted her hand away. She turned to Lilith, her fists clenched, eyes little slits of anger.

"Stop acting like you know me!" she screamed at her. "You know *nothing* about me!" Lilith's face broke. Her hair swayed gently in front of her face as a daze wandered over her eyes.
~~~

"Quilla-" she started, pain scraping her voice.

"And if you're smart," Quilla turned away, trying not to notice how much the pain in Lilith's eyes hurt her. "You'll stay far, *far* away from me."

Chapter Twenty Four
Nikolai

"I just don't get her!" Lilith paced around Nikolai's cabin angrily. Her fists were clenched and her strides were long. Anger seemed to pulse like a beating heart. "One second she's treating me like a close friend and the next she's telling me to buzz off!"

Nikolai looked up from the book he was reading. His legs were crossed and his chin rested on his palm. "She's quite peculiar, isn't she?"

Lilith scoffed. "What is her problem?" she flung herself at Nikolai's punching bag that was hanging in the corner of the cabin. Her fists hit it relentlessly, each punch harder than the last. "She's terrified of her own emotion to the point where she doesn't admit she has any!" she repeatedly punched a singular part of the bag, all of her anger being channeled into the one piece of cloth. One extra hard hit caused the bag to cave in, Lilith's fist jammed into it and sand spilled out, falling like water.

Lilith pulled her fist out, dusting the sand from her knuckles. "Sorry."

Nikolai sighed. He set his book on the table and opened one of the drawers to his desk, grabbing a small string and needle. "Catch." He said as he tossed the string to Lilith. She caught it with one hand, studying the needle carefully. "Hope you know how to sew."

She pulled the needle from the thread. "How hard could it be?"

Nikolai gave a small laugh. He then slouched back into his chair, picked up his book, and began to read again. His thoughts drifted from page to page, scanning the words. Master Killen had given it to him, it was titled, The Mental Way to Slay a Dragon. It was supposedly to help with his state of mind. Even though Killen often talked about a space free of judgment, the many passages about crippling self-doubt made Nikolai feel quite attacked. One memorable paragraph described a situation where a man had skill beyond any of his other opponents, but when the time came, he flunked. Not because of his lack of skill, but lack of belief in it. The story was uncannily close to many of his previous failures, which he had strived to forget about. Of course, Killen was right about his poor state of mind, but it still stung.

"Argh!" Nikolai closed his book as he heard the frustrated scream. Lilith was standing over the wrecked punching bag, sand covered the floor like a pool of blood. Her chest was rising up and down quickly, her legs bent in a fighting stance. It looked as though the string and needle had been thrown to a far corner of the room.

Nikolai raised his eyebrows. "That's coming out of your paycheck."

She sighed, brushing her hair out of her eyes. "That's fair."

He stood, placing the book on his desk with an unnecessary slam. "I'm hungry, I'm going to breakfast." He strode out the door, Lilith trailing close behind him. The deck outside was polished, a light breeze ruffled his hair as the cold morning air ran through it.

Nikolai lifted a hatch. Below it was a set of polished stairs. Once down, he gazed at the cafeteria. Bowls of porridge lined several seats of a long table. Steam rose from the hot food.

Lilith raised her eyebrows. "Well, this is impressive." She strode past him, taking a seat at the table and blowing on her breakfast. Nikolai sat down beside her, taking a spoon of porridge and stuffing it in his mouth.

He quickly regretted the decision, spitting the food back into his bowl and rubbing his tongue against his shirt. "Hot!" he said after wiping his tongue.

Lilith nearly fell over laughing, tears beaded at the corner of her eyes as she let out a chain of giggles. "Oh, how princely!" she said between laughs. Nikolai chuckled a bit, enjoying the warm feeling inside him.

"I'm glad we're sharing this together." He said. Lilith gave him a confused expression. "Not the oatmeal. The conversation. Like the moment, or something."

Lilith just laughed. "I'm glad we're friends too."

Nikolai gazed at the empty chairs in front of them, all of the crew had already sat down to eat, or had already eaten. "Speaking of which, where's your other friend?" Lilith raised an eyebrow. "You know, the reason my punching bag is nothing more than a pile of sand."

"Huh." She let out a small laugh. "My guess is she didn't sleep well last night." She took a bite of porridge, clearly not as hot as his had been a minute ago.

"She sleeps?" Nikolai asked, taking a second attempt at breakfast.

"Depends on the day."

Nikolai looked up the stairs. "You stay here, get acquainted with the crew. I'll find Thorne."

Lilith took a bite of food. "Good luck."

"Thanks, I'll need it." Nikolai headed up to Thorne's quarters. The wind was starting to pick up, and the ocean had become more turbulent. He opened the door, slowly. Inside were two beds. The first one was a mess. The blanket was half on the floor, and the pillow was in the dead center of the mattress. The other was made perfectly, the blanket hung down like a curtain.

Nikolai looked around. The lights were off, and no window shades were open. All he could smell was roses.

"Thorne!" he called out. "It may come as a surprise to you but your body needs food, especially when you're about to commit treason."

"Shut. *It.*" Nikolai's gaze shot upward. Sitting on one of the ceiling beams with her legs crossed, was the con queen. Her eyes were closed and her breath seemed to be coming out in rhythms.

Nikolai was struggling to hold in laughs. "You meditate?" he asked, nearly doubling over.

"How amusing." Thorne rolled her eyes and hopped down from her perch. She crossed her arms. "And yes. I meditate. Skills aren't the only thing that matters in a fight you know."

Nikolai scoffed, remembering his master's many lessons. "Oh, I know."

Thorne pulled on her jacket. "Sure you do." She walked towards the door, turning her head right as she was about to walk out. "Oh, and for the record, I've committed treason, war crimes, and many other things that can land me the death penalty. And I am, *very*, proud of them."

This time it was Nikolai's turn to roll his eyes. "I will never understand you."

"And I, you." With that she headed out the door, her long coat trailing behind her.

The wind was blowing at full strength now, the boat moving at a high speed because of its newfound force. In the distance, he could see an island, rocks were poking out of the water like jaggers. On the island was a large, square building.

"We're closer than I thought," Nikolai said. "Man your stations, be ready! I'm not planning on engaging in a fight, but I want to be ready if we find ourselves in that kind of situation!"

"Where should we dock, Sir?" Rex asked, suddenly appearing next to him. His posture was as straight as ever, and his uniform was poised and tidy.

"No need," Thorne answered. "Once we get close, we can swim to the Archives."

"Uh, no." Lilith materialized next to them. "We can't."

The two glared at each other for a while, Nikolai standing awkwardly in between. The tension was so real you could cut it with a knife. Eventually, Thorne sighed. "Fine. You got a boat, pretty boy?" she turned, searching the deck. "Preferably a small one with oars."

Nikolai led them to a boat hanging off the main deck. It was held up with a pulley system that could lower it into the water. Oars were positioned on the sides. The boat itself was in a pretty bad state; a couple of holes were in the oars, and the wood was chipped, but overall, it was usable.

Nikolai gestured with his hands to beat up the boat, leaning down and smiling. "Only the best." He said in a mischievous tone, enjoying this a little too much.

Thorne's lip curled. "I hate you." The two climbed into the boat, positioning themselves in a position to row. Nikolai grasped the wheel attached to the pulley system, slowly turning it and lowering the girls into the water. At the last second, he let go of the wheel, letting the boat freefall until he heard a splash.

He leaned over the edge, both girls were still in the boat, but they looked slightly sprayed and very annoyed. "Oops, slipped." Thorne looked ready to hurl a knife at his head.

The girls picked up their oars, begging to paddle away. "Wait!" Nikolai held up his hand.

Lilith turned her head to look at him. "In, out. Don't break anything. We got it, thanks."

"That's not it." Nikolai pinched the bridge of his nose, not believing he cared about this. "Be careful, okay?"

Lilith gave him a small, reassuring smile. "Always am!" with that, the boat turned and he watched them slowly row into the distance.

Chapter Twenty Five
Quilla

The wind blew hard around the Archives. Trees looked as though they could topple over at any moment, and the harsh sea looked as if it would swallow you up in just a second.

A large, square building stood in the middle of the island. Inside, was all the information the Empire held dear. Its steel walls were indestructible, the only entrance in the front was heavily guarded, and anything abnormal got blown to bits.

Patrol marched around the building, their blue suits blowing in the wind, only staying still where their armor clung. They clutched the swords at their hilts, clearly cautious with the cloudy, windy day.

One wearing dark silver held up a hand, stopping the march suddenly. He scanned the open sea. "Look!" he said, pointing to a small, old boat that was pulled up onto the rocky shore. He pulled out his sword, already in a fighting position. "Someone's here."

The patrol armed themselves, taking slow, steady steps. Suddenly, they all whipped their heads around. A silhouette was outlined in the distance. She was tall and slim, her hair blowing in the wind along with her long coat. She strode towards them with confidence, hands clasped behind her back.

"Freeze!" the one in silver shouted. "Put your hands up and get on your knees, we need to escort you off this island, ma'am."

The woman gasped, covering her mouth with a hand. "Am I not supposed to be here?" she asked in a shocked voice. "I had no idea, *commander*." The patrol looked at each other warily. Something wasn't right. The woman put her hands up, lowering herself to the wet leaves.

Just as her knees touched the ground, the first arrow flew by. It landed in the center of one of the soldiers' chests. He fell to the ground just as another arrow shot past, impaling another soldier.

"Take cover!" the silver commander yelled frantically. The men scrambled, trying to find refuge from the nearby sniper.

Quilla got up from her knees, drawing two knives like claws. She strode around like a lion, hunting for its prey patiently. The leaves under her boots crinkled with every step.

"No one wants to come to play?" she spotted one hiding behind a tree. "I'm disappointed!" the blade spun out of her hand and into the man's throat. He crumpled to the ground as wine-colored blood leaked from the wound.

Just then, another one charged at her. She turned quickly, dropping into a fighting stance, but her sniper had it taken care of. Another arrow flew into his chest, causing him to fall at Quilla's feet.

Just as she straightened her posture, the sound of footsteps crept into the night sky. Not just one pair of feet, but the entire battalion. Their swords were pointed and every angle was blocked, but Quilla just smiled. At the last second, she jumped. She spun in the air, disarming several swords with her hands. She landed with her blades between her fingers, like they were a part of her.

Her knives slid across the warm flesh of the soldiers' throats. They crumpled at her feet, causing the wet leaves to turn a crimson red. The second wave wasn't far behind. One tackled her from behind, his grimy hands clamped around her neck. Quilla froze for a second, then threw her head forward and sent the man flying.

She clicked her gloves. Blades sprouted along her knuckles. The last of the attackers swung at her, but she was ready, dropping into a fighting position. One went at her from the top, but she quickly dragged her blade along his stomach. Quilla then ran, charging at the rest with speed. She slashed at their throats, sending them toppling to the ground in a bloody mess.

Quilla stood straight, wiping the blood on her hands against her coat. The island surrounding the Archives was now eerily silent. Only the screams of the fallen remained, some murmured, some only echoed.

But... there was something else. Quilla furrowed her brow in concentration, trying to figure out where the exhausted panting was coming from. Her head whipped around as her eyes found the singular silver sprinting towards the woods. A smile crept along her lips as she drew a knife and hurled it at the sprinting man. It caught the fabric of his clothing and pinned him to a tree.

"Going somewhere, *commander*?" she strode to him with blades resting in her palms. He struggled against her knife, but the blade wouldn't budge. His black hair hung over his terrified eyes as he realized that death would follow soon.

His eyes suddenly grew bigger with a new revelation. "I know you!" he exclaimed, but Quilla shoved a blade into his heart before he could continue.

"No." She jutted out her jaw, "You don't."

She let the commander's lifeless body fall to her feet. Lilith materialized behind her, wiping the blood on her arrows against the inside of her coat. "Well, three minutes in and we already made shit of the League's plans. As far as disobeying orders go, that's a new record!"

Quilla scoffed. "Could've helped a bit, couldn't you?"

Her partner shrugged. "Yeah, but you always said to watch the master at work." Quilla tilted her head in doubt. "Plus, I ran out of ammo."

Quilla rolled her eyes. "Come on." She beckoned. "We need to get out of here before the next shift change."

The two girls ran to the back of the building with long strides. Quilla could feel the cold air biting her nose. Once they reached the back, she stopped abruptly.

An exasperated sigh escaped her lips as she saw the vent. It was at least three stories in the air, and the Archives were all steel, too slippery to climb on. She turned to Lilith, "Any ideas?"

She threw up her hands. "I thought you had this planned out?"

Quilla put her hands on her hips. "There was limited time! If it was up to me, I would have scoped this out *before* we attempted the heist! So do you have an idea, or not?"

Lilith growled. "Of course, I have an idea."

Quilla watched as she removed an arrow from her quiver. It was one of the red ones, the tip was as sharp as a sharpened knife. She then pulled out a coil. The string was clear, but it looked strong and stretchy.

"Don't you use that to restring your bow?" Quilla asked.

"Usually, yes." She said, tying the string to her arrow. "But in tough situations, I've learned to improvise. Can you hand me one of your knives?"

Quilla tossed her a serrated one from the inside of her coat. She caught it with one hand, not looking up from what she was doing. Her hands cut the string gently, leaving a lot of material to work with.

"Remember when you sent me, Soren, and Rye on that lab heist?" she asked, loading her bow with the red arrow.

"Granite Labs? Yes." Quilla responded skeptically. "To retrieve some new prototype Gillen needed. What about it?"

She fired the arrow, it landed right above the vent. Lilith tugged the string harshly, but the arrow attached didn't budge. "When we were escaping, they released some kind of genetically modified dog on us. Used this trick to get over their big brick wall." She grasped the coil tightly, putting her feet on the steel wall of the Archives. She started climbing, cautiously moving up the wall with her makeshift grappling hook. "You're welcome."

Quilla sighed. She grabbed the string and climbed after her, carefully making her way to the vent.

Lilith reached it first, she yanked the vent door and it popped open with a clang. The two then slipped into the silver vent. Quilla yanked Lilith's arrow from the steel and handed it to her, then placed the door over the vent. It was surprisingly roomy, both of them could crawl comfortably, but it was unpleasantly dark.

Quilla felt her way around the dark corner. "I memorized the way there, just follow my lead."

"Oh, that would be a great idea! That is if I knew where you were." Lilith said in a sarcastic tone.

She scoffed, grabbing her wrist and placing it on her ankle. "Now you know where I am. Follow me."

They weaved through many corners, Quilla leading the way and Lilith's hand on her ankle, trying to keep up. The vent was dusty and even though she couldn't see, Quilla could feel the soot on her hand. She frequently stopped to brush it off on her coat with a frustrated growl. This was not a pleasant experience that she was eager to endure again.

Finally, they reached the end. Light peeked out of the hatch's shutters, finally letting her eyes see again. She sped up her crawl, desperate to get to the end of this tunnel. Before popping open the vent, she paused, peeking through the little slits. Two patrol guards were walking outside. Their blue uniforms signified they had the rank of bronze.

"What are you waiting for?" whispered her partner. "We can take them!"

"Yes, but if we take them we alert the entire building we're here!" she retorted. "I at least want to make it seem like we were listening to anything those Dove guys said!"

Lilith growled something under her breath, but Quilla wasn't paying attention to her anymore. Her eyes were on the guards, who were walking past the vent. Their posture was shrinking, clearly exhausted from their long day at work. Once they turned the corner, she popped open the vent hatch, jumping to the ground without making a sound.

"Ugh!" Lilith exclaimed quietly once they had reached the ground. "I don't care what Nikolai's paying us. I am not breaking into this thing again!"

"Once you have your money, you won't have to," Quilla told her. She then hurried along the wall, her feet not making a sound.

Lilith followed her, it felt as though their shoes were barely touching the ground. They stayed on the center of their feet, gently padding on the shiny floor. The halls were dark gray and circular. Pillars curved around the walls like a textured pipe. It was surprisingly bright, the murky light shimmering off the metal.

Quilla crept around the edge of another corner, stopping at a set of massive doors. The two of them were in a giant, square room, tiny pipe-like tunnels departed off of every corner. The doors were a different type of metal, looking more like a solid iron than steel. Wooden bars crossed them horizontally, and two stone owls were perched at the top.

Quilla pushed the doors and they slid open with a creek, revealing an even larger, dark room. She sighed happily and turned, "Welcome to the Archives!"

Chapter Twenty Six
Lilith

Lilith walked into the vast room. Shelves that were several stories tall were lined in rows. The room gave an eerie brown glow, as if it was lit up purely by candlelight. Each of the shelves had a tiny slit, as though meant for paper.

Quilla strode over to one of the shelves. She pulled a small piece of paper from her cloak, clicking a pen in her other hand. "What was her name again?"

"Alohi Windlem," Lilith said plainly. Quilla jotted the name down quickly, then strode over to one of the nearby shelves. She held the paper by the edge and stuck it into the slit.

Quilla stood back as the shelf rattled. The several sheets of paper that rested on it seemed to click and separate until one spewed out of the tiny slit. The rattling stopped, and the room was as quiet as when they first entered.

"The shelves are arranged alphabetically. Find anyone or anything's name, and get all the information the Empire has on them." She reached into her coat and grabbed several small sheets of paper, handing them and the pen to Lilith. "I'm assuming you have some questions, this place has the answers."

She took them, searching her mind for anyone she had unsettled disputes with. Her mind then flashed and she headed to the farthest shelf. On the card, she wrote *Polar Zinglor*. Anger bristled on her skin as she thought of his face. She shoved the card into the slot, eager to get rid of the aura the name held.

The shelf shuttered, and papers clicked and shifted. Lilith watched from down below, patiently waiting for her answers. The shaking suddenly stopped, and the tiny slit spit out a small pamphlet. She ripped it from the shelf, opening it aggressively.

At the top of the sheet of paper read his name; next was his date of birth and family heritage. Lilith skimmed most of it, her finger trailing the words. Eventually, she stopped where the paper read the address. *434 Grand Hill*, the rich side of town. Lilith took out the pen and jotted the information down, hoping to use it later. She continued to read, finding that he went to school at Sea Cliff University and that he had a *wife*.

She fondly imagined holding a knife to Polar's sweetheart's throat. In a perfect reality, he would be sobbing and begging for a mercy that would never come. Lilith would savor his pain. Keep it bottled inside a special memory. She would murder all of the people he loved, but leave him with the guilt and the sorrow of a broken failure!

She shuddered, breaking out of this thought to the revelation of how horrible it was. She had been spending too much time with Quilla.

Her hands grasped the pen again, a new idea popping into her head. She crouched on the floor and wrote the name, *Terrace Cole*. She wrote it neatly, not an ink smudge out of place. When she was done, she brushed the words with her finger, trying not to pay attention to the hurt that came with the loss of her father.

Lilith gently placed it into the slot, watching the shelf shutter and click until it made a halting stop. She took the pamphlet gently, trying not to leave any creases.

Her knees hit the floor hard when she read the word at the top. She cradled the pamphlet against her heart as several tears rushed down her cheeks. She opened it again, hoping to find another description, but the same word remained. *Deceased*.

She read through the pamphlet, her heart aching at every word. Memories of her father rushed through her head. She remembered when she was little, they would do target practice together.

~~~

"Look where you want the arrow to go." He told her, straightening her head gently with his hands. A seven-year-old Lilith held a bow and arrow that was much too big for her little body. She pointed it at the target, a tree trunk that had been flipped over. Its rings were prominent, making it the perfect bullseye.

"Pull the string back." Her father instructed. He was a tall man, his hair was long and had a brownish-red look to it. He wore a sleeved shirt and baggy shorts that had dirt smeared over them. Lilith did as he said, struggling to pull the stiff bowstring. "Breath in." He told her in a whisper. She took a large, exaggerated breath, puffing out her cheeks to hold it in.

Her father laughed. "No, not like that!" Lilith released the air she had been holding. "It has to be relaxed, calm, it's supposed to center you."

Lilith inhaled again, this time taking a slow, natural breath. Her father nodded. "Now," he told her. "At the same time, breathe out and let go of the string."

As soon as her fingers uncurled around the bowstring, Lilith knew the aim was off. She breathed out too hard, and her hand slipped, causing the arrow to fly into a nearby bush.

Lilith screamed in anger, slamming her bow on the ground. But her father did not react; instead, he knelt, putting his hands on her shoulders.

"Lilith, it's not the good shots that make a good archer, but your reactions to the bad ones." He picked up the bow and handed it to her. "If you give up after your first bad shot, then you will never have a good one."

Lilith reloaded the bow, pulling back the string and taking a relaxed breath at the same time. She looked at her father and smiled. Her tiny hands shifted the bow, lining it up with the target. Then, in one fluid motion, she let go of the string, exhaling while she did it. The arrow flew into the stump, not in the center but on one of the middle rings.
~~~

She jumped with joy, throwing her hands up and hugging her father. He had a smug expression on his face, looking at Lilith with proud eyes.

Even at that early age, Lilith never looked for perfection. All she expected from herself was improvement. It was what her father taught her, and what she would one day pass on to her own kids. Perfection doesn't exist, but with improvement, you can accomplish far more even if it did.

~~~

Lilith hugged the pamphlet, memories of her father seemed to float around it. Her eyes stung with new tears and her cheeks felt sticky with old ones. She wiped her eyes with her sleeve and carefully tucked the pamphlet into her jacket.

She took out another slip of paper, a new idea popping into her mind. She took the pen and quickly wrote down the name– *Quilla Cercel Thorne.*

She remembered seeing Quilla's peculiar middle name when she was signing forms for Gillen. She wrote it in a slanted cursive that Lilith could barely read, but over the years she made it out.

Lilith stuffed the slip into the slot, watching as the shelf shuttered. But it seemed to go on for longer this time. She watched as the papers clicked and slid, but minutes went by and the shelf kept shaking, as though it was going through all the papers twice. All of a sudden, it stopped and the eerie quiet of the archives returned. A small piece of paper popped out of the slot.

Lilith took it gently but stumbled back as she read the words. Her hand flew to her mouth to keep her from gasping. She blinked, making sure she read the words correctly, but sure enough, in black lettering, she read– *file does not exist.*
~~~

Chapter Twenty Seven
Alohi

The cafeteria felt different after her escape attempt. Instead of being small and afraid, she felt like she ruled the place. No one was bowing to her, and she was painfully aware of the watchful eyes of the guards that followed her every move. She was surprised that they even let her in the cafeteria after her big escape.

After she had been knocked out, Alohi was thrown back into her small cell. Of course, she was unconscious at the time. But when she woke up to the blank, gray ceiling, that's what she had guessed happened.

Until now, she had no idea what had happened to Joshua and Nathaniel. She found her heart pounding with anxiety at the thought that her partners had suffered a much greater fate than she had. So when she saw them in the cafeteria, she was more than thrilled.

As soon as she saw the old man's snow-white beard and the inmate's shiny head, she ran over. They were eating the slop that was served in the cafeteria, trying to get enough of it into their body so that they could survive another day in the mines. Hopefully, they wouldn't have to spend too many more days in that awful place.

"Hey!" she chimed as she met them. The two of them looked at her with dull faces. "I'm glad you're alright."

Joshua's eyes were as gray as the room around them. All he did in response was nod.

Alohi sat down next to them, leaning against the concrete wall. "So," she started, her tone soft and positive. "When are we going to try again?"

They looked up at her. Nathaniel's face was soft and apologetic, but Joshua's was hard as a rock. "We *aren't*."

Disappointment sprang into Alohi's eyes. "What do you mean?"

Joshua stood up, anger radiating off him. "I *mean* I'm not going to try and escape again."

Nathaniel nodded solemnly. "I'm sorry, Alohi." He said in an apologetic tone. "But we're lucky we only got off with a slap on the wrist. Next time, we won't be as lucky."

Loud, dry cackles rose from Joshua's throat. He may have been laughing, but there was no trace of humor in his tone. "A slap on the wrist?" he exclaimed after he pulled himself together. "Is that what you call this?" he rolled up his long sleeves to reveal bloodied bandages going all the way up his forearm.

Alohi's jaw nearly hit the floor. She just looked at his arm, gaping. "Josh-"

"No." He interrupted. "Whatever you have to say, politician, I don't want to hear it. You may have been the one to organize this whole charade, but I'm the one who paid for *your* failure." The inmate turned away from her, his voice barely a whisper. "I don't want to see you. Don't talk to me, Alohi, *ever* again."

Nathaniel stood up next, placing a frail hand on her shoulder. "Sorry kid." He said with apologetic eyes. "It's for the best." With that he walked away, not looking back once.

Alohi was stunned. Sorrow and guilt plagued her mind as she watched them helplessly. For a moment, she couldn't move, her emotions holding her down like chains. Then they were replaced with pure, unfiltered rage.

With clenched fists, she grabbed a glass plate from the food line. She then climbed onto an empty table and smashed the thing against the ground.

The noise was ear-splitting, like a thousand knives clattering to the floor at once. All eyes turned to her, curious and expecting.

Alohi looked at them with a blank expression. Now that she had their attention, the words wouldn't come out of her mouth. She stood, frozen, unable to produce even a sentence when she had a speech prepared before.

No. she clenched her fists. *Not again, I will not fail again.*

She opened her mouth, not exactly sure what was going to come out. But as soon as her lips parted, instincts took over. Her years of practice, years of pain, years of paying this world everything she had, was finally paying off. She had been giving since she was a child, and now it was time to receive her due.

"This sucks." Surprisingly, those were the words that first came from her throat. The room mumbled, curiosity flying around like birds. "I'm not just saying that because I had a bad day, I'm saying that because this whole system is rigged." Confidence had fueled her, poised at her fingertips and ready to come out in loud, inspiring words. "We never got a fair chance as a child, at least I didn't. Instead of helping us, the Empire locks us up in facilities like these to keep us away from the public eye. We do their dirty work, this was our destiny from birth, and we never got the chance to change it!"

The guards at the door started bristling, their hands noticeably hovering over their weapons. Alohi summoned her confidence again, the powerful feeling running down her arms and out her throat.

"I am so done!" she exclaimed. "This is a never-ending cycle. We fight to survive the only way we can, and then we get locked up for it. Our kids, born into the same unfortunate situations we were, inherit the sin and live the same lives their parents, their grandparents, their family for generations have lived." She took a breath, steadying her voice. "It's a cycle, and no one will dare break out of it because of the harsh punishments. But if we don't at least die, we're submitting to our fates. I don't know about you, but I am not ready to give my life to some unlivable *bullshit*!"

Alohi smiled as cheers flew around the room. The guards looked at each other anxiously, unsure of what to do. All of a sudden, more plates were thrown to the ground. A chorus of shatters sang throughout the room, yells of rebellion joining them.

The inmates charged at the doors, fury fueling their footsteps. The guards had drawn their weapons and were slashing them at the criminals. Blood sprayed everywhere as more and more inmates rushed to join the fight.

Alohi leaped down from the table she was standing on. The distraction at the door was enough so that she could get out.

She wove around the prisoners, making sure to steer clear of any blades. Through the crowd, she saw the doors. The gray hallways were just a few footsteps away, all she needed to do was get past one guard.

Alohi slipped under his shoulder and darted into the hallway. The chaos of the cafeteria had softened to only muted yells. She kept running, her legs carrying her faster than ever before. She was so close, she could make it!

All of a sudden, something grabbed her clothes. She craned her head to see a soldier dressed in all silver. A slick smile spread across his face as he looked down at Alohi.

"Where do you think you're going?" he rasped through teeth so white they looked translucent.

Alohi scrambled against his tight grip, but it was no good. The soldier's hold on her never softened as he dragged her back to the cafeteria.

The loud chaos of the cafeteria had vanished. In its place, was the peace of submission. The prisoners were seated at their tables, most of their limbs bound by restraints. Alohi felt a tinge of guilt as she saw the bloodied bodies of her fellow inmates on the ground. Though she tried to block the thoughts from her head, she knew that those lives were on her. She had blood on her hands, even though she never held the blade.

The silver soldier pushed her to her knees. In front of her were Nathaniel and Joshua. Her two friends were also kneeling on the ground, a defeated look painted on their faces.

Alohi understood immediately. "No, no, *please*!" she begged. "I was the one who planned the escape, I was the one who started the riot! Kill me, not them!"

All the soldier did was chuckle, the strong mint smell that came off him was nauseating. "Let this be a lesson!" he called to the audience of restrained prisoners. "These people that speak inspiring words of a better future are nothing but a *ruse*. Their words are trickery, given to them by Satan to mesmerize you to do their bidding." Shame flooded Alohi. Tears stung in her eyes, begging to breach her waterline. "All the while this prude tried to escape on her own, letting her fellow comrades die at other's hands."

Alohi looked up to see blades being held to both Joshua's and Nathaniel's throats. Her chorus of begging started again. "*Please*! Not them, it was me! *Kill* me!" her voice was hoarse, barely able to reach anything above a rasp.

All the soldier did was beam. "Someone has to carry the guilt." He then turned to Nathaniel and Joshua. "Any last words?" his voice was sick, a cruel pleasure lacing every word.

Nathaniel was silent, but Joshua looked straight at Alohi, his eyes full of fury. "Politicians," he growled. "The reason I hated the way I lived, and the reason I died." The swords then ran across their throats in one, fluid motion. Blood sprayed from the wound as the two of them fell to the ground.

Alohi let out a cry as she watched the life fade from their eyes. Tears spilled down her cheeks as she watched the crimson blood continue to leave their bodies. A cold rush ran over her, and for a moment she thought the blood was leaking out of her too.

"Let's go." The soldier said dismissively, then dragged her out of the cafeteria.

The gray halls felt gloomier than usual. Tears still leaked from her eyes and slid down her cheeks. She didn't care about the scrapes the rough concrete floor was leaving on her bare skin, she didn't care how pathetic she looked at that moment. All she cared about was the blood on her hands. Her friends, allies, were all dead because of her.

She was pushed inside a small room. The walls were a smooth, dark gray and the room itself was a square. On the far wall, was a pair of restraints. The door locked behind them with a click. Alohi was pushed against the wall, her arms yanked up by the soldier and pressed against the cold bonds. She struggled against the metal, pushing her wrists against the cold surface.

Her heart almost stopped when she saw the soldier pull out a knife. It was long and shiny, its blade serrated. The man had a sick smile on his face as he approached her.

Her eyes were wide as a full moon, a fear like no other slithered around her. "No..."

The man pressed the side of the metal against her cheek, it glided down her neck and stopped at her shoulder. He turned its blade so the serrated tip pointed to her skin. Then, all of a sudden, he pressed it into her flesh. The sharp, jagged edge ripped into the skin of her arm like paper. Pain spread from the cut like wildfire, consuming her arm in a terrible, persistent aching. Her head became light when she saw that blood was gushing from the wound.

A scream ripped from her mouth. Tears poured from her eyes as the knife continued to run down her arm. She clenched her restrained fists, trying to distract herself from the unbearable pain.

The knife finally slid out of her wound, but the pain lingered like an insult, unrelenting. She let her head hang, gasping for breath. Tears still ran down her cheeks, and her heart was beating as though soon it wouldn't.

"Please..." She begged her captor in a weak voice. "Stop..."

But the soldier just smiled sadistically. He pressed the cold metal to her wrist, as if trying to plot a point to start.

"Look at you." His voice felt like its own blade, carving up her mind like butter. "You beg for your safety because you couldn't take it for yourself." He jammed the knife deep into her skin. Her head jolted back, a scream rising from her throat. "You thought yourself worthy to challenge my men and escape? I was under the impression that you may be a problem, being so close to Nikolai Lone and all." He laughed, ripping the skin down to her elbow.

"But I must say I was disappointed!" the knife reached her shoulder, and Alohi could feel the warm blood pouring from her wound and the pain that spread from it. Her fists clenched and teeth grit. But nothing could distract her from the terrible pain. She felt the man's hot breath come close to her ear, and she shuddered with fear of what he was going to do next, but all that came from him was a whisper. "You're just *weak*!"

The pain of the wound dulled as those words were spoken. They rang out in her head. *Weak, weak, weak*! That was what she was. She was never able to take care of herself. She couldn't gain her father's love unless she did something with herself, and of course, she chose the option that was less than. She wasn't loved because she was incapable. She was *weak*!

The soldier unhatched her restraints and she fell to the ground. He picked her up by the collar, dragging her feet on the ground. She was barely conscious, her head felt dizzy and her stomach nauseous. She only saw the gray ground passing beneath her as she was dragged back to her cell.

Once the man opened the door, he threw Alohi to the ground and slammed the door. She just laid there, curled up on the floor, cradling her arms. Tears stung in her eyes, but they weren't from the physical pain. Her heart ached and shame seemed to linger around her like a raincloud. The revelation dwelled in her head, refusing to leave. She tried to shake the feeling but she couldn't. No matter how hard she tried, she would never get out of this prison. She was *weak*.

Chapter Twenty Eight
Nikolai

Nikolai aggressively looped the rope through itself. His hands were dry and swollen but his heart was pounding. He watched the sea anxiously, waiting for the small boat he lent the girls to come back.

Fear pounded in his head, sending his thoughts into a spiral as his brain tortured him with possible disasters. Although he was far from fond of Thorne, he would never find himself wishing harm upon her. And he had become friends with Lilith, therefore he would be deeply hurt if she got hurt while on a mission he sent her on.

Have you met those two? Said a slim voice of comfort in his head. *If death looked them in the eyes they would challenge him to a fistfight and win! They'll be fine.* The voice gave no solace; even if they did come back, there was the chance that they wouldn't come back with the information. And then... then...

He didn't want to finish that sentence. Thinking about Alohi's current situation was a death trap. He couldn't let fear drive him into a ditch. *Eyes on the goal,* that was what he always told himself. Emotion was never supposed to be a component. It made people distracted, *weak.*

~~~

He remembered after he lost embarrassingly. It was just a sparring tournament, held purely for fun, or at least that's what it was for most people.
~~~

The pain did not hit him when Tnil disarmed his sword a few seconds in, or when he got too exhausted to run any longer and he fell to the ground. The pain did not hit when Tnil pointed her blade at his throat. It did not happen after the match when he got booed by the crowd, or the whispers that doubted how worthy he was to be the White King.

No, the pain started when he entered his house. He remembered creaking the door open. The large house was dark, a single candle burning on the table, the flame flickering lightly. He came in with slow steady steps. As soon as he passed the door, his father grabbed him and shoved him against the wall.

"Wanna explain that?" his strong grip left bruises on Nikolai's shoulders. "Disarmed in the first minute? Laughable!" he threw him against the floor. "You're *laughable*!"

Tears stung in his eyes. Guilt flooded him, shame exploding in every part of his head. "I'm sorry, Dad!" the tears left his eyes and flooded down his cheeks. "I'm so sorry!"

His father smiled wickedly. "You will be!" he took Nikolai by the collar, pulling him off his feet. "Don't cry again! You hear me? You will never cry again!"

He drew shaky breaths, they were racked with sobs. Self-hate dwelled. He wasn't good enough, he wasn't worth his life. He was weak!

All Nikolai wanted to do at that moment was fight back. But all he could murmur to him was a weak, feeble, "Sorry." His father shook him rapidly, pounding his head against the wall.

At that moment he realized that he could fight back against any opponent. Any but his father. He would never fight his father. Because through all the abuse, through all the hate, he was still his father, and even though it would have been better if he hated him. He could never.

~~~

"Nikolai?" Rex's deep voice broke his memory. He quickly stood, wiping the tears that slid down his face.

Nikolai peered down to see his first mate climbing up the ladder. In his calloused hand was a cup of hot tea. The liquid sloshed around in the mug as his friend made his way up the mast.
~~~

"You've been up here for a while." Rex chimed in a happy tone. "Thought you might-" he stopped, noticing his tear-stained face. "Are you okay?"

Nikolai cracked a fake smile. "Yeah of course!" his tone was raspy, but the barest tint of fake joy laced it. In the moment, it was the best he could do.

A compassionate look spread across Rex's face. He sat down next to Nikolai, handing him the hot tea. The warmth that came from the cup was comforting against his numb fingers.

"I know you're ranked higher than I am, and I may be overstepping my role," Rex kept his eyes trained on the turbulent ocean. "But I want you to know, Nikolai, there were times that I didn't think you would make it."

Nikolai furrowed his brow. He had never brushed death so closely that there were doubts about his survival. "Really?"

"Not physically, of course." Rex clarified. "But I've known you since you were fourteen. I've been your first mate since you were fourteen. And after you lose, you look so disgusted with yourself. I've seen you withhold food, I've seen you lock yourself in that training center and work until your legs just can't do it anymore." A tear rolled down his cheek. "There have been countless times when I thought I would be reassigned to a different captain. Countless times where I just stayed in my room, dreading the letter that I thought was sure to come, telling me that something had happened to you."

Shaky breaths rattled between the two of them, only the gentle brush of the wind filling the silence. "But then, just when I had given up all hope, you would knock on my door and tell me that there was a new job. That we were going back out to sea. That we were trying again."

A gentle smile spread along Rex's lips. "I guess what I'm saying is that no matter what you were faced with, you bounced back. I know you don't have the best relationship with your father, and your life so far has been hard. But-" his voice cracked, something Nikolai had never seen his first mate's tone do. "I think of you like you were my own son and Nikolai, I want you to know I'm so, *so* proud of you."

Tears stung in Nikolai's eyes as he looked at his friend. He opened his mouth to speak, but nothing came out. Even if he could talk, he wasn't sure he could say anything worthy of what Rex had just told him.

Nikolai threw his arms around his first mate, pressing his face into Rex's coat. Tears slid down his face as he hugged his friend tighter. Rex wrapped his arms around him, laying a gentle hand on his head.

Neither of them wanted to let go. Some part of Nikolai felt that if he did, he would never see Rex again. So he held on tight, not daring to let go.

"Look!" Rex exclaimed as they broke from each other's embrace. "What's that?"

Nikolai's teary gaze looked out onto the ocean. There, paddling across the wavy water, was the small boat he had lent Thorne and Lilith. The two criminals were rowing back at an alarming speed, their wild hair flapping in the wind.

He slid down the ladder excitedly, quickly wiping his tears. Thorne and Lilith were rowing close to the ship. He ran to the pulley system, eager to hoist the girls up.

"Did you get it?" he asked once they were on the ship. He didn't even try to hide the giddy feeling rising in his throat.

Thorne handed him a pamphlet. He opened it excitedly and his heart ached with longing. Alohi's name was imprinted at the top of the paper. The font was black and plain, but just the thought that she was alive made his heart beat faster. "Thank you."

Thorne put her hands on her hips. "Don't get too excited yet, Lone." She said in a sarcastic tone that so blatantly belonged to her. "She's not safe yet."

Nikolai rolled his eyes. "Don't remind me." He pushed back any emotion and looked at the two girls. They looked unharmed, only their hair was messy and their eyes were dazed from exhaustion. But there was something different about Lilith. Her eyes were unfocused, as though her mind was wandering down a new path. She quickly brushed past Thorne and headed to her room, her partner not even noticing.

The criminal prodigy handed him another pamphlet. "She's being held in Rock Highland. It's a prison camp in Courna that uses their occupants to mine iron, gold, and other elements. The good news is that it's not the Empire's most high-security prison," she sighed, dusting dirt off of her tailored pants. "The bad news is that the only way to get in unnoticed is where the minecarts go out. It's incredibly dangerous. If you got hit by those... well, to put it plainly, you won't be moving anytime soon. I'll need more time to study, do you by any chance have a map of it?"

Nikolai smiled. "Any known Empire military base, I've got a map of it."

"Impressive, Lone, even I can admit that." She cracked a smile. "I may have to break into your ship when the need calls for it."

Nikolai chuckled. The thought of him waking up to get a drink of water and seeing Thorne studying one of his maps seemed obscure, but also incredibly in character for the young criminal. "That would be a war crime."

"I'm no stranger."

There was a long silence, none of them had anything left to say. Thorne turned to leave for his map room.

Something caught his eye. "You have blood on your shirt."

Thorne looked down at a red stain on her white blouse, quickly covering it with her coat. "It's not mine."

Nikolai's eyes narrowed. "That's precisely what I'm worried about. How much trouble did you cause?"

"We killed a squadron of patrol guards."

Nikolai put his hands over his nose, frustration boiling his blood. "Ignoring how morally unjust that is, did you at least hide the bodies or get rid of the evidence?"

Thorne cracked a smile along her lips. "Now where's the fun in that? I need to leave a signature somewhere."

Nikolai sighed. "Well if they didn't already know we were coming, they know now. We begin phase two at daybreak; for now, go study. You'll need it." He started to walk away, then turned his head. "Oh, and for a signature, I must say I prefer the roses."

Chapter Twenty Nine
Lilith

Lilith sat on her small bed. The bedroom was made of polished wood and beams stretched across the ceiling like a pipe system. Quilla's bed was across from hers. It had thin black sheets and was made as neatly as humanly possible.

Her feelings about her partner were mixed. She knew Quilla's past was unknown to most if not all, but she was always sure that there would've been some record of it. She knew if she had faked her death, which was relatively possible, that she would still have a file. The Archives had been around way before Ghan's Empire. They had every record within two hundred years. She knew Quilla was skilled, but to evade any record; that was near impossible.

She gazed at Quilla's side of the room. A bag hung at the end of her bed. It was black and red, a hatch hung over the top that was sealed with a small, shiny button. The bag tempted her. The urge to seek out answers felt as though it was pulling her towards it.

No! She told herself. *The last person you would ever want to breach trust with is Quilla.* The voice of reason made a point. Her partner would gut her if she even touched her stuff. But curiosity pushed on, and eventually, she couldn't help herself.

Lilith slowly walked towards the bag. Her head turned to the door every second, making sure Quilla wasn't turning the handle. She knelt down and carefully opened the hatch. Inside she found a knife sharpener, several additional knives, clothes, and a small notebook.

Lilith slowly raised the notebook out of the bag. It was almost all black, a pattern of roses engraved into it. In the center was a gold pentagon. On each of the five sides was a weapon. A sword, an arrow, a spear, a knife, and a throwing star.

She opened the book carefully. On the first page was a drawing. Two small girls were sleeping against a wall. They were leaning against each other, one head on the other's shoulder. They looked young, maybe five or six. Their dirty, tattered clothes hung loose on their body. One had dark, messy curls that sprouted in all different directions. The other had hair that was as straight as the horizon. It ran down to her chin and was as dark as her black eyes.

She turned the page, gazing at the rough pencil marks. This time there were five children, they looked around ten.

The two from before were playing; wrestling each other to the ground while the others watched, laughing. They all wore black clothing with traces of gold. One boy had short dreads, like little leaves unfurling. His skin was dark, and his smile was brilliant as he played with the others. He stood trying to separate the two girls, but his face cracked a smile, joy seeping through his features.

The second boy's hair was wild. It was short but sprouted in all sorts of directions. His uniform, which was neat on the others, seemed to be intentionally ripped near the sleeves. He had a mischievous expression on his face, as though he was enjoying the aftermath of a situation that was his doing.

The third child was a girl with even curlier hair than her friend. It was let loose and puffed over her head. She was laughing in the corner of the page, her eyes closed and teary.

Lilith turned the page again, but this time she saw a completely different side of the five children. They all had an assortment of weapons, each wielding them like it was all they had ever done. A group of wild cats were roaming around the room, their mouths hungry and teeth pointed. Each of the children were going toe to toe with one of the animals, even though they all looked relatively young. The first curly-haired girl had mounted one of the lions. She had one knife positioned at its throat and a hand waving in the air, warding off any other attackers.

On the next page, she found only the curly-headed girl. She was embracing an older man. He was slim, wearing a tailored blazer that went down to his knees. The girl looked happy, enjoying her father's affection. The man's face, however, was crossed out angrily. Pencil marks pressed into the paper where his face would be, as though they were knives slashing to make him bleed.

The sudden change of emotion made Lilith gasp as she turned the page. It was only the first two girls, but they looked older, around twelve. Tears leaked from their eyes. Their dark hair was blowing in the wind. The building they were in looked like it was coming down, flames danced angrily around the walls and rubble.

The straight-haired girl had a throwing star pointed at her friend's throat, her face painted with pain, as if begging herself not to do it. Her friend's knives were lowered to her sides. She looked as though she was begging, not for her life but for something else.

She turned the page carefully, curiosity burning. But instead of two girls, only one remained. In the place of the straight-haired girl was a pile of rubble. The lone one was on her knees. Tears ran down her cheeks, her eyes closed. On her chest, she cradled her friend's star.

Lilith's head whipped around as she heard the doorknob turn. She quickly closed the book and rolled under Quilla's bed. She heard her partner's boots click as she strode across the floor.

Lilith didn't dare breathe; she knew that Quilla could sense anyone hiding in a room. She could feel all of it, the vibrations in the floor, the near-silent sound of breathing. Lilith stayed on the floor, clutching the book to her chest. Her muscles tensed, not daring to move.

Quilla leaned down, opening her bag and rummaging through it. Her eyebrows furrowed as she searched for the object. Lilith felt her chest tighten as the thought came over her like an icy breeze. *She's looking for the book!*

"God dammit," Quilla said under her breath. "It was here a minute ago!" she stood, giving the room one last glance and heading for the door. Frustration came off her like a fragrant perfume.

Lilith gasped, rolling out from under the bed and staring at the ceiling. That was a close call that she didn't want to encounter again. She stood, carefully placing the book under Quilla's pillow. She would think she left it there, if Lilith was lucky.

She crept towards the door, opening it just a crack to see if her partner was still outside. But Quilla had gone somewhere below deck. She slipped out the door and headed for the bow.

Chapter Thirty
Lilith

The shores of Couna were rocky and icy. Nikolai's ship had taken a painfully long time to dock, and both she and Quilla had become impatient. Lilith was drumming her fingers against the ship's railing, waiting to finally get to work.

Quilla's long, dark hair blew in the wind. Her eyes were focused on the icy shores. Lilith couldn't help looking at her. Anger always seemed to linger around her partner, but just now she was realizing something else. Her eyes, as clouded as they were, had a faint sparkle. It was as if a spark of life had returned with this mission and was waiting to turn into a flame.

Nikolai materialized next to them. His black hair was more messy than usual, his clothing also seemed less fitted. She noticed bags under his eyes, a sign he hadn't slept in days.

"A couple of things you should know about Courna." He said promptly. "They aren't very sociable. A couple of strangers usually means bad news. So I wouldn't ask anyone for help. At all."

Quilla turned to him. "No need, I have the heist plans memorized. We won't be asking for help."

Lilith turned to her partner. "Well, that's great. But do you know how to get *to* Rock Highland?"

Quilla raised an eyebrow. She then opened her mouth, presumably to come up with a witty response, but Nikolai interjected.

"She has a point." He told them. Lilith raised her chin in triumph. "Courna is hard to navigate. The forests are thick and the snow is deep. If you're not careful you'll die of hyperthermia before you even make it to the prison."

Quilla put her hands on her hips. "So how do you suppose we get there, pretty boy?"

Nikolai smiled keenly. "We stowaway." He straightened his back, tightening his posture. "There are trains going to the prison. They carry prisoners, supplies, and plenty of Empire soldiers, so we'll have to be careful. If we get on one of those, they take us right to the prison."

"*Us?*" Quilla asked skeptically. "I thought it was just me and Lilith."

Nikolai cleared his throat. "Change of plans. I want to be there when rescuing Alohi."

Quilla's eyes widened. "You don't trust us?"

"No." He told her, his voice staying poised and calm. "Your talent is breaking in, but I could be useful in a fight. I want to be ready for anything, even the improbable."

Quilla looked at him with a distasteful glare. "I don't think-"

"*I* think that's a great idea." Lilith intervened. She could almost feel Quilla's glare pressing into her skin. "We don't know the terrain that well. Besides, he has a point. We might need him if things get messy."

"Thank you." Nikolai bowed his head. "I need to see her again, as soon as possible." Lilith smiled. Alohi and Nikolai's relationship was gold. Built on trust and love, she envied what they had. The absence of it in her own partnership was painfully noticeable.

Quilla rolled her eyes. "Fine. But if you're too slow you'll be left in the snow." She turned on her heel and headed for the crow's nest, her long hair blowing behind her.

Lilith turned, glaring at the turbulent ocean. Her fingernails dug into the wood, frustrated at her partner's stubborn demeanor.

Nikolai rested his elbows on the fence next to her. "So, you and Thorne?"

"What about us?"

Nikolai sighed. "Did something happen? Sometimes you seem so close, but now it's like you can't stand five minutes around each other."

Lilith turned to him, taking a breath. "We had a fight when you left. Quilla's always been distant but now she seems almost unstable. It's like she doesn't know how to act around people, although I see her do it flawlessly around strangers. Just not me."

Nikolai looked at her. "You said she was afraid of her feelings, right?" Lilith nodded. "Thorne is confident with other people because she couldn't care less if they lived or died. But you, Lilith, I think she cares about you. And well, she doesn't exactly know where to go with that, leading to her lashing out in strange ways."

Lilith laughed. "She doesn't care about me!" she looked out onto the sea. "She cares about my shooting. According to her, it would be a *big hassle* to train another shooter with as much talent as me."

"Maybe," Nikolai smiled. "But if I were you, I wouldn't completely turn your back on your partner." He turned on his heel, heading back to his cabin.

Lilith looked behind her. Quilla was perched on the crow's nest. Her long coat was blowing in the wind with her hair. She was sitting on the taffrail, her heels dangling in the air. She looked so carefree, as though her problems and secrets had drifted away in the wind.

Lilith watched her own braid fly in the wind, a red streak woven into it. Her and Quilla's fashion sense was surprisingly different. Her partner seemed drawn towards the more professional look, whereas Lilith took towards jeans and a t-shirt, typically paired with a sweater. She often admired Quilla's ability to stay so poised in stressful situations. She wondered if the way she dressed empowered her, or hid something besides her blades.

The ship slowly came closer and closer to the docks. Beyond them was a small town. Every house was made of bricks, each had a small chimney with smoke coming out of it. Lights lingered in the windows as an eerie, yellow glow. Tracks ran through the town, going far into the woods. The sun was beginning to set into the mountains far beyond.

The ship lurched, and some of Nikolai's crew leaped from the deck to tie the boat down. The ice glimmered on the dock, clear as air. The cold of the place nipped her nose, and she could feel her cheeks turning bright pink.

Quilla appeared beside her, "I already hate this place."

Lilith gave a cocky laugh. "Keep an open mind, it's cold and eerie. You have a lot in common!"

She glared at her. "If you were anyone else, I'd gut you where you stood."

Lilith gave a teasing smile, "I'm just too good at what I do."

Quilla scoffed, "If only."

Nikolai materialized beside them, holding some very warm-looking clothes. Lilith silently thanked the universe. Her hands wouldn't be shaking with cold on this mission.

He handed them a jacket and shoes. They appeared to be made out of leather and laced with some sort of fur. As she pulled on the clothes, a sense of warmth flooded over her.

Nikolai stood in similar attire. His hair was messy and his two swords were strung across his back. "We need to leave soon, gather your stuff." He told them. "We're already short on time.

Lilith silently checked over herself. All she needed was her bow and quiver, which were resting on her back. She figured they would figure out food and water on the way.

"We're ready," Quilla told him.

"Good," Nikolai answered. The three of them strode off the ship and onto the cold icy rocks of Courna.

Chapter Thirty One
Nikolai

The sun had set behind the mountains long ago. Thorne, Lilith, and Nikolai waited at the tracks anxiously. Lilith had cleared off a bench from snow and looked like she was about to drift off to sleep. Thorne was leaning against a lamp post, her arms crossed and her eyes bored. Nikolai stood waiting, his swords drawn at his sides and his eyes wide as a deer, ready for a train to come zooming by at any second.

"It won't kill you to sit down, Lone." He heard Thorne's sassy tone behind him.

"I want to be ready." He told her, eyes still trained on the tracks.

Thorne scoffed. "Do you know how long trains are?" he could almost feel her eyes rolling. "It's not going to take you a whole ten cars to get up off of a bench."

Nikolai didn't even blink. "Again, I want to be ready."

Thorne sighed, and Nikolai felt his blood pressure rising. Each scrape of a word that rang from her mouth had him breathing heavier. "You're so dramatic."

He felt his hands tighten into fists. He flew around, glaring at the crime lord. "You don't get it, do you?" he said through a clenched jaw. "I care about her more than anything! And she is in danger!" his legs started walking towards her, almost without his permission. "I won't rest until she does!"

Thorne looked unbothered, she only raised her eyebrows and shook her head. "You can't see your own weakness."

Nikolai let out a shrill laugh. "Of course!" he cackled. "Of course, you would see that as a weakness. You've never loved anything!"

This seemed to anger her. Her eyes tightened into slits and fire ignited in her gaze. She stood up straight, eyes focused on him. "How dare you!" the two advanced on each other, Nikolai almost felt the urge to reach for his swords and he could see Thorne's hands lingering around her knives.

All of a sudden they heard a whistle. The tracks started shaking and in the distance, he saw a chain of smoke. Lilith stood from her spot on the bench, dusting the snow from her coat. "Um, guys." She told them. "Train."

All three of them stood by the tracks as the massive machine moved towards them. It was at least three stories tall and had a snow plow attached to its front that looked like it could cut someone in half.

Nikolai bent his knees as it raced towards them. From a distance, he saw it had handles on its sides. Lilith bent down on one knee, putting her hands out like a step. Thorne's snow boot planted on her palms. As the train came whooshing by, she was launched up into the night sky. Thorne flipped in the air, landing on top of the train like an acrobat.

He jumped next, grabbing one of the handles on the side of the large machine. His feet dangled as he struggled to find a place to put them. They finally rested on a small, icy pipe. He carefully climbed the engine, making his way to the top.

Lilith started running with the train, her partner running in the opposite direction. Nikolai followed her, struggling to keep his balance on the icy roof.

"Grab my legs," Thorne told him through the cold wind. Then, without warning, she dove off the side of the train. Nikolai lunged for her, grabbing her ankles at the last second.

"This has to be the stupidest idea you've ever come up with!" he yelled through the howling wind.

Lilith grabbed Thorne's outstretched hand, lifting into the air. "Not even in the top five!"

"Shut it!" Thorne growled, still hanging over the train. "Pull me up!"

Nikolai started tugging the girls onto the room. The icy surface made his shoes slip and he had to hook his boot around a handle. Once Thorne was up, she lifted her partner. They all lay on the snow, panting. Time seemed to fly, and none of them wanted to get up.

"So," Lilith finally spoke. "What next?"

Thorne sat up, dusting off her jacket. "Now," she said. "We get in."

The three of them stood and started making their way to the end of the train. The snow on the roof was slippery, and they occasionally had to duck for overhanging branches. It was late now, maybe midnight, and the train would be getting there at the break of dawn. Nikolai was anxious to get to sleep.

Once they got to the end, they hopped down onto a small ledge at the side of the caboose. The tracks flew by with the train's alarming speed, and the ledge was slippery with ice. His hands were grasping whatever small holds he could reach, careful not to fall on the dangerous tracks.

Although Lilith looked as frightened and uncomfortable as Nikolai was, Thorne seemed to swing from hold to hold, as though she was afraid of nothing. Her jacket and long hair swung behind her.

He rolled his eyes. *Show off,* he thought pettily, but he couldn't help but envy her skill.

They slowly made their way between the two cars. They were coupled together by a steel latch, and a small piece of metal was placed between them, serving as a bridge. On each car, was a door.

Nikolai reached the entrance, panting. Thorne was already waiting, Lilith by her side. "Took you long enough." She said in her sarcastic tone.

He ignored her, peaking in the car in front of the caboose. Men, women, and children were chained up in rows. Their arms and legs bound to the car. They wore rags that were ripped and stained. Their feet were bare and blistered. Some had sores on their pale, dull faces, indicating they were sick.

He felt a hand on his shoulder. Jolting around, he was surprised to find it belonged to the girl he had nearly punched just minutes ago.

"This is what the Empire does to people," Thorne told him, he could almost sense sadness in her voice. "Most of these people are innocent, here for crimes they didn't commit. Meanwhile, the wealthy people can bribe and hire courts that are on their side, leaving the less fortunate to suffer for their wrongdoings."

Nikolai tilted his head. Maybe his earlier statement was wrong. Maybe Thorne did care about some people.

She grasped both his shoulders tightly. "That's why you have to win. You have to make sure this *never* happens again!" the passion in her voice was unmistakable. She turned, opened the door to the caboose, and headed inside.

Nikolai followed. The inside of the car was dark. Wooden boxes littered the inside. Most were empty, but some were filled with tools, blankets, and most importantly, food.

Lilith jammed her arrow into the lock, with a click, it opened and the top slid off. She reached inside, grabbing a can of what looked like soup, and tossing it to him and Thorne.

Nikolai shook his head. "I'm pretty sure this is considered stealing."

Lilith raised her eyebrows. "Oh, how terrible!"

Thorne caught the soup with one hand. She jammed her knife into the metal lid and passed the blade to her partner. Nikolai did the same, drinking the soup like coffee.

His mouth tingled as the liquid hit his lips. The taste of salty potato and beef was the best thing he had all day. He ate every bit, licking the can when he was done, and throwing it in one of the empty bins.

He dabbed his mouth with a handkerchief, wishing he had more. "So," he asked. "What are you going to do after all of this is over?"

Lilith smiled, tossing her soup can into the empty box that Nikolai's lay in. "I'm going to buy a property in the mountains. Get a life, have children, and forget this ever happened."

Nikolai smiled back, but he couldn't help envying her. They had both been trapped in a cage for years. But she was getting set free soon, whereas he would never be let out of his. "How about you, Nikolai?"

"I guess I'll just continue to live the life I've always led. Training, missions from my dad, and expected to kill Ghan's heir."

Thorne's eyebrows shot up. "His heir?"

Nikolai sighed. Grabbing a can of tomato juice and sipping on it. "About seven years ago, Ghan publicly announced that he had an heir. We didn't get to see her, but I know she was around ten at the time. Meaning she should be seventeen, the same age as me. We also know she's been trained by Ghan from birth, in leading and fighting. It's part of the reason I am expected to train so hard; if I am even to come close to beating her, I have to be insanely good."

Lilith leaned against a nearby crate. "Why would Ghan even need an heir? I thought Thine did it by elections."

Thorne growled. Her voice was laced with irritation. "They did, until Ghan found out how to control the entire planet. He figured out that each country didn't have the resources to survive without one other, so he linked them. Courna provides water and metals, Salenian provides most of our meat and seafood, Woodran provides agriculture and lumber, and Thine provides gold and sand. Ghan controls the distribution, if anyone rebels, they're left with little to no resources. So, in short, he can do whatever he wants, because if anyone tells him no, they'll die of starvation." She turned to Nikolai. "Speaking of which, how does the League get food and supplies?"

Nikolai smiled menacingly. "A little trick I like to call hijacking."

Lilith laughed. "You two might get along better than you thought!"

"So," Nikolai asked Thorne. "What are you going to do once you have your money and this is all over with?"

Thorne hesitated, reaching back to touch her neck. "Actually," she said, her eyes trailing the floor. "I want to join the League of Red Doves."

Chapter Thirty Two
Quilla

Lilith's eyebrows shot straight up and Lone choked on his drink.

"What?" asked Lone, trying to regain his poised demeanor. "Did I hear that correctly?"

Quilla rolled her eyes. "Yes, I want to join the League of Red Doves."

"Okay, just wanted to make sure my mind wasn't tricking me." Lone set his drink to the side.

"So why the change of heart? Have you finally given up your vengeful lifestyle?" asked Lilith, hope brimming in her tone.

Quilla scoffed. "If anything this decision enhances it. I want to hurt the Empire, and petty crimes aren't doing it for me anymore." She cracked a smile, her tone turning more sadistic. "And let's be honest, your pathetic little rebellion needs all the help it can get."

Lone growled, "What makes you so sure that we'll let you in?"

Lilith huffed a laugh. "Have you met her?" she scoffed. "She'll stay at Shina until she gets in. Meanwhile, causing havoc you couldn't even imagine."

Quilla smiled. "As delightful as that would be, I have a valid reason." Lone raised his eyebrows in question. "I've spent my life dedicated to taking down the Empire. I know every move he has made, and every move he will continue to make. Every resource, every strength, every *weakness*!"

"What is his weakness?" asked Lone skeptically.

"I guess you'll have to wait and find out."

Lilith yawned. "I don't care what you do, Quilla, just don't involve me in it." She laid down, using her coat as a pillow. "I'm going to sleep."

Quilla tried to ignore how much that sentence hurt her. It was better that they felt no attachment to each other, Lilith had the right idea. Maybe a part of her thought that maybe, after all those years in Hanslack, they would become close; in a way other than business.

Her mind gave her a mental punch in the face. *Don't you dare!* An angry voice hollered at her. *If you care about anyone, ever, it'll end in flames.*

~~~

That night her dreams were filled with little kids who tumbled through the halls, screaming and laughing with joy. They were covered with dirt and mud, their knees bare and skinned. Their voices were painfully familiar as they called her name, hollering for her to join them.

The halls were dark blue, with shiny steel lining the walls. A ten-year-old Quilla stood in the center of it all, the kids circled around her, holding hands with each other, skipping and singing. Smiles spread across their little faces.

She skipped next to one with pencil-straight hair, the girl's ripped training uniform matched the several scratches on her face.

The little girl stopped skipping. A smile glittered on her face as she reached into a pocket and pulled out a small trinket. It was a carved knife, made only of wood. The carving was sharp and perfect, not a dent or a mark. "I made this for you!" she said in a small, but proud voice.

Quilla took it, smiling at the girl. "Thank you!" she told her, tucking her knife in her pocket. The girl's smile brightened, joy springing into her eyes.

"Come on!" the other children said to her, pulling at her wrist. Quilla laughed, running with them as they dragged her along the halls. They ran fast, eventually leading her to a large, dark room. The ceiling was high and the walls were painted a dark blue. A staircase led to a throne in the middle of the vast area. Sitting there, looking almost bored, was a lean, well-dressed man.
~~~

When the children walked in, he smiled, standing and striding down the staircase. He bent down in front of them, chuckling to himself. "What did you guys get yourselves into?" he asked, approaching a girl with fluffy hair. He stroked her cheek and the girl laughed, beaming at the man. "Lamia, you're a mess."

He bent down next to the two boys. One had long hair and beads were strung in the front two strands. The man rubbed some dirt off of his face, then brushed the hair out of his eyes. "I thought you of all people would be able to stop this, Casimir." The boy stood up tall, puffing out his chest.

He then moved to the other boy. He had wild, short hair that looked as though it hadn't been brushed in years. "But I suppose this is your doing, isn't it, Ezekiel." The boy giggled mischievously, pulling out a small trinket from his trousers. It was round, and covered in something that looked like oil. The little boy threw it and the ball crashed into the wall, mud exploding as soon as it made contact.

The man looked stunned. His face hardened as he turned back to the children. "Who made that?"

The girl with straight hair beamed with pride. "I did!" her joyous tone faded as soon as he saw the man's hardened face. He was angry, his eyes lit up with flames. He wound up his hand, about to slap the girl across the face, but Quilla stepped in front of her, shielding her with her small, child body.

"Stop!" she said, her voice tiny, but powerful. Courage radiated off of her, not a hint of fear clouding her small, round eyes. The man paused, looking at her with a blank expression, then his poised demeanor returned with a calm smile.

"You should all get some rest." He told them. The children skipped off, as happy and bright as before. All except the girl with straight hair, who hung her head low in shame. Quilla turned to follow, but the man grasped her wrist.

She gasped for air, eyes wide. That hand, that firm grip was so familiar. She turned around, looking into his black eyes.

Her heart stopped beating. It was so, unmistakably him. His cold smile, calm conduct. Nothing scared her more. The man brushed her hair out of her eyes, stroking her cheek gently. "My dear daughter." He said in a soft, kind voice. "You need to keep her better under control."

Quilla stammered, her heart beating fast, every muscle telling her to run. "Cerce isn't dangerous, just clueless." She told her father. "She could be a real asset if we just gave her a chance."

Her father laughed, bending down next to her. "You aren't given chances, my darling, you make them for yourself. That is why you are so ahead of your siblings," he pulled a golden blade out of his pocket. "And that is why I want to make you my heir."

Quilla felt the air leave her body. "I'm not ready!" she begged. "I-I wouldn't know where to start!"

Her father stroked her cheek again. He handed her the blade. It was lined with a pattern of roses, a small crown engraved at the hilt. Quilla ran her finger down the detailed pattern, not believing what she was holding "Shh." He told her. "I'll help you. And you'll have your siblings for advice. Meanwhile, I will train you personally to become the greatest empress the world has ever seen." He stood, wrapping an arm around her shoulder and leading her to his throne. "You and I are going to do great things together."

<center>~~~</center>

Quilla woke up in cold sweats. Her ears were still ringing with her old father's words. That was a time she strived to forget about. That is, at least, once he was dead.

The tracks clicked in the cold night as the train ran along them. She was huddled in a corner next to several boxes. Dawn was creeping along the horizon, meaning they were almost there. She sat up, trying to shake her dream out of her head.

Next to her, Lone and Lilith slept. He was huddled in a little pile, his coat draped over him. Lone was snoring loudly, sounding like an elephant. Quilla silently laughed, making a mental note of this to use as blackmail.

Lilith was using her coat as a pillow. Her hair was down and sprawled out around her head like a mane. The red streak was apart from the other brunette strands, falling on her cheek and running down her neck. Goosebumps littered her tan arms and she shivered with a light breeze.

Dammit! Her mind cursed at her as she took off her jacket. *God dammit, Thorne.* She gently placed it on her partner, making sure to cover her shoulders. Lilith stopped shivering and Quilla sighed.

She walked over to the train door, opened it, and leaned against its frame. The landscape of Courna seemed so peaceful. The morning's first rays of sun shimmered on the soft snow. The trees were decorated with little icicles that hung down like ornaments. As pretty as it looked now, she knew that it would become a death trap as soon as she was off the train. Some of the crooks that Link harbored came from this place. They had been cast out, left to die in the snow. The stories they would tell would be horrific. They had been buried in snow or burned for witchcraft, and Quilla knew that it wouldn't be much of a challenge for them to find a reason to kill her. She preferred to stay as far from civilization as possible.

Chapter Thirty Three
Lilith

The rattle of the train woke Lilith up. Her eyes slowly opened to reveal the sun peaking through the open door. She had a coat draped over her, the hood covering her shoulders. She sat up, pulling the coat off of her and looking at the incoming light.

Quilla was standing in the doorway. She was facing away from Lilith; her brown, curly hair blowing softly in the wind. She was wearing a white blouse, black lace ran down her arms and neck. It was tucked into black, high-waisted pants that flared out at the bottom, just covering her heeled boots.

Lilith stood, walking over to her. She leaned against the door next to her, watching her hair blow in the wind. Quilla turned, gesturing to the jacket she was holding. "I believe that's mine."

Lilith shook off her awkwardness. "Oh, yeah." she handed it to her, watching as she pulled it on.

They stood there for a while, silence haunting their presence. The trees and snow blew by with the speed of the train. They watched as the sun rose, its rays peeking through the branches. Little droplets of water fell on the leaves from the melting snow.

"It wasn't all bad, was it?" asked Quilla, looking at her with black eyes. "You know, Hanslack?"

Lilith shrugged. "I mean what do you expect?" she looked at the sky, trying to keep herself from getting emotional. "It was a life of crime and dishonesty."

"Yes," argued Quilla. "But sometimes, I would have fun. You know, when we would pull off something thought to be impossible. I enjoy the looks of disbelief."

Lilith sighed. "Do you remember my first job with you, when we broke into that mercher's house?"

She nodded. "Servil Huston. We disintegrated his entire third floor!"

Lilith laughed. "It was just the two of us! And then, when the rubble came crashing down while he was having dinner, we peeked in the room with bags of money and jewels over our shoulders!"

Quilla smiled, a glimmer of nostalgia glimmered in her black eyes. "We waved, then bowed. I still remember the look of shame when he found out two fifteen-year-olds had destroyed nearly his entire life!"

A grin curved along Lilith's lips as she remembered the warm memory. "When we got back to the Link, we traded those jewels like candy, laughing all night." She rolled up her sleeve, showing a silver, metal bracelet. "I remember being so impressed when you stole this right off his sleeping daughter. She didn't even move!" she remembered watching as a fifteen-year-old Quilla loomed over the bed of a girl the same age as her. Her long fingers gently unclipped the bracelet and gently slid it off the girl's manicured hands. "I still don't know how you did that."

Quilla cocked her head to the side. "It takes a special kind of silence."

"I guess it must be a you thing." Lilith shrugged. "You know, being a criminal prodigy and all."

Quilla laughed, her gaze wondering. "I don't know why people call me that." Her tone was light, an airy laughter lifting her rasp. "I'm no prodigy."

In the distance, was a large building. It was a triangle, at least twenty stories tall. The trees cleared and surrounding it was a bunch of small buildings. The train sped past the last of the forest and the rest of the structure came into view. Rocks and rubble were being cleared out by tiny carts on rails. They emerged from little tunnels that looked unfinished.

Quilla turned. "Lone's still snoring." she gestured to Nikolai, who was sleeping with his coat pulled over him. His sleep looked so deep, that even a loud whistle couldn't wake him. Quilla strode over to his unconscious body, an aura of frustration radiating from her like a gloomy cloud.

"What are you doing?" asked Lilith, raising an eyebrow.

Quilla rolled her eyes. "Waking him, obviously."

She laughed, cocking her head to the side. "The boring way?"

Her partner smiled, showing her fang-like teeth. She then put both of her hands above Nikolai's ear. She glanced at Lilith and she nodded. All of a sudden, Quilla slammed her two hands together, making a loud clap.

Nikolai's eyes flew open. He sat straight up, throwing his jacket at Quilla. Lilith fell over laughing, enjoying the glare she got from Nikolai and her partner's mischievous smile.

He got up, fixing his clothes and his awful bedhead. "Why do you feel the need to do this?"

Quilla leaned against the wall of the train. "It was her idea." She gestured to Lilith.

Lilith raised her arms. "Yeah, but you acted on it."

Nikolai shrugged. "Whatever." He looked out the door and at the large building. "We're almost there. Follow me." He pulled on his coat and raced out the door. Quilla and Lilith followed.

The tracks flew by under them, the train clicking as it flew through the countryside. Just around the next turn, was the clearing.

"We can't be seen," Quilla told them. "We have to jump."

Nikolai groaned. "I hate your plans."

"Just countdown, Lone. You aren't going to get hurt without my direct involvement."

Nikolai clenched his fists. "Oh, how reassuring!"

The turn was nearing, and neither of them looked ready to jump. If they weren't off the train soon, the entire mission was off and they would be caught. Lilith shoved both of them off the train and onto the ground. She then leaped off, landing on her feet.

Nikolai had face-planted into the snow. His swords had come out of their hilts and were lying next to him. Quilla had done a little better, but not much. She was lying face up, her hair sprawled out in the white fluff.

Nikolai lifted his face, dusting off the snow that stuck to it. "Little warning next time?" he asked angrily, dusting off the rest of his body and finding his two loose swords.

Lilith laughed. "Now where's the fun in that?"

Quilla stood. Her hair was slightly wet and she had that dangerous look on her face again. The one that everyone feared. It was ambitious, Lilith saw it every time she was about to pull off a job or a fight was forming. Whenever that look crossed her face, she knew her partner was unstoppable.

"Come on!" she gestured towards the woods, then turned to run.

Nikolai held out a hand. "Stop! You'll sink into the snow like it's eating you!"

Quilla stopped, leaning against a tree. "In that case, we take the fun way!" she scrambled up its trunk, disappearing into the thick of the branches.

Lilith smiled, running toward the tree at full speed. She jumped and grabbed the lowest branch, hauling herself onto it. It wasn't nearly as graceful as what her partner had done, but she hadn't learned nothing from Quilla; and snipers needed to be in high, unlikely places.

She gestured to Nikolai, who was carefully making his way over to the tree. Lilith laughed to herself, encouraging him to move faster. He rolled his eyes and broke into a run.

"You two are the most reckless people I have ever met." He told her as he climbed up the tree in a much more graceful way than Lilith expected. "You leave me generally wondering how you've stayed alive this long."

Lilith rolled her eyes. "Remember what Quilla said: keep up, or you'll be left in the snow." She then sprang from her branch, grabbing onto the next. Nikolai kept an even pace with her; surprisingly light on his feet.

Quilla was perched on a distant branch, watching the activity down below. People in Empire uniforms hauled rocks onto a waiting train. They had swords and bows strung across their backs but looked as though they were half asleep.

"Lilith, cover us. Lone, you're with me." She told them authoritatively, her eyes trained on the target.

Nikolai raised an eyebrow. "Uh-huh, and what are we doing?"

Quilla looked him in the eye, glaring. "Playing chess," just as the words left her mouth she flew from the branch, drawing her knives in the air and hurling them at the guards.

Nikolai flew down after her, swords already drawn and ready to fight. Lilith grabbed her weapons from her back, loading her bow with a red arrow. She pulled back the string, ready to aim.

As soon as Quilla reached the ground, she clicked her gloves; blades sprouted from her knuckles. "Good morning!" she said in a cheerful voice as she slashed her blades like claws.

The two fought back to back, several guards came rushing at them at a time. Lilith fired, picking away the ones she could. She breathed out as she let the arrow fly, watching it land in a body with an exhale. She reloaded, adjusting her aim to make sure she only hit the enemy, not her allies.

Quilla was fighting off three people at once. One came from the back, slamming his fist into shoulder blades. Quilla turned; she grabbed his hand and flung him over her shoulder. He landed face-up in the snow; but as soon as he tried to get up, Lilith fired an arrow right at his throat.

Her partner looked at her, smiling with cruel joy. Lilith raised her hand to her forehead, saluting her. Quilla turned, swinging her blades at the oncoming opponents.

Nikolai was fighting on the opposite side of her. He swung his long swords in quick, strong movements. But unlike the last time he saw him fight, he was stabbing those soldiers without a second thought. Anger seemed to flare in his eyes as he swung his blades.

Lilith fired at random, shifting from branch to branch to get a better angle. She shot an arrow at a man who was engaging Quilla, striking him in his chest, then at the one who was dueling Nikolai, the arrow landing in his head.

Suddenly Lilith felt something brush by her. Goose bumps formed on her arms as a chill came over her. She quickly sprang to another branch as another arrow flew by her neck. Scanning the battlefield, she loaded her bow, ready to fire at any given time.

She heard a bowstring release, the air seemed to change, as though it was parting. Lilith turned around quickly, holding up her bow directly in front of her face. An arrow soared into the wood, directly in front of her face.

But the arrow was pointing towards the battlefield, meaning her opponent was in the woods. Lilith leaped from branch to branch, scanning for another archer. The trees were thick and cold leaves brushed her cheek. Through the branches, she caught the barest glimpse of a man. He wore a gray uniform, his weapon strung to his back.

Lilith loaded her bow, adjusting her aim to the silver that was running from branch to branch. She fired, aiming at his chest, but the silver ducked. As soon as the arrow went over his head, he was on the move again.

Lilith reloaded, firing quickly. The man sprang back, balancing himself on a tree trunk. He slipped behind the bark, using it as a shield.

Arrows flew at her at an alarming speed. She could feel the wind shift as they whistled by her head. She ducked, swinging from branch to branch and using her bow as a shield. The silver kept firing. His aim was flawless, making it so Lilith had to dodge every one. She felt one brush her loose hair, taking a couple of strands with it as it flung into a nearby tree.

Lilith was getting closer to the shooter, meaning it was much easier for him to shoot at her. She grabbed an overhanging branch, hauling herself up.

She scaled the upper branches, they were smaller and could hold much less weight. Her feet were kept light, balancing on each for only a second. The silver was pointing his bow in several directions, trying to figure out where she went. Lilith carefully drew an arrow from her quiver, holding it like a knife. She reached the tree the silver was hiding behind, and carefully climbed down its fragile limbs.

She didn't make a sound, her boots padding on the wood. The silver didn't bother to look up, making his demise so much easier.

All of a sudden, Lilith leaped from her perch and onto the same branch as her opponent. The silver swung around, loading his bow, but Lilith was too quick. She jammed the arrow into his throat.

Blood spewed from the open wound as the man choked, falling to his knees. Lilith yanked the arrow from his neck and watched as he fell through the trees, landing in the soft snow.

She leaped down next to him. Blood leaked onto the snow, making it a deluded red. Life slowly drained out of his eyes, fading by the second. Lilith took two fingers and closed them, whispering a tiny apology.

On his now still chest, was a silver badge. She plucked it from his clothes and disappeared back into the trees.

~~~

"Where were you?" asked Quilla angrily as Lilith approached her and Nikolai. Their clothes were bloodied, and their hair was messy and wet. Dead bodies of bronze soldiers lay in the snow. Nikolai was cleaning off his swords with the inside of his coat, it looked like he was struggling to get all the sticky blood off.

Lilith dropped the silver badge at her partner's feet. "You're welcome."

Quilla raised an eyebrow. "Impressive." She picked up the badge and handed it back to her. "It's a valuable trophy, I recommend you keep it."
~~~

Lilith took it, but instead of tucking it away, she threw it deep into the woods. "My pride doesn't come with my kills."

Nikolai wiped his forehead. "Let's get moving, it won't be long until they find the mess we left."

The snow was thick, and Lilith's boot sank in at least halfway every time she took a step. The ice had unfortunately made its way into her socks, and now she felt her feet squish. Quilla was in front of her. She took long strides, just trailing Nikolai. Her curly hair flew behind her, the cold air whipping through it. Lilith didn't think she had ever seen her so alive.

Nikolai, on the other hand, was more serious. His eyes had been trained on the goal ever since they got to Courna. The joyful boy that she had joked with on the ride over seemed to have disintegrated.

The tunnels were small and rocky. It looked like they had been carved by hand. Rails came out of the dark hole. They were rusty and used. Rock Highland must not be eager to change out their equipment.

Nikolai waited anxiously outside the tunnel. "We have to wait until the next cart comes. We're going to have a five-minute window to get inside. If we get run over, our torsos are going to look similar to how meat looks out of a grinder."

Lilith's eyes widened as he said the last part. Of course, it was true, but she found it easier not to imagine the worst and just pray she didn't have to come by it.

Nikolai bristled near the tunnel with his arms crossed. His muscles never relaxed, his eyes never shifted from the dark hole. Lilith didn't think she even saw him blink.

"You know," she told him in a kind voice. "You'll be better in a fight if you rest for the time we have."

Nikolai stayed silent, eyeing the tunnel. He fiddled with his hands, anxiously cracking his knuckles. His eyes were wide, and goose bumps had formed on his arms from the cold.

Lilith walked over to him, putting a hand on his shoulder. "Hey," she said gently, "She's going to be alright. We'll have her back by nightfall."

Nikolai kept his gaze turned away. "You don't know that."

"But I can hope." Her tone was light and kind. "And we've broken into many high-security fortresses. How hard can this one be?"

Nikolai simply shrugged, as though the information was meaningless.

Lilith gave him a compassionate smile, persisting. "When I'm worried I-"

Nikolai got up quickly, his teeth were grit and his eyes were angry. He slapped Lilith's hand away and advanced on her. "You can't talk!" he yelled, his voice a furious rasp. Lilith backed into the snow. "You're just a rotten criminal, you've never had anyone who cared about you!" his face changed, shifting to her former slaver, holding his whip in a rough hand. "You've never had a purpose!" Polar Zinglor was standing in front of her. That sick smile plastered on his face, a knife balancing on his hand. She tripped on a rock and fell, the cold snow chilling her spine. "Never had a legacy!"

An accent rang through the air, strict and terrifying. "Take one more step and I'll make sure your legacy ends, right here, right now!" Quilla had stepped between them. Her long hair blew gently in the breeze. Her eyes were angry, focused only on Nikolai. Lilith saw her blades were out, and she was ready to use them.

Nikolai looked at his hands, his eyes widened and his fiery demeanor shifted. He looked at Lilith, sorrow and regret shimmering over the anger that once burned in his gaze. "Lilith, I-"

Quilla cocked her head. "Don't bother."

Just then a cart rushed out of the tunnel, full of rocks and rubble. They watched it sail by, checking for patrol. Her partner gestured towards the tunnel. "You first, Princely." Quilla jutted out her jaw, her voice angry and threatening.

Nikolai sighed, ducking into the tunnel and crawling along the tracks. Quilla and Lilith watched him go, waiting until he disappeared into the darkness.

Once he did, Quilla extended a hand to Lilith. She took it, rising to her feet.

"I'm going to kill him." breathed her partner.

Lilith glared at the tunnel, jutting out her jaw. "Not if I do first."

Chapter Thirty Four
Alohi

Alohi was lying on the concrete floor. Her muscles ached from being used in the mine, and the cut on her arm still stung. It wasn't a normal wound; those would have ceased hurting at least a bit. But this one was still burning. She cradled it, tucking her knees to her chest and lying in the fetal position.

Tears ran down her cheeks; not because of the pain, but the shame that came with it. Her mind could think of all kinds of insults to throw at her. She was useless, she was unloved, she was weak.

She swallowed, trying to make this sadness go away. It was like she was trapped, not just in this cell, but in her mind. No matter what memories ran through her head, no matter the distractions from cold reality, she couldn't find a space where she could feel okay about herself.

So instead she lay on the floor. She didn't have the energy to move. Guards had placed food near the door a few hours ago, but she hadn't touched it. The thought of eating right now appalled her.

Suddenly the doors opened. Alohi didn't bother to turn, she just sunk more into her sadness, only dreading what the day was about to bring. But instead of the cold voice of the prison guards, she heard an even colder, crisp accent. "Morning, Windlem."

Alohi turned around to find a lean woman standing against the door frame. Her features were so sharp it felt like they could cut you. She had brown curls that strayed and ran down her face in strands. They covered black eyes that matched the dark knife she was balancing on her finger.

"W-who are you?" Alohi uttered.

The girl strode to her, walking with wide strides. She extended a hand, on it were gloves that covered no higher than the base of her long fingers. "Quilla Thorne."

Alohi scrambled back, but if this girl was who she said she was, it would do no good. "The criminal prodigy?"

Quilla clucked her tongue. "No, the duck." She started walking towards the door, her heels clicking against the concrete. "Come on, we have limited time!"

Alohi stayed where she was, glaring at her. "I'm not going anywhere with you,"

Quilla slowly turned around, tilting her head to the side. "Look, you're coming with me no matter what. Whether you're conscious or unconscious while with me is entirely up to you." She leaned against the wall again. "Besides, your boyfriend sent me."

Alohi raised an eyebrow. "My what?"

The crime prodigy jutted out her jaw. "You know, black hair, terrible style, and a bit hot-headed when it comes to heists."

Alohi's eyes widened. *Nikolai's here! I'm getting out of here!* She jumped up, sprinting out the door, eager to find her friend. Just as she crossed the frame, she stopped at a sword pointed at her throat.

Guards dressed in dark blue surrounded the doorway. They all had either swords or arrows pointed in her direction. A cold chill ran down her spine, terrified of what was to happen next.

Quilla walked next to her. Alohi couldn't tell if her calm aura infuriated or amazed her; either way, it was out of place. The con queen stood with her hands clasped behind her back and a gentle smile on her lips.

"Quilla Thorne." The closest guard smiled. "After all these years, we finally know your face."

The crime prodigy only laughed, tilting back her head. "Plenty of people have seen my face, but none ever live to tell the story."

Alohi leaped back as an arrow sailed through the crowd, landing in a guard's throat. They all turned, frantic to locate the archer. Alohi's breath escalated, wondering if the guards were the next target or she was. Another arrow flew directly into another guard's throat, and a third barely a second after. Panic erupted, arrows from the guards flew in random directions, while the mysterious archer kept shooting with amazing precision.

Quilla gave an ambitious smile. "Gentlemen, allow me to introduce you to my apprentice archer and right hand; Lilith Cole."

Arrows flew down, one after the other. Alohi couldn't quite see where it was coming from, but the archer never missed. The guards fell, one by one, as the arrows soared into their throats. Quilla just stood there watching the scene while Alohi was bracing herself for an arrow to come soaring right at her.

The chaos continued, the few that were still alive tripped over the fallen bodies, before they could get up, an arrow soared directly into their throat. Blood leaked from the open wounds and onto the floor. Alohi felt slightly dizzy, she begged herself not to faint.

The last guard was wide-eyed, he ran frantically around the room, pointing his sword in random directions. His legs were bent and his arms extended, it looked like he was expecting an arrow to come to end his life, but one never did.

Instead, a girl leaped down. She had long, golden brown hair that was woven into a braid. The red streak that ran through it was the same color as the blood she had just spilled. She wore black bell bottom pants and a rust-red leather jacket. Her eyes were a brilliant shade of green that sparkled in the light. She had a black arrow in hand, red streaks ran down its sides. Her feet padded along the floor, not making a sound.

The guard frantically looked around, turning with his sword outstretched, but the archer just weaved beyond his view with a crude smile on her face. Her hands with the arrow were clasped behind her back. She walked in a circle, just barely avoiding the man's line of sight.

Suddenly she stopped moving. The man turned to face her, fear glazing over his eyes. He charged at her, sword outstretched and face angry. The archer swerved to the side of him, knocking the sword out of his hands with just a slap. She then took the arrow, stabbing it into the man's spine.

The man crumpled to the ground, blood pouring out of his wound. He breathed rapid, short breaths. His eyes sparkled with panic as the revelation that death was waiting just beyond the corner hit him. The girl knelt down, tilting her head almost with curiosity, and then jamming the arrow directly into his throat. The man struggled for just a split second, then lay still and silent.

Alohi's eyes were wide. Her breathing was rapid and scared. The girl walked over to them, putting the red arrow back in her quiver. "Could've helped?"

Quilla shrugged. "You looked like you were having fun. Wouldn't want to spoil that."

The archer scoffed, striding over to Alohi. She braced herself, unsure of what horrors the girl had planned for her. But then, unexpectedly, she held out a hand. Her warm smile glowed and her eyes sparkled with friendliness.

"Lilith Cole." She grinned, completely switching personalities. "But you already knew that, due to my partner's dramatic introduction." Alohi could sense the crime prodigy's glare. "Alohi Windlem, right?"

She took Lilith's hand; it was rough and calloused. Alohi gave a tiny nod, unsure if Lilith saw it. "Yes." She said, using the only bit of fake confidence she had at the moment.

The archer nodded. "Figured." She turned to her partner, reaching to grab her bow that was strung around her back. "We need to go, before-"

Suddenly sirens blared and the bright light that once filled the halls was replaced by a terrible red. Alohi braced herself. She hadn't a clue how to fight, but she wanted to be able to run whenever the time called for it.

Quilla gave an angry growl. "Before that." The two of them started running towards the caves, dragging Alohi by the wrist. "Better get back to Princely before he wets himself."

Alohi was barely able to keep up with the two girls. They took long, fast strides, their feet silent as rats.

"Why are we heading towards the caves?" she asked as they opened the large doors. Inside was a familiar dark, rocky hall. "It's not going to work!"

Quilla rolled her eyes. "And why is that?" she cracked her neck. "This is the way we went in, I don't see why it would be any different on the way out."

Suddenly they heard a growl. They raced around the corner to the large cliff. Down below, on the sandy ground, was a giant creature. Its jagged teeth and mane told Alohi it was a lion, but the paleness of the creature was strange and unhealthy.

Drool and blood ran down its mouth in a stream. It was howling; charging at a man holding two blades. His hair was wild and his legs bent in a fighting stance. He had familiar, kind, gray-blue eyes that were focused on the animal. His coat was torn and tattered, and he had a cut on his forehead.

Nikolai looked up onto the cliff, his eyes lightened and his lips curved into a smile. His gaze was set on her, something that looked like relief and pure happiness. Alohi felt like rushing down there, collapsing in her friend's arms.

But just then the creature rammed its head into him, sending him flying through the air and crashing into the sand. "Nikolai!" Alohi hollered.

Quilla gave an exasperated sigh. "Lilith, shoot that thing from above. I'm gonna go save Lone's sorry ass." She then ran, sliding down the ladder and yelling. "We left you alone for two minutes and you engaged with a wildcat?"

Lilith loaded her bow, and Alohi felt anxiety crawling up her legs like a virus. They were so close, Nikolai couldn't die now.

"Hey," Lilith's kind voice interrupted her terrible thoughts. "He's tougher than he looks." She shot at the animal, the arrow just bouncing off its leathery skin. "Shit!"

Lilith loaded another one, this time taking more time to aim. She kept shifting the bow's angle, unsure of what to aim at. The monster kept attacking, Quilla and Nikolai fending it off as well as they could with their blades. The few attacks they got slid off the lion's skin as if they were hitting it with twigs.

Quilla charged at the cat's head. Her knives slashed out like claws and her eyes filled with fire. She leaped at the creature, trying to land on its back; but the monster spun, swinging its leg right into her stomach. She was hurled back, knocking her head against the cave wall. She crumpled to the ground, sinking in the sand. She lay there unmoving, her knives slipping out of her loose grip.

Alohi saw something flicker in Lilith's eyes, anger mixed with panic sparking like a flame. She fired at the monster, arrow after arrow bouncing off his scales. Just as quickly as they fired, another reloaded.

"Stop!" Alohi told her. Lilith held her fire, anger still burning bright. "Aim for the eyes. There's no way your arrow won't penetrate the pupil."

Lilith loaded an arrow. The archer closed her eyes, breathing controlled breaths. She pulled back her bowstring, opening her eyes and fixing her aim on the lion's eyes. She inhaled, finding her placement one last time, exhaled, and fired.

The arrow soared through the air. The cat growled, slowly moving towards Quilla's unconscious body. Alohi's breathing tightened as she watched the arrow get closer. Seconds seemed to be longer than minutes; anticipation made her shake.

The arrow hit the lion's eye straight on. The beast howled, clawing the arrow wedged deep into his skull. The animal turned away from Quilla, frantically trying to make the pain go away. Alohi and Lilith scrambled down the ladder, tripping over their own feet.

As soon as Alohi's feet touched the sandy ground, she rushed to Nikolai. He was standing in a corner, his blades were out and his eyes were alert. As soon as he saw her running towards him, his face softened. They ran towards each other, embracing in a warm hug. It felt as though it would last forever, and she would stay there gladly. Nikolai's arms squeezed her tightly and she buried her head in his chest. They didn't say a word, only soaking up each other's presence. When they finally pulled apart, all she could manage was, "I missed you."

Chapter Thirty Five
Quilla

"Quilla?" her eyes slowly opened to find her partner standing over her. "Quilla!" Lilith's braid was messy, little strands of hair hung over her eyes. She was shaking Quilla's shoulders, her green eyes wide.

Quilla sat up, coughing. The taste of blood lingered in her mouth; her head ached and her cuts stung. She felt a wave of nausea coming, and quickly pushed it down. Her vision cleared, and she realized that it wasn't just Lilith who was kneeling beside her, but Lone and Windlem.

Lilith laid a hand on her back, but she brushed it off, getting to her feet. As soon as the wave of dizziness hit and the nausea worsened, she wished he hadn't done that. Her arms flew out to catch her balance and her legs turned to noodles. Lilith's hands flew to her shoulders and this time, Quilla didn't try to stop it.

Lone crossed his arms. "Woah, Thorne." His cocky smile wasn't helping her nausea. "You just got knocked unconscious by a cat."

Quilla groaned, "Oh, do shut up." She headed for the ladder, trying to look less unbalanced than she was. "Let's go before that thing realizes we're still alive."

The beast was howling in a corner of the cave. It clawed at its eyes, trying to grab an arrow that was lodged deep into his pupil. Quilla turned to her partner. "What did you do?"

Lilith crossed her arms, proud. "There was no way we could penetrate the skin, so I shot it in the eye."

Quilla's mouth nearly dropped. To shoot something that precise, not to mention on a moving target required a lot of skill. Her apprentice was truly a master of her craft.

They all headed up the ladder. Her head still ached from the earlier impact, and her nausea hadn't ceased. Though climbs were typically easy for Quilla, this one was much more challenging. Her ribcage hurt from the impact and she could feel that skin had been torn under her shirt.

Once they reached the top of the ladder, they sprinted towards the door. The sand their feet picked up turned to dust in the air. "Wait!" Quilla's head turned as she heard Windlems's voice. "Where are we going?"

Quilla didn't stop running, her legs still pounding the sand. "The main entrance. We might be able to pick the lock and get out there."

She felt a hand grab her wrist. She stopped, turning around to see Lilith's hand holding her sleeve. "We can't get out there, it's suicide."

Quilla looked at them. "I know." Her gaze shifted to the ground. "There wasn't supposed to be a plan B. Plan A was supposed to work out!" she glared at Windlem. "But *someone* failed to tell us about the mutant guarding our escape route."

Windlem threw up her hands. She had dark skin and curly walnut hair. Her eyes were sky-blue. She wore something that looked like it was supposed to be a prison uniform, but it was reduced to stained rags. She had large, open cuts on her forearm and her hands shifted in a way that looked as though she was trying to hide them.

Quilla started running again, turning the sharp corner and sprinting down the hall. Her hair flew behind her as she turned the corners she had memorized. A grin spread along her lips as she realized that the others were far behind her.

She stopped, waiting for them to catch up. The hard footsteps and heavy breathing told her that they weren't far behind.

"How are you so fast?" Lone's winded voice asked.

Quilla turned, brushing hair out of her eyes. "Would you believe running from the authorities?"

Nikolai glared at her. "No." His gaze then shifted. In front of them was a large wooden gate. It was plated with gold around its edges. A giant, fancy lock was latching two handles together. Quilla grabbed a knife from her inside pocket.

"I might be able to pick it." She said, striding towards the door. Just as she jammed the knife in the lock, she heard loud footsteps. There were many of them. A storm of blue uniforms with some silvers sprinkled around the front charged at them. They had weapons drawn and firing. Quilla ducked as an arrow sailed over her head. She turned, facing her crew.

"Get your weapons out." She ordered, then turned to the politician. "Oh, wait."

Windlem glared at her while Lilith and Lone drew their weapons. Lone charged, blades out at his sides. He slashed the opponent as though it was easy, not caring as they fell to the ground in death. His eyes were angry, his fists clenched and posture so straight it radiated furiosity. A vicious smile spread along his lips as the blade slid through the throats of his opponents. Quilla recognized the anger in his eyes. She had seen it in the mirror.

Lilith fired at random, adjusting her aim every time. But the battle was coming closer, and a sharpshooter was meant to be away from the battle; killing from above, not in the dead center.

Quilla turned, twisting the knife around in the lock. It was complicated, different components needed to be hit in the right way at the right time. Her eyes narrowed, trying to remember any vague information she knew about lock picking. Sweat beaded on her forehead as she heard footsteps come pounding closer.

Quilla shoved the knife deeper into the keyhole, twisting it aggressively. Although she turned the knife, there was no click, no sign that the lock had opened. She yanked it out with a jolt, trying again. The footsteps were getting closer. She heard slashing and screaming in the distance, and turned her head to make sure it wasn't any of her crew.

They were all fine. Lilith fired at an alarming speed and Lone looked as though he could explode with anger. Windlem was standing in the corner, doing nothing as expected.

Focus, Thorne! The voice in her head told her. She turned back, sticking her knife in the lock and twisting. No click, it just got stuck. "Fuck!"

"Quilla," Lilith appeared beside her, leaning against the door. "I've known you for two years, and never seen you successfully pick a lock. So with all due respect, give me a try."

She groaned, stepping aside as her partner leaned down and tried the lock.

In front of her was a battle. Lone was fairing well. He was surrounded by guards, fighting them with precision and power. They crowded around him, their weapons swung and blocked from all directions as he slit several men's throats with just one clean swing.

Quilla inhaled. She squeezed her fists and blades sprouted from her gloves. She breathed out, walking slowly towards the oncoming competition.

Inhale. She ordered. *Exhale.* She sprinted into the competition. *Inhale.* She slashed the throat of an incoming guard. *Exhale.* She hurled a knife at a silver sprinting at her. *Inhale,* She landed on a man's back, jamming her blades into his spine. *Exhale.*

The rancid smell of blood and sweat filled her nose. She gagged as she breathed the hot air. But she kept breathing. It kept her in check and it would keep the situation slower in her eyes than in others. It gave her the upper hand.

Lone was fighting a couple of feet away. The anger in his eyes had not ceased. He had blood splatters all over his bare arms. His coat had come off somewhere, and now he wore a stained, white t-shirt. A man in blue snuck up behind him, his sword pointed at his head. Quilla lunged at him, knocking the sword out of his hand. The man flung himself at her, his fist extended. She ducked, slamming her fist into his stomach. The man doubled back, trying to recover, but Quilla was too quick. She slammed her boot into his head. With the impact she heard a loud crack. The man's eyes rolled back in his head and he collapsed.

"With me!" she yelled at Lone. He backed up, swords now in a defensive position. They fought back to back, covering each other as the incoming guards came rushing at them.

"On your right!" he yelled as a silver swerved at her. Quilla threw a serrated knife at him. It landed on his head, blood trickled down the wound and he fell. The next wave wasn't far behind. It felt like the fight would never end.

"Argh!" Quilla hollered as a blade sunk deep into her thigh. Her hands rushed to the wound on her upper leg, instantly being covered with blood. "Care to warn me, Lone?"

He quickly stabbed her attacker. "I don't have eyes in the back of my head!"

The pain was horrible. She had been nauseous before, but now she was actually salivating. Tears leaked from her eyes as she shut them, trying to ease the unbearable sting.

"I've got it!" Lilith cried. Behind her, the door had swung wide open. Outside was the rough, snowy landscape of Courna. Stables with horses were stationed just out the doors. A perfect escape route.

Quilla stood. The pain in her leg was excruciating, but she pushed through, risk and adrenaline taking over her senses. She limped to the doors, hurling knives at the incoming opponents.

Lone fought beside her, his blades flying around like birds. Blood sprayed around them at an alarming rate, but the opponents kept coming even faster. She narrowed her eyes, breaking into a run and sprinting towards the doors. Her blades were drawn and slicing anyone in her way like meat.

"Let's go!" she yelled at her crew, gesturing with her hand for them to follow her. All four of them sprinted towards the stables. They were wooden and a heavy blanket of snow fell on the roof. Inside were horses of all colors, their manes looked unbrushed and the horses themselves looked nearly starved.

When they reached them, Windlem reached out to a midnight black one. The horse retreated, its eyes wide and scared. She stood her ground, slowly moving closer to the terrified animal. The horse paused, letting her get close but ready to bolt at any second. She laid a hand on its face, gently petting the animal.

Quilla whipped her head around. The forces of Rock Highland weren't far behind and her leg pain had not ceased. A massive amount of blood leaked from the wound and she was beginning to feel lightheaded. "Can we get a move on, Windlem?"

"Can you be patient?" the politician hissed. "He's clearly scared!"

Quilla limped past her to the next horse. It was a dark brown color, scars ran down its back and its mane was tangled. She reached into her coat, grabbing a small bar. She opened it and extended her arm to the animal.

The horse cautiously walked towards her, taking the bar and eating it in one bite. He then lowered to the ground, letting her climb on his back. Quilla threw a bar to Lone and Lilith, gesturing for them to get their own horse.

"Come on!" she ordered, the pain in her upper thigh now making her impatient. "We need to go!"

The four of them mounted their horses and took off. The wind ran through her hair, and her nose and ears started to feel cold and numb. The landscape flew by on the back of the fast animals. Quilla felt the air shift. She ducked as an arrow flew by their heads. She risked a glance behind them, the mob was charging at them on horses, arrows flying from every direction. "Lilith!"

Her partner rode next to her on her own, murky brown horse. "On it!" she drew her bow and started firing at the guards. They fell off their horses as the arrows hit them directly in the chest.

Lone rode behind her. His long, black blades were drawn and it looked like he was trying to engage with the mob.

"Those won't do much good in this battle, Lone!" she yelled at him. "Get in front of us, Lilith is our only line of defense now." His horse swerved, riding directly in front of Windlems.

Quilla spotted thick woods ahead of them. Pine trees that were three stories tall were crammed into a forest. "We ride in there!" she yelled at them. Lone looked behind, a skeptical look crossing his face. She shot him back a glare.

Arrows flew over their heads and Quilla could hear the hooves of horses getting closer. The sound of a bowstring going off behind her suddenly stopped with an ear splitting snap.

"Lilith!" Quilla yelled at her partner. "What the hell is going on?"

"My string broke!" the archer yelled back.

Quilla's eyes narrowed. She pressed the horse's neck, urging it to go quicker. They were just a couple of feet from the woods. The horses galloped faster, so close to the trees. Lone and Windlem crossed into the forest and faded from view. An arrow flew by Quilla and she swerved just in time. The second pair of horses passed the first tree and ran into the thicket of branches.

Quilla swerved around the trees. They came one after another, threatening to whack her right off her horse. Just as she weaved around another one, an overhanging branch came at them. She raised her hands, grasping its rough bark and pulling herself up. Lilith followed, jumping off her horse and balancing on the branch.

Their horses ran off, finally free from his oppressive captor. Quilla gave a small, silent prayer for them, secretly hoping that they would find their way to live a good, long, happy life.

Shouts flew through the woods as the confused guards struggled to find them. Arrows flew into random trees below them. They stood on the branch in dead silence, not even daring to breathe. Quilla's wound burned in her leg. She closed her eyes tightly, trying to distract herself from the agony.

The yells faded, and the horses galloped deep into the woods. They looked at each other, unsure if it was safe to speak. Finally, Lilith broke the silence. "So, what now?"

Quilla looked out into the woods, trying to find the other half of their gang. "Now we find the two incompetent hyperbole that got us into this mess."

Chapter Thirty Six
Nikolai

Nikolai and Alohi rode into the deep woods. The silence was thick and heavy. None of them dared to speak, and Nikolai didn't think he could if he tried. Alohi's brown, curly hair was down loose and her clothes were tattered. Her dark skin seemed to glow in the light reflecting off the snow.

Their horses had slowed to a light jog, and they weaved around the trees in what seemed to be a relaxed motion. Nikolai bit his lip, not knowing if he should say anything. The awkwardness was unusual. Usually, Alohi was the only one he could really talk to without the intense fear that he would say something wrong. But now it felt like any word would turn her away and she would never talk to him again.

"Stop!" he finally said to break the silence. Her horse came to a halt, and she turned around. Her blue eyes sparkled and her hair hung over her face. Panic instilled in him as he realized he had no idea what he was going to say.

"Uh." He paused, scraping his mind for stuff to say. "You look... reflective."

There was an awkward pause. *God dammit*! His head was already beating himself up. *What kind of complement is that?*

Alohi crossed her arms, raising a skeptical eyebrow. Nikolai felt the air around them tighten. His lungs seemed to stop breathing and anxiety rose in his throat.

She then burst out laughing, pushing him playfully. Tears of joy leaked from her eyes as she giggled. If Nikolai could bottle the sound and listen to it every second of every day, he would. Her happiness was like music, her smile like art. Soon, Nikolai was laughing, tilting back his head in joy.

"There!" a deep yell broke the joy, and through the woods, Nikolai saw horses rushing at them.

"Go, go!" Nikolai hurried. Alohi turned, pressing her horse's neck to urge it to run. Nikolai pressed his own horse's neck, but the animal didn't seem to be in any rush. It started a low gallop, but it wasn't enough. Arrows flew towards them, direct, precise, and about to strike a deadly blow to their throats.

Just then a hand grabbed his shirt. He watched as Alohi got lifted from her horse's back, and him next. Their horses scrambled off and he was lifted onto a branch. The yell of guards came closer, and through a small part in the leaves, he saw arrows and horses running by.

Thorne and Lilith were perched on the branch above them, their clothes were tattered and Thorne's wound seemed to be more bloodied. They raised their fingers to their mouths, gesturing to keep quiet.

The chaos of battle faded into the woods, the yelling dulled and the sound of hooves turned nonexistent. The four of them stared at each other for a while, unsure if it was safe to speak.

"So," Nikolai started skeptically. "How much of that did you guys hear?"

Lilith laughed. "Most, if not all."

"That was some marvelous flirting skills, Lone. Maybe I should take notes." Thorne said in a teasing tone.

Nikolai rolled his eyes. "Oh please, if any man had an interest in you, they would get stabbed not even a second after their first word."

"Hm." She pushed her hair to one side of her shoulder. "Any *man*, maybe."

"Guys," Alohi inquired, breaking the tone of sarcasm. "As fun as it is in the trees, I'm long overdue for a bed. So if we could please focus our attention on finding a place to stay, that would be great."

Thorne raised her eyebrows. "Well, would you look at that- Windlem has a tongue."

Alohi scoffed, glaring at the criminal prodigy. Though they had just met, Nikolai could just sense that their relationship was going to be comical.

"I saw a small hotel ahead." Lilith told them. "It's in a small village, fairly out of the way. We should be able to lay low there for the night."

Thorne groaned. "I do not feel like socializing."

Nikolai rolled his eyes. "Well, that's too bad. Lilith, where is it?"

The archer climbed the branches, peeking her head out over the top of the trees. "To your left, Nikolai. Just keep heading in that general direction, and we'll get there eventually."

Thorne smiled, looking at him and Alohi. "Try and keep up." She then leaped into the trees, swinging on different branches and then disappearing into the deep brush.

Lilith flashed them a smile, and swiftly followed her partner through the woods, vanishing along with her. Nikolai turned to Alohi, she was glaring after them, her eyes focused.

He laughed. "You'll get used to it." He then jumped to another branch and extended a hand to her. "You coming?"

Alohi smiled, placing her hand in his. It was surprisingly soft and light in his palm. They then leaped from branch to branch, together at last.

~~~

Dusk had broken when they peeked their heads out of the trees and looked at the small town. The orange and pink light decorated the plain white snow.

Thorne and Lilith were standing on a brick road. Little shops and houses lined the path, people in old fashion dresses and trousers stood along the buildings, looking skeptically at the two crime lords.
~~~

Thorne had her knives out and was balancing one on her finger as she leaned against a lamppost. Her wound had left a stain in her pants, and there was a giant tear on her upper thigh where the weapon had impaled her. She looked slightly pale, as though she was barely able to keep herself from fainting.

Lilith was restringing her wooden bow next to her. The once tight braid was now loosely woven and tangled. She kept glancing at her partner, but quickly looked back, as though she was afraid Thorne would notice.

Nikolai and Alohi hopped down from their branch, walking up to the two girls. Thorne glared at them, her eyes aflame with what looked like severe pain. "Took you long enough."

He growled but didn't say anything. He had already taken a wrong step today when he advanced on Lilith, and he wasn't one to make the same mistake twice.

The looks they got from the civilians were judgemental and sharp. Some hurried their children inside, and some pulled out they're knives and bows. Nikolai often felt the urge to stop and clarify that they weren't anything to be afraid of, but Thorne kept walking. She took long strides and her boots clicked against the ground with every step. The wound in her leg seemed to vanish, but she still had an awful, focused expression on her face. It was as if nothing else mattered anymore, just her goal.

The hotel was perched on the right side of the street. Lamps were on either side of the small staircase leading up to the front door. The building itself was a dark brown, spikes on metal fences lined the small balconies. Small windows with bars on them seemed to belong to different rooms.

Thorne strode up the staircase, her long coat flowing behind her as she threw open the door. Nikolai could just feel the bad decision that he was about to walk into.

Inside looked like a dark bar. The people inside all had knives and glasses of what looked like hard whiskey. Music played that felt way too upbeat compared to the dull surroundings. In the center of it was a check-out desk that appeared to also be serving hard alcohol. The man working wore all black with his hair pulled into a high ponytail. He had tattoos that ran down his bare arms and piercings in about every place possible.

Thorne strode up to him, anger surrounding her like a raincloud. Alohi quickly hurried up to her, stepping in front of her long strides.

"Quilla," she laid a hand on the crime prodigy's shoulder. "Maybe it's best if I do the talking."

Thorne stepped aside, leading Alohi to the tattooed man. "Then, by all means, Windlem, do the talking!"

Nikolai didn't understand how Alohi wasn't shivering with fear at that moment, but she walked up to the man with confidence, placing her hand on the counter. "Excuse me!" she said in a bright tone, the bartender didn't answer. She tried again. "Excuse me!"

The bartender turned, looking their group up and down. "We don't serve vigilantes." He then turned around, getting back to his drinks.

Alohi laughed. "Oh, this is all a big misunderstanding!" she lied. "We're not vigilantes, we just got a little roughed up during a hunting trip, that's all!"

The bartender rolled his eyes, "What do you want?"

Alohi tilted her head, a kind smile spreading on her chapped lips. "Just two rooms." Nikolai was amazed that her bright persona hadn't shifted.

"And what do you have to pay for these rooms?" the bartender huffed.

Thorne slammed a fistful of kangue onto the table. "Will this do?"

He laughed. "We don't take Thine money."

Alohi began to open her mouth, but Thorne brushed her aside. "My turn, Windlem!" she opened her mouth to protest but closed it as she realized that Thorne's knives were out.

The criminal prodigy slammed the knife into the countertop. The blade firmly stuck to the fine wood like an arrow that had been shot into a target.

The bartender turned towards Throne, eyeing her with fury. "That-" he slammed his fist on the counter. "Was expensive!" caution drifted over the room as the bartender's own knife gleamed in his hands.

"I-" she cocked her head to the side, "Don't care." Thorne yanked the knife from the wood, hoping behind the counter. The bartender lunged at her, but he was too slow. Thorne ducked and pushed the muscular man into the counter. As soon as he tried to get up, she jammed her knife into the man's hand.

He hollered with pain as Thorne removed the blade. Blood sprayed all over the bartender as he crumpled to the ground, still wailing from the pain.

The crime prodigy, however, was perusing his selection of alcohol like a library. Her long fingers traced several bottles, gently brushing the tips of her fingers against the glass.

Thorne finally grabbed a large bottle with clear liquid inside. Her black eyes admired the liquor with what looked like curiosity. When she was done gazing at the alcohol, she placed the bottle on the counter.

Picking up the bartender by the shirt, who was still clutching his bleeding hand, Thorne hurled him onto the counter. She hopped onto the fine wood, picked up the wine bottle, and popped it open. The liquid fizzed and bubbled over, trickling onto the ground.

Thorne tipped her head back and took a large swig of the wine. "Château Lafite, if I'm not mistaken. Incredibly expensive. Would be a shame if-" she grabbed the bartender's wounded hand and poured the wine on the wound. He hollered as the alcohol hit his bloodied flesh. "-It got poured out."

The counter was now covered in a mixture of wine and blood. Nikolai was trying hard not to hurl, and it looked like Alohi and Lilith were trying to do the same. Thorne, on the other hand, had hopped down from the counter and was tipping over the other bottles of alcohol. They fell to the ground as her hand brushed them off the shelves, shattering on impact.

"Here's the deal!" Thorne knelt down to where the bartender was crouching, still clutching his wounded hand. Pure fear sparkled in his gaze as it met the criminal prodigy's black one. "You give us two rooms, I'll stop."

The bartender swallowed. The power and confidence that once radiated off him had disintegrated into a trembling fear. "And if I don't?"

"Then your alcohol won't be the only thing you're losing."

The bartender's eyes widened as he realized that if he refused, he might not get to keep all his limbs. With this new revelation, he rushed to a small cabinet. Still cradling his arm, he handed Thorne two silver keys.

Thorne's eyes lit up and her lips curled into a fanged smile. Nikolai watched as she flipped her dark, unruly hair out of her gleaming eyes. "Pleasure doing business."

Chapter Thirty Seven
Alohi

"Good god!" that was the first thing that Alohi said as the door to their room closed. "Good god! How am I supposed to spend the rest of the journey with *her*?"

The room was large. Two small beds were placed next to each other with nightstands for each. They had a window that gave them a view of the entire village. Nikolai walked up to it, gazing at the landscape below. "I find it works well to just not get in her way."

She scoffed, falling back first onto her bed. "I get that the man refused service, but he was just doing what he thought was right." She turned to look at Nikolai. "And let's be honest, we looked like trouble. He didn't deserve to lose a hand!"

Nikolai collapsed beside her. "It's not amputated, just a bit demobilized." He turned and smiled. His blue-gray eyes met hers, and they gazed at each other for a while. Nikolai's hair was wild, but his smile was kind. He had a large gash on his forehead that was still leaking blood.

"One second." Alohi told him, getting up. "I'm going to go get something for that." She grinned and disappeared into the bathroom, coming back with a wet cloth.

Nikolai sat up, waiting for her with his hands folded. She sat down and dabbed it on his head. As soon as it came in contact with his skin, he winced. Alohi jolted away. "Sorry."

He gave a small laugh. "No, it's fine." His hands brushed hers as he took the rag and dabbed it on his forehead. It came away bloodied, the cut producing more of the red liquid just as soon as it was wiped away.

Nikolai sighed, throwing the cloth on the floor. "Well, that's not going to do much."

"I'll get another one." Alohi offered, standing up. But as soon as she started walking Nikolai grabbed her wrist.

"Wait!" he gently pulled her onto the soft mattress. Still gently grasping her hand, Nikolai turned it, revealing her red cuts. "Alohi, what happened?"

She sighed, trying to block the awful scenario out of her head. "Before you got to me, I tried to get out on my own." She looked at her cuts. "It was pretty feeble. A man caught me, chained me up, and ran his knives down my arms."

Nikolai's eyes filled with horror. "Alohi, I'm so sorry."

She scoffed. "Don't you dare pity me. I'm just weak, it's something I have to get used to living with." She stood, heading to the bathroom to get towels.

He quickly stepped in front of her stride. Their eyes locked and there was a sternness in Nikolai's gaze that she barely saw. "Don't ever say that again!"

Alohi kept walking to the bathroom. "It's true. I am weak. At least in the category of fighting." She looked down, remembering her father's dark words. "That's what my family thinks, at least."

Nikolai reached into a black cabinet. "No offense, but anyone who says that is a delusional asshole." Alohi raised her eyebrows, Nikolai barely used profanity, and when he did, it was for something he was passionate about. He pulled out a bundle of bandages. "Sit down, I need to wrap those up."

Alohi hopped onto the counter, holding out her cut forearms. With a damp towel, he started dabbing her wounds. She fought the urge to wince at the sudden sting, but eventually, the cold of the water felt good, as though it was washing away her pain.

Nikolai dabbed her arms again with a dry cloth. "If anything, I'm the weak one." He told her, looking down at his work.

Alohi almost laughed. "Oh, of course," she said in a sarcastic tone. "Nikolai Lone, the child prodigy and the future king of Thine, is a weakling."

He gave a light smile. "It's not just skills that make you strong, it's your mind too." He started wrapping her wound in bandages, looking down. "And when you were gone, my mind snapped."

Alohi's eyes softened. "What do you mean?"

Guilt clouded over her friend's face. "You know Lilith, the archer? She's really nice once you get to know her."

Alohi gave a small smirk. "She killed twenty people in cold blood just in the last hour."

Nikolai shrugged. "That too. But she's considerate and kind. She was forced into her current predicament, and doesn't want to be following along with the..." he paused, trying to think of the right word. "*Unusual* methods of her partner. I honestly think you two would get along."

She scoffed. "We'll see about that."

Nikolai finished wrapping her right arm. "Anyway, when you were gone, I wasn't sure if you were... you know..." he rubbed his neck self-consciously. "Still alive. So with this worry, I wasn't exactly like myself. I felt angrier than usual, as though I would go through any boundary to get to you. When we were waiting to get into the tunnel, I guess Lilith sensed my unease and tried to comfort me." He sighed, taking another roll of bandages. "But, instead of letting it happen, I turned on her. I said some pretty bad things that I think affected her. It was like she was scared of me, for at least a little while. And honestly, I think I was scared of myself."

Alohi laid her bandaged hand on his shoulder. "Honestly, I don't think it matters." His eyes widened at the sharpness of her tone. "Once we're home, they'll be on their way and we'll be on ours, so what does it matter if there are some unfortunate feelings?"

Nikolai bit his lip anxiously. "Actually…" He started, his voice small. "Thorne is joining the League of Red Doves."

Alohi jumped to her feet. "What?" at first, she was appalled and considered hiring a hitman to take the prodigy out. Then her brow furrowed as the revelation hit her. "Actually, that might not be too bad."

This time it was Nikolai's turn to act surprised. "What?"

Alohi shifted her gaze. "She's undeniably skilled. It takes a special kind of talent to break into an Empire base, not to mention doing it with ease."

Nikolai laughed. "She has a giant gash in her leg."

"But we don't! Quilla may be ruthless, but she knows how to get the job done." Alohi chimed, enthusiasm starting to creep into her voice. "We don't have to like her, but we do need her." She strode out of the bathroom and sat on the soft bed. "And let's be honest, the League needs all the help it can get."

Alohi felt Nikolai's tone shift. "You're sounding a lot like her right now."

She laid down on the pillows, letting the soft cushion engulf her. This comment filled her with cruel pride. Quilla Thorne wasn't weak. She smirked, "Maybe that's a good thing."

Chapter Thirty Eight
Lilith

As soon as they entered the room, Quilla collapsed on the floor. Lilith's eyes widened as she rolled up her pants to reveal a wide gash on her upper thigh. Blood leaked from the wound as fast as water and the skin around it was beginning to turn purple.

"You're hurt!" Lilith exclaimed, rushing to her partner's side.

"No kidding!" Quilla's eyes were shut in pain. The once fiery gaze that burned on her features was now blank and tired.

Lilith reached into her quiver, pulling out a small bottle of disinfectant alcohol, bandages, and stitching materials. She rushed into the bathroom, grabbed a small towel, and rushed back out. She poured a hefty amount of alcohol onto the cloth. "This might hurt a bit." Before her partner could object, Lilith gently pressed the cloth into her wound.

Quilla's nails dug into the floorboards. Her eyes shut in pain and her teeth pressed tightly together. She took large, rapid breaths, and beads of sweat formed on her forehead. Her hair was messy, strands of it ran over her clenched eyes.

Lilith gently removed the cloth. It came away soaked with blood. Worry and concern filled her as she grabbed the stitching supplies. She threaded the needle with a thin thread and angled it at Quilla's wound.

As soon as she was about to begin, Quilla's hand grabbed her wrist. She supposed the grip was supposed to be tight, but instead Quilla's touch was cold and fragile. She was breathing hard, her chest rising and falling rapidly. "I don't need your *pity*!"

"This isn't pity," Lilith told her, gently removing her limp hand from her wrist. "This is compassion and *caring*."

Quilla tried to scramble away, her leg clearly causing her a lot of pain. "I can do it myself!" her black eyes glared at Lilith. Quilla reminded her of a scared, wounded spider.

"No, you can't," Lilith said in the calmest tone she could manage. "You're obviously barely staying conscious as is. You're going to bleed out if we don't get that fixed. It's already getting more infected by the second and I would rather not go through the alcohol thing again. So for the love of god, Quilla, stop being so stubborn and let me work on it!"

Although she was still glaring at her, Quilla relented. She laid her leg on the floor, her back resting on the wall. Lilith stuck the needle into the wounded flesh, and a pang of guilt shot through her as her partner flinched.

Lilith wove the thread through the wound. It was getting late. The light reflecting on the snow outside their window was slowly fading. The orange sun was dipping behind the forested mountains.

She and Quilla sat in silence. Both of them were exhausted and making conversation seemed like an unnecessary effort.

Lilith was halfway through stitching now. The wound was slowly closing, and the bleeding seemed to have slowed.

"How did you get it?" Lilith asked. "The wound?"

Quilla's eyes were still closed. "Some asshole snuck up behind me and stabbed my leg. Personally, I blame Lone's bad eyesight."

She laughed. "So, place your bets: how long do you think before he tries to fist-fight one of us."

Quilla's lips spread into a smirk. "The real question is how long will it take for us to meet our wits' end and take a swing at him."

"Oh okay, so sunrise tomorrow, with you and him," Lilith said with confidence.

Quilla tilted her head to the side. "Uh-huh, and where will you be while this is happening?"

Lilith finished stitching Quilla's leg and reached for the bandages. "Watching while drinking whiskey and eating popcorn."

"I speak from experience when I say that's a terrible combination." She flinched as Liltih wrapped the first layer of bandages around her leg.

She stopped. "Too tight?"

Quilla looked at the ceiling, gritting her teeth. "No, that's fine."

"Uh-huh." Lilith nodded skeptically, loosening the bandages. "So, League of Red Doves?"

"What about it?"

"You're just going to leave your life in Hanslack? Why?" Lilith asked. Quilla had built a reputation from the bottom up, and she wasn't the type to watch years of work burn.

Quilla's hard glare returned. "Hanslack is a cage for me too. I want to be free as much as you do."

Lilith doubted that. The crime prodigy always seemed to enjoy the look of pain on other's faces, or the thrill of stealing. A caged bird suffered and plucked its feathers, but Quilla seemed far from that. If anything, her partner fit the role of cager than the caged. "So if you're there unwillingly, who put you there?" Lilith didn't know why she asked this, she knew the answer.

Quilla's face tightened like it did whenever someone asked her to discuss her past. "It's none of your concern." Words Lilith had gotten used to.

"Ghan, right?" Lilith asked as she finished bandaging up her leg. "That's why you hate him."

Quilla rose to her feet, still looking unstable, but angry. "I told you to *leave it*!"

"No!" Lilith's own eyes lit up with anger. "You've been playing a dangerous, vengeful game and using my life as a pawn! I deserve to know the reason!"

Quilla's eyes were glittering with fire. "You act like you haven't been using me for your own goals!" her tone was rich with spite. "I'm a criminal, I'm a narcissist, I'm a monster! That's what you believe! Yet you walk around with me as though we're partners! So wake the hell up, we've been using each other as pawns for years!"

Lilith laughed dryly. "Well, that explains it! All the times you had me learn the hard lessons on the streets, all the times you used me as bait or leverage! You never cared for me! Hell, Nikolai's right, you've never cared for anyone!"

With this, Quilla's face softened and her eyes dropped to the ground, now full of regret. "You wanna know what Ghan did to me?" she rasped. "He killed my sister, and turned the rest of my siblings against me. So yes, I don't care about anyone; but I did care about them."

Lilith's mind flew with the pictures from Quilla's notebook. The little kids, fighting and laughing together. They were her family, and Ghan stole them from her. Lilith could relate to that, painfully. "Quilla, I-"

Quilla turned on her heel, heading out the door. "I'll sleep in the hall. After all, you don't want to sleep with a *monster*."

Chapter Thirty Nine
Nikolai

Nikolai padded into the hall quietly, careful not to wake Alohi. It was still dark outside, the early morning birds were still silent. It was cold in the hotel; it sunk through him as he snuck out the door and into the corridor.

No lamps were lit yet, so the room was dark. From what Nikolai could see, old pictures of people hung on the wall. The floor was lined with a thin, stained carpet. Large plants in pots were lined along the hall, looking like terrifying creatures in the dark.

Nikolai was dressed in a dark blue coat and black trousers. He wore a white, collared shirt that was wrinkled. His swords were strapped to his back, ready for him to grab at any second.

But the hall was almost completely empty as he slowly made his way down a carpeted set of stairs. Below was the quiet setting of the bar. The mess from the earlier day seemed to have been cleaned up, and all that was left was a small stain of blood and alcohol. I'm the dim moonlight, he saw a figure sitting at the bar.

Her long, curly hair was unbrushed, and strands hung over her eyes like a ripped curtain. She was slouched at the very counter that she nearly destroyed the night before. With her was a small shot glass filled with dark alcohol.

"Have you been drinking all night?" he asked her.

Thorne turned her head, she had droopy eyelids and bags under them. "No."

Nikolai raised his eyebrows skeptically. "So you slept?"

"Also, no." Thorne tipped her head back and downed the shot.

Nikolai sighed. "So what exactly have you been doing all night?"

"I've been making myself useful." She got up and strode over to the library of drinks behind the counter. "I scouted a route to the docks, it looks all clear on horseback." She grabbed a bottle of rich, red alcohol, and poured it into her glass.

"Give me some," Nikolai told her, the regrets of the earlier day finally catching up to him. Thorne pulled out a small glass and poured the red liquid to its top.

He grabbed it and took a small sip. The bitter taste burned his tongue. Nikolai choked, swallowing it quickly and gagging.

"First time?" Thorne asked, downing hers all in one go.

Nikolai wiped his mouth with his coat. "Yeah."

"You'll get used to it." She told him. "So, what are you so down about?"

Nikolai rested his forehead on his palm. "The Empire prisons, what are they like?"

Thorne sighed, her face creasing with immediate understanding. "I can't tell you. It's only going to make your guilt worse."

Nikolai turned to her with begging eyes. "Please, I- I need to know what she went through in there." He stared at the red alcohol still sitting in his cup.

"It's not good." Thorne took another shot of wine. "Whenever someone comes back from one of those places, and they rarely do, their sense of self is almost completely destroyed. The prisons are designed to make you feel helpless and less than. Has your friend changed at all?"

He sighed, rubbing his temples. "Alohi was always empathetic and kind, no matter what. That's why we clicked." Those times seemed so far away, especially now. "But last night, she seemed almost..." He trailed off, not exactly knowing what he was going to say.

"Like me," Thorne said solemnly, keeping her head down.

"Yeah." Nikolai felt a pang of guilt saying that, especially to her face. "Have you ever been in an Empire prison?"

Thorne drank her alcohol in one swig. She looked down at the wood, emotion glittering in her eyes. "Of a sort."

Nikolai took the bottle away from her, figuring it was better if she didn't have anymore. "And what kind of sort is this?"

Thorne looked at her hands, "I prefer not to say," she straightened her posture, flipping the hair out of her eyes. "But I can say that it's an experience that shaped me. My life revolves around revenge for the people who hurt me and the people I loved."

Nikolai decided not to press on. He could understand a sensitive topic, especially one that involved the Empire. "So, is Alohi going to be consumed with vengeance?"

Thorne shook her head. "I doubt it. My best guess is her self-esteem took a big blow, that's it. She was also only in there for a few weeks, whereas I was in a prison for seven years, not to mention the developing stages."

Nikolai was beginning to understand the reason behind Thorne's methods. "How old were you?"

She rubbed her temples. "I was put in there at five years old, escaped at twelve."

"You were a criminal before you could spell?"

Thorne tilted her head back and laughed, dry and humorless. "No. I was kidnapped because I was thought to be useful. After I escaped, Hanslack was the only place to go, so I learned to survive the only way I could."

Nikolai's heart stung with sympathy. "I had no idea, I'm so sorry."

Thorne glared at him. "Don't pity me, Lone. I did what I had to do, and now it's done."

Nikolai passed his thick wine to Thorne- she deserved to drown her feelings. "You shouldn't have had to. None of us should have had to do what we had to do to survive." They gazed at the dark bar for what felt like minutes; contemplating what their lives were, and what they could have been.

"So," Thorne chugged the shot. "Why do you and Windlem hate Ghan?"

Nikolai cackled, the noise sudden and out of place. "That's the thing, we don't." His tone was lighter than it should have been, and he in no way found this conversation laughable. But the humorous tone slid off his tongue so easily. "Don't get me wrong, what he does to people is terrible and the world would be much better off without him. But personally, I don't hold a grudge against him. It's my father who does, although as far as I'm concerned it's more of a political fight for power." He tilted back his head, looking at the ceiling. "As soon as I was born, I was put into sword fighting lessons. By the time I was five, people considered me a prodigy. But I hated every second of it. I never wanted to be the White King, and I never wanted to fight. But as my father always said, *destiny* doesn't give you a choice."

Thorne looked at him with black, angry eyes. "Destiny's an asshole."

Nikolai felt tears start to form in his eyes. "Yeah, it really is!"

"So what about Windlem?" Quilla asked. "Does she want the life she has?"

He looked out the window onto the harsh landscape, the sun was beginning to come up, giving the snow an orange reflection. "Her situation is similar. Her father believes that to be of worth you have to be good at something. For her, it was either fighting or having an influence politically, so she chose the second one. Her sister, Ranine, chose fighting. She's an excellent warrior."

Thorne gave a hard laugh. "Come now," she said, pulling a knife from her coat and sticking it into the table. "That girl couldn't kill a duck if it sat on her feet."

Nikolai glared at her. Though he was objectively a better fighter than Ranine, she was a close friend. "I guess, in some ways, it's a good thing."

She looked at him skeptically. "What is?"

"That all this happened. Ghan ruining your and Lilith's lives, the grudges he created ruining me and Alohi's. I would never have met Alohi if her family hadn't sought refuge in the League of Red Doves and you would have never met your archer if she hadn't been enslaved in the Grave Desert."

Thorne snorted. "Believe me, Lone, me and Lilith's relationship is *purely* professional."

Nikolai rested his chin on his palm. "Oh really?" when he watched the two, they reminded him of two birds. Thieving food from others plates and laughing as they flew into the trees. They seemed inseparable. "Well, on a lighter note, without the Empire's involvement, I wouldn't have met you."

"Oh please." Thorne unstuck her knife from the table and fiddled with the blade. "Don't pretend that every second with me isn't anything less than agony."

Nikolai smiled. "If I hated every second with you, I wouldn't be having this deep conversation would I?" he drummed his fingers against the table. "We may have different methods, but I don't hate you." This wasn't a lie. Though he and the crime prodigy quarreled often, he had grown quite close to her.

Thorne twisted her knife into the counter. "A terrible decision, really."

"Not really." He told her. "I don't want to have an unpleasant relationship with someone who has the power equivalent to an army."

"Flattery doesn't work on me, Lone."

Nikolai laughed. "Trust me, I am trying to gain no favor. I guess what I'm trying to say is, I'm grateful for your help now and in the future." He stood, walking towards the stairs. "Thank you, Quilla."

For just a second, her eyes softened. She sat up straighter, a surprised look crossing her face. Then, she smiled gently. "You're welcome, Nikolai."

Chapter Forty
Quilla

Quilla was looking out the barred window. The sunlight came over the trees and leaked its light onto the white snow. The town wasn't up yet, villagers were probably still in their cozy homes. Some part of her longed for the comfort of a home of her own. It still amazed her that some children got that luxury right out of birth, with no blood-curdling work to earn it.

Of course, she never got that; well, not that she could remember. It was a long time ago that her life was no different than that of an average child. She only had a few memories of her parents, and even those hurt too much to run through her brain.

She was already beating herself up for spilling so much of her past to Nikolai. Of course, he had asked for it; but that didn't mean she had to explain where she came from.

But you didn't! A crude voice told her. *And let's hope you never do, it would be better if you forgot your home*! But she couldn't, no matter how much she tried, she couldn't forget where she came from. Even though it was reduced to vapor right before her eyes, she couldn't forget it.

She moved away from the window, clicking her boots against the ground. The wound in her leg was hurting much less than yesterday. Lilith had done a good job.

She bit her lip as she remembered her conversation with her partner. The combination of the oversharing she did with Nikolai and Lilith could be enough information to piece the entire story of her past together. Luckily, the two would probably never cross paths again after this mission. It would just be her, Nikolai, and Alohi.

Oh no, she realized as her brain fully processed that thought. Though she and Nikolai had become closer, she was fairly sure Alohi had some rather negative feelings towards her. The mix of limited morals and passion for stabbing seemed as though it would become fairly repulsing to the morally bound politician. However, she had never come across someone who worked in politics and also had a complete moral code intact.

Quilla turned as she heard footsteps coming down the stairs. Lilith was wearing baggy clothes, her hair was down and messy. She yawned and started browsing the bar.

"Where's the coffee, Quilla?" she asked in a voice cracked with sleep.

Quilla strode to the bar. "Do you not care for how people perceive you physically?" she asked in a judgemental tone.

Lilith turned to look at her. "Do you have no care for how people perceive you morally?" a fair comeback. "Coffee, Quilla."

She leaned against the counter. "Wouldn't know." Her shot glass was still sitting on the wood, traces of the alcohol still lingering.

Lilith looked at it, then at Quilla. "How drunk are you?"

She scoffed. "Oh please, it takes more than a few shots to break my tolerance."

Her partner laughed. "Ah yes, a resistance to alcohol at seventeen, how healthy."

Quilla glared at her. "I never expected to live this long in the first place."

Lilith shrugged. She opened up a drawer and pulled out dark brown coffee grains. "Want some?" Quilla just glared at her. "Fine." She put a tea kettle on the old stove and switched on the flame.

Her partner strode over to the wooden counter. "How are you feeling?"

Quilla looked out the window, her eyes slits of anger and hatred. "Physically or mentally?"

"Physically." Lilith clarified. Even though she was turned away, Quilla could feel her wretched sympathy.

"Like I've just walked through fire."

"And mentally?" Lilith asked, nauseating pity lacing her voice.

"Like I've just walked through magma."

Quilla could feel Lilith's prying green eyes digging into her back. "Do you want to talk about it?"

Quilla narrowed her eyes. The pity in her partner's voice was making her want to vomit. She turned to her, her eyes angry little slits. "When have I ever wanted to talk about it?"

Lilith was about to open her mouth, but just then Nikolai and Alohi came down. They were dressed in warm, puffy clothes. Scarves were wrapped tightly over their mouths, and fuzzy hats were barely covering their eyes.

Quilla's eyebrows shot straight up. "You look ridiculous."

Nikolai seemed to be raising his covered eyebrows. "We won't get hyperthermia."

"Lucky you."

Lilith had poured the now hot liquid from the kettle and into her cup. She now sat at the bar drinking the steaming, brown liquid. "So," she said, sipping her coffee. "What's the plan?"

Quilla stood straighter, like whenever she was about to explain a scheme. "Today we ride to the docks where the ship is. It's going to take a while, so I'd stalk up on supplies here, or plan to not eat." She walked over to the bar and sat on a stool. "Remember, the soldiers from Rock Highland are going to be looking for us, so be discreet."

Nikolai raised an eyebrow. "Do you just expect us to trust that you know where you're going?" he asked skeptically. "There could be any type of obstacle in the way that even you couldn't prepare for."

Quilla's lips curled into a mischievous smile. "Well, Nikolai, since you so *eagerly* volunteered, you are more than welcome to inform us of any obstacles that await our arrival."

Nikolai groaned. "And how exactly would I get that information?"

Quilla raised an eyebrow. "As a councilman, aren't you supposed to know a bit about all countries, not just the one you were born in?"

"Actually," Alohi butted in. "He's not a councilman, I am. And I can tell you that Courna is a popular meeting spot for pirates."

Lilith sipped her coffee. "I thought pirates mostly lingered around the outskirts of Salenian."

"Typically, they do." Answered Alohi. "But Courna is the second largest country, following Thine, of course, with not many rivers or canals for transportation. People either travel by train, or by horseback. And when they travel, usually they have something to deliver."

"And the pirates steal it." Nikolai sighed. His eyes were downcast, as though the harsh realities of the world were just dawning on him.

"Well," Quilla started. "If it eases your worries, the route we're traveling on isn't commonly attacked by pirates. Besides, they know better than to attack a handful of powerful vigilantes."

"Oh really?" Nikolai straightened his posture. "And how exactly do you know this?"

"I've worked with a couple once or twice."

Lilith choked on her coffee. "What?"

Quilla scoffed. "Keep in mind, Lilith, that you have only been in Hanslack for two years. Whereas I have been there since I was twelve. Me and Gillen did a job with them when I was fourteen." She growled, remembering her unfortunate relationship with the gang lord. Back then, they had been close. She had once seen him as a father figure. But not anymore, never again.

Nikolai knit his brow. "How do you plan to get these horses?"

Quilla laughed, he knew damn well how they would be getting the horses. "What do you think? Asking nicely?"

Nikolai and Alohi groaned, but Quilla just smiled. How much these two dreaded what she and Lilith did every day made her laugh.

"We better get going." Lilith had downed the rest of her coffee in one swig. She got up and started searching the cabinets. "Anyone know where the food is?"

With this comment, Quilla realized she hadn't eaten anything yesterday. Her stomach growled with the newfound feeling of hunger. Although, she was just as nauseous as before.

Nikolai and Alohi joined Lilith in searching the cabinets. She watched as they found dried fruit, jerky, and bread. She saw Nikolai stuffing a bottle of what looked like alcohol into a small potato sack.

Quilla strode over to him and their eyes met. She pulled out the bottle of liquor and raised her eyebrows. Nikolai crossed his arms, staring at the dark liquid.

"I thought you didn't like alcohol?" she questioned.

Nikolai growled. "I thought it might be helpful."

Quilla looked at the bottle. Anger swirled in her head. She had spent countless nights with this bitter drink, trying to drown her past in the narcotic. "Trust me, Nikolai." She slammed the bottle against the counter, glass shards flew everywhere and whiskey splashed out. She felt Lilith and Alohi's head turn. "It's not helpful, at *all*."

She handed Nikolai what was left of the broken bottle, and strode out of the room. Her heels clicked against the floor as she headed outside. A fresh coat of snow had fallen on the small town.

The paths were slippery with a light crust of frost. Icicles hung from any place they could. Though the stables were only a few blocks away from the hotel, Quilla's hands were already going numb from the cold.

A small building with a large yard made the stables. Through the window, she could see the sleeping horses, cuddled in hay. She picked up a rock that was nestled in the snow and strode over to the window. Her hand wound up and she slammed the rock into the glass. It shattered on impact, leaving little shards resting on the cold snow.

Quilla hopped through the window and onto the soft hay. The horses were still sleeping soundly. These ones, unlike the ones the Empire harbored, looked well-fed and rested. Their bellies were plump and Quilla didn't think she saw a bone on their backs. Each looked jacked and ready to run at least twenty miles without rest. Their manes were brushed and silky, some were braided while others were let down loose and wavy.

Quilla approached a light brown one. The animal had white spots running down his muzzle. She ran her long fingers through his loose, silky tail. Whomever the owners were, they had taken good care of this one.

Quilla scratched under the horse's chin. He gently waved his flowy tail, letting her know he was enjoying it. She slowly made her way to his side, running her fingers through his light fur. "You will do nicely,"

Her eyes flew to four saddles in the corner. They were large, big enough to hold a person and some supplies. She picked up one and dusted the hay off of its leather surface. The saddle had bags and compartments attached to it; perfect for storing their food.

"Are you the caretaker?" a small voice behind her asked. *Shit!* Quilla had to fight the urge to draw her knives and fling them at whoever had said that. Instead, she slowly turned around, plastering a kind smile on her face.

A little girl stood just outside the door. She was holding a ring with keys, explaining how she got past the locked door. Her blonde hair was woven into two braids, not a strand astray.

"I thought the caretaker came in the afternoon." The little girl sniffled.

Quilla walked up to her and knelt down on her knee. The girl's blue eyes sparkled with curiosity. "Well," she said, still smiling. "The truth is I'm not a caretaker."

The girl took a step back, fear consuming her face; but Quilla just laughed. "Don't be afraid," she lent her hand. "What's your name?"

She looked at Quilla with wide eyes, it seemed every emotion was lingering in her gaze. The curiosity was mixed with fear and caution. "Trilly."

"Well, Trilly." Quilla gave a gentle smile. "Do you believe in royalty?"

Trilly nodded her head excitedly, hope sparking in her once fear-clouded eyes. Quilla felt familiar cruel glory spreading across her face; flames ignited in her lungs, burning her heart until nothing remained but ashes. "Well, would you believe I am a princess?"

The little girl made a face, piercing her lips in doubt. "No," she said flatly. "Prove it."

Quilla reached into her coat and pulled out a knife. It was all black, its sharp tip shining with reflecting light. The girl's face shifted to a fearful expression, but curiosity still brimmed the light in her eyes.

"Princesses are not how they say in the stories." She ran her fingers along the black blade. "They don't have long, pretty dresses, and they aren't beautiful. They don't believe in kindness, and they most certainly don't believe in love." The girl's eyes widened. "In fact, most princesses are monsters. They feed on power and pain. They don't have morals. And for the most part, they don't care if they live or die, only that they have power."

Trillys lip wobbled, she turned to run, but Quilla grabbed one of her neat braids, holding the girl in place. Trilly's eyes were terrified, tears ran down her red cheeks as she took quick, panicked breaths. As soon as her mouth opened to scream, Quilla's knife slid to hover over her throat.

"So here's what's going to happen." She whispered in Trilly's ear. "You are going to go back to your warm house, and you're going to creep back into bed. When your parents wake up, you're going to pretend like this *never happened*." She pressed the knife further into the girl's warm skin. "And if you don't? I'll kill all these little horses, one by one. Then I'll kill your family, and all your little friends." Quilla tilted her head. "But I won't kill you." She gave a hard laugh. "No, someone needs to feel the guilt."

Quilla removed the knife from Trilly's throat, letting the little girl run through the large door and out into the street, her little braids flying behind her. Quilla tucked her black knife back into her coat and dusted off her knees.

She wasn't serious, of course. She didn't have the time nor the will to come and ruin that poor girl's life. All she needed was for her to be scared enough to keep their little secret. If word got out that a vigilante with dark hair and merciless knives was in this town, the Empire's men would be quick to storm this place; searching every nook and cranny until they were in custody.

Quilla grabbed four muscular, groomed horses by the reins and led them out into the cold streets. The steeds followed obediently, as if it was already apparent that she was their new owner.

Chapter Forty One
Alohi

Alohi, Lilith, and Nikolai were standing just outside the hotel. The cold drifted through Alohi's curly hair, making her shiver. They each had bags over their shoulder, filled with food and other supplies they smuggled from the cabinets inside.

Quilla had to be late now. Although she didn't have the slightest clue what time it was, she was sure that the con queen was a little behind schedule. It felt like they had been waiting in the snow for at least thirty minutes, and Alohi's hands were about to go numb.

She wouldn't dare mention her thoughts to Quilla's face. Per reasonable explanation, Alohi found her terrifying. Even though they were around the same age, whenever they were next to each other she felt like Quilla was years older than her. Her short temper and easily deployed skills made her a force Alohi didn't dare aggravate.

However, she couldn't help but admire her confidence; or rather, her ability to do what she wanted and not let anyone else dictate that. Alohi let out an exasperated breath, watching as it turned a misty white in the cold air and drifted away like a feather. What she wouldn't give to have that ability, to not be affected by the opinions of others.

She was a people pleaser, and she hated herself for it. If she could just not care about what anyone thought of her, she would be free. But of course, she couldn't do that. Her reputation depended on how well others liked her, whereas Quilla's depended on how much they didn't.

Around a corner came Quilla riding on a midnight black horse. Her coffee brown hair flew behind her along with her dark coat. Running next to her were three other horses. Their bodies were muscular and their maines combed. Each looked as though they could run for hours at a time without rest.

"Sorry about the wait." She chimed as the horses pulled in front of them. "I ran into some... complications."

Lilith raised an eyebrow. "What kind of complications?"

Quilla hopped from the horse's back, dusting off her thighs. "A child walked in on me while I was readying the horses."

Alohi's jaw dropped and horror sparked in her eyes. She couldn't imagine the fate that had landed on that poor kid. Knowing Quilla, the child would be lucky if it had a swift death. More probable scenario; they had lost their limbs and were currently bleeding out on the cold snow.

"Oh, close your mouth, Alohi." Quilla rolled her eyes. "I didn't kill her, just gave her a good scare."

Alohi still had her doubts. The con queen didn't seem capable of just giving a scare. Nonetheless, arguing would lead to a messy fate of her own.

They started loading the food into the saddles. The sun was high in the sky when they started riding. The back of her horse was cramped, and the animal's lumpy back was digging into her tailbone; even through the saddle.

"Couldn't you have gotten a thicker saddle?" she asked, her tone a little frustrated.

"If you would rather have the comfort of a roomy cell back at Rock Highland we can drop you off." Lilith retorted. Though Alohi couldn't see her face, she could tell she was glaring.

Nikolai turned around abruptly. His horse was positioned at the front of the pack. Behind him was Quilla, whose steed matched the dark style of the criminal prodigy. Lilith's horse trotted behind her partners, and the animal looked eager to break into a run. Alohi brought up the back; however she was still struggling to get comfortable on her horse.

"Oh relax." Quilla retorted in a sharp tone. "She was only kidding."

Nikolai clucked his tongue. "You can never tell with you." He turned around, guiding his horse further into the woods. His hair was messy, and his clothes wrinkled. But at the same time, he was just as stunning as ever.

Typically his hair was combed back, not a strand astray. It outlined his sharp edges and terrifying demeanor. That is, at least, to those who fell for it.

Alohi had learned to see beyond the sharp glares and cold projectile voice. Of course, she had noticed that those particular features softened when she was near. She supposed she might look similar: confident voice, cold and merciless while in argument. But when she saw him, she let her guard down. As if she was finally free from the chains and shackles of her reputation.

Now that she thought about it, Quilla had the same features. What Alohi had seen of her was absolutely terrifying; but maybe there was a sweet spot in the middle, beyond her thorns and thick skin. Maybe there was more of a human being beyond what was projected as criminal royalty.

She snuck a glance at Quilla. She was looking directly into the rising sun, as though actively trying to blind herself. Her brown, wild hair whipped in the wind as her horse sped through the countryside. She and Nikolai felt like siblings. Though they might seem hostile on the outside, Alohi guessed that they had a lot in common. Skilled, cunning, and sarcastic when needed; their personality traits aligned. Then again, they certainly squabbled like siblings.

The ride continued for what felt like days. Alohi's tailbone was sore from the constant bumps of the horse. Her eyes were droopy and every part of her felt exhausted, even though it was the steed who did the work. She had to stop herself from leaping from the saddle in joy when she saw the gray ocean in the distance.

"We're almost there!" she exclaimed. The ride had been largely quiet, everyone seemed to be lost in their own thoughts. Breaking that silence almost seemed wrong.

She turned to see Quilla scanning the area. In front of them was a break in the trees where a village stood. Its yellow lights flickered like birds flapping their tiny wings. Beyond that was the vast ocean, and sitting there was the ship.

Though it had only been a few weeks, it felt so long since she had seen something from home. The ship's soft, polished wood shined in the sunlight and the sails drifted in the gentle wind.

Her horse galloped through the city streets. Eyes turned to look at them as they passed. Why wouldn't they? All four of them were bloodied and scarred. Their clothes were torn and wrinkled; and if she looked how she felt, she probably had bags under her droopy eyes.

As they approached the ship, she saw the silhouettes of Nikolai's crew. Their friendly faces made her smile. They looked deep in conversation, leaning against the rail of the boat.

When the horse reached the dock, Alohi leaped off its back. She landed on her heels, probably bruising them, but she didn't care. She raced to the deck, feet pounding against the ground and probably smiling more than she ever had.

The crew saw her as she ran up the ramp. Rex turned; his uniform was tailored to fit his muscled body, and a pin was fastened perfectly to his chest. She reached him and jumped into his arms, embracing him in a tight hug.

Even though this wasn't her crew, it still felt like they were family. She had insisted on coming on so many long trips with Nikolai that they all knew her well.

She ran to hug every one of them, enjoying the smell of home that they had brought with them. *Home.* That's where she was going. Finally, *home.*

A hand grasped her shoulder and she turned to find Nikolai smiling beside her. "They all volunteered to come." He told her. "They all wanted you to be safe."

Those words made her smile. This was her family, her home, and they cared about her. "Thank you. For all of it."

"Here!" Nia was standing in front of Alohi, holding a steaming cup of tea. "I thought you might want it." Her blonde hair blew chaotically with the strong wind of the ocean.

Alohi took the warm liquid, taking a dainty sip. "I never thought I'd taste your spectacular cooking again!"

Nia's brother, Wesley, appeared next to him. "It's not that hard to make tea. All you have to do is boil water and flavor it."

Alohi laughed as she took another sip of the warm liquid. Nia shot her brother a look of annoyance that only spawned between siblings. "Well, some people, not naming anyone, burn everything they touch. That includes water."

Alohi burst out laughing as Wesley gave her sister a playful nudge. "Technically, it was milk!"

"How did you manage that?" Alohi asked through a burst of cackles.

"Don't worry about it." Wesley shrugged. His playful expression vanished as his eyes flew to her arms. Some of the bandages that Nikolai had wrapped around it had come off. The long scar still hadn't healed yet and was still a raw red. "Oh god, Alohi, what happened?"

Nia grabbed her wrist, gazing at the large gash. Alohi quickly pulled it away, hiding the wound behind her back. "It's fine." Her eyes flew to her floor. "Nikolai's had a lot worse."

Nia put an arm around her shoulders, compassion glimmering in her wide eyes. "That doesn't mean we can't be worried about you." She led her to the cabin. Her warm touch was comforting against Alohi's cold skin. "And it doesn't mean we can't help bandage you up."

Chapter Forty Two
Lilith

As soon as the two criminals got to their small chambers, they collapsed on the bed.

Lilith looked at Quilla. Her black eyes were exhausted and her curly hair fell over her face in strands. She felt the strong urge to take some of the strands and tuck them behind her ear, but she restrained herself. If she did that, she probably would end up with a knife impaled in her chest.

"Hey, Quilla?" she asked in a sheepish voice.

Her partner turned to her, the usual fight in her eyes had vanished and was replaced by an exhausted gaze. "Yes?"

"About that night in the hotel." She swallowed. "I'm sorry, I shouldn't have asked you to share those... *things.*"

Quilla only shrugged, standing from the bed. "It's done, it can't be undone."

Lilith opened her mouth to respond but swiftly closed it. She realized she didn't exactly know what her partner meant. "I mean it. I know it can't be undone, but I'm really sorry."

Quilla turned to look at her, black eyes boring into her green ones. "Don't be, Lilith. It's fine." Her tone was dismissive, fierce. Lilith took a small note of where her bow and arrows were placed on the bed.

Quilla's long fingers picked up her small notebook from her own bed, gently stroking the rose-decorated cover. Lilith sat up, her eyes trained on the booklet of secrets. "What's that?" her tone was laced with a fake curiosity. She knew damn well what it was.

"It's nothing," Quilla whispered.

Well, that's not true. Although she had gone through the book before, she felt a pang of regret. She knew Quilla's past was a tragic one, and she would share it if she was ever ready. So probably never.

Quilla placed the sketchbook in her bag, then moved to sit next to Lilith. She tilted her head back, her brown hair falling behind her like a curtain. "I'm exhausted."

Lilith lay back on the bed. Her head felt heavy, and with the current state of her brain, she didn't think she could even do simple math. For a moment, she just wanted the mattress to swallow her, and bring her into the dark oblivion that was sleep.

Just as she felt unconsciousness drift over her, a giant *boom* rattled the ship. Quilla hopped to her feet and drew her knives. Lilith did the same, loading an arrow into her bow, ready to fire.

Another loud sound rattled the air. Lilith pointed her arrow in different directions, ready to kill any attacker at first sight. Then she heard a bone-rattling crack.

Her eyes flew frantically to the ceiling. Terror took over her body as she saw it was falling towards her. She rolled out of the way as a large beam came plummeting at her. It landed with a crash, just inches from Lilith's skull.

Dust and debris filled the air as more wood came crashing down. "Quilla!" she yelled through the chaos.

"I'm alive!" Lilith felt a wave of relief as her partner's crisp accent cut through the air.

Just then, the floor under her broke. She felt the air rushing past her ears as she fell. Wood and debris plummeted around her, and nails and sharp objects scraped her skin, drawing blood that fell with her. It felt as though the drop was forever. She felt every cut, every hit. She felt all the terror that seized her.

When she hit the water, it felt as if hundreds of icy hands were clawing at her skin, trying to break in and freeze her heart. She opened her mouth to scream, but frigid water flooded her lungs. The salt seeped into her cuts and stung her eyes.

The surface sparkled above her. It looked so peaceful, but so far away, so far from her grasp. Above her, she could see the explosions destroying the ship. Red and orange sprayed the air. It was almost beautiful, but her mind knew it was so destructive.

This is it. A voice told her. *This is where you die.* The revelation sank into her mind like a grain of sand landing in a pool of water. She didn't scream, she didn't try to fight it, instead, she just let the cold water carry her to her death.

<div align="center">~~~</div>

She remembered back in the desert. It wasn't even the second day, and her arms felt as though they couldn't lift a twig. Her legs as though they couldn't carry her another step. But she still had to lift those goddamn pieces of wood. That goddamn hot steel to build those goddamn stupid tracks.

The sun burned on her back, as usual, her hands were swollen and her skin dry. The endless horizon had that weird, watery appearance. At least she thought it did at that moment, or it might have been that she hadn't eaten or slept in days.

But she kept working. For if she stopped, she would get beaten without mercy by the guards in blue uniforms. She would have been crying, but her body didn't have that much water to spare.

Her father was working next to her. His clothes were torn and his eyes were tired. He kept his gaze firmly planted on the tracks, just one nail at a time. Lilith hated to see him like this. He was usually so strong, and so resilient. To see him broken down to bits made her want to sob.

Suddenly she felt a slash across her back. She fell to the ground just as a boot slammed her head into the iron of the track. She heard a horrible crack and felt hot blood pour out of her broken nose. Tears welled in her eyes as the pain sunk in. Her arms were being held against the burning sand as a whip slashed against her back.

"Agh!" she cried as another slash cut her into pieces. "Please!" she begged. "Stop!"

Just as Lilith said those words, the lashing ceased and her hands were released. Her head slowly turned to reveal her father with bloody fists tackling a guard. His teeth were clenched and his eyes fierce with a fury that she had never seen in him. Guards surrounded him, grabbing his wrists and legs. A terrified scream ripped from his lungs.

"Let him go!" Lilith shouted at them. The number of men dragging her father away had risen to at least ten, but none of them listened to her. He struggled against their restraints, screaming and yelling with anger like no other.

Lilith watched in horror as they grabbed a tuft of his hair and bashed his head against a steel track. He screamed, getting louder with each hit while the other men kicked his rib cage and slashed his back.

"*Please*!" she sobbed. "Please, I'm *begging* you. Please stop!" her voice cracked with tears as she pleaded for a mercy that would never come.

She watched as the angry fire that once filled her father's eyes vanished and was replaced by nothing more than a glaze. She watched as his skull slowly caved in and blood sprayed out of it onto the sand. His screams died slowly until even his breathing had ceased.

"No!" she shouted as the guards dropped his body at her feet. They walked away laughing and cheering for the death of her father.

Lilith cradled his battered head in her arms. She didn't care that his blood was getting on her legs. "No." She whispered, putting her forehead against what used to be his. "Please don't go, please don't leave!" tears from her eyes landed on his pale skin. It was still warm with life but his eyes were nothing but empty. "I didn't even get to say goodbye."

~~~

Her current tears faded into the icy water as she drifted further to the bottom. She knew she was running out of air when her stomach tightened and her nose breathed in more of the salty water. Soon she would drown, soon she would see her father. Soon this nightmare of a life would be over.

But she didn't want it to be. It might have been more than a nightmare so far but she still had so much more to do. She wanted to travel, she wanted to see the Empire fall, and she wanted to help with its destruction. She wanted to live her life.

Black oblivion started to creep along the sides of her vision. She looked at the now even more blurry surface, saying goodbye to the life she had once known.

Suddenly a hand reached in front of her, grabbing her shirt and pulling her to the surface. She felt the black slowly closing in on her eyes, but the surface was getting closer rapidly. *Five feet*, she told herself, *four feet*. She clenched her fists, trying desperately to stay conscious, *three feet*. Her breath felt as though it would burst from her body. *Two feet*. Every second felt like an eternity. *One foot.*

Lilith burst through the surface as if she was breaking ice. At first she tried to breathe, but all that happened was thick, uncontrollable coughing. Water and something that looked like blood came out of her mouth like a flood. When she finally got it out of her system she gasped, breathing sweet, cold oxygen.

Her vision had cleared and reality came into view. Nikolai's ship was torn into a thousand pieces that littered the water like seagulls swarming a school of fish. Fire danced around the larger ones while others were soaking wet.

"I have *got* to teach you how to swim." Lilith now realized that the spiteful tone had come from Quilla, the one and only reason she was staying afloat right now. She had her arm around Lilith's waist and was kicking the water rapidly.
~~~

"No thanks." She told her, grabbing onto a small piece of wood and using it as a flotation device. "I wouldn't last five minutes before you got frustrated and tried to drown me yourself."

Quilla rolled her eyes. Her hair was soaking wet and she had bruises all over her body. Her leg wound from earlier was clearly causing her a lot of pain, although she would never admit it. But through all of that, she had a look of ferocity on her face. No, *fear*.

"What?" Lilith asked, amazed that she wasn't breaking down in a panic herself.

"Nothing." Quilla turned away. "Let's head to shore, I can't swim for much longer."

Lilith kicked through the ice-cold water. Her body had almost become completely numb, so much so that she found herself wondering if her toes were even still there. The waves lapped against her head, pushing water into her mouth. She spit it out immediately, deciding that she despised the ocean.

The waves got larger as they got closer to the shore. Lilith was panting hard, whether from the cold or because she was desperately out of shape, she didn't know. It was just a couple of feet now, she felt the sand brush against her boots.

The waves crashed into her, sending her toppling to the ground. The sand was much harder than she expected, bruising her ribs. The white water flew around her, pushing her down and not letting her break the surface. She felt panic rise around her as she ran short of breath.

The wave flattened and the water released her. Lilith was lying on the sand, panting. Her head ached and the cuts on her arm stung. She took rapid, large breaths, trying to make up for the lost oxygen.

She turned her head to see Quilla beside her. Her hair was wet but still had those messy curls. Her long coat still hung across her shoulders and her blouse was stained with what looked like blood.

Quilla's eyes were tired and glazed, not focused on anything. She had sand dusted on her cheeks. They made eye contact, staring at each other with a mix of exhaustion and disbelief that either of them was still alive. It was almost as though they were afraid to break eye contact, and if they did, one of them would be launched back into the frigid ocean.

Footsteps surrounded them, kicking up sand. Shouts and screams echoed around the beach. Lilith looked up to see Empire soldiers standing over them, swords pointed directly at their heads.

Neither of them tried to struggle, neither of them tried to run. Though it didn't happen often, they knew when they had lost. And now, they had just lost.

Chapter Forty Three
Nikolai

It didn't matter how hopeless the fight was. Nikolai Lone *never* surrendered.

That was why he was currently in the freezing water, swords drawn and eyes alert. Alohi was swimming beside him, trying to find a clear path back to shore. His crew was scattered in the water, weapons drawn.

His ship was destroyed, fire skipped along the larger pieces of wood while his crew held onto the small ones. The water was deep and the bottom couldn't be seen. He spit as cold water splashed his mouth, the salt vile on his tongue.

"Alohi?" he yelled frantically.

"There's no clear path. The soldiers have the entire beach!" her voice was panicked, but he barely heard her over the roar of the waves.

She was right. The beach was covered in Empire soldiers. Some of them were lined on the beach with bows and arrows. Nikolai's eyes widened as they loaded and fired directly at them.

Arrows flew over his head, splashing in the water. He and his crew watched as more deadly weapons came soaring over them.

Suddenly a horrible scream ripped through the air behind them. Nikolai turned to see an arrow right in Nia's neck. Blood dripped from the wound as she slowly sank into the sea. The water around her was turning an awful, murky red as her blood spread through the salty sea.

"Nia!" Wesley swam over to her, panic painting his face. "No! No! *No!*" he cradled her lifeless body in his arms, tears running down his cheeks. "You aren't done, you can't die like this!" he shook her limp shoulders. "*Nia!*"

Nikolai's head whipped around as he saw an arrow flying directly at them. "Wesley!" his voice was shrill as he frantically splashed towards him. The boy turned his head too late, or maybe he wasn't even trying to avoid the weapon flying towards his head.

The arrow landed on his forehead. Blood sprayed from the wound as soon as its blade entered his flesh. Nikolai watched as the gleam in Wesley's brown eyes vanished, replaced only by a daze.

"No!" Alohi swam towards them as both of the siblings sank into the frigid ocean. "*No!*" the water splashed as she kicked towards the corpses, but it was no good. They sunk deeper into the murky water, still grasping each other tightly.

"Nikolai! Alohi!" their heads whipped around to see Rex. His uniform was soaked and his eyes tired, but the fight in his gaze still gleamed with life. "Get underwater."

They dove under the turbulent waves, watching arrows fly above the water's rough surface. Nikolai's eyes stung as the salty water seeped into them. He felt his breath running short, his lungs tightened as they craved the cold sensation of air.

His stomach strained, eyes still tightly trained on Rex and Alohi. *Just keep eye contact.* He told himself. *Don't breach the surface!*

But it was too much. Nikolai took a deep breath, still completely underwater. Cold water rushed into his nose. Without telling them to, his hands propelled him towards the surface.

As soon as he broke the water, air filled his lungs. It was cold, relieving, and full. Nikolai gasped for a while, watching arrows fly over his head. The calmness he felt was out of place. He was watching bombs like fireworks.

He turned around, still feeling dangerously tranquil. His eyes widened and his heart quickened as he saw an arrow fly right towards his head. Time seemed to slow as the dangerous weapon got closer. He couldn't move, fear had paralyzed him as death looked him right in the eye.

Just as the arrow was about to impale him, something jumped from the water. Nikolai watched helplessly as Rex exploded from the sea. Little gray droplets surrounded the commander as he fully propelled himself out of the ocean, right in front of Nikolai.

The arrow hit him square in the chest. As soon as the weapon made contact, he was propelled backward, falling into the glacial water. Blood flooded from the wound and mixed with the murky liquid as the closest thing Nikolai had to a loving father sank into the water.

"*No!*" Nikolai cried as he rushed over to Rex. The fight in his eyes was fading quickly. "God no, Rex, you can't leave!" he grasped his hand, pulling him to the surface.

Nikolai cradled his limp head in his arms. Tears rolled down his cheek as he shook Rex's shoulders. "*Please!*" he cried. "Don't go!"

Alohi appeared next to him, sorrow brimming her bright blue eyes. "Nikolai." Rex choked, his voice was weak. "Let go."

"No!" he wailed. "I'm not losing you. We're going to make it out of here!"

Rex reached up and stroked Nikolai's cheek. His fingertips were cold and clammy. "*You're* going to make it out of here." He raised a shaky hand to his forehead, saluting him one last time. "Go change the world, captain. I'm so, *so* proud of you."

With the last of his strength, Rex rolled out of Nikolai's arms, sinking into the water, and disappearing forever.

"No!" Nikolai hollered, tears flooded from his eyes and his legs fell limp. There was barely anything keeping him afloat now, and some part of him just wanted to sink into the water like his friend.

"Nikolai!" warned Alohi. He turned around to see a massive ship just feet from their heads. It was so big and so close that he could only see the bow. It was painted silver that looked as if it couldn't be chipped. Men in blue uniforms loomed over the taffrail, holding a giant net that looked like its main purpose was catching fish. Unfortunately, he and Alohi were now the fish.

He pushed the water away, desperately trying to propel himself through the water. But the ship was moving ten times faster than he ever could. The net swallowed him like a giant maw. All he could do was watch as he was raised and caught.

He and Alohi were hauled up to the ship. There, he got a better view of the massive vessel. It had white sails that looked as though they could cover houses. On it were hundreds of men. They bustled about, some pointed swords and arrows at them, while others rushed to do additional things to accommodate their newfound prisoners.

The net was placed on the ground and Nikolai watched as their rope cage fell, only to be replaced as several guards surrounded them and bound their wrists.

He felt his swords get removed from their hilts on his back, and several hands patted him down. Goosebumps formed on his arms, whether they were from the cold of the water or even colder fear, he did not know.

He felt hands grip his arms and haul him to his feet. A sword was pointed at his back as he was led to a small hatch on the floor. He stood tall, trying to hide how uncomfortable and fearful he was at that moment.

A soldier in blue opened the hatch. The room inside looked small and dark. He was shoved into the hole without warning, landing on his back with a hard thump.

Alohi came tumbling town after him, landing just inches from where he lay on the hard ground. He gazed up as the hatch closed, still refusing to believe he had lost. There had to be a way up, there had to be a way out of this mess.

The room that they were in was dark. A few bared, tinted windows provided the little light it had. It was a hardwood that looked as though it would splinter you if you rubbed it the wrong way.

"Well, would you look at who it is!" Nikolai's head fell in exasperation as the crisp accent cut through the air.

He groaned. "Why are you still here?"

Quilla held up her hands, they were bound together with a thick rope. "Same reason you are, Princely."

Nikolai sat up and rolled his eyes. "Oh, really? I could have sworn I heard you say that 'no prison could hold us' back at Shina." He told her, mimicking Quilla's accent poorly.

The crime queen growled at him, showing her fanged teeth. He felt grim satisfaction for winning this petty argument.

"Well, if you too want to stop bickering, we should talk about how we're going to get out of here." Lilith chimed. She was sitting in the corner next to her glaring partner. They were both soaked head to toe and had numerous cuts scattered around their bodies. Nikolai thought that Lilith's eyes were more wide, their usual bright green glow had dulled. She looked almost... scared.

"I agree." Alohi sat up next to Nikolai. "We need to figure out a way to get out of here, or at least survive what those Empire scum have planned for us." She was rubbing two stones together anxiously, Nikolai supposed it was a method of keeping herself calm.

Nikolai gazed at the hatch. "I don't think there's any way out of this."

"Well, Nikolai," Quilla rasped. "Since you're clearly the expert, I think we should take your word for it." She smiled manically, clearly eager to regain her stance as the winner of their previous argument.

"I never said I was good at escapes." Nikolai smiled, this winning streak with Quilla wasn't going to last long, and he wanted to enjoy it. "I just implied you were *bad* at them."

"I wouldn't call it *bad*; after all, I did rescue your girlfriend from Rock Highland." She retorted, raising an eyebrow.

"*We*, Quilla," Lilith told her.

The con queen shrugged. "Sure. Anyway, I wouldn't count yourself out of luck yet. Empire ships aren't the most advanced part of the dynasty, and are easier to overthrow."

Alohi raised an eyebrow. "What do you mean?"

"I mean the Empire uses trains as their finest mode of transportation. So naturally, their sea travel is less competent." Quilla told them, her voice proud and knowledgeable. "If we're able to get out of here, we can kill the captain and sail right into the waiting hands of the League of Red Doves. As incompetent as your little rebellion is, I feel as though they could take on a few inexperienced sailors."

Nikolai gave a small chuckle. There were so many things wrong with this plan he didn't know where to begin. "Well, that's great, Quilla. But none of that will be possible until we get out of here." He held up his bound hands. "And I'm assuming none of you have a weapon on you."

"I don't need one." Everyone turned to look at Alohi. She held up two free hands, the stones she was rubbing together earlier held between her fingers.

"How did you-" asked Lilith, looking completely bewildered.

"It's flint," Alohi said proudly. "Rub it together enough and it'll spark. Nestle that spark in something flammable, and it'll start a flame. That flame destroys whatever flammable item that gave birth to it," she held up the remnants of burnt rope. "In our case, cotton."

Nikolai felt his wrists getting hot already. "I think I'll keep my skin, thanks."

"She's going to untie you, not burn you, imbecile." He could almost feel Quilla's eyes roll from her sarcastic tone.

Alohi approached him. Her long fingers touched his wrists as she untied him. Nikolai felt his stomach turn and he began to feel self-conscious about how sweaty he must be.

Once they were all untied, they stood, rubbing their sore wrists. His were red and the rope had left an indent on his skin. "Well," he stretched, finally feeling the weight of the day coming down on him. "What do we do now?"

Alohi looked at the way they came through. There was a ladder, but the hatch had been locked. "I'm assuming that way is out of the question."

Quilla grasped the barred windows with both hands. "Let me give you a lesson on breaking and entering." She pulled against the bars, breaking them off with a snap. "The way you came in..." She kicked the yellow stained glass with her high-heeled boot. It shattered into a million pieces. "Is never the way you get out."

Chapter Forty Four
Quilla

Quilla was hanging outside the window she had just broken. Her sweaty hands loosely gripped the small ledge that was keeping her alive. Below her, the sea tumbled and tossed in on itself. Waves crashed against the side of the boat, causing cold drops of water to fly up and hit her.

Lilith looked out of the broken window. Her messy, wet braid was flying in the wind, and her green eyes sparkled as they did with the excitement of an escape. "How's it coming?"

"Oh great!" Quilla retorted, her tone nowhere near as positive as her partners had been. "I'm climbing a slippery boat with little to no handholds, surrounded by Empire soldiers; and if I fall I'll plummet back into the frigid ocean and be left to die!"

Nikolai poked his head out of the window, shoving Lilith inside. "So not great, I'm assuming."

"Obviously!" Quilla turned back to the ship. She still had a while to go, and the constant splashes from the sea weren't helping. Her hand reached for the next little dent between the boards. It might have been the smallest, most inconvenient hold there was, but it still held her weight and allowed her to move up a couple of inches.

After a couple more tedious minutes, Quilla reached the taffrail. Her hands grasped the fence and she hauled herself over it. The boat was filled with Empire soldiers. Men in blue hauled crates and tended to the sails while others played with their swords and arrows, striking poor, fake blows at one another.

She ducked behind some boxes, not daring to risk being seen. The hatch they came through was just a couple of feet away. Soldiers guarded it with swords and bows.

Quilla furrowed her brow, there was no way that she was going to get around them without killing. But doing that would alert the entire boat of her presence.

She peeked into one of the crates and smiled with cruel joy. In it was gunpowder. She grabbed a handful of it, smelling the toxic scent. All she needed now was something to light it with.

A spark caught Quilla's eye. She turned to look at soldiers near a cannon. A string was lit with fire, burning towards the giant machine. Her footsteps silently padded towards them, gunpowder in hand. She crept behind crates until she was only a couple feet from the cannon.

The men cheered as the large ball flew into the air with a boom. Smoke drifted off into the distance as the men rethreaded a string within the cannon. The fire sparked on a match, and the string was lit.

You have one shot. A voice told her. *Don't blow it.* Quilla wound back her hand with the explosives. The string was getting smaller as the spark burned away. She furrowed her brow, centering her concentration. It was like throwing a knife. Gently, but with purpose. Follow through, but be relaxed. And don't think, never think about it.

The first time Quilla heard this advice she nearly threw her knives on the ground and stormed out of the room; for at that moment, none of that made sense. To her, gently and purpose seemed like opposites. Over time, she had learned that they went hand in hand with each other, just as organization and chaos did.

The fire had almost reached the cannon. Quilla threw the powder without thinking. It scattered in the air like dust, leaving nothing but a grayish tint to the air. No one would have noticed it unless you knew it was there.

Quilla held her breath, anticipation filling her. It was as though time slowed, seconds became minutes, and words became as long as phrases. Then... chaos.

The air exploded. The first one was small, like a firework, but then the rest of the airborne gunpowder went off, and fire erupted from nothing.

Quilla was propelled back, smashing her head against the crates as more explosions went off. Confusion took control of the ship, soldiers from every post ran to investigate the explosions, only to be pushed back by more clouds of fire.

Her ears were ringing and her eyesight was blurry. Quilla looked over to the hatch. It was left unguarded, but locks still forced it shut. She approached the small door, looking around to see that no one was looking at her.

Quilla pressed her fingers against the cold metal of the lock. Lilith was right, lock picking was not her most dominant skill; but if she really tried, and applied just enough pressure, she could get one open when she wanted to. The lock was stubborn, not wanting to open at her unauthorized hand. She pressed harder, on the verge of just kicking the door open in frustration. Finally, the lock clicked and opened.

She flung open the hatch and leaned over the edge, gazing into the dark room. "Wake up!" she called in a sing-song voice. "Time to go."

Her crew appeared below. Their eyes were wide and fists clenched. "What was that noise?" asked Alohi, referring to the chaos that had sprouted from her hand.

Quilla smiled. "A handful of gunpowder and a couple of Empire idiots." She watched as their eyes widened with shock. She savored the powerful feeling in her body, not wanting to let it go. "Now come on, it won't distract them for long."

They hurried up the ladder, one by one. The gunpowder was still creating a great distraction for them. Soldiers screamed at one another, urging for the explosions to stop. Quilla looked at them with a smile. Sure, organization was okay and it worked well. But she preferred if things were messy and tangled. She enjoyed the scramble. She craved chaos.

As soon as they were all there, they ran to the cabin. There was no need for sneaking about, the explosions made a few escaped prisoners the least of their problems; and through the commotion, she doubted anyone saw them.

The cabin was located towards the stern. It was larger than Nikolai's had been. Stairs lead to the top of it which had another, smaller, cabin located on top.

Quilla threw open the door and they strode in. Inside was a large room. It was mostly carpeted, and a large table was positioned in the center that was made nicely. A ladder that led up to the second cabin was positioned in the corner. Around it were potted plants that looked as though they were from all four regions.

On the table were their weapons. It looked like someone had stacked them there without a second thought. Quilla rushed over to her stack of various knives, running her fingers along the sharp blade. She tucked them one by one into her coat, as though reuniting with a close friend. She pulled on her gloves, enjoying the powerful sensation the blades inside brung.

Lilith and Nikolai picked up their weapons gently. It was as if a part of themselves had been taken away, and they were finally reuniting.

"Guys," Alohi chimed from a corner. "We need to go."

All three of them glared at her. "I guess you wouldn't understand," Lilith answered. "'I don't need a weapon.'" She mocked Alohi's previous phrase in a squeaky tone.

Alohi shrugged as they walked towards another door. "I'm just saying that relying on a certain tool is a liability. Being able to exist without one would be helpful."

Quilla narrowed her eyes into a sharp glare. "As far as I've noticed, you're the only liability I see."

Alohi glared back. "Thanks, Quilla."

They started walking towards the ladder. Quilla headed up first, knives sprouted along her knuckles as she clicked her gloves. She didn't want to take any chances on what she would find once she reached the top.

A silver soldier sat at a wooden table. His feet were crossed as he watched the chaos happening below through a large window. The room felt cozy and the warm smell of baked goods snuck into Quilla's nose.

Her breath almost stopped as she saw what was lying on the table. Just next to him was a black book. It had golden, familiar edges, and her entire past inside.

The cozy atmosphere the room had brung was gone. It suddenly felt like she had been thrown into icy water, being pulled out and dunked again like a cruel torture method. Her vision felt blurry, and her legs shook with anxiety. There was only one thought that crossed her mind as the silver picked up her book. He had to die.

Chapter Forty Five
Lilith

Quilla's blades gleamed as she leaped from the ladder. Her hair flew around her as she fired her knives. They knocked the book out of the silver's hands and it landed on the floor with a bang. The criminal prodigy had an angry look in her gaze; not ambitious, just rich with fury. "That's mine."

The silver only stood, raising his eyebrows at Quilla. The sharpness of his curves were well-fitted and his uniform looked tailored and smoothed. A grim smile spread across his face. "Is that so?"

Quilla answered by firing a knife at his head. It brushed his combed hair as he ducked. The silver drew a long sword, pointing it at Quilla. They charged at each other, both eyes angry and eager to fight.

Lilith reached back to draw her bow, but someone grabbed her wrist. Alohi was positioned right next to her on the ladder. "I don't think she wants you to help." She told her, gesturing to Quilla. "This looks pretty personal."

She was right. Her partner had that hunger in her eye. It appeared every time she wanted to kill someone, every time it was personal. But that didn't mean it wasn't hard for Lilith to watch.

She felt herself flinch as Quilla was pushed against the wall. The silver held her by the throat and pointed his blade at her chest. Her partner's glare was a bright flame, it felt as though someone would die just from looking into it. But the soldier still stood, looking dangerous and powerful.

"I already read your little book." Lilith didn't think it was possible for her partner's face to get more vengeful, and yet it did. "I never thought I would meet you. But here I am," he said in a cocky tone that made her want to vomit. "I am holding the life of R-"

Quilla brought up her knee into the soldier's stomach. He doubled back in pain as she advanced on him. Her knives were drawn and her eyes were angrier than Lilith had ever seen.

She watched as her partner threw a knife into the silver's wrist. He howled with pain as blood splattered everywhere. Lilith thought she smelled the wretched stuff as Quilla impaled the other limb with a second blade.

The red liquid had soaked the con queen's hands. She stood, running her red fingers through her hair and watching as the man squealed in a pool of his own blood. Her jaw clicked and she tilted her head, as if looking at a piece of artwork. Her bloodied hands pulled a serrated knife from her coat and tossed it in the air like a toy. "Now your life is in my hands." She told the silver as she knelt down and slid the knife across his throat. The life faded from his once powerful, proud eyes, and was replaced by a daze. "And I just shattered it."

Quilla stood. They all watched in awe as she wiped a drop of blood sliding down her chin. The power in her eyes had dulled, only leaving an unreadable gaze. She strode over to where her book had clattered to the floor, picking it up with gentle hands.

Lilith left her perch on the ladder and walked over to her. The once clean carpet was stained with red and the body of the man lay there motionless. She quickly stepped around it, careful to avoid touching any part of the corpse.

Her partner was looking down at the small book. Her long fingers stroked the black cover. The book itself looked water-stained, she hoped for Quilla's sake that the contents inside were still legible.

Lilith laid a hand on her partner's shoulder. Quilla took a sharp breath and spun around, dropping into a battle stance. She tucked the book into her jacket, but Lilith could see her hand hovering close to it.

"Hey," she put her hands in the air, plastering a kind smile on her face. "It's going to be safer in my quiver."

Quilla looked at her skeptically, her eyes glimmering with something that Lilith had never seen on Quilla's face. She reached into her coat and handed her the book, watching every movement with careful eyes.

Lilith tucked it in her quiver, smiling innocently. Quilla's sharp glare returned, but this time laced with skepticism. "I want that back."

"Wasn't planning on keeping it." Lilith flipped her loose braid off her shoulder, turning to Nikolai and Alohi.

They were standing over the silver's body with terrified eyes. Or was it disgust? Lilith couldn't tell. All she knew was that Alohi looked ready to add a vomit stain to the already bloody carpet, and Nikolai's eyes were filled with a mix of pity and fear.

"You owe us an explanation." Nikolai had an expectant glare plastered on his face.

Quilla looked at him with black eyes. "I don't owe you anything."

"Yes, you do." Alohi argued. The usual complacent expression on her face was replaced by a furious one. "You strayed from the plan to kill a man in pure cruelty."

Fire ignited in Quilla's gaze. She showed her fang-like teeth and clenched her jaw. "You want to see my cruelty, Windlem? Because that wasn't even close!"

Lilith could feel the tension in the room rise. Nikolai strode up to her, about to grab Quilla's collar and probably engage in the long-awaited fight. Just as he got close, the ship rattled with a massive *boom*.

They all fell to the ground as the ship shook. *Not again*, Lilith felt slightly nauseous, remembering the last time a ship made that kind of sound. She wasn't in the mood to take another swim.

"What was that?" Alohi asked, getting off the floor.

Nikolai clenched his fists, climbing to his feet. "Pirates."

They looked into the distance, a ship was coming towards them. It looked huge, but its sails were torn and the wood looked unpolished and unkempt.

"We should stay here." Quilla inquired. "This isn't our fight yet, and it's probably best we don't change that."

Lilith looked at her, raising an eyebrow. "I think whatever the outcome of this battle is, we'll have to fight the winner."

Nikolai ran a hand through his hair. "What if we got on the pirate ship? I would much rather fight a couple of pirates than a hundred Empire soldiers. Wouldn't you?"

Quilla's expression shifted to a studious one. "Really depends on the pirates."

They all looked at her in shock. "That was supposed to be rhetorical." Nikolai informed her.

The criminal prodigy shrugged. "Like I said earlier, the Empire's sea travel operation is one of its weak links. Pirates have been doing it for centuries. You really think that they won't be able to kill a bunch of vigilantes?"

Lilith smiled viciously. "If the vigilantes are us, then I think they'll have a hell of a time trying."

The ship was approaching fast. Men in ragged clothes were perched on the bow, waving swords with excited faces. Another cannon fired and shook the ship with an ear-shattering boom.

Their hands flew out, trying to steady their balance. "What if we were to hijack one of the ships while they're fighting?" asked Alohi, cautiously trying to regain her balance. "We could just run away with one of them."

Quilla tilted her head. "That's... actually a good idea." She smiled at Alohi, placing a hand on her shoulder. "Maybe you aren't the weak link. Maybe it's *someone else*." She made an accusatory look in Nikolai's direction.

Lilith thought she saw pride glimmer in Alohi's gaze. As though she had just gotten a compliment from a celebrity she admired. She couldn't imagine why the political prodigy would seek validation from a criminal who dwelled in the lowest ranks of Hanslack. To Lilith, it seemed to go against all her supposed morals.

The pirate ship had gotten no less than a foot away from their own. The chaotic, unruly men swung onto the dock, their swords out and swinging. The neat, Empire soldiers met them in rows, their swords and bows drawn and firing.

Quilla turned on her heel, rushing towards the ladder. The rest of the crew followed, struggling to keep up with the con queen as she slid down the ladder. Her heels clicked on the polished wood and her hair flew behind as though the wind ran its hands through it.

They pushed the door open to find a chaotic battle. Swords clashed and arrows flew in every direction. Blood splashed into the sea as more and more soldiers rushed to aid their side.

Quilla walked through the battle like it was only a crowded market. She simply swerved around arrows and ducked as swords stabbed in her direction. The rest of them, on the other hand, had a lot more common sense. Lilith had ducked behind a crate while Nikolai and Alohi were creeping closer to the taffrail.

Lilith rolled her eyes, barely believing how reckless her partner was. She sighed, then ran from her shelter to grab her. Arrows fired in every direction. She felt the air change, as though it was parting for something dangerous. She ducked, letting the arrow fly over her. Quilla was still heading towards the pirate ship with alarming speed. Lilith ran to her, grabbing her wrist and pulling her behind a crate.

"Are you serious?" she asked, her eyes panicked and infuriated. "You could have been killed!"

"No." Quilla's eyes matched her anger. "Neither side is firing at me, and I know how to avoid crossfire."

Lilith had to fight the urge to slap her. "The way you avoid crossfire, Quilla, is simply by not *walking directly into it*!"

Her partner sighed, rolling her eyes. "Let me show you." Quilla grabbed her wrist, pulling her from behind the crate and into the battlefield.

Oh, she is so dead! Thought Lilith as they weaved through arrows and slashing swords. That was, at least, if they were to get out of this situation alive. Her head swam with millions of thoughts and worries. All her legs wanted to do was turn and run in the opposite direction.

Quilla, on the other hand, looked calm and ready. Her eyes were focused on the pirate ship, but she moved in all sorts of directions, dodging the arrows that came flying at them.

They reached the taffrail and Quilla dragged her over. They leaped from the Empire ship to the pirate one. As soon as her boot landed on the splintered wood, the air changed. The fresh, clean wind was replaced by an oily, thick taste. Ripped sails loomed over them like ghosts, just waiting to attack.

Quilla turned to her. The wild, chaotic gaze had returned to her eyes as strands of hair flew around her face. "See?" she dusted off her shoulder. "Not a scratch."

Lilith glared at her, hating that she was right. "Nikolai and Alohi aren't across yet."

"That's their problem." Quilla turned, heading towards what seemed like the cabin. "They'll get across eventually."

Lilith growled, her partner always had an interesting way of doing things, and unfortunately, it was always effective. She followed Quilla to the cabin, taking note of the creaking boards beneath her feet.

The door was a rusty metal, and from the looks of it, it might have weighed a few tons. To her surprise, when Quilla turned the handle it slid right open, revealing a dark, flame-lit room.

Her partner let out an exasperated breath. At a large desk, sitting in a throne-like chair, was a pirate. Their long hair was a tangled, braidlike mess. Tall, heeled boots were perched on the table and a long, ripped coat hung off their body like the ripped sails of their ship. A happy, but fearful aura filled the room as the pirate smiled, showing a set of bone-white teeth, with a singular gold one glimmering.

"Quilla!" they sang. "What a wonderful surprise!"

Chapter Forty Six
Nikolai

Nikolai and Alohi gaped as they watched Quilla pull Lilith through the battlefield and onto the pirate ship. Arrows narrowly missed them and swords brushed their hair.

The two looked at each other as the con lords escaped, disbelief and confusion lacing their faces.

"We aren't doing that, right?" asked Alohi in a hesitant tone.

"Oh, god no," Nikolai responded as an arrow flew directly over their heads. "I'm reckless, but those two take it to a whole new level."

"Yeah." Alohi's gaze shifted to the pirate ship. "I hope I never have to go on a mission where Quilla's in charge."

Nikolai laughed, wishing the same thing. But he knew that any mission that Quilla was on, she led. "I don't think you'll have much of a choice in that matter."

"Right," Alohi said in an exasperated tone. "We should try and get past the battle. They'll be waiting."

The two of them crept along the taffrail, Nikolai's swords were drawn and Alohi walked closely to him. Arrows flew around them in every direction. Blood sprayed from the open wounds of Empire soldiers, but not a single red drop from the pirates. Despite their messy, unorganized attacking style, she couldn't see a single pirate corpse on the ground.

Nikolai dove to the side as a spare arrow flew at his chest. His breath rose and fell as quickly as the crashing waves. Alohi knelt beside him, ducking for cover. They slowly stood, watching the sky for arrows.

"We need to just make a break for it," Alohi yelled over the raging battle.

Nikolai sighed. He knew she was right, but the thought of that still made him want to vomit. He grabbed her hand, taking a large breath. With that, they sprinted into the battle.

Arrows flew in every direction and swords clashed. Thick blood sprayed Nikolai's cheek and he fought the urge to gag. The adrenaline of the battle seemed to be contagious, and he was catching the cold.

He could feel his mind spinning with thoughts and fears. Everything seemed to fade away. He kept his eyes trained on the pirate ship, legs still pounding on the floor.

He and Alohi reached the taffrail and lunged over it. They only had a split second to look at the sea below, deep and out of control, and then they landed on the splintered wood.

The pirate ship was calmer than he expected. It almost had an eerie feel; as though something dangerous was lurking in the ghost-like sails, and would pounce at any moment.

The two walked cautiously to the cabin, the floorboards creaked under their feet. The door to the cabin was open, and the room was dimly lit. Quilla and Lilith stood frozen near the entrance. Sitting at a desk, with their feet on the table, was a pirate.

"Why haven't you killed him yet?" that was the first thing that came out of Nikolai's mouth as he approached the two girls. He regretted it as soon as the pirate smiled.

"I like this one!" they said with a toothy grin. "Quilla, why don't you introduce me to your friends!"

All eyes turned to look at the con queen. Her cheeks were flushed red and she palmed her face.

"You know them?" Alohi asked, stunned.

The pirate gasped, clutching their chest dramatically. "You mean she never told you about me?" they jumped from their chair and put a hand around Quilla, who looked ready to murder everyone in the room. "I'm basically her older sibling."

Nikolai must've broken his ribs trying not to laugh. He couldn't begin to imagine what blackmail he was going to use this moment for.

"Florian," Quilla told the pirate, clearly trying not to push them off of her. "Would you be so kind as to move your arm?"

Florian obliged, lifting their arm and running a hand through their thick, braided hair. Quilla dusted off her shoulder and straightened her posture. "Nikolai, Alohi, Lilith, this is Florian." She introduced. "Florian, this is my crew."

The pirate smiled, extending a ringed hand to the three of them. No one took it and they shrugged. "So," Florian sat on their desk and crossed their legs. "Why were you on an Empire ship anyway?"

The four of them looked at each other, neither of them wanting to answer. "They... blew up ours and took us captive," Nikolai answered nervously.

This seemed to leave the pirate shocked; their sea-green eyes widened. "You let them do that?" they exclaimed. "Honestly, Quilla, given the amount of wanted posters with your name on them, I would have thought you would know better."

Quilla glared at Florian. "Technically, it was Nikolai's ship, and he was in charge."

Guilt and grief took over him like a wave. She was right. It was his fault that his crew had died. It was his fault that they were in this mess. Hell, it was his fault that Alohi was captured in the first place. Now that he thought about it, he was lucky that she was still talking to him. He bit down on his lip, hard. The taste of blood lingered in his mouth and pain burned from the bite.

Florian looked at him with curious eyes. The pirate leaned down, studying a broach fastened to his shirt. They smelled of seawater, and their close proximity did not help his anxiety. "Is this the Lone family crest?"

Alohi jutted out her jaw. "You couldn't find another jewel more hideous."

Florian's eyes widened with newfound excitement. "Oh ho ho! Did you steal this, boy? Perhaps I underestimated you."

Nikolai cleared his throat, straightening his pin. "Actually, sir, I'm Nikolai Lone."

Florian threw back their head and cackled. "Y-you-" they said through mouthfuls of laughter. The pirate had to stabilize themselves to regain control. "You're a prince!" Nikolai felt his cheeks flush as the pirate went into another fit of laughter. "I'm gonna call you Princely!"

"Taken," Quilla said plainly, crossing her arms in the corner.

Florian shrugged. "What are you doing with the Red Doves lot, Quilla? I thought your sole purpose was just to create chaos."

Quilla yawned, her expression was nothing less than extremely annoyed. "Well, I can do that a lot better with the might of an army, can't I?"

Florian punched Quilla's shoulder, maybe a little harder than they meant to. "Has she always been this moody?"

Lilith laughed. "As long as I can remember."

Quilla gave her a death glare while the pirate crossed their arms. "And who might you be?"

"Lilith." She said in a bright tone. "I'm Quilla's partner."

Florian's face lit up; they turned to the con queen, excitement brimming their eyes. "You got a girlfriend?"

Both the girls scrambled away from each other. "Not like that, you imbecile!" Quilla breathed heavily, eyeing Lilith. "In crime!"

Florian slapped their forehead. "Ohh!" they eyed the two girls, still on opposite sides of the room. "You keep telling yourself that, Kiwi."

This time Nikolai couldn't keep his laughter contained. He and Alohi burst out in harmonious cackles, watching as Quilla's dignity died a slow, humiliating death.

"Shouldn't you be helping your crew with the Empire ship?" asked Quilla, trying to change the subject.

Florian peaked out the door, gazing at the battle ahead. It looked as though the only bodies were Empire soldiers. The pirates had moved on to pillaging the ship and drinking large amounts of alcohol. "I think they have it under control." Florian shrugged. "Well, since your ship obviously isn't usable," Nikolai felt his heart sink. "I suppose you could use that one once we're done with it." They gestured to the pillaged Empire ship. "For a price, of course."

Quilla smiled. "Good to know you haven't gone soft, Florian."

The pirate flashed a toothy grin. "Right back at you, Kiwi."

"Where do you think you're getting this money?" Alohi chimed with her arms crossed. "The League will not be happy with all these extra expenses."

Florian rolled their eyes. "Trust me, my dear, it's no secret your little rebellion can't afford a pot to piss in." Well, they certainly were Quilla's sibling. "I believe you can pay the expenses out of pocket?" they gestured to Quilla.

The con queen growled, pulling a small sack of coins from her black coat. "One way or another, this is coming from the Lone family savings."

Nikolai shrugged. "Just make it discrete. As long as I'm not blamed, I don't see the issue."

Florian laughed, planting a jeweled hand on Nikolai's shoulder. "I still like this one!" they gestured to the open door. Pirates loomed outside, slowly making their way back to their own ship and mooning over their loot. The Empire ship was left unharmed, and the corpses of soldiers were thrown into the unforgiving sea. Florian started pushing them out the door, as though they had somewhere to be. "Well, as wonderful as it was meeting you all, we must get going. Enjoy your trip!"

Chapter Forty Seven
Quilla

Waves lapped against the ship as Quilla steered it towards Shina. She had learned to use the stars to guide her way to her destination, and right now, there were plenty of them. They glittered in the midnight sky like spots of white paint. The cold sea air was salty and tangy as it blew around her, occasionally sending drops of frigid water that landed on her skin.

They had agreed to take turns on steering duty, and Quilla had agreed to take the first shift. Staying up wasn't hard for her, and she had plenty on her mind anyway. The suspense on why this happened was killing her.

The Empire's attack was too swift. She should have known better, it was too easy for them to get Alohi and get out. They must have known that they would be more vulnerable at sea. Once they had gotten on Nikolai's ship, Quilla had let down her guard, thinking that the threat was over. She was cursing herself for that mistake now and was contemplating how she would redeem herself.

There was no way that the Empire could have known they were coming unless they had been there to watch over their plans. Even if they were informed after the Archives mission, there was no way that they could form an attack plan that fast. Besides, how would they even know where the ship was, and plant explosives in it before they got there?

Something was missing. Throughout this whole charade, there was something that Quilla missed. Something that slipped right under her nose before, and she would be damned if it did it again.

Her head flew around as she heard footsteps coming towards her. She felt her hands fly to her knives, ready to impale the oncoming attacker.

"Are you ever not on edge?" Lilith raised her eyebrows as Quilla tucked her knives back into her coat.

"It's good to be on edge, then no one would come at me by surprise." Quilla told her partner, getting back to the steering wheel. "And shouldn't you be in bed? The shift change is not for another hour."

Lilith shrugged. "I couldn't sleep, it seems too probable that we could get attacked again."

Quilla crossed her arms. "Look who's on edge now."

Her partner laughed, dry and humorless. "Don't you feel the same? It's been so chaotic lately that it's hard to predict what's going to happen next."

Quilla gazed out into the endless sea. The waves shimmered in the moonlight while they crashed against each other. A cold breeze ran through her hair like a comb. "I don't think it's a coincidence."

"And why is that?" Lilith crossed her arms, as though in doubt.

"The Empire blew up Nikolai's ship around two days after we entered the Archives. To plan something like that takes time, and how would they even know where our ship was? It's not like we weren't discreet, there's no way they could even know what train we took to get there. To think they made a lucky guess just isn't probable." Quilla told her. "There had to have been a weak link. Someone who has other loyalties, but is stationed inside the rebellion. And they had to be near the plans."

"So…" Lilith started, biting her lip. "There's an Empire spy in the League of Red Doves that got to the plan for the mission, and they reported back to their boss." She put a hand on her hip. "Look, even if this was true, why would they wait until we were on the ship? There's a lot less risk in just putting more security on Alohi's cell than waiting until we were almost free."

Quilla grinned. "Because they weren't interested in keeping Alohi, but finding a new prisoner. One more valuable, one more *powerful*."

Lilith rolled her eyes. "You?"

"I'm not that cocky." She tilted her head. "Nikolai. He's the League's prince. Imagine the bargaining chip that his capture would be. The entire rebellion would yield just at the thought of his torture."

Lilith leaned against the taffrail. "Hm, okay, so I'm assuming this is what you're going to be doing until you have some poor chap in custody."

Quilla shrugged. "I have to earn their trust somehow, don't I?"

Lilith tilted her head. "Well, I prefer to earn it by *following the rules* and *doing as they ask*."

"Since when are you joining the League of Red Doves?" Quilla asked, raising an eyebrow. "What happened to forgetting this ever happened?"

She shrugged. "Maybe your vengeful ways are wearing off on me."

Quilla sighed in exasperation. "Finally!"

Her partner's eyes stayed dull. "What? Were you afraid that you would have to train another archer?"

Quilla's lips parted, remembering her previous phrase. "I never meant that."

Lilith crossed her arms. "Really? It felt like you did." The words crept through her grit teeth like blood leaking from a fresh wound. Pain brimmed every syllable.

Quilla took her hands off the steering wheel, cursing herself for walking over to Lilith. She wasn't supposed to care about her, she wasn't supposed to regret what she had said. But the pain and the guilt in her heart was overwhelming, and she needed to make it right.

She placed her hands on her partner's shoulders, ignoring all the voices telling her not to. Lilith's loose braid blew gently in the wind, her green eyes were wide with shock and her thin lips parted. The cold sea air suddenly warmed, and the distinct smell of salt was replaced by perfumy flowers. "You are so much more to me than an archer. It's important that you know that."

Lilith's gaze hardened, her eyes turning to flames. "Why?" she asked in a spiteful tone. "Do you need to boost my confidence for one of your missions? Or- or are you setting me up to get destroyed by someone else?"

Horror spread through her. She hadn't done that, had she? She wouldn't set her up like that. She would never. "No!" she blurted, the word coming out harsher than she meant it to. "What-" she took a breath, silencing the anxiety and self-blame that was burrowing in her skin. "Whatever I did to make you think that, I'm so sorry. You are more to me than an archer, you're more to me than my partner in crime. You're my..." She trailed off, almost afraid to say the word.

Lilith crossed her arms, still looking unconvinced. "Say it."

Quilla took a breath. She could feel her hands shaking. Every inch of her screamed at her to shut up. Every instinct was telling her to retreat into her cold demeanor. "I-" she stammered. Lilith's expecting eyes were looking at her with intensity. "I-"

Chapter Forty Eight
Nikolai

"Am I interrupting something?" Nikolai's cool, poised voice broke through the air.

The girls were standing closer than he had ever seen them. Pain glazed over both of their eyes, and their knuckles were turning white from clenched fists. The air around them was still like ice, and Nikolai could swear that Quilla was paralyzed. The con queens black eyes gazed at her partner with an unreadable gaze.

"Yes, you definitely are," Lilith responded, her voice cold. "But it wasn't important anyway."

Nikolai saw something fade in Quilla's face, as though she had just lost a battle. Lilith strode away, anger blowing behind her like a mist.

As soon as the archer left, Quilla slapped her own cheek, hard. Her hand made a large, red implant. "I'm such an *imbecile*!"

Nikolai's eyes widened. "Slapping yourself isn't going to fix that."

The criminal prodigy put her hands on the taffrail, looking out into the sea. "Well, it's not exactly going to hurt anything, is it?"

He raised his eyebrows, eyeing the bruise on her face. "Right." He took the wooden wheel of the ship. "So what were you talking to her about anyway?"

Quilla turned. Her hair hung over her fiery eyes in curly strands. "It's none of your concern."

Nikolai shrugged, he wasn't about to push Quilla into telling him anything. "Do you care?"

Quilla kept her head turned to the sea. "You're going to have to specify."

He laughed, a bright, cheerful noise. "Oh please Quilla, you know exactly what I'm talking about."

The crime queen rested her forehead against her temple. "I don't know." She kept looking at the ocean, her gaze unwavering. "Every time she talks about her time in Hanslack, she says she hated it. And that's what it was supposed to be- terrible. That's what *I* promised. But her time there, that's her time with *me*. And if she hates Hanslack, then she hates me too."

"So," Nikolai began. "Do you hate her?"

Quilla's head whipped around, her eyes shone wide and panicked. "*No!*" she covered her eyes. "I shouldn't care about her, but I don't hate her. I never hated her!" her head turned back to the sea as if it was a retreat. "I was always hard on her because I saw her potential! If she wanted to survive, she needed to learn those lessons the hard way, but I- I never let her get *seriously* hurt."

Nikolai's eyes widened. "Quilla," he started. "What did you do?"

The crime prodigy's breath fell short. "She-" her voice cracked with regret. "She always had impulse problems, and I thought the only way to fix them was to learn the consequences. I had noticed them before, and I knew they could be destructive if they got out of hand." Her breaths kept coming, heavy and rapid. "On her first night out on the streets, some guys started picking on her. She stabbed one of them and they ganged up on her. I was on the rooftop. I just watched them kick her, and- and one cut her shoulder. She was on the concrete, cut and bruised when I finally decided to step in. I only scared them away, and left her bleeding on the ground." Her voice was racked with sorrow and guilt. "She was only fifteen..."

Nikolai took a breath, trying to process this new information. "So were you. We're all still just kids."

"No," Quilla said in a solemn tone. "We were never *just* kids."

He took a breath, not believing what he was about to share. "It was my fault Alohi was taken." Quilla looked at him. "We were hijacking trains. It was going so well, and everyone was actually having a good time. We saw one coming, and Alohi wanted to take it. Herself and a few men." He pressed his temples. "Little did we know, it was a trap. That train was filled with a couple of 'silvers', as you call it. They didn't stand a chance. Those men died. Alohi was the only one that survived." At that moment his poised structure fell apart. "It- it was my fault. She didn't have any training, and I- I should have been with her. I can't even battle a force full of silvers, Alohi didn't stand a chance." A tear rolled down his cheek and he felt more dwelling in his eyes.

Quilla's shrill laugh broke the air. It was dull and humorless but somehow went on for almost half a minute. Nikolai could almost feel his blood pressure rising.

"Oh please, Nikolai." Quilla turned around and leaned against the taffrail, her hair hanging in front of her eyes like that of a mad woman. "You weren't the one that threw her in that cage and slid a knife down her arms."

Nikolai clenched his fists. The con queen may have gotten on his final nerve. "Oh, and were you the one that beat Lilith to a pulp and left her bleeding on the pavement?" his sarcastic retort came out harsher than he meant it.

Quilla pushed off the taffrail and approached him. Her eyes narrowed into black slits while her hair blew behind her like the pieces of a shredded flag. She cracked her neck to the side, showing white, fanged teeth. "I'll leave you bleeding right now."

He saw Quilla reach for her knives, but he waved her off. "I know better than to fight you." A petty smirk spread across his face that he knew would hurt much more than any slash he could do with a blade. "I'm not a dirty, loveless, delinquent."

Quilla's jaw jutted out, her eyes turned to stone and her face became sour. She turned on her heel and disappeared into the cold night.

Nikolai watched her go, the anger he had still lingering. After he was sure she was gone, he fell into a small ball, burying his head in his hands. All previous emotions were taken over by sadness and guilt. His mind seemed to be punching him, over and over and over again.

Even though he wasn't the one who placed those bombs, it was his fault that he lost his crew. They were his family, the ones who loved him *unconditionally*, and he had led them into a death trap.

The memory of deluded blood in the salty water racked his brain. The thick feeling still layered his hands like an oil. Their blood, and so many others, were on his hands.

He pulled his hair vigorously, trying to pry the guilt out of his head. Those men had real families. Ones who weren't put on a crew together just to fight. They had real, blood families that loved them. Those families, those *kids*, would suffer because of a mistake that *he* made. It was him that would have to break the news to their families. He would have to watch mothers, fathers, husbands, wives, and kids fall to the ground in grief as he told them of the terrible tragedy. He would watch as they slowly connected the dots back to him. They would blame him, and they had every right to.

"What did you say to Quilla?" Alohi's voice broke the air. "She's throwing knives at one of the masts and it looks like she's pretending it's your face." Nikolai lifted his head to see that she was striding up the staircase, her nightgown gently swaying in the wind. "Are you okay?" concern laced her voice as she saw his tear-stained face.

Nikolai stood up, brushing the salty drops off his cheeks and blinking away any extra tears. "Fine!" he said in the most joyful tone he could manage.

Alohi put her hands on her hips, fixing her expression to one of great doubt. "Nikolai, how long have we known each other?"

"Going on five years, I believe?"

She nodded. "And you would think that after all that time, I would be able to see through your poised illusion."

Nikolai took a sharp breath. "You would think that, wouldn't you?"

Alohi rolled her eyes as she strode up to Nikolai and put a hand on his shoulder. "What's going on?"

He huffed a fake laugh and brushed off her hand. "Nothing's going on, seriously."

Alohi groaned. "Fine," she crossed her arms and leaned against the taffrail. "You don't want to talk? I'm sure Quilla would be more than thrilled to practice her knife throwing on *live* targets." Her lips quirked into a semi-evil smile.

"Okay," he relented. "I guess I'm just processing..."

Alohi's expression morphed back into a considerate one. "Processing what?"

Nikolai gulped. He knew if he started talking about it tears would escape from his eyes. He took a breath, looking towards the dark night sky. *Don't cry.* He chanted to himself. *Don't you dare cry!*

"It's my fault they died." He blurted, falling back to the ground. "I should have told them to get off the ship, I should have just come alone. They didn't have to be there, I could have told them they couldn't come. And- and now they're dead! They died painful, hard deaths and I didn't do anything. I didn't even retrieve their bodies. My crew- my *family*, are lying at the bottom of an icy ocean, and I stood there and watched." Tears streamed down his cheeks, the emotions pouring out like a river. "I don't even know why you still talk to me! I'm the reason that you got captured in the first place. I'm the reason you had to be in that awful prison. All of this is my *fault*!"

Alohi's mouth dropped. Tears welled in her own sympathy-coated eyes. "Oh, Nikolai." She leaned down, embracing him in a tight hug. "None of this was ever your fault. You couldn't stop me from getting on that train even if you tried, and if I knew Rex and the rest of the crew, there was no way that you could have stopped them from coming. It was their choice, they knew the risks."

"Yeah," Nikolai took another breath. Guilt still welled inside of him, but now it had lessened, as though it was just the remnants of a crash. He buried his head in Alohi's arm, letting his terrible thoughts drift away like the wind.

Chapter Forty Nine
Alohi

The morning gulls squawked outside the room Alohi lingered in. Through the walls of the boat, she could hear soft waves lapping outside. She was sitting on a messy bed, her legs crossed over one another. She had barely slept a wink last night, even though she usually enjoyed sleeping out on the ocean. The darkness was too much of a reminder of the past couple of weeks; and right now, she was trying as hard as she could to forget that.

The room smelled of tangy salt. Her thoughts were immersed in the book she found on one of the jumbled shelves, the world of dragons and magic distracting her from the dull, predictable world. The words bounded off the page and entered her mind, creating scenes of chaos and beauty with every sentence.

"Morning, Alohi." She was so concentrated on her book that she didn't see the con queen enter the room.

"Quilla!" she closed her book with a snap. "To what do I owe the pleasure?"

She stood leaning against the door frame, a cup of steaming coffee in hand. "I need your help." Alohi raised her eyebrows, it was highly out of character for Quilla to ask anyone for help. "You dabble in politics, correct?"

"You could say that," Alohi responded, getting up from her perch on the bed. "What do you need?"

The criminal prodigy sighed. "As you know, I want to join the League of Red Doves, but I'm not sure your-" she paused, trying to find the right word. "*Executives* are going to take kindly to my proposal." She took a sip of her black coffee. "I need your help to convince them of my use."

Alohi raised her eyebrows. "Why do you need me to do that?" she asked skeptically. "You seem perfectly capable of proving a point."

Quilla ran a hand through her hair, her gaze wandering to different parts of the room. "Yes, proving that I'm ruthless; however, being a skilled killer is different from being of worth."

"Right." Alohi didn't quite agree with that phrase. As long as Quilla had that undeniable skill, there was no way that she wouldn't be of use. "So why get me to do it? Nikolai has much more influence than I do, he is the future emperor after all."

Quilla scoffed. "Let's not get ahead of ourselves now, you do have to win the war before he'll have any power." Alohi clenched her fists, the previous failures of the League were no secret, and the criminal prodigy didn't waste any time bringing them up when they may work in her favor. "As for Nikolai, he and I aren't on the best terms at the moment." This she already knew.

"Fine." Alohi relented. "I'll get you into the League of Red Doves, but you have to do something for me in return."

Quilla smiled mischievously. "And what would that be?"

"Train me." Alohi lifted her chin, trying to seem more confident than she was.

Quilla almost dropped her coffee. "In thievery? If I'm being honest, Alohi, I don't think you'd like it."

She rolled her eyes. "No. In self-defense. I want to make sure I am never helpless like that *again*."

"Fair enough." Quilla subsided. "Why not get Nikolai to do it for you, I think he may be a better teacher than I would be. At least in *your* case." A devious smile lit her face as she said the last part.

Alohi was fighting the urge to slap the con queen across the face. "He has enough on his plate, I don't want to bother him with this."

Quilla jutted out her jaw. "Oh, but you feel perfectly content with burdening me with it?"

Alohi smiled cruelly, an expression that had never crossed her face before. "I don't much care what burdens you."

To her surprise, Quilla's lips curved into a grin equal to her own. "I knew there was a reason I liked you."

A thunderous rumbling took over the cabin. Alohi's hands extended out to catch her balance, while Quilla barely looked phased. Instead, she strode to the small shaded window on the opposite side of her quarters.

Once Alohi had regained her balance, she hurried to the site. Right outside, was the glistening harbor of Shina. Lights shined down on them as boats sailed in and out of the port. Each carried around a hundred armed men.

Her eyes widened as she heard a boom. The ship rumbled as more cannons fired in the direction of their ship. Quilla drew her knives, holding them like claws ready to strike.

"It's the ship!" Alohi realized. "They think we're the Empire!"

Quilla groaned, muttering a swear-cluttered insult under her breath. She turned on her heel and rushed out the door, looking eager to fire the knives she had in hand.

The deck outside was a world of chaos. Fire danced along the tattered wood and explosions came frequently. Nikolai was jumping up and down frantically, waving his arms in the air. "They don't know it's us!"

Lilith appeared next to them, her braid was messy, and her clothes were tattered. "The hell do you think you're doing?"

"I'm *trying* to let them know who we are!" he hollered back, panting.

Alohi watched as several other explosions demolished the bow of the ship. Smoke filled the air and water crept onto the deck, making her scramble back.

"Well, obviously your plan isn't working!" Quilla yelled over the flames. The boat started tipping and water crept up its edges. Alohi felt herself sliding down the boards into the waiting ocean. "I say abandon ship!"

She quickly grabbed the taffrail that was now almost completely vertical. Quilla wrenched her knife into the boards of the ship, holding onto it with one hand. With the other, she grabbed Lilith's wrist. The archer was looking at the water like it was lava waiting to send them all to their flaming death. Alohi had grabbed Nikolai's hand, and her grip on the taffrail slowly slipped from both of their weight.

"I can't swim!" Alohi heard Lilith yell as the wretched smell of smoke filled her lungs.

"Well, we *all* can't survive in fire." Quilla's cold accent shot back. "So you better pray your quick learning skills kick in or one of us is strong enough to carry you on our backs!"

With that, Quilla tugged the knife out of the deck and fell into the water. Alohi looked at Nikolai, letting go as he gave her a swift nod. They slid down the wood, getting splinters in their backs as they fell.

The water was cold, the smoke and debris had made it a filthy gray. It tasted toxic and salty in Alohi's mouth, and she spit it out as soon as it crept through her lips.

"I can stand!" exclaimed Lilith, a relieved smile spreading across her lips. Alohi let her feet fall to the ground, her shoes landed in soft mud that seemed to be laced with sand. She fought the urge to gag as her feet sunk further into the gunk.

Quilla rolled her eyes. "Lucky you."

More explosions rained down on them, demolishing the ship around them. Alohi quickly dove under the murky liquid, as though the water above her would provide any sort of protection.

She felt a hand grab her wrist, and she was pulled to the surface. As her face broke the water, she saw Nikolai pulling her to shore. His eyes were padded with determination and focus. Fire and canons fell on them like heavy rain.

Quilla and Lilith were ahead, but it looked like they were more annoyed at the situation than scared. The crime prodigy's calm demeanor had been completely removed and replaced with pure annoyance. She was dragging the archer through the water, not looking back at the scene behind her.

Alohi and Nikolai were propelled forward as an explosion went off behind them. She flew through the air, the rough water glittering below her. She could taste blood in her mouth as she crashed into the water. Her new wounds stung as the salt seeped into them. She could feel the ground beneath her, it was more sandy than the previous, and the water only went up to her knees when she stood.

Red Dove soldiers lined up along the shore. Their bows were loaded and pointed at her. Anger and frustration boiled in her blood. She could feel her face getting hot, even though the water around her was next to freezing.

She flipped the curtain of wet hair over her eyes to the back of her head. "If *anyone* fires an arrow, or explodes something else-" she took an exasperated breath. "I swear to god, I will have Quilla gut you."

Their eyes widened and their bows lowered. All fire vanished from their eyes and was replaced by awe. Their mouths dropped and their weapons clattered to the ground. "Alohi Windlem?"

She strode out of the water, her clothes soaked and dripping. The dry sand felt heavenly as she padded along the beach. "In the flesh." She tilted her head expectantly, "Now can someone please get me a towel?"

Chapter Fifty
Lilith

Lilith was sitting in a small tub. Warm water surrounded her, soaking into her dry, battered skin. It was just now that she realized how many scrapes and cuts burdened her flesh. When she got into the tub, it felt like every inch of her was stinging. And it was even worse once she had to use soap.

A nice, shy girl named Ika had shown them to their room, and she had mostly remembered the way. The League of Red Doves was like a maze, and she wasn't completely convinced that the halls didn't shift around while no one was looking.

Of course, she was sharing a room with Quilla. Her partner had let her use the bathtub first; which to her, felt a bit like an unfortunate insinuation, but she wasn't complaining.

Tensions between the two of them had been unsteady ever since that night on the ship. But Quilla's hesitation intrigued her. The criminal prodigy's struggle to say a small phrase brought up a lot of questions, especially because she rarely struggled to do anything.

Lilith leaned back, letting the water cuff her ears. She could feel her loose hair floating lazily in the warm liquid. Her eyes closed, resting after days of intense events. This was the first time she had rested in days, and it felt as though she wasn't supposed to be doing it.

She looked down at the arrow wound implanted in her stomach. It was still red, and a soft scab had formed over it. The pain still lingered, but only an eighth of its original. She was glad the wound hadn't been that bad.

Lilith lifted herself out of the water, ringing out her hair as she did so. Her bare feet stepped over the walls of the tub and padded on the cold bathroom floor. She looked in the large mirror, admiring her bare body.

The water had washed away the dirt and sand, but there were still the old scars and new cuts that no amount of water could erase. She turned around, noticing the large whip lashes that left brutal, red marks on her back. They were ugly, and at that moment, all she wanted was for them to vanish.

There was one that stuck out. It was a knife wound on her shoulder, drawn by a man in Hanslack when she was only fifteen.

~~~

She remembered walking through the cold, rainy streets. She had finally gotten brave enough to leave her small room in the Link and venture out into the new city. The feeling of anxiety lingered inside her chest, thoughts of the worst raiding her head. Looking back, maybe it would have done her well to listen to those thoughts.

She took small steps and held onto the bow in her hand like it was her life. She only had three arrows, but to her, it felt as though they were her only chance of surviving. Rain clattered on the ground, hard drops pouring on her hair.

The glittering lights of Hanslack surprised her. If you hadn't heard of the city's crude reputation, you wouldn't be so hesitant to admire its beauty; but unfortunately, the city had shown Lilith its dark side many times before.

But the lights had relaxed her, and the darkness and patter of the hard rain seemed to soothe her scared soul. It was as though all her problems disappeared, her fear melted and instead, she strode through the dark streets, almost skipping. But although her fear disintegrated, so did her caution.
~~~

"Hello, little girl." The deep voice came from a dark corner. Lilith stopped, her smile faded and curiosity came over her. "What are you doing all alone?"

Lilith tilted her head. "Who are you?"

Three dark figures emerged from the alleyway. Black, leather coats hung off of them like capes. They looked only a little older than she was, but their thick, muscled arms and yellowed grins told her that they were much more dangerous. One lit a cigarette and puffed smoke from his mouth.

"Oh," one widened his eyes and tilted his head, as though mocking her. "I'm a nice boy who wants to play with you."

Lilith bit her tongue. She could sense mockery when she heard it, but she wasn't ready to let anger control her again.

"Really?" she asked skeptically.

His friends laughed, giggling like hyenas. "Sure." The grim smile from before crept across his lips. "Do you wanna play?"

Her hands shook. Danger was an old friend of hers, and she wasn't willing to stick around to see him. "I have to go," she said quickly, walking quickly into the darkness.

The group of men followed, their footsteps loud and obnoxious. She could feel the air get colder and goosebumps form on her arms. She took rapid breaths as her steps got longer, trying to get away from these horrible men.

"Where do you think you're going?" she felt a hand grab the collar of her shirt, hot breath ran down her spine as one of the three men pulled her towards them.

She felt anger seize her, it ran up her spine like electricity, lighting up her eyes like fire. Her head spun with caution and fear, but it didn't matter, the wretched emotion was in control now.

Lilith grabbed an arrow from her small quiver and jammed it into the man's shoulder. He screamed and fell to the ground, clutching his gushing wound. The other men's eyes lit up, anger dwelling on their faces. All while her anger released its hold, leaving her defenseless. Only Quilla's earlier warning rang in her head: *they'll kill you if you're lucky, but if you're not, it will be a much worse fate you'll suffer.*

First, one of the men picked her up and slammed her on the cold concrete, leaving her in a deep puddle. She felt her teeth chip in her mouth as her head hit the curb. Next, the cigarette that a man once smoked was being pressed into her skin. She screamed, the agony and pain unbearable.

She felt a knife being pressed into her shoulder. Its cool blade cut her skin so easily like it was only paper. Another ear-shattering scream escaped from her throat as blood ran down her arm and mixed with the muddy water.

That's when they started kicking. She felt their boots dig into her torso and step on her head. Tears poured from her eyes and into her pool of blood. Ribs cracked as their pointed shoes stabbed at her torso, again and again and *again*.

"*Please*," Lilith begged through hard sobs. "Please stop."

Suddenly the kicking stopped. She felt someone lift her chin and a terrible, smokey breath hit her face. "But don't you know?" tears rolled down her cheeks as the man's long fingernails dug into her face. "Girls who don't follow the rules get punished."

Horror overtook her as she felt hands on her pants. The man's greasy fingers crept under her clothes. She would have kicked, she would have fought back, but fear and pain had paralyzed her. A horrifying thought plagued her as she realized, *they're undressing me*!

Suddenly, the hands touching her were pulled away. Her head lifted just enough to see a small, hooded figure taking on all three men. Blades slashed and cut, but it seemed like the only flesh being torn was her attacker's. Soon they were running from the hooded figure, limping and clutching their open wounds.

Lilith felt someone kneel beside her. The smell of roses tainted the air, along with the distinct smell of blood.

"I warned you." Quilla's cold accent cut through the air. She stood, her long, flowy coat blowing in the wind just above her heeled boots. "If you make it back to the Link, I'll teach you how to fight."

With that, she strode into the night, leaving Lilith clutching her bleeding arm as rain poured clattered down on her.

~~~

That memory always made her flinch. It was the night that she learned what Hanslack really was. Just another prison, another cage, but this time the people who dwelled in it were angrier.

"Can you hurry up?" an angry voice shouted, followed by an obnoxious knocking on the door.

"I'm coming!" Lilith responded, pulling on her robe and heading out.

Their room was small, with only a set of beds and another set of small desks. The walls looked as though they had been bleached white, whereas the floor was a murky gray. The whole room smelled of fresh paint that made Lilith's nose crinkle.

"We really need to redecorate," said Quilla, putting her hands on her hips.

"What do you mean?" Lilith questioned, cracking a smile. "It seems right up your alley."

Quilla growled, then rolled up her pant leg to reveal the purple wound on her upper thigh. It looked better but was far from being healed completely. "You need to rebandage this."

Lilith nodded obediently, but silently cursed the con queen out in her head. She wasn't in the mood for bandaging up Quilla's reckless wounds.

She strode over to her, sitting down next to her partner. Quilla's bare knee rubbed against her leg as she handed Lilith the bandages. She sat there, not sure if she should move her leg away or scoot it closer.

"Lilith." Quilla's accent chimed. "Bandages."
~~~

Lilith nodded, starting to unwrap the lint that already covered Quilla's thigh. Her fingers brushed the con queen's soft skin as she slowly unwound the cloth.

She barely breathed during this process. It was surreal that she, a seventeen-year-old who had grown up on a small farm in Salenian, was tending to the wounds of a notorious criminal. When she had first met Quilla, she was afraid to walk too close to her, as though afraid she might catch the cold of vengeance. But now, the criminal prodigy trusted her enough to tend to her wounds. It was both a tremendous honor and a bit insulting.

"Quilla." Lilith broke the silence. "After you get all your... vengeance, what do you plan to do?"

Quilla looked at her with an unreadable expression. "You answer that question first."

Lilith shrugged, removing the last of the bandages and reaching for the fresh ones. "Try and forget, I assume."

Quilla looked down at the floor, her eyes sparkled with an emotion she still couldn't identify. "Sometimes there are too many scars to forget."

Lilith looked at her with curious eyes. "No matter the severity, scars will always fade."

The con queen gave a small laugh. "I wasn't talking about the physical ones." Her smile was dull and it looked like all energy was drained from her face. "No matter how hard you try, your mind will *never* let you forget."

"I guess you would know." Lilith's tone came out more spiteful than she thought it would, but Quilla wore her vengeance too clearly on her sleeves to forget easily. "So, I answered the question, now it's your turn." She lifted her chin as she bandaged up the con queen's thigh. "What are you going to do after your vengeance is served?"

Quilla laughed. The sound wasn't humorous, but soft and dry. "Die."

Lilith stopped wrapping her leg, not sure if she heard her partner correctly. "What?"

Quilla shrugged. "After I serve my grudges, my life will have no meaning anymore, no *purpose*. As far as I'm concerned, as soon as my debts are paid, I have no purpose in this world anymore."

Lilith was speechless. She opened her mouth to say something, but nothing came out. "What-" she stammered, not sure if there was anything to say at this moment. "Quilla, why?"

The con queen furrowed her brow. "I thought I had explained that already."

"No, I just meant-" shock brimmed every syllable, and she couldn't quite find the words to describe her emotions at that moment. "You've built a reputation, a *dynasty* in Hanslack. Why would you leave that?"

"Lilith." The calmness of Quilla's tone was infuriating. "Those who stay in Hanslack until they reach old age become shameful, disgusting bastards. Think of Olan. I may be a legend now, but as soon as my bones grow old and my hair grays, I'll be no more than a disgrace to the city. If I die, the legend continues. Think of it as a way to preserve my exalted reputation."

There were no words left to say. There was nothing that Lilith could do to change her partner's mind. Nothing that she would believe, anyway. She continued wrapping Quilla's leg, bandaging a bit tighter than necessary.

"Too tight?" she asked hopefully.

Quilla furrowed her brow. "No?"

Lilith nodded, then continued to pull the bandage until Quilla's circulation was sure to be cut off. "How about now?"

Quilla snatched the bandage from her hastily. "Okay, got it, you're pissy." She limped to the bathroom, occasionally using the wall for extra support. "I'll do it myself."

Lilith was hesitant to let her go after their previous conversation. She was hesitant to even let Quilla out of her sight. But from what she understood, as long as Emperor Ghan lived, so would the criminal prodigy.

Once she was gone, Lilith collapsed on the bed, spreading her arms out and letting herself sink into the soft mattress. All the stresses from the past few days melted away. Then she realized.

She had escaped. She had done it. She was a part of the League of Red Doves, or at least she would be soon. Hanslack was in the past, and so was her life as a petty criminal. This was a new chapter, this was the part where she helped people, where she made sure that others didn't have the same terrible fate as she did.

With newfound life, she jumped from the bed. She found jeans and a small jacket in her small closet and pulled them on. Her long fingers weaved her braid into a neat pattern that hung over her shoulder. She strode over to the door, but her hip brushed something off of its perch on her desk and it clattered to the ground.

She looked down, finding her arrows spilled in a mess, but as she leaned down, she found something else. Quilla's book was sprawled out on the ground, its pages were ruffled and water-stained. It was opened to the back, which had a small pocket with something sharp emerging from it.

Not able to control her curiosity, Lilith picked it up. She reached into the pocket with care, pulling out a small throwing star. It was bronze-gold and looked rather old. She furrowed her brow in curiosity; she had never seen Quilla with a throwing star. Even though knives were her traditional weapon, and they were quite similar, she hadn't even mentioned the object. It might have been a trophy or something worth a lot of money; but then Quilla would never bring anything of worth on a trip like this, or in such a loose pocket.

She tucked the star back into the pocket gently, not daring to even risk a tear. She closed the book with a snap, but as soon as she saw the back cover, her mouth dropped.

As mysterious as her partner was, she never dreamed of something like this. There, on the back of Quilla's rose-patterned book, was a blue triangle. A simple shape, but the symbol of the Empire.

Chapter Fifty One
Quilla

"So." Alohi chimed. "What are we working with here?"

Quilla had gathered herself, Alohi, and Lilith in the library to discuss their plans for their upcoming meeting with the council. They were sitting in a vast room with more shelves than she could count. The lighting was dim and the warm room smelled of freshly baked goods.

Alohi had changed into a white blouse with black lace lining her neck. Now that she had cleaned up, the girl looked less like a prisoner and more like, well, a politician. Lilith was sitting across from her wearing a black sweater and flared pants, her bright green gaze watching Quilla.

"Working with what?" Quilla asked in a spiteful tone.

Alohi sighed, brushing her two front strands of hair out of her face. "I mean, what can you offer to the League?"

Quilla jutted out her jaw. "Simple, criminal prodigy and I can throw a knife with perfect aim." She folded her arms. "What more is there to offer?"

Alohi pressed her fingers against her temples. "Keep in mind, this is an operation that is supposedly run through a standpoint of morality, so I don't think saying that you're a *criminal prodigy* is going to help your chances."

Lilith scoffed. "Come now, we all know politics has no more morality than common thievery." She was right. Quilla knew many politicians back in Hanslack who could have been sicker than her.

"I'm not going to argue with you on that." Alohi confided. "But the fact remains, in order to be successful, people have to believe that politicians have your best interest at heart. How would it look if we were harboring a criminal."

"Two criminals." Lilith corrected.

"Not exactly," said Alohi. "You have the sympathetic story, the morality, and the skills to make you a great fit for the League of Red Doves. Anyone could blame your time in Hanslack as a desperate attempt for survival. Whereas your partner," she looked accusingly at Quilla. "Isn't so easily forgiven."

"So I need a sob story?" Quilla groaned, hating this place more by the second.

"Well, having one wouldn't hurt." Alohi concluded, "Do you have one?"

Quilla turned away, brushing her hair over her eyes. "Not for your ears, or any of the councils for that matter." Even if she was willing to share what made her the rotten heathen she had become, it wouldn't do much good. If anything, it would just turn the odds against her more, even though that seemed faintly possible.

Lilith looked at her with narrow eyes. Scheming was rarely an emotion she saw on her partner's face; yet there it was. It was as though she was trying to figure out how to break into a facility.

"Fine." Alohi sighed. "In that case, we may have to use other methods."

"What if we didn't give them a choice." Quilla ran a hand through her hair. "They needed me before, right? So what if another problem arose, and they need me again?"

The politician crossed her arms, frowning. "That's the thing, they don't need you anymore."

Quilla bit her tongue, heaving a sigh. "Yes, but if there was a *problem* that only *I* could solve, then they would have no choice but to let me join!"

"Right, but there isn't a problem!" Alohi tilted her head, her face slowly filling with annoyance.

"But if there was-"

"There *isn't!*" she slammed her fists on the table.

Lilith covered her eyes in exasperation. "She's saying we create a problem."

Alohi's eyes widened. "That's treason!"

Quilla shrugged, "Only if we get caught," she said in a light tone. "And besides, you don't have to participate, just advocate. Lilith and I will do all the illegal things."

"No." Alohi leaned back in her chair, shaking her head. "We do this honestly, or you find a new advocate."

Quilla and Lilith looked at each other. Understanding shimmered on both of their faces. Each of them needed to join, and Alohi was their best bet of getting into the League.

"There is an alternative." Alohi sat up as soon as the words broke Quilla's lips. "We believe there's a spy in the League; and given that I've been a spy before, I think I am best equipped to find them."

The politician paused, as though processing what had just been said. "That could work. But just checking, there is a spy and you're not planning on going on a wild goose chase to find an imaginary traitor?"

Quilla smiled, showing her fang-like teeth. "Would I ever lie to you?"

The politician looked down, focusing on her notes. "I wouldn't put it past you." She said, clicking a silver pen. "Go, I'll figure out the speech. Meet in the assembly hall at noon, and don't be late." She waved a hand at them, signaling to them to leave her alone.

Quilla and Lilith strode out the door. Quilla figured it was best to keep her hopes for the upcoming meeting low. It was no secret that the prissy members of the League of Red Doves weren't particularly fond of her, and probably anxious to never speak to her again. To hear that she wanted to stay would certainly cause a stir.

"So," started Lilith as soon as the doors to the library shut. "How are we going to find this weak link? It's not like we have a lead or anything."

Quilla looked forward, gazing out into the bright halls. "The spy needs to be in contact with the Empire somehow, so we're going to find out how they're staying in contact."

Her partner raised her eyebrows. "And what do you plan to do after you find this spy?" she asked skeptically. "The League might not need you anymore after this."

Quilla smiled, ambition lacing her eyes. "I'm going to work my way up, just like I did in Hanslack." She strode into the white halls, her heels clicking with every step. "Make no mistake, my apprentice; a craving for vengeance is a powerful weapon, and *no one* is more hungry than I am."

Chapter Fifty Two
Nikolai

Nikolai opened the door to his house wearily. It was a grand entrance, the wood engraved and laced with gold paint. On the center of the door was a simple crown, large jewels engraved in its points. The Lone family crest.

The door creaked open to reveal his opulent house. Vast staircases curved around banisters and royal red carpets. His father had really gone for the royal theme, as though attempting to carve into Nikolai's mind the fact that they were prestigious.

He padded into the room, anxiety and fear thumping in his heart as his feet gently landed on the soft carpet. This house was no home, but a place where he was reminded of how worthless he was if he didn't perform. His breath quickened and his hands shook. Maybe, if he was lucky, he could slip to his room without his father noticing he was home.

As soon as he stepped on the stairs, a stone-cold voice rasped from the living room. He felt the hairs on the back of his neck stand straight, his breath slipped from his lungs as a lump formed in his throat. "Nikolai."

His father's voice was calm, but he had heard it too many times before to expect it to be kind. His hands had started shaking, he felt his teeth dig into his tongue as fear trapped his body in a black net. "Come to the living room."

He had to convince his legs not to run, not to carry him away, as far as they could from this new danger.

"I'm coming." Just for those two words, he silenced his fear and anxiety.

His feet carried him into the living room reluctantly, where his father was sitting in his laced armchair, whiskey in hand. A tailored, striped suit hung off him in neat lines. His white hair was combed back, not a strand astray. His mustache looked sharp enough to impale someone.

"Sit." Grandez Lone told him, gesturing to the empty lounge chair beside him. Nikolai did as he was told, planting himself on the edge of the chair.

The two sat there for a second, just looking at the blank wall in front of them. Nikolai didn't dare speak, he wasn't even sure he could. His father just sat there, sipping on his amber alcohol.

"What-" he started, every inch of him telling him not to talk. "Why am I here?"

His father downed his whiskey, milking the cup for the last drops. "You're here-" he took a breath, setting the empty glass on the table. "Because you failed."

Nikolai's eyes widened. The fear had engulfed him. Black clouded his vision as his breath left him completely.

His father stood from his chair, slamming his glass on the hard ground. The shards flew everywhere, not leaving any trace of a cup. Anger lit up in his eyes like a wildfire and his lips curled down to reveal whiskey stained teeth.

"Families?" his voice was almost questioning, but the rage in his posture remained powerful and unwavering. "Mourning!"

Nikolai stood up, his instincts of danger taking over as he backed up. "Ship?" his father asked through a face full of rage. "Blown to bits!"

Nikolai tripped over something, falling to the floor with a loud bang. But his father kept getting closer. He was an opponent that Nikolai wanted to hurt, he wanted to kill. But there was no way he would ever lay a hand on him.

"Crew?" godforsaken tears formed in his eyes. *No!* Panic swept over him. *Not now, any time but now!* "DEAD!" his father's angry voice shook the walls. The tears rolled from Nikolai's eyes, little beads of horror.

His father picked him up by the collar and slammed him against the wall. His head hurt from the impact, but every sense was paralyzed. Fear was holding him hostage, bonds of black tight around every limb.

"I'm sorry!" that was all he could manage through ugly sobs. "I'm so sorry!"

Nikolai felt a fist slam against his face. "Don't cry!" his father's voice boomed again. "Men don't cry! Crying is for kids! And failures!" his father laughed, ugly, dry, and so, so, scary. "Which... I guess you are.." A fist came hurling at him, but this time at his gut.

He fell to the floor, clutching his stomach with both hands. "I raised a failure!" he yelled at Nikolai, kicking him again in the ribs. He no longer had air to breathe, all he could do was gasp and claw at the ground.

"I'm sorry!" he sobbed, tears still streaming down his cheeks. Those were the only words he could manage to say, the only ones that could touch his lips. "Please, Father!"

All his father did was turn away, his eyes still slit with anger. "You are not my son until there is something to be proud of." Those words, so calm, so poised. But they hurt so damn much.

Nikolai watched as his father strode into the next room, stepping on the broken glass from before. All he did was lay there, gasping for air. He could feel his bruises aching all over, little splotches of pain.

After what felt like hours, he stood. His legs were wobbly and his breath shallow, his arms flew out to catch him. He leaned against the wall, all his weight leaning on the plain white drywall.

His legs shook, every part of him did. *One step at a time.* He breathed to himself. His foot landed on the carpet. *Good. He chanted. Another one.*

Just a couple more, he coaxed as he took another agonizing step. *We're almost to the bathroom.* The trip up the stairs was agonizing, every inch of him felt achy and painful.

As soon as he reached the bathroom, he collapsed onto the cold tile. He let the cool floor sink into his skin, as though it was melting away the bruises and cuts that burdened him. He let it touch his cheeks, his stomach, his ribs. Everything before the strength to stand finally came.

Nikolai stood, taking off his shirt and gazing at the blue splotches all over his body. It was muscled, but it looked more lean and pale than usual. His hair was ruffled and his eyes were puffy and red.

It was awful, gruesome. He shouldn't have any of the wounds that plagued his body; but the only thought that crossed his mind was, there's no blood.

He deserved to bleed. He deserved to have all the pain in the world. His crew, Alohi, Rex. It was his fault that those terrible things had happened to them. They had bled, fought, and died for his mistakes. It was only fair that he did as well, whether it was from an opponent's hand or his own.

Don't! A voice screamed at him. *Once you do it, there's no turning back!*

Do it! Another chimed. *You fucking deserve it!*

Nikolai drew his swords, looking at the shiny blade. No! No! No! A million whispers chanted in his head. If he did this there was no turning back.

Yes! Yes! Yes! A million more screamed as he lowered the blade to his wrist. *Failure, disgrace, weak!* They were too much, the insults floating in his head like a hurricane. *Do it!*

Don't!

Do it!

Don't!

DO IT!

"AGHH!" Nikolai screamed. He slid his blade across his wrist. Bright red blood flooded out of the wound, dripping down his arm.

The pain lingered for a bit but was not at all unpleasant. The voices in his head shut their mouths, quiet and content.

Nikolai sank to the ground, leaning his exhausted head against the wall and closing his eyes. He could feel the sting. He could feel the blood dripping. And he could feel a gentle smile curling around his lips. His breath returned, and a sense of calm washed over him, and then...

And then he laughed. It wasn't large, or humorous. It was a small chuckle, as though he was enjoying a small joke he made himself.

As he stopped, he sunk deeper into the cold of the floor. The laughing ceased and he stared up at the bright ceiling, smiling to himself. The feeling was airy, light, unlike anything he had ever felt. It was as if he had detached from the rest of the world. As if he wasn't human anymore. And he liked it.

He lay there for hours. Time wasn't real anymore, nothing was real. It was only him and the bathroom, nothing else mattered. The floor had taken him, swallowed him, made him unmoving, unthinking. It was bliss. The only thing he felt was the light sting on his wrist.

But then it was gone. The cut stopped bleeding and scabbed over. Stopped *stinging*. The feeling was gone, but the panic was back. Anxiety, shame, anger, sadness. They all rushed back over him in a powerful wave.

He sat up, curling into a small ball and breathing heavily. The voices were back. It was all too much. A thousand thoughts flew in his head, hitting and punishing him. But one single sentence overcame all of them.

Do it again.

Chapter Fifty Three
Lilith

The large meeting hall of the League of Red Doves still felt like a massive power trip.

Just in front of them, was a massive jury. Jumbled voices talked in hushed voices as if they were trying to tell a secret. Above the jury, sat the council members, with Nikolai and his father sitting in the center.

The only difference from the last time that she was here was that Alohi had replaced her sister on the high throne that represented the country of Woodran. The young politician was shuffling through her notes, stopping once and a while to reread something. Next to her other older colleagues, she looked... well, seventeen.

Lilith and Quilla were positioned at a lower level. The League had supplied them with two splintering wooden chairs that looked like they belonged in a prison rather than a courtroom. When she sat in them, it felt as if something had twisted in her back.

Quilla sat beside her, reading a paper that she had written herself. Her black eyes darted from one side of the page to the other like she was watching a game of tennis. Lilith had convinced her partner to make her a part of the investigation, or at least in the council's eyes. She wasn't keen on sharing her story, she wasn't even sure she could do it without breaking down in ugly sobs. And she did not need any excess judgment from Quilla.

"Look at Nikolai." The criminal prodigy had stopped reading her script and tapped her shoulder. "He looks terrible."

Lilith gazed up at where the politicians sat. Quilla was right, Nikolai did look terrible. He was thinner than usual, and his pale skin highlighted a giant bruise on his cheek. His posture was hunched and his eyes dull. But the most noticeable thing about his appearance was the long sleeves that he seemed to be holding above his palm.

"Why is he wearing sleeves like that?" Lilith murmured in Quilla's ear.

She was glaring up at him, black eyes in focused slits. "No one does that without a reason."

"What's his reason?" Lilith asked.

Quilla huffed a dry laugh, "How should I know? I'm down here with you."

A loud voice rang across the room. Grandez Lone was standing up, his mustache more pronounced than ever. He cleared his throat and his eyes shifted into angry triangles as he realized everyone was still talking.

"QUIET!" the murmurs hushed, and everyone positioned to face him. The anger faded from his face and his hands clasped behind his back. "Ladies and gentlemen of the court, we are gathered here today to decide if Lilith Cole and..." He wrinkled his nose at the name. "Quilla Thorne... may join the League of Red Doves."

Quilla's lips curved into a vicious smile. She raised a hand to her forehead and saluted the old man. "I know what he's voting for." Her cold accent whispered to Lilith.

"Miss Windlem," Grandez Lone stepped aside, gesturing for Alohi to come onstage. "The floor is yours."

The young politician stood, a slim smile crossing her lips. "Good afternoon, ladies and gentlemen." She chimed in a loud voice. "I know that many of you find yourselves at the high point of your life right now. Here you are, sitting with power, money, and a found family that will support you through anything. A throne that you have built yourself, from nothing but sticks and rocks." Lilith wanted to vomit. She knew that Alohi was just building up the flattery that would work in her favor later; but right now it was making her queasy. "But do you remember a time when life wasn't this easy? Do you remember those sticks and rocks from which you came from? The anguish and defeat that accompanied them?" she paused, letting her words sink in. "I do, and I remember the anger I felt when I found out the Empire burned my home to the ground. I remember wanting to get them back, I wanted *revenge!*" now she was getting somewhere. "And I would do *anything* to get my vengeance. I'm sure all of you have felt that urge before, because we all have one thing in common!"

Alohi inhaled, power surging through her. "The Empire had hurt us, all of us. And when we were at our lowest, the League of Red Doves extended a hand. It gave us a home, something to eat, a purpose!"

Her tone shifted, becoming darker with constructed sadness. "But what if another hand reached out to us? Another opportunity to serve our vengeance. I know if it was me, I would have taken that hand without a second thought." She paused, letting her words find her audience. "That is what happened to my friends down there. At their lowest, becoming a criminal was the only way that they could survive."

Lilith rolled her eyes. Alohi was making it sound like her time in Hanslack was something she should regret. The problem was she didn't. If she hadn't become Quilla Thorne's right hand, then she wouldn't be half the person she was today.

"That's great." Intervened Raya Spin, the councilwoman from Courna. "But if we start accepting every poor soul that needs our help, then we'll become less of a rebellion and more of a refugee camp. How effective will that be against the Empire?"

This raised a round of murmurs around the court. Some glared at Alohi, while others kept their hateful stares completely centered around Quilla and Lilith.

All the young politician did was raise a hand. The talking stopped abruptly as all eyes turned to her. "I'm glad you asked." She said with a smile. "To address your concerns, I would like you to turn your attention to my colleague, Miss Thorne?"

Quilla stood, straightening her posture and flipping her hair behind her. "Thank you, Miss Windlem." A grim smile spread across her lips as her eyes flew over her speech. "But let me ask you, is the League of Red Doves really a successful organization even without refugees? I mean, you send soldiers into battle and not even half of them come back. Remind me again, what happened in Brighan?"

Glares fired down on Quilla, but she still stood confident. "You're not training your soldiers, your weapons are of very little quality, and you expect a couple of teenagers to do your bidding for you." She gestured to Nikolai and Alohi, who looked back at her with horror. "Honestly, and then you act like winning this war is going to be a piece of cake. In the Empire's eyes, you aren't even an opponent, just a mild annoyance destined for extermination. Besides, what do you plan on doing if, by the slim chance, you do win? From where I stand, all that would change is who's dictating. It wouldn't be a change of government, just a change of tyranny." The room was like a thin sheet of ice, a wrong step and it would shatter. "Personally, I don't see how Grandez Lone is any better than Theodore Ghan."

The ice broke. The room exploded. Shouts and insults rained down on them like flowers. Quilla just stood there, accepting them like flowers. A slick smile spread across her lips as she stood there with her hands clasped behind her back.

"How dare you!" was used a lot by several angry voices.

"Dirty delinquent!" typically followed.

"What do you know?" was also scattered amongst the defamation.

"Next time," Lilith whispered in Quilla's ear with grit, angry teeth. "I'm doing the talking."

Quilla turned to her; her eyes were wild with fire and her fanged teeth shone in a vicious smile. She was enjoying this. "Have you no faith in me?"

Lilith shook her head. "After that speech, not much."

The con queen smirked, cocking her head to the side. A loud voice boomed over the room. Everyone's heads turned to see Grandez Lone's red, angry face.

"Thorne," he said through whistling teeth. "If you must insult us more, continue."

"I must." Quilla continued. "But lucky for you, I've already gotten my worst criticisms out, so this small one won't feel so bad." She ran her fingers through her long, curly hair. "There's a spy in your facility. How do I know? On our mission to Rock Highland, our ship was ambushed. The crew, aside from me and my other comrades standing in this room, didn't make it." The mournful hush fell over the room, and Lilith saw Nikolai's face turn a pale green. "Yes, yes, very sad." Quilla hurried on. "Anyway, there is no way that the Empire could have predicted where we docked our ship. Not to mention the battalion of highly skilled soldiers that they had just lined up at the beach. Even if they were warned of our arrival by the men at the Archives, that wouldn't be nearly enough time to create an attack plan that precise."

She paused, letting her words resonate with the room. The councilmen looked at her with confused, sad, and slightly angry faces.

"What are you suggesting, Quilla?" asked Nikolai, his voice was raspier than usual.

"To put it simply, there's a rat in the League, and it's been reporting all our plans to the Empire. As a spy myself, I know exactly how I would infiltrate this place. So if you let me stay, I will find whatever weak link is holding you back, and smoke them out!"

The murmurs and whispers fell silent, just for a second. Then the room erupted with laughter. Lilith's face turned bright red as the horrific cackles pierced her ears, but Quilla just stood there, her face emotionless.

"You think-" Grandez Lone spat between laughs. "That we would harbor two criminals just because you think there's a spy?"

Quilla pinched her lips. "Well, that," her tone was blank, as though she was just stating a fact. "And the fact that if you don't hire me and my partner, it will look pretty bad for advertisement." The council members' eyebrows shot up. "If I'm not mistaken, your reputation precedes the League of Red Doves as an organization where all, no matter their race, birthright, or *history*, are considered equal." She was right; the rebellion was fond of painting itself in a godly light. Lilith had heard plenty of rumors that the organization was a safe haven for misfits. Clearly, those statements had been a little shifted from the truth. "It would be a shame if I were to go back to Hanslack and tell everyone how *tyrannical* the League really is. Especially when so many of them have considered joining the League themselves."

Grandez Lone heaved a sigh, his mustache twitching as he did so. "Oh, but Miss Thorne, if you keep making these threats you won't leave this room alive."

Quilla just laughed, her evil smile curving her lips. "I'm not sure you want to do that." The cruel, ambitious tone had drifted into her voice again. Lilith knew the voice well. Whenever it was used, victory was just seconds away. "I sent a messenger hawk to Hanslack this morning holding a note with the *exact location* of your base on Shina. If they don't get another letter from me, with my signature, within the next twenty-four hours, my associates at the Link will deliver your location to the authorities. The Empire will blow your little base to bits in a matter of hours."

Horror filled the courtroom. Gasps and shouts sprayed from the audience while the council members just sat there, stunned. Lilith's jaw dropped so violently she thought it might hit the floor.

"You're bluffing." Grandez Lone breathed.

Quilla cocked her head to the side, confidence and power radiating off her like a storm. "Are you really willing to take that chance?"

The council members talked in hushed whispers, horrified looks still stained their faces. After a while, Alohi turned to the audience, standing up straight and mustering courage that obviously wasn't there. "I believe the council has a decision to make."

Quilla bowed her head. "Take your time."

Lilith looked at her with shock. "Did you actually send our location to Hanslack?"

Her partner gave a light smile. "Of course I did."

Lilith drew a sigh. "With instructions to deliver it to the authorities?"

Quilla shrugged. "That, or burn it with my instruction."

Above them, the council, with Nikolai and his father, were huddled in a bunch. You could sense the tension from where they were. Angry words sometimes drifted down, letting the entire audience get glimpses of their conversation.

Eventually, Grandez Lone turned towards the audience. His brow was furrowed and his face worried. "After careful consideration," he began, his voice laced with frustration. "We would like to welcome Lilith Cole and Quilla Thorne to the League of Red Doves." He took a breath, as if the words were having trouble coming out. "Welcome to the rebellion."

Chapter Fifty Four
Alohi

There was no applause after the announcement rang. No murmurs, no insults, no disagreements of any kind. Instead, the court just seemed to accept their new members with no emotion. They quietly picked up their things and left the stands like they had somewhere else to be.

Alohi had to fight the urge to sigh with relief when Nikolai's father called out the verdict. She would be lying if she said she didn't have doubts that the case would go their way, especially when Quilla opened with about five different insults aimed directly at the organization.

But it didn't matter. Even though the crime lord had used some... unusual tactics to join their ranks, it had worked all the same. And now Alohi was going to be trained in self-defense by her. Excitement brimmed in her bones as she skipped down the stairs and towards the two criminals. The future was looking bright. Especially compared to these last few weeks.

As she approached the bottom floor, she was met by the bustle of the court. Men and women rushed everywhere, talking in hushed voices and looking wearily at her. Chaos overwhelmed her, most of these people were quite a bit taller than her, and a lot of them weren't exactly fond of her.

Through the disarray, she heard a familiar voice. Her eyes lit up as she saw her sister in the crowd. Ranine's brown eyes shone along with her dark skin. Her curly hair was held together by a dark blue ribbon.

"Alohi!" she screamed delightfully through the crowd. Alohi's legs were running towards her sister before she commanded them to. They met in the middle of the crowd, embracing in a tight hug.

She would have stayed in the embrace forever if she had allowed herself to. It had been so long since she had seen her older sister and Ranine's arms felt more like a home than the League of Red Doves ever had.

"You were amazing!" Ranine exclaimed as soon as they pulled apart. "I never saw you defending criminals though, you seem far too pure for that."

Alohi huffed a laugh. "Well, maybe I've taken a liking to these particular criminals." She crossed her arms, changing her voice to a sound barely above a whisper. "Or maybe I convinced them to train me in self-defense."

Rainine's jaw dropped. "You? Interested in fighting?" she shrugged doubtfully. "Why not just get Nikolai to teach you? He seems skilled enough."

"Maybe I admire the way she acts," Alohi answered. "And the way she fights."

"Oh yeah!" the excitement had returned to her sister's voice. "The one that completely *destroyed* Grandez Lone! She was awesome! What was her name, Quin?"

Alohi must've broken a few ribs trying to contain her laughter. "Quilla."

Ranine placed a hand on her back. "Well, I thought *I* did an amazing job filling in for you as the representative for Woodran."

Alohi cocked her head to the side. "Oh really?" she said in a playful tone. "And how is that?"

Her sister scoffed. "Well, I didn't run out of the room laughing because of the way Grandez Lone's mustache moves when he talks." She placed a hand on her chest dramatically. "I believe that deserves a medal on its own!"

Alohi nearly fell over laughing. It was a feeling that she hadn't felt in a long time, pure unfiltered happiness.

"So," she managed after the giggles stopped. "Why talk to me now? I mean, it's been nearly two days since I've returned!"

Ranine's face turned from festive to horrified. She grasped Alohi's shoulders, sorrow watering in her eyes. "Alohi, I am so sorry." She said in a serious tone. "Dad sent me away on a mission for some reason, and I only realized you were back when I-"

Alohi smiled at her, warmth flooding her blue eyes. "Relax, I know how Dad can be. I grew up with him, didn't I?"

Ranine huffed a laugh. "We are sisters." The stress left her face and was replaced with a neutral expression. "So, have you seen them yet?"

Even with the vagueness of the sentence, Alohi knew exactly what her sister was talking about. Their parents. "No, I'm kind of avoiding it."

Ranine heaved a sigh. "They were really worried about you. Well not Dad, but Mom was. I would have to come over to their house in the middle of the night and console her because she couldn't stop weeping. She got night terrors, about you and what they were doing to you."

Alohi breathed, not wanting to talk about her nightmarish experience in Rock Highland. "It was terrifying." She said in a mournful tone. "But it's over now! And with Quilla's training, it won't ever happen again."

Ranine clapped her hands together with excitement, as eager to change the conversation as Alohi was. "Speaking of which, I need to talk to her in person! Do you think she would want to be invited to dinner?"

Alohi shrugged. "I don't think she would turn it down." For some reason, her mind couldn't picture the crime prodigy at a dinner table, eating with other people and enjoying a peaceful conversation.

"Turn what down?" the sister's heads snapped around as she heard Quilla's crisp accent cut through the air. Lilith was standing beside her, hands in her pockets.

"Hi!" excitement brimmed Ranine's voice as she extended a hand. Quilla took it hesitantly, furrowing her brow. "I'm Ranine, Alohi's sister! Do you want to have dinner with us?"

Lilith smiled, opening her mouth to answer when Ranine held up a hand. "Not you."

Alohi watched as the archer's face sank. She shot her sister a nasty glare, hoping that would convey the message.

"Sure," Quilla said hesitantly.

Ranine let out a tiny squeal, excitement radiating off her. "Great! We can talk about how much *bullshit* the Lone's are! Ooh! And then we can brainstorm the best way to rob a bank! I've heard you're good at that!" her sister was hopping up and down now. She quickly grabbed a dumbstruck Quilla by the wrist and pulled her out of the crowded room.

Alohi laughed as she watched them go. She then turned to Lilith, who was watching the door. "Don't worry about my sister, she's just really excited that someone finally agrees with her views on the way this place is run." She placed a hand on Lilith's shoulder. "And don't worry, it's my house too; you're invited to dinner."

The archer huffed a laugh. "That's not what I was worried about." She turned to Alohi, her bright green eyes gleaming in the white light. "Do you ever get the feeling that someone is keeping something big from you?"

Alohi shrugged. "Only about every time Quilla opens her mouth." She could tell by Lilith's disgusted expression that this wasn't the answer she was looking for. "I'm going to go find Nikolai. He was a lot more quiet than usual." She headed for the stairs, turning at the last second. "Oh, and by the way, welcome to the League of Red Doves!"

All Lilith offered was a small smile, worry quickly replacing it. Alohi headed for the stairs. Whatever she was worried about, it wasn't her job to fix it. Besides, knowing the two criminals, she would find out soon enough.

When she reached the top, all she saw were four six empty chairs. One for each of the council members, Nikolai, and his father. She furrowed her brow, heading to the bathroom.

"Nikolai?" she called into the white room.

"Hey, Alohi." He rasped back.

She padded into the tiled, shiny bathroom to see him hunched over the granite sink. His eyes were clouded and his hair, which was usually slicked back, hung over his eyes in strands.

"What are you doing?" Nikolai asked in a voice that wasn't his. "I thought you had left."

Alohi's worried expression intensified. "I wanted to check on you." She managed a smile. "You were very quiet during the meeting today."

Nikolai huffed a sigh, placing a hand on his forehead. "You sound like my father."

Her eyes widened, shock filling her voice. "Did something happen?" she asked, "Nikolai, I'm worried about you."

She walked up to her friend, laying a hand on his back. As soon as they made contact, he gasped. Her hand was brushed away and Nikolai retreated to the other side of the room.

"Nikolai-" she started, panic rising in her voice.

"I'm fine, Alohi." He brushed past her, heading for the exit. "Don't follow me."

Chapter Fifty Five
Quilla

Being acquainted with Ranine Windlem was surprisingly... pleasant.

Though she was quite a bit older than Quilla, the girl was almost childish. Her competitive nature made her an excellent opponent when it came to knife throwing.

"How do you do that?" she threw her hands up as Quilla landed the fourth bullseye. They were standing in the center of the training center, throwing their blades at a rubber mannequin.

"You're not flicking your wrist," Quilla answered. She placed her hands on Ranine's, copying the motion. She nodded, grabbing another knife and hurling at the manekin. It bounced off its chest with a clank and clattered to the floor.

"Ugh!" she exclaimed, throwing the rest of her waiting knives against the hard ground.

"It takes practice." Quilla consoled, "I've been throwing knives since I was five."

Ranine raised her eyebrows. "Who taught you, your parents?"

The Quilla's eyes flew to the ground. Sorrow that should have never been there sunk into her skin. "My parents are dead. I don't remember them."

Ranine's jaw dropped, horror filling her face. "So who raised you?"

Quilla shrugged, shaking off the horrible feeling. "I'm a child of chaos, she raised me to be unpredictable; and a student of discipline, he taught me to be unbreakable."

Ranine just stared at her for a while, an unreadable emotion painted on her face. Then she tilted her head and pierced her lips. "You certainly are unpredictable. I don't think any of us in that courtroom saw your massive string of insults coming."

Quilla huffed a laugh, the memory of Grandez Lone's stunned face was one that she looked back on fondly. "Yes, well, I'm not one to kiss the ass of a cocky, ancient politician."

"Oh don't worry." Ranine rolled her eyes. "My sister did enough of that for both of you."

Quilla raised an eyebrow. "I thought you two were close?"

"Oh, don't get me wrong, we are!" Ranine reassured. "But Alohi never had guts. It's part of the reason she became a politician, it was either that or a fighter."

The Quilla hurled another knife at the manekin, it struck its rubbery throat in the dead center. "I would have chosen a fighter one hundred times over. Politics is much too scary."

Ranine watched her knife stick into the mannequin, admiration and competition brimming her eyes. "Same here." She strode over to a nearby weapon shelf, grabbing a bag full of throwing stars. "I think my father agrees with the two of us. He and Alohi always had a rocky relationship." Ranine's long fingers picked up the silver star. With a face full of rage, she hurled it at the manikin. "I hate him for how he treats her!" she launched five more throwing stars at the manekin. One landed in its forehead, one in the throat, the chest, and two in the stomach.

This time it was Quilla's turn to look shocked. The way Ranine's hand twisted when she threw the weapon, the way she stood on one leg at the end of her form. It was wretchedly familiar.

Ranine tilted her head back, brushing loose strands of hair out of her eyes. "Best you've ever seen, huh?"

Quilla was still gaping. "Almost," she conceded. "What does your father do to Alohi?"

Ranine went to retrieve her stars. "It ranges, when we were really young he would beat her, but now it's just emotional damage."

Alohi never seemed like a child of abuse, she was always so sunny and polite. But she guessed everyone had to put on an act. "Like what?" she asked, sympathy brimming her voice.

Ranine shrugged. "Mostly just calling her a failure, not feeding her, not talking to her for days. It was usually caused by her not doing well in politics." She hurled the throwing stars back at the manekin. The poor dummy had become dismembered from all the slashes and was no more than a rubber blob.

"Did he not do that to you?" Quilla inquired, she felt bad for asking questions, but at the same time this information felt important. Espccially if she was going to be training Alohi.

"Oh, of course he did," Ranine said in an almost joyful tone as she hurled the rest of her stars at the rubber. "Whenever I didn't score well in a combat tournament, or when I didn't practice hard enough." Her eyes turned to the floor. "But I was always the favorite. And it wasn't all bad; he would teach me how to fight, how to kill. And he would seem so joyful when I got it! But as soon as I failed, all that joy would fade, and shift into cold anger." She clapped her hands together, the aroma changing from sad to brimming with excitement. "But anyway, who do you think the spy is?"

Quilla gave a light smile. "I honestly have no clue." She turned to Ranine, taking a small envelope out of her pocket. "But I do need to deliver this, sooner rather than later."

Ranine raised an eyebrow. "What's that?" she asked skeptically.

"The letter telling my comrades in Hanslack not to deliver your location to the authorities."

Ranine's jaw dropped, her eyes brimming with excitement. "You actually did it?"

Pride sunk into her body. "Sure did."

Ranine squinted at the letter. "What would happen if you don't send it?"

Quilla thought about it for a while. "Well, I assume the Empire would come with ships and fire cannons at your base until the island itself sinks into the water."

"Well, you better get going!" Ranine told her, already pushing Quilla out the door.

She laughed, stopping Ranine from shoving her any further. "That's the thing, I don't know how to get there."

"Oh," Ranine tilted her head to the side like a confused pigeon. "Do you know where the docks are?"

"Yes," Quilla answered. "I had to get in somehow, didn't I?"

Ranine let out a laugh. "You and I both know there's always another way to get into a building." She put a hand around Quilla's shoulders. "Anyway, the League sends out all its letters by falcon, and the cages are just beyond the farthest dock. People will send them out for you."

She nodded, silently memorizing Ranine's words. "Thank you. I look forward to having dinner with you and your family."

Ranine let out a stout laugh. "That'll definitely be interesting."

Quilla turned on her heel, not knowing what else to say. Although if there was any silence, it would have been quickly filled with Ranine's chatter. It seemed as though the girl could talk for hours without stopping, which was honestly fine with her. If someone was talking, it didn't necessarily mean she had to listen.

It was better that she got to the messaging port anyway. Not only did she need to send out the letter to Hanslack to make sure that this place didn't get blown to bits; but she needed to check the other letters. If there was a rat, they would need to communicate with the Empire somehow, and this was the way to do it.

Of course, she wasn't eager to tell anyone about her investigation. The League of Red Doves hadn't exactly believed her when she voiced their obvious problem. But she did need to prove her worth somehow, and eventually blackmail just wouldn't work anymore. She needed solid, undeniable proof or a confession from the spy themselves.

The docks were much busier than usual, soldiers shouted and rushed to ships. Some had swords and bows in hand, while others carried medical supplies. No one noticed as she strode past the bustle. Her black coat made it hard to pick her out from the crowd.

Though she didn't always show it, her heart ached for the soldiers who were wounded in battle. The Empire would keep taking from them until they didn't even have limbs to give, and she knew firsthand how hard it was having your enemy beat you over and over and *over* again.

When she reached the messaging port, her senses were overwhelmed with the smell of bird dung. She wrinkled her nose at the stench, and a nauseating feeling took over her stomach as she saw the wet bird droppings on the ground.

Bird cages were towered higher than the eye could see. Ladders rested against the giant wall of wires, making it easy to get to the higher cages. Majestic falcons squawked loudly, as though begging to come out of the cage.

"Afternoon, ma'am." Quilla's head whipped around as she saw a short boy looking at her. He barely looked over sixteen, and his hands were full with a stack of paper. "Can I help you with anything?"

"Yes, actually." She said, pulling the letter from her pocket. "I need this delivered to Hanslack as soon as possible."

The boy shrugged, "Sure thing." He shifted his posture and a couple of the letters he was carrying fell to the ground. "Do you mind... putting it on top of the pile?"

Quilla did so, being careful not to spill any more letters. "Anything else I could do for you?" the boy asked with a sly smile.

This was where she got him into a trap. The young ones were always more compassionate, and much more naive. Quilla wobbled her lip and sniffled. She summoned fake tears to her eyes, which wasn't hard considering they were already watering from the stench. Before she knew it, tears rolled down her cheeks and she fell to the floor.

The boy dropped his letters and kneeled beside her, placing a hand on her shaking shoulders. "I'm sorry," she muttered through fake sobs. "I- I shouldn't be crying."

"That's okay." He consoled. "Let it out."

Quilla looked up at him with wide, teary eyes. "My- my husband. They sent him to Brighan a week ago. And I- I haven't heard anything from him. I know half the people they send there don't return. Bu- but I don't know what I would do if he..." She trailed off, burying her head in her hands. "I know your postal system isn't the most efficient, so if there was any letter that came through, I need to know it wasn't thrown out!"

The boy gently stroked her back. "I'll make sure it's not," he told her in a soothing voice. "If there's any letter from Brighan, I'll make sure you're the first person that knows."

"Really?" Quilla wiped her tears from her puffy eyes. "You would do that?"

The boy smiled gently, "Of course." He offered her a hand to stand. "And if you ever want to have dinner sometime to... talk about it?"

Quilla took a deep, shaky breath. "That would be nice." She dried the rest of her fake tears with her coat.

"What's your name?" he asked, offering her a handkerchief.

Quilla held up a reluctant hand, noticing the brown stains on the thing. "Lamia, and you?"

The boy tucked the handkerchief back in his pocket. "Aden. It's nice to meet you, Lamia."

"And you," Quilla said in the kindest voice she could manage. "Well, I'll be going, but thank you for all you did."

Aden waved a dismissive hand. "It was nothing, and I'll make sure your letter gets mailed right away."

Quilla raised a dainty hand to her chest. "What a lovely heart you have." With that she turned on her heel, heading for the door. Her mournful expression had vanished and was replaced by a cruel smile. That poor sap would be asking around for a lovely, kind woman with long brown curls and wide eyes. But all he would receive for that description was a ruthless vigilante that kept threatening the League.

All the while she would have her spy in due time. She knew that the rat would be communicating with someone in Brighan, that being the capital; and all letters from there would be immediately turned over to her.

She smiled sweetly to herself. All in due time, she would work her way up here, all she needed was to be patient.

Chapter Fifty Six
Lilith

Lilith collapsed on her bed. That meeting was exhausting, and she still couldn't believe they had gotten into the League after Quilla's spiteful performance. She could almost feel the angry stares that followed her as she walked back to her room. It was as though every corner she turned, a new person was judging her for something.

She was starting to have doubts about joining this rebellion. She could have just left, taken her money, and built a nice life for herself. Found a romantic partner, had kids, and lived in a small town where no one could find her. But she was romanticizing it. No matter how hard she tried, her history wasn't something that she could erase.

Would she tell her future friends about her past, or would she practice archery in the dark when her children had already fallen asleep? It wasn't realistic to think that she could ever exist without a bow nearby- she wouldn't feel safe.

But she was lying to herself, a normal future was out of the range of possibilities at this point. The ways of thugs and thieves had been engraved in her mind, and her thirst for vengeance wouldn't fade easily. She supposed that was the real reason that she couldn't forget about the past few years. The thought of watching her enemies burn was the thing that got her up in the morning, and that hadn't happened yet.

Besides, she did have something to do in the meantime. Her trust for Quilla was growing slimmer by the second, and she needed to find out what was going on.

She walked over to her partner's small black book. Every time she got near the thing, it was like a dark aura consumed her. Its blackness swallowed her, maybe because it was from the Empire; or maybe because it held secrets that were never supposed to be uncovered.

Either way, curiosity with a pinch of caution had overcome her, and she decided it would be best to find out whatever tales this book was hiding.

She tucked the dark thing into her small bag and headed for the library. The white halls were blindingly bright as always. It appeared almost dreamlike, as though none of it was real and she was imagining it.

The only splash of color that was seen was when she got to the vast entrance of the library. Of course, the doors were dark wood and towered at least twenty feet above her. The gold plating was scattered amongst the design. It seemed like everything the League had was obligated to look grand.

She pushed open the doors and strode into the building. The library's dark essence was relieving compared to the usual blinding halls of Shina. The entire building smelled of old paper, and the silence was thick but comforting.

The click of her shoes echoed against the enormous walls as she walked to the front desk. A woman sat in a chair, reading a small book that could fit in your pocket.

She lifted her head as she saw Lilith, a kind smile spreading on her lips. "Hello," she chimed in a dreamy voice. "What can I do for you today?"

Lilith reached into her bag and pulled out Quilla's small book. "Do you have any books on this symbol?" she asked, pointing to the five-sided shape on the front.

The librarian just gazed at it for a second, her eyes focusing on little slits. "We might." She told her. "Follow me." She beckoned for Lilith to come as she got up from her desk.

They strode through the tall shelves, ladders and steps were scattered along the books, most likely placed to reach the higher books. It was like a rainbow of dark colors, something for everyone's interest. Here, there was no boredom, this was a place that held no secrets, where all mysteries could be solved.

At least, that was what she hoped. If Quilla was associated with the Empire in any way, she needed to know. Maybe this was all some elaborate plan that had been in place for years. To get into the League and destroy it from the inside. Maybe all of Quilla's spiteful words towards the Empire were a ruse, and she was the spy that she was supposedly so eager to find.

The librarian suddenly halted. She paused, looking at the array of books. Then knelt and pulled a small one from the shelf.

Disappointment flooded over Lilith as she was handed a children's book. It was no more than a couple of pages, but on the weak paper cover, was the five-sided symbol.

"This is unfortunately all we have." The librarian told her. "That topic is fairly scarce around here. Mostly used as a tale to scare children."

Lilith nodded as the librarian strode away, leaving her with the small book. As she opened it, she was met with small drawings with no color. Five children were standing in a row, their backs turned and fingers intertwined. Just beyond them, was a massive explosion. If it had been real, it would be the largest bloom of fire she had ever seen.

Just below the illustration, was a sentence. *When Lunan met hell, only five crawled out.*

Lilith turned the page and her eyes flashed with familiarity. She quickly reached into her bag, pulling out Quilla's sketchbook. As she flipped it open, she saw the same faces that lingered on the children's book. The five children, one of whom she supposed was her partner, were standing with weapons out. A sword, something that looked like a needle, a bow, a knife, and a throwing star. They wore a tight training uniform that was laced with gold. Standing behind them was a skinny, well-dressed man who looked no older than thirty.

Ezekiel, Lamia, Casimir, Cercel, and Rosalie. Trained by Satan himself. The words seemed to glitter beneath the children. Lilith could have been certain that the little girl smiling in the middle was a seven-year-old Quilla. Her curly hair and dark eyes were always a dead giveaway. Though her name was eerily absent from the list.

She turned the page, seeing the children fighting a large puma. Sharp teeth bared and claws unsheathed, but the creature looked as though it was being beaten terribly. Blood ripped from its wounds as the children, not looking a day over ten, continued to make more deadly wounds on the cat. The one she suspected was the future criminal prodigy had mounted the beast and was slitting its throat while her siblings fired their various weapons.

Below, the caption read, *defeating beasts from hell, each child was a danger to be reckoned with. But one stood above the rest.*

She turned the page, running her finger against the page as she saw Quilla's young, pale face. She looked around ten years old, a wide smile spread across her face. She was beaming down at a large crowd, waving to the strangers. Behind her, stood the same slim man from before. He laid a hand on her back and was beaming with the same energy as the child.

Rosalie Ghan, the leader of the Golden Class and the heir to Satan's throne.

Lilith's mouth dropped as she read the passage. She was sure that was Quilla's face. Positive. The con queen had barely aged. She had to fight the urge to slam the book closed and never think of this story again. But curiosity and fear told her to carry on and turn the page.

The picture showed two girls. One was the supposed Rosalie Ghan, and the other had impossibly straight hair that looked like it must have been a wig. They stood in a large room that looked like it was about to collapse on them. Flames danced around the walls, cracks were littered around them and little pieces of debris lingered on the ground.

Rosalie was holding a long knife, anger flared in her eyes. Her sister's face was plastered with fear. The girl's mouth widened with shock and her eyes glittered with pain.

But the Golden Heir ran from responsibility...

Lilith turned the page, eager to find the next part of Quilla's story. But all she found was the straight-haired girl lying on the ground, blood pouring out of a massive wound on her stomach.

The passage below was aggravatingly simple. *And left Cercel bleeding.*

"What?" Lilith exclaimed as she turned the page just to find the back cover. "This can't be it!" she slammed the book on the ground, anger radiating off of her. "Where's the rest of it?"

She stopped, feeling the rage lingering inside her. She took a breath, sighing as the air left her lungs. What was she talking about? She had all the information she needed.

Everything made sense now. Quilla's middle name was Cercel, her first kill. Her weird obsession with roses was a reference to her real name. The rose tattoo on the back of her neck covered the one that marked her as an Empire soldier.

When Lunan met hell, that was the first line. Lunan must have meant Lunan Renel. Quilla was Renelian, that must have been where her accent came from.

Rosalie Ghan, the name was stamped in her head like a tattoo. That last name. Horror ran through her as she made the revelation. Quilla Thorne, better known as Rosalie Ghan, was the daughter and heir to the tyrannical emperor that she claimed to hate so much, Theodore Ghan.

Chapter Fifty Seven
Nikolai

Nikolai was in a daze.

Or, to word it better, he was in euphoria. At this moment, sadness did not exist. His pain was forever dulled by the rush that enthralled him. Feelings weren't real, they weren't relevant. And besides, at this moment, he didn't feel them. Because emotions were for the sane, and sane people didn't cut themselves.

The cold blade had slid across his skin more times than he could count in the last day. He hadn't gotten a wink of sleep, and if he was honest, he didn't think he could sleep. Every time he stopped, every time he put down the blade and let the wound scab over, he craved the cold press of the knife. The feel of his blood dripping down his arm was a warmth that he felt in no other place, and the scars he got from the sensation were proof that his pain was real.

He looked at his wrist. Several, vertical lines ran down it like a barcode. They were all scabs, and most would still bleed if you picked at them too much. He knew they would leave scars. He had been cut by others so many times he could recognize which wounds would leave remnants of their pain, and he had definitely cut deep enough.

The wound that he currently had was dripping down his wrist in crimson lines. The knife had dug deep into his skin, and more blood was coming out than usual.

But the painful sensation was dulling, and now the intense emotions were coming back. Terrible grief, guilt, and shame haunted his conscience, and without the fresh wound, they were unbearable.

Nikolai got up off the bathroom floor, using the counter to support his weight. He ran cold water against his raw wrists, letting the stinging feeling soak into his skin. The water filled his cupped hand and he splashed it against his pale, tired face.

He needed to go to the training center. He needed to swallow his pain and practice his craft. If he took one more day off his skills would plummet, and people would notice.

Air left his lungs as he exhaled, trying to clear his mind of emotions. He brushed his hair back and pulled on his training uniform, white pants, and white t-shirt. It was plain but easy to move in; and its simplicity and regularity gave a sense of security.

There was only one problem. His wounds were on display. They stood out like a bear in a group of ducks, right on the back of his wrist.

He rummaged through the drawers of his bathroom. The once organized hygiene products were now a giant mess that he would procrastinate cleaning later, but he needed something to cover the scars.

He felt his heart rest in his chest as he pulled a pair of black gloves from the drawer. They were long enough to cover his elbow, and flexible enough that they wouldn't compromise his movement. As he pulled them on, a new sense of security flooded over him. He had been grounded, somehow the gloves had brought him back to sanity.

A sigh escaped his lips, but the anxiety still lingered. It would get worse once he left the house. Hell, it would be unbearable once he left the bathroom. He couldn't fight like that, he could barely walk with the fear clogging his throat. Unfortunately, there was only one way to rid himself of the nauseating feeling.

Nikolai took the glove off his hand, gently placing it on the counter. He then drew his sword, pressing the cold metal against his bare wrist. With one fluid motion, he slid the blade across his flesh.

The anxiety was gone, along with every other emotion. The only thing that Nikolai could feel was the warm sensation of blood dripping down his wrist.

A slick smile crossed his lips. This was the feeling he had when he was about to win a fencing match. This was what power felt like, and he liked it.

~~~

The giant doors of the training center slammed behind him as he strode into the massive building. The fresh wound hiding behind his glove still stung, the pain was creating confidence that Nikolai hadn't had in days. It may have been false, and it might have terrible consequences later, but right now, it would make him perform well.

His face lifted as he saw a tall figure standing in the middle of the sparring ring. His long, tiger-patterned coat hung off of him like a flag. The manicured nails were laced with gold and there wasn't a strand astray from his long hair.

"Master Killen!" Nikolai beamed. His voice was so high-pitched and excited it made him sound like a child.

"Nikolai!" Killen turned, a smile spreading across his lips. They ran to each other, embracing in a tight hug.

Both of their smiles still gleamed on their faces as they broke apart. Killen put an arm around him as he led him to the sparring ring. "So," he started in a teasing tone. "I've heard you've become good friends with two criminals."

Nikolai scoffed. "Oh come now, Master, you and I both know that you aren't above breaking a couple of laws."

"Touche," Killen said. "But it's not like I disapprove of your relationship, I think it's good that you get an opposing perspective." He wrinkled his nose. "You know, other than your father's one-sided view."
~~~

Nikolai laughed. One of the many things that he and Killen bonded over was their mutual disgust for his father. "Careful, he pays you, doesn't he?"

"Not enough."

"Well," Nikolai said with a slick smile. "Even if he didn't pay you, I'm just too pleasant and you would come back just to hang with me."

His master pointed a sharp, manicured finger at his chest. "Don't get cocky, you're not that pleasant."

There was a pause, then both of them broke into harmonious laughter. It was a sound that he had missed dearly.

"So, where have you been?" Nikolai asked after wrapping up the spurt of giggles.

Killen gave him a side-eye. "Nosy much?"

Nikolai raised an eyebrow. "Come on, I know you're *very* eager to spill all of the gossip to me."

Killen clutched his chest dramatically. "Gossip? Me? I am *appalled* that you would ever think such horrendous things." Nikolai rolled his eyes as his master's serious face broke into a mischievous smile. "So, there's this mercher, Servil Huston, I believe. Anyway, he has a daughter that keeps getting robbed, or she just loses her things, I really can't tell. Anyway, he paid me a lot of kangue to train his daughter in self-defense."

"Is she any good?" asked Nikolai.

Killen let out a laugh. "Oh, she's *god awful*!" he said. "In the end, me and her came to an understanding that she didn't want to learn and I didn't want to teach. So it's our little secret that I got paid for free and she didn't learn dog shit."

Nikolai smiled. "Well, aren't you persistent."

"Hey, I can't coach effort. So if someone doesn't wanna learn, why bother teaching?" Killen retorted.

"That's why you're so lucky to have me!" a cocky smile spread across Nikolai's lips.

"Well, I did miss you." His master relented. "So anyway, how was your mission? Did you get Alohi back?"

Nikolai's breath caught in his throat as the grief rose to the surface. "Yes." He said with a nod. "She's doing quite well." He had developed quite a skill for covering his pain with a poised demeanor, now he just hoped that Killen didn't see right through it.

His master paused; an unreadable expression lingering on his face. "Wonderful!" he finally said. "I like that girl, it would be a horrible shame if any harm had come to her."

Nikolai heaved a sigh of relief. "Yeah," he muttered. "It definitely would."

Killen clapped his hands together, an excited smile crossing his glossed lips. "Anyway, I have a special surprise for you."

A smile spread across Nikolai's own face. "Really?"

"Indeed." Killen clapped his hands twice and about a dozen masked, armored men sprang from the high walls of the sparring ring.

Nikolai glared back at his master. "Really?"

"You've been away too long, my little prodégé." His sarcastic tone was a bit too enthusiastic. "Have fun!"

Nikolai quickly turned to the men coming at him. He drew his long swords, the familiar weight of the blade gave him a powerful feeling. A slick smile spread across his lips as he swung at the first man. He stepped to the left, but Nikolai just swung his other sword at him, slashing his chest plate.

The man looked at the mark on his armor and left the ring with his head down. Meanwhile, two other soldiers came charging at him, blades pointed at his chest. Nikolai took a small step back, letting the two run into each other. Through the confusion, he slashed both of their chests.

"Ha!" adrenaline coursed through Nikolai's veins. Another soldier came at him from behind. He felt the air change, and as soon as the man touched him, he threw him over his shoulder.

He landed on the ground with a thump. Nikolai jabbed his heaving chest with his sword, and the soldier got up and left the ring.

Three more people came charging at him. One leaped in the air, his sword swung above his head. All Nikolai did was duck, the man flew over him uncontrollably and landed on his teammate, sending them both to the ground.

The third one was smarter, he kept his balance wide and unpredictable. Nikolai swung at him in a smooth slash, but he ducked, going for Nikolai's legs. Nikolai jumped just in the knick of time, landing on his opponent's sword. The soldier looked confused for a second, fear lingering in his eyes. Nikolai then slashed his sword against his armor.

The man got up and left the ring as Nikolai scanned the area for more incoming soldiers. None came, he was alone.

His head whipped around as the sound of clapping came from the entryway. He turned to see Killen striding towards him, his long coat swaying at his feet. His master had a slick smile plastered over his face and his white teeth shone as he spoke. "Well what do you know, you're just as spectacular as I remember."

Nikolai took a small bow. "Maybe even more."

"Let's not get too cocky." Killen's eyes glimmered with mischief. "You have yet to beat the master."

His jaw nearly hit the floor as his master drew the long sword from his cloak. Killen never fought him, never even raised a blade. It was a huge honor to finally have the chance to fight the master swordsman.

But he couldn't. His wound that he had made earlier was healing, the pain wasn't nearly as relieving and the feeling of euphoria was fading quickly.

His breath quickened, and he could feel nausea knocking on the door. It was as though the floodgates suddenly opened inside of him; and now grief, fear, shame, and sadness were pouring into his mind. The nausea had broken into his stomach, and he could feel the bile rising in his throat.

He let his swords clatter to the ground as he ran past Killen. The swordsman looked stunned. Playful only a minute before, Killens expression cemented into one of concern.

"Nikolai!" his master called after him, fear lacing his voice.

Nikolai barely heard him, all that touched his ears were the voices. Hundreds, thousands lingered in his head. So many different voices, different accents. But they were all telling him one thing.

Cut.

Chapter Fifty Eight
Quilla

"What do you mean there's no letters?"

Quilla had Aden in a chokehold against the disgusting walls of the messaging port. The fear and confusion that lingered in the boy's eyes brought power to her. By now, he had probably figured out that the fragile girl that supposedly went by Lamia wasn't an accurate description of her.

"I swear." He sobbed. "There's been nothing from Brighan in the last couple of days, I wouldn't dare lie to you!"

Like hell you wouldn't. Quilla rolled her eyes, pressing her elbow deeper into his neck. "It's the capital of Thine, for crying out loud. The League sends doomed soldiers there *everyday*! Do you really expect me to believe that once they leave this wretched harbor they have no line of communication?" she knew this place was incompetent, but she had to give the Lone's some credit.

"Please!" he gagged. "I can't breathe!"

Quilla drew an exasperated sigh and released him. She crossed her arms as she waited for the kid to catch his breath.

"I swear on my life, there were no letters from Brighan," Aden said, still leaning heavily on the wall. "I checked all of them, some even twice."

"Hm." She shrugged, pulling a serrated knife out of her cloak. "Check them again." She held the blade to his quivering throat. "Or I will make sure it's on your life." She pressed the knife deeper into his tear-stained neck, savoring the droplets that ran down his skin. Then she released him, tucking the knife into her cloak and turning away.

Anger and frustration radiated off of her. It was very possible that Aden was telling the truth and there were no letters from Brighan. It was even more possible that the rat was using other methods of communication, after all, it was what she would do.

Her threatening methods were more used as an outlet for... some chaotic emotion that she didn't quite know how to deal with. If she couldn't pull this off, the League would find a way sooner or later to kick her out of their base or better yet, assassinate her in her sleep.

At least, as long as she was training Alohi, she had a council member on her side. The politician had proven to be quite useful on the courtroom floor. Quilla was curious about how she would do on a battleground.

Alohi's first training session was long overdue, and she was sure both of them were eager to get started. It was something that Quilla had come to look forward to. A break from all the memorizing and searching for any kind of clue on who may be the information leak had started to sound quite appealing.

As soon as she pushed open the doors to the training center, she saw Alohi's waiting face smiling up at her. The politician was wearing loose shorts that looked like they were barely staying on her waist. She had a black tank top that was equally as loose and was beaming harder than Quilla had ever seen anyone's lips stretch.

She squinted at Alohi's outfit. "What are you wearing?"

"Well, I thought it would be appropriate!" she placed her hand on her hips. "I've never had a fighting lesson before, so I had to steal some of Ranine's clothes."

Quilla raised her eyebrows. "You would have never guessed."

Alohi looked like she was about to bounce off the walls with excitement. "So, what's first?"

She led her along the vast floor of the training center. "I was thinking I would show you how to throw a knife, that's typically a good place to start in terms of self-defense."

Alohi stopped, biting her lip. "Quilla, wait." The con queen stopped mid-step and turned to face her. "I don't want to learn how to handle blades or shoot arrows. I don't want to learn how to kill people. I never want that kind of power in my hands." She sighed. "All I want is the basic knowledge on how to defend myself if those..." She paused, as if the words weren't coming out of her mouth. "*People* ever come back."

Quilla crossed her arms. "Empire soldiers, Alohi, it's only going to get worse if you don't say it." A sense of compassion rolled over her. There was a time when the same thoughts had once crossed her mind, where she didn't want to wield something powerful enough to take someone's life. Those feelings were long gone, and sometimes she marveled at the irony of her old beliefs and what she had become. "And it's going to take more than some *basic knowledge* to even phase those soldiers."

Alohi rubbed the back of her neck. "I just don't want to hurt anyone, my job is helping people." She eyed Quilla's coat, where her blades rested. "And knives hurt people."

Quilla sighed, her exhale tainted with obvious frustration. "Fine," she said through an exasperated breath. "Hand-to-hand combat never hurts anyone, permanently, that is." This was a flat lie. She had been quite close to someone who could kill people with only a jab of a needle. They had known all the weak spots along the body, and how to paralyze every muscle. But Alohi didn't need to know how dangerous that craft was.

"Great!" the politician's bubbly personality had returned. "Where do we start?"

Quilla held her arms out and widened her posture, looking like a strawman. "Hit me."

Alohi looked taken aback, her blue eyes widened with shock. "What?"

Quilla rolled her eyes. "I like to meet my students where they currently stand, and the best way to teach is to build off of what skills you've already acquired." This wasn't a lie, though she knew that, in terms of fighting, Alohi had little-to-no previous talent. All she was trying to figure out was how terrible the politician really was.

"But I might hurt you." For a moment Quilla didn't think her student was serious. But there wasn't a trace of sarcasm on Alohi's face, and this sent her into a spurt of cackles.

"Trust me, Alohi," Quilla told her after regathering herself. "You're *not* going to hurt me."

Alohi's face remained concerned, but she nodded solemnly in agreement. Her hand curled into a fist, and with all the strength in her arm, she punched Quilla in the stomach.

The con queen barely flinched. Alohi however, was left shaking her hand in pain. "Jeezus, Quilla!" she exclaimed, her face scrunched with pain. "Do you have iron abs?"

Quilla shrugged. "No," she said plainly. "But *you* have the worst form I have ever seen."

Alohi's eyes narrowed into tiny, fiery slits, as though trying to mimic her own glare. "Fine." She said through grit teeth. "How would you do it?"

Quilla took Alohi's wrist gently. "May I?"

The politician scoffed. "Do I have a choice?"

A cruel smile spread on her lips. "If you want to learn, I guess not." Quilla's long fingers curled around Alohi's, tightening her hand into a fist. "First off, you want to punch with your mid-knuckle, not that flat part of your fingers. And second, don't put all your weight into your punches, that's a good way to wind up on the floor with a knife to your throat. You want your punches to be quick and fast, strength doesn't matter as long as you hit the right places."

Alohi furrowed her brow. "What do you mean, *the right places*?"

Quilla shrugged. "Typically pressure points. My personal favorite is around the neck or collarbone. Sometimes, with enough practice, you can paralyze someone. I had a friend who used needles to do so."

Alohi's eyes widened. "Permanently?"

She let out a long laugh. "Only if you hit them hard enough, which for your case, seems out of the range of possibilities." She let out another laugh as she saw Alohi's mimicking glare. "If not, the paralyzation usually wears off in about twenty minutes. A dangerous skill in battle, all the same."

"So it's not harmful?"

Quilla scrunched her face. "Essentially."

"Great!" she crossed her arms. "How do I paralyze?"

Quilla rolled her eyes. "Learning this skill takes years of training, and you can't even pack a punch." Her tone was deliberately demeaning.

Alohi scrunched her face in a way that would imply she was angry. She saw her hands tighten into fists as anger radiated off of her. Quilla didn't even bother to move when her fist came plummeting towards her. But instead of landing in the center of the stomach, the politician aimed for just below the ribs.

Quilla doubled over as every molecule of air was knocked out of her lungs. She gasped, clutching the area where Alohi's fist hit. Maybe she had underestimated the girl. Under the right circumstances, she could be a real threat.

"Oh god." She hurried over to Quilla's side, concern and regret lacing her voice. "I'm so sorry, I don't know what came over me."

Quilla stood up slowly, holding up a hand. "Maybe I should stop underestimating you."

The smile returned to Alohi's face. "You think?" she crossed her arms as a sadistic smile crossed her face. "Now teach me how to paralyze or I'll punch you again."

Chapter Fifty Nine
Alohi

As it turned out, Quilla did not know the right pressure points to paralyze someone. All the criminal prodigy had offered to teach Alohi was how to fight, but the art of debilitation she had to learn herself.

So now she was sitting on the hard, cold wood of the library, looking through the stacks of books around her about human anatomy. Quilla was right about one thing, there were plenty of deadly pressure points around the neck. The problem was that you needed to be able to reach under the collarbone to hit them. She could see why someone would want to use needles to get under there, they could break the tendons without much effort.

The weird thing was, no matter how hard she looked, there was no record of anyone who had ever used this skill. In fact, there was no record of it being possible. It wasn't a deadly technique, so whoever it was used on would at least live to tell the story. But of course, whomever the con queen associated with probably knew how to keep a low profile.

Her gaze shifted to the clock. Both hands were positioned exactly at the six. Her eyes widened and she scrambled to put her wall of books back on the shelves. The dinner with their crew was in thirty minutes, and she wasn't even close to ready.

She ran out of the library and into the blindingly lit halls. She had sprinted the path to her and Ranine's quarters before; sometimes running for fun, sometimes from something. As soon as she had reached sixteen, she had moved out of her parent's house and in with her sister. Living life without the relentless pressure put on her by her father was like having a bar of iron lifted off her shoulders.

She and Ranine always got along well, and her sister had welcomed Alohi into her house with open arms. Since then, life has been much easier. They had limited contact with their father and tried to find comfort for their mother as much as possible.

The marriage wasn't exactly prospering. Since she and Ranine had left, all of their father's unquenchable anger had been taken out on their mother. Whenever they asked her about it, she always claimed that it wasn't that bad. But she always bristled when her husband was near, and seemed to sit as far away from him as possible.

Alohi opened the small door to her home. It wasn't exceptionally large, since most of her and Ranine's profits typically went to their parents, but it felt like more of a home than any of Shina ever had. The walls were painted a light blue, and a few white carpets were scattered around the floor. The entire house smelled of freshly baked goods that made her stomach grumble.

"Alohi?" her sister called from the kitchen. "Where have you been?"

Ranine was planted in the kitchen. Her clothes were stained with what looked like flour, and her hair was pulled into a messy bun.

"Quilla's teaching me how to fight," Alohi responded, walking next to her sister.

Ranine's eyebrows shot straight up. "I still can't believe you're still doing that," she said. "Like, on purpose."

Alohi glared at her. "Yes. I'm learning how to paralyze people."

Ranine's eyes flashed. "Huh," she said quietly, looking down at her cooking.

Alohi peered over her shoulder curiously, her sister was chopping dozens of vegetables, each the perfect size. "What are you making?"

Her sister shrugged. "It's a salad, I thought that was pretty obvious."

Alohi smiled, touching her shoulder. "Do you want help?"

Ranine gave her a horrified look. "Oh god no!" she exclaimed. "I don't know how you do it, but every time you touch something, it's no longer edible."

"Hey!" Alohi protested as Ranine burst into laughter.

"Now go get changed." Her sister pushed her playfully. "You smell disgusting."

Alohi gave her a gentle push-back and headed for her room. Her sister was right, she couldn't cook if her life depended on it, but Ranine had quite a talent for it. And it seemed that she was quite eager to impress their guests.

Her room was small, just a bed and a desk pushed closely together. But it felt like it belonged to her more than anything. She had decorated the room with blue lights that gave the walls a soft glow, and a carpet that swallowed her feet as she walked on it.

Inside her small closet was an array of fancy, uncomfortable clothes. It was expected, as a council member, to always be wearing something respectable. Which usually meant that she was itching the entire meeting and ripped off the outfit as soon as she got within the comfort of her own home.

But tonight, she wasn't expected to put on a show or stay poised. This was just a dinner. And though she hadn't known Quilla or Lilith for very long, they felt like, well... friends.

She pulled a pair of jeans and a plain T-shirt from the hangers. It had been so long since she had worn any of them, but they felt more hers than any of the outfits in her small closet.

Her head ached from her hair being pulled back into a tight bun for so long. She reached back and tugged the wretched rubber band from her hair, letting it loose. Her tight curls fell from their once poised position to a comfortable mess.

She looked at the person in the mirror. They barely looked like her, at least not the her that she let people see. This was who she was, the person that she enjoyed being. But unfortunately, this self barely made an appearance.

Her nose wrinkled as she noticed the large scars on her forearms. They had mostly healed, but the redness made them quite noticeable. They were ugly, and they showed that she had been beaten. It showed weakness.

She tore through her desk drawers. She needed something, *anything* to cover it. She needed them to go away, even if it was only temporary.

A smile spread across her lips as she pulled a pair of white gloves from the mess. They ran all the way down to her elbow, and a feeling of safety washed over her as she pulled them on. No one else could see them, no one else could see she failed, but more importantly, she couldn't see the scars.

There was suddenly a loud banging coming from the kitchen. Alohi's head whirled around towards the living room. Excitement brimmed inside her as she ran from her room and towards the obnoxious knocking.

Her sister, however, had beaten her to it. Ranine was standing near the door, a giant grin planted on her face and arms wide. The girl looked like she was about to burst with excitement.

No wonder, her one and only idol was standing at the door. Quilla's tucked and tailored outfit made the rest of their clothes look like nothing more than rags. The con queen wore a rose-patterned button-up with a stainless, black coat pulled over. Below her flared pants, were healed boots that looked like they could do more damage than any of her waiting knives.

"Hello Alohi." Quilla's crisp accent broke Ranine's mindless chatter. "You look... better than your sister."

Ranine gave her a sharp glare. "Hey!" she crossed her arms. "I cooked dinner. Of course I look a little less decorative than you two."

Quilla looked her up and down, a skeptical scowl plastered on her face. "You look like an elderly sparrow who decided to take a dry bath in flour."

Alohi let out a laugh. Quilla's description was uncannily accurate. "Still as charming as ever I see."

The criminal prodigy strode over to her, the light smell of roses following her path. She threw herself onto the couch, crossing her legs and leaning her head back. "I hate this place already."

Alohi sat next to her, placing her hands in her lap. "So you miss Hanslack?"

Quilla gave her a look. "I didn't say that. But everyone here pretends that they are oh so kind and righteous." She rolled her eyes. "When really, the only moral compass they have is a roulette wheel. At least in Hanslack, we know how vile we are and wear it on our sleeves. The less of a conscience, the more respected." She wrinkled her nose. "Here, whoever's best at hiding their iniquity lands on top of the dog pile."

Alohi just looked at her, disbelief staining her eyes. "Okay." She looked down at her hands, not exactly sure how to continue the conversation. "I wouldn't use those exact words, but I won't say I disagree with you."

"Ha!" both their heads whipped around to see Ranine icing a small cake. "No truer words have ever been spoken!" she said with triumph. "Anyone who ever touched the world of politics can burn in hell for all I care."

Alohi shot her a look, waiting for her sister to process what she just said.

Ranine's hands shot up, innocence burning in her eyes. "Not you, of course, dearest sister."

Alohi smiled smugly, turning back to Quilla. "So, where's Lilith?"

"I have no idea." She groaned, leaning her head back against the pillows. "We aren't attached, you know."

Just then, a loud obnoxious knocking came from the front door. Alohi looked at Quilla, a slick expression spreading across her face. The con queen, however, looked wearily at the door. "There's your answer."

Alohi stood and walked over to the door. She opened the door to see Lilith. The archer was dressed unusually nice. She wore a dark blue turtleneck dress that went down to her knees. Gold lace ran down the fabric along with shimmering golden shoes. Her hair was still in its usual braid, but attached to the ribbon that was holding the weave together, was a star.

Quilla stood up jarringly from the couch. The two stared at each other with unreadable expressions. Both girls' eyes were focused on each other, their stare unwavering. It felt as though their gaze wouldn't break even if it was cut with a knife.

"Nice blouse." Lilith finally broke the silence, still glaring at her partner.

"Nice hair tie." Quilla's crisp accent rasped back.

"Wonderful!" Ranine chimed from the kitchen. "I think we're just waiting on one more?"

Alohi furrowed her brow. "Nikolai's usually never late."

"I haven't seen much of him lately," Lilith shrugged. "Maybe he's busy?"

Ranine scoffed. "Lone's are always busy."

Her sister was right, but Ranine always had an unusual spite for anyone who came from that family line. Alohi was still worried, Nikolai hadn't seemed like himself lately, and it felt like something was off. Really off.

Just then, a gentle tapping knocked against the door. Alohi sprang to open it, turning the knob to find her friend standing at the door. He looked weary, large bags hung under his dim eyes. The usual white, royal clothes hung off of him, but this time they were wrinkled and unfitted. Lying beneath his loose sleeves, were a pair of black gloves.

They looked at each other, silence like a void between them. "Nice gloves." Nikolai finally rasped. His voice was dry, as though he hadn't drunk anything in weeks.

Alohi smiled lightly. "I like yours too."

Quilla broke the silence with a loud cackle. "You look terrible, Nikolai."

All he did was turn to her and nod, all his fight was gone and replaced by something *else*.

"Foods ready!" Ranine strode from the kitchen, carrying a large chicken.

She smiled, gesturing for everyone to sit. Despite the obvious tension between the four of them; she was half starved, and though she hated to admit it, her sister was an excellent cook.

They all took their seats, the smell of warm food penetrating the awkwardness. These four people may be drastically different in every way shape or form, but to her, this was the closest thing to family she had. Their differences made them unique, and the mixture of talents made them dangerous and unpredictable, like on their way back from Rock Highland.

But now they didn't have to worry about getting through a platoon of guards or breaking into anything. For now, all they were doing was eating, and it was nice.

"You made this?" Lilith asked through a mouthful of chicken.

Ranine smiled with pride. "Yep, ever since I moved out I developed quite a hobby for cooking."

Alohi nodded in agreement, the chicken was flavored perfectly. Tints of spice and greens floated around her mouth. "When you live with her, you get to have this every night."

Lilith's green eyes perked, and Alohi thought that the archer might actually be considering sleeping in their home. "She's lucky too." Ranine's teasing voice said. "Alohi burns everything she touches."

Her sister broke into a laugh, and Lilith joined her, filling the room with spouts of joy. But Alohi's eyes were on Nikolai. He sat at the end of the table, poking at his chicken. The once playful glow in his eye was replaced by just a gaze. Now that she thought about it, he looked unusually thin. His cheekbones were sharper and it looked like an infant could fit their hands around his wrist.

The other one who hadn't touched her food was Quilla, but unlike Nikolai, Alohi wasn't worried. The con queen sat glaring at her partner; she seemed to be watching the small star in her hair. The gold thing swished back and forth when Lilith laughed with Ranine. But Quilla's eyes never wavered, and she wouldn't be surprised if the criminal prodigy was planning on grabbing the thing right out of the air.

Alohi's focus turned to Nikolai. Though her teachers' petty grudges were interesting and at times hysterical, her empathy won out. She reached out to touch Nikolai's shoulder, then stopped. He looked dazed, as if he was in a trance. And he didn't seem to do too well with touch the last time she saw him.

"Hey Nik," she said lightly, using the nickname she'd given him as a child. "Guess who's teaching me how to fight?"

Nikolai smiled. It was small, but it seemed to bring a world of color to his face. "Who?"

A mischievous grin spread across Alohi's face. She pointed discreetly to Quilla, who was still watching Lilith with intense eyes.

Nikolai's eyes widened with shock. "What?" disbelief brimmed his whisper. "Her?" he leaned forward. "I feel like the first order of business is to ask if you're hurt."

Alohi chuckled softly. "Punching her stomach is the equivalent of ramming my fist full force into concrete, but other than that I'm fine."

Nikolai's gaze just kept getting more enthralled. "You got to punch her?"

Alohi knew if Nikolai knew this next piece of information he would explode from excitement, but she didn't care. "Well, the first time it hurt me more than her, but the second time I knocked the wind out of her."

"HA!" all heads turned as Nikolai leaned back in his chair, laughing.

"Care to tell the rest of us what's so funny?" Quilla's stone-cold accent cut through the air.

"You-" he gasped in between giggles. "Alohi knocked the wind out of you?"

All heads turned to Quilla, but she remained perfectly calm, only combing a loose strand of hair from her eyes. "She hit me just below the ribs, I can't help that my lungs are there." She shrugged. "Besides, the girl has some real talent, she could be a real threat someday if she worked at it."

Alohi had to bite her lips to stop herself from beaming. The compliment from Quilla had released a hurricane of warm feelings inside of her. She was fighting the urge to run up and hug her. Actually, the reason that she wasn't doing that was because she knew she would end up with a knife in her back.

"Is that so?" the icy rasp banished every warm feeling from inside her. Her breath stopped, it felt like ice had encased her. She had dreaded hearing that voice, and if it was her choice, she would never hear it again. Her head slowly turned to see her father's slim silhouette standing in the doorway, a sick smile spread on his face.

His eyes lit up with an achingly familiar gaze. "Hello, Alohi."

Chapter Sixty
Lilith

Lilith didn't recognize the two people standing in the doorway, but by the way everyone at the table stopped breathing when they spoke, she supposed they weren't exactly welcome.

The two strode in, and she could almost see the panic rising off of Alohi. One was a tall man, he had dark skin like the two sisters, but his hair was straight and long, pulled into a ponytail. The woman trailed behind him, looking small. Her hair was equally straight, but it looked as though she was trying to hide her face with it.

"What are you doing here?" Ranine asked through grit teeth.

The man shrugged. "I was told you were having a dinner party." The man said in a cold rasp. "And I'm a bit offended that you didn't think to invite your own *parents*." He smiled, showing large, tusklike teeth. "Especially when you were having two *legends* joining you."

He extended a jeweled hand to Lilith and Quilla, eyes glimmering with expectation. The con queen quickly slapped it away, meeting the man's hopeful eyes with a rock-hard glare. "Even I have standards, Windlem."

Lilith did the same, slapping his hand away with a cold expression. All the man did was shrug. He pulled a chair from under the table and sat next to Ranine. "Lindsay, be a dear and get me some chicken?"

His wife nodded, her hair still hanging over her face. But the man wasn't satisfied, he banged his fist on the table, anger wrinkling his face. "What are you? Mute? Talk to me!"

Lilith instinctively reached for her bow, while Quilla's hands reached inside her coat for the waiting blades. Just then Ranine's hands landed on their wrists, slight panic lingering in her eyes. "Don't." She ordered. "You'll only make it worse."

"Okay," Lindsay muttered. It was barely a whisper, but thankfully the man seemed satisfied.

"So?" he asked through a mouthful of chicken. "What are you planning on doing now that you've joined the League?"

Lilith looked at Quilla, skepticism lingering in both of their eyes. Her partner gave the slightest shake of her head, and they turned to the man.

"Our business is none of yours," Lilith said with all the confidence she had.

The man wrinkled his nose. "Oh please." He wiped a trickle of juice that leaked from his mouth. "What have I ever done to deserve your distrust?"

Anger was radiating off of Quilla like her rose perfume. "Typically, I trust who my friends trust, saves me a lot of blood." She looked at Alohi and Ranine. "And they seem to have a pretty negative interpretation of you."

The irritation seemed to be rising in him. "Oh, what do they have to complain about?" he glared at the two sisters. "We gave them everything. We're the reason they're so successful today!"

Alohi muttered something under her breath. She had her head resting against her arm while she glared at her plate, stabbing it with her fork like the chicken was her father.

"What was that?" her father yelled angrily, slamming the table.

Alohi stood, an anger that Lilith hadn't seen in the politician glimmered on her face. "I said we gave *you* everything!" she slammed her fist on the table. "Most of our salaries go to you! The *only* reason you live in that big fancy house with all your gourmet food and velvet clothes is because of *us*!" she hollered, fire lighting in her eyes. "What do you think is going to happen to you when I turn eighteen and control where my money is spent? I will leave you without a pot to piss in!"

All her father did was laugh, dry and humorless. "Oh, Alohi." He said with a poised smile. "You're adorable."

"I disagree." Ranine's cold voice broke the silence. "I'm twenty, I can manage my own money. So why am I still paying you?"

Their father sat back in his chair. "Because, honey, I'm in good with the court system. If you withhold a *penny*, I will take everything you have." He shrugged. "Besides, I made you. You two wouldn't be half the people you are if it wasn't for your father's loving, kind support."

Both sisters broke into loud, obnoxious cackles. She had never seen Alohi laugh like that. Ranine, she expected it from, but Alohi was always so kind.

"Oh," Alohi rasped through dry laughs. "You were *oh so gentle*, making us choose between killing and profession debatably less moral." She was obviously talking about politics, she had made it clear before that she didn't exactly approve of the methods and ambitions in the line of work. "Ha! And when we failed, we didn't eat. I had to *claw* myself out of a burning fire because you didn't think I was good enough for life. Me! Your own *daughter* didn't deserve to live!" tears sprang from her eyes, but anger still remained on her face.

The man got up suddenly, striding over to Alohi and grabbing her by the throat. Lilith felt her hands fly to her bow while Quilla, Ranine, and Nikolai all reached for their weapons. But it was too late.

Her father threw Alohi against the wall with all his might. The room echoed with the loud bang, the walls shook as she crumpled to the ground. Before the man could take another step, all four of them had cornered him

Lilith had an arrow loaded and aimed directly at his throat. Quilla had her knives drawn like a deck of cards while Ranine held throwing stars in the same way. Nikolai had drawn his swords, and the quiet demeanor from before had vanished. All of them thrummed with pure, unfiltered rage.

"If you take one step forward…" Nikolai's rasp was barely a whisper, but every inch of it was soaked with anger. "You'll be so dismembered even your mother won't recognize you."

The man froze, raising his hands in the air. "Oh come now, it's just a little bruise."

Lilith looked at Alohi, still lying on the ground. "She's unconscious."

Ranine grit her teeth, the girl looked as though she was about to hurl one of her stars at her father. "I think you've outstayed your welcome."

"I agree." Quilla's cold accent chipped in.

The man shrugged. They let him through as he strode out the door, grabbing his poor wife and dragging her into the hall. Lilith didn't take her eyes off of him until there was nothing left to see.

As soon as he left the room, they all crowded around Alohi. Nikolai knelt, grabbing her by the shoulders. "Please be okay!" he pleaded. "Please, please, *please*!"

Ranine pushed him aside, grasping her sister and shaking her. "For the love of god Alohi, you've survived worse than this. Wake up!" she screamed, shaking her.

Tears ran down their faces. Lilith had only known the politician for a bit, but somehow they seemed like family. She couldn't die like this, this was supposed to be a happy night. There was no way that this would take her down.

"Alohi!" now it was Quilla's turn to kneel next to her. "You're not done, you don't get to give up!" she took a breath, as if she was actually scared. "I meant what I said, you have so much potential! And I'll be damned if all that goes to waste!" Lilith had never seen her partner beg for someone to open their eyes; typically it was her that was bringing death upon people.

All of a sudden, Nikolai wrapped Alohi in a tight hug. Tears streamed down his face as he rocked back and forth. *"Please*, Alohi!" he sobbed. "I can't lose you too! Not again!"

The politician's eyes suddenly flew open. She wrapped her arms around Nikolai, cradling him in a tight hug. The rest joined, wrapping their arms around each other, tears still running down their faces.

After a while, they pulled apart. "My head hurts," Alohi said, cracking a small smile.

Nikolai laughed, his cheeks still wet with tears. "I'd be concerned if it didn't."

Ranine was studying the back of her sister's head. Blood had mixed with her now messy hair and was dripping down her neck. "We should get you fixed up."

Alohi's shaky hand reached back, touching the wound. Her eyes widened as it came back completely bloodied. "Yeah," she said, her voice equally as shaky. "We probably should."

Nikolai and Ranine helped her off the ground. Every inch of Alohi shook, and Lilith wasn't sure how stable she was. They helped her to the bathroom, taking careful, slow steps.

It surprised her how concerned Quilla was. It wasn't usual for her partner to show any compassion, and she couldn't help but feel a little jealous. The criminal prodigy hadn't shed a tear yet, but you could see in her black eyes that she was a little worried.

Of course, it could be a ruse. She was from the Empire; and as far as Lilith was concerned, Quilla's motives were purely for herself. After all, why would she kill her sister in cold blood if it wasn't selfish?

Lilith was still having trouble picturing her partner as the Golden Heir to Thine's throne, but it did explain Quilla's tremendous amount of skill. Ghan must've been an excellent teacher. The only thing the book didn't explain was her partner's tremendous hate for the tyrant. Of course, that could also be a ruse.

At this point, she was wondering if every fact Quilla had told her was a lie. It was possible that the only reason she had decided to rescue her from the Grave Desert was because she needed an archer. Quilla had always been cruel, but compassion had sparked at times; and some part of Lilith always believed that her teacher had some sort of kindness deep, *deep* down.

But she did kill her sister. That was why she had chosen the outfit she did. The dark blue was to show connection to the Empire while the gold lacing symbolized the Golden Class. But the thing that got her partner's attention was the small star woven into her braid; a tribute to Cercel, the sister killed.

Nikolai and Ranine set Alohi down on the bathroom floor. The politician looked more tired than Lilith had ever seen her. Her eyes looked like they were barely staying open, and she had massive bags beneath them.

"Nikolai." She rasped, beckoning him down to her.

He rushed to her side, worry still burning in his eyes. "What is it?"

She pointed at the clock on the wall. "You have a meeting in ten minutes."

Relief flooded Nikolai's face. "Don't worry, I'm not going."

Alohi's tired eyes widened. "You have to, your dad's going to be furious."

"I really don't care, I'm staying with you."

Ranine rolled her eyes. "Nope," she said, already pushing Nikolai out the door. "She said she didn't want you, now go. You don't have to go to your stupid meeting but you can't stay here."

Alohi held up a hand. "I didn't-"

"Welp he's gone now." Ranine sighed. "You should probably shower, and then we can patch up your wound."

Her sister nodded, helping herself up with the help of the counter. Alohi still looked terrible, but at least she was walking by herself. Kinda.

"Quilla, I have a bottle of cleaning alcohol in my closet. Lilith, get a towel from the kitchen." Ranine turned back to Alohi, helping her to the shower.

The two ran from the room, eager to find their assigned things. But in truth, Lilith was thrumming with anxiety. At the slightest opportunity, she was eager to get away from Quilla. After all, she wasn't sure if she was going to get stabbed.

She scrambled into the kitchen, grabbed the towel, and rushed out. Her gold heels clicked on the floor in a rushed fashion. The irony was obvious, she sounded like her partner.

She slowed her pace, trying to calm herself. If she was about to do this, she needed to be in a calm state of mind. All emotions needed to be dulled, silent, and ineffective. She took a breath and entered Ranine's bedroom.

It was a small room, just a bed, a desk, and a closet. Its simplicity was surprising, given the woman that inhabited it. The only thing that fit Ranine's rambunctious personality was the messenger hawk that sat on her nightstand, cleaning its feathers. Quilla was standing in front of the open closet, reading a small piece of paper that looked like a letter.

Lilith took a silent breath, silencing the doubtful thoughts from her mind. Every inch of her shook, anxiety soaking through her. She clenched her fists, she needed to be confident if she was about to do this.

She inhaled again, banishing the fearful thoughts. Then, with every ounce of confidence she had, she opened her mouth.

"Hey, Rosalie."

Chapter Sixty One
Quilla

Quilla's hands released the letter she was holding, the piece of paper fluttered to the ground, not making a sound. She felt her heartbeat in her chest as her breathing stopped. Suddenly the room became hot, sweat begged to come out of her pores like the crystal tears that had sprang to her eyes.

As she looked up, she was no longer in Ranine's room. Instead she stood in the dark halls of a place she once called home. The Golden Palace. Back in Thine. But it wasn't safe, the walls were aflame and falling apart. Rubble crashed in her path as she tried to sprint around the crumbling building.

She quickly turned a corner only to stop. The last time she had ever heard the name, the last time someone had called *her* name. "Rosalie?"

Cercel's voice was tainted with curiosity; so innocent, so pure. Quilla turned around to see her sister standing behind her. Her pencil straight hair swayed gently in the wind of the fire. "What are you doing? The attackers went that way." She pointed in the opposite direction.

"Cerce." Quilla's voice was shaky, "This- this is all wrong. Everything that father is doing, it- it isn't right." She grasped her sister's shoulders. "We need to find the rest of the Golden Class, and we need to run. We can make it, we can lead normal lives!" she paused, looking away frantically. "But- this is just cruel."

Cercel's eyes glittered in the fire. For a second, her face was unreadable. But then it shifted, anger curling on her lips. She shoved Quilla's hands off her shoulders. "Did you *just* realize that?" her voice was shrill. "I mean for heaven's sake, Rose, he blew up our country!" rubble crashed from the ceiling with a large boom. "Yes, it's terrible. But who cares? We have each other, and soon we'll be running everything!" Cercel grasped her shoulders. "Everything is *finally* going our way. Father trusts me now! He loves me! He loves *us*! So enough with your little identity crisis and let's go drive these thugs away for good!"

Cercel offered her a hand, and Quilla ached to take it. She wanted to go back; she wanted to hug her sister and never let her go, but she couldn't.

"No." Her voice was barely a whisper. "No, I won't live with innocent blood on my hands. I won't join the man who destroyed my home and took my life hostage. I won't be just another pawn in his game!"

Her sister just stood for a second, looking at her horrified. In a slow movement, she drew a throwing star with a shaking hand. A tear rolled down her cheek as she bared angry teeth. "If-" she started, swallowing her sorrows. "If you leave- you're a traitor."

Quilla's eyes widened. "Cerce-" tears rolled down her cheek, one after the other. "Cerce, please."

Cercel advanced on her. Her eyes, once filled with innocence, were angry and vengeful. "I won't let you!" she was in full sobs now. "I- I won't let you leave us! I won't let you leave me!"

Quilla's legs were frozen, she couldn't move, only stand and shake. "I- I never meant it like that!" more tears spilled from her eyes. "Cerce, *please*!"

But her sister showed no relent, instead charging at her with fire in her eyes. "You're the terrible one, Rosalie! You're selfish, and cruel, and- and you never let anyone else share the spotlight!" she was getting closer, throwing stars drawn at her side. "I *hate* you!"

Quilla couldn't move, she was paralyzed. But she saw the rubble fall before Cercel did. Right over her, flames dancing along the rocks. "Cerce! No!" she called, holding out a desperate hand.

Cercel looked up a second too late. Quilla saw her eyes widen in horror, then the rocks crushed her.

Dust flew around the halls, she felt the little particles enter her lungs. She couldn't breath; the halls were too hot with fire, and everything was too much. Quilla dropped to her knees, more tears spilled from her eyes as she gazed at the rubble in front of her.

"*Cerce*!" she meant to scream, but her voice couldn't make more than a horrified, squeaky sound. "Cerce! Oh god please don't be dead!"

She started frantically digging through the rubble, her hands ached and little cuts stung on her fingers. The rocks felt heavier than anything her shaky hands had ever lifted. But she kept digging, she had to find her!

As she lifted a big rock, she saw her sister's golden throwing star laying on the ground. It gleamed in the fire light, as though it was brand new. She picked it up and cradled it against her chest, pretending it was actually her.

Yells sprouted from around the hall. Quilla looked around frantically. *They* were coming, and they were going to take her back. There was no time. She needed to go.

She gently tucked the throwing star into her bag. All she had in there were her knives and a small notebook. Then she ran. She didn't know where she was going, or how her life was about to change; but she knew she wouldn't stop running until she was somewhere no one could catch her.

~~~

Quilla came out of her flashback in cold sweats. The room seemed to be closing in on her and the oxygen in her lungs had suddenly been divided by ten. Her limbs shook as Lilith strode around the room.

The archer's heels clicked against the ground, an emotionless expression spread across her face. *How?* The familiar voice in her head hollered. *How the hell did she find out?*
~~~

"So, Rosalie Ghan's your real name?" Quilla flinched at the phrase. "You're the heir to the throne of Thine, and the leader of the Golden Class?" Lilith asked, tilting her head to the side. "Why am I even asking?" she huffed a laugh. "I know the answer. Well, at least you *were* all those things."

Quilla clenched her jaw as her partner continued. "I never knew you as someone who ran, Quilla. You always taught me that responsibility was a gift, and that declining it was a sign of weakness. Now I see what a hypocritical thing that was. After all, you killed your own sister just to escape a *gift*."

Now she had done it. Quilla felt her hands tighten into fists, and all of a sudden she wished she could draw her knives. "How dare you!" she looked up, her eyes in slits. "I did what I had to do!"

Lilith laughed. "Oh? Stabbing Cercel in cold blood was what *you had to do*?" her lips curled back into a growl. "How do I know you aren't going to pull out a knife and stab me at any second?"

"I didn't stab her!" Quilla strode around Lilith, her hands hovering close to her knives. "I don't know what shady source you got your information from, but clearly you have some facts mixed up." She flipped the stray strands of hair from her eyes. "First, I didn't stab my sister, she was crushed by rubble. And I don't know where you've been, but in case you haven't noticed, Theodore Ghan is a pretty messed up guy. For heaven's sake, he blew up my country, my *home*! So if you haven't figured it out, he wasn't exactly father of the year either. I ran away because I realized how morally unjust it was, not because I didn't want to be Empress."

Lilith paused for a second, her green eyes filled with curiosity. Then she tilted back her head, a dry laugh ripping from her throat. "Come now, Quilla, any morality you have is bleeding to death on a table. And you really expect me to believe that Cercel *died* under rubble?"

Quilla's breath stopped, the burst of confidence she had just a second ago was gone. "She's not dead." She was fighting to keep tears from spilling from her eyes. "She's not dead." The words were more for herself than anyone else.

Lilith rolled her eyes. "She is!" her scream was shrill. "You killed her!"

Quilla's hands still shook and tears lingered in her eyes, but the grief had turned to pure, unfiltered rage. She felt her teeth press together and her hands curl into fists. With one, smooth motion she lunged at Lilith.

The archer saw it coming, quickly jumping to the side, but Quilla wasn't done yet. She dropped herself to the ground and swept her legs under Lilith.

Lilith started to fall, yet her eyes stayed alert and ready. As soon as she hit the ground, she bounced back up like a spring. Her punches came faster than Quilla could have ever expected, pounding her in the face.

Quilla fell to the ground, clutching her bloodied nose. The warm trickle felt achingly familiar.

Her eyes flew to Lilith as she heard an ear splitting cackle. "To think I'm fighting Emperor Ghans daughter, and *winning*!"

Quilla felt the anger fly back into her heart. She stood, knives now ready at her grasp. "I am not Ghan's daughter!" she hurled the knife at Lilith. The archer ducked just in time, the knife brushing her hair. "I am not the leader of the Golden Class. I am not the Golden Heir. I am not Rosalie Ghan!"

Lilith tipped Ranine's desk over, shielding herself behind it. Out of the corner of her eye, she saw her bow being loaded with arrows. "No, you aren't!" Quilla dove to the side as one of her partner's arrows fired at her. Her eyes widened with horror as she realized it had red stripes. "Rosalie Ghan was a person. She cared about people!" more arrows plummeted towards her, Quilla twirled around them, barely dodging in time. "That person burned, and all that's left is the scarred skeleton that lives just to hurt others!"

Quilla jumped onto Ranine's bed, drawing her knives like cards. She hurled them one after another at the archer, who was still cowering behind the desk.

"That's a bold assumption!" Quilla sprang over to the other side of the desk, knives ready. Lilith already had an arrow loaded, but something sparked in her eyes as she saw Quilla. Suddenly the innocence had returned to her face; it was the same look she had when they had first met each other in the Grave Desert.

The small amount of hesitation was all Quilla needed. She quickly knocked the bow out of Lilith's grasp. Her hands then flew to her archers limbs, pinning her to the ground.

"I am not a skeleton of Rosalie Ghan, she was a skeleton of me!" Lilith squirmed under her, reaching for her bow, only to have Quilla kick it farther away. "And I do what I have to do to survive. Do you think the Empire just forgot about me? No! They're looking for me, every minute of every day. That's why I changed my name! That's why I'm the wrath of Hanslack! That's why I use people to my advantage!"

Lilith drove her knee into Quilla's stomach. She felt the air leave her lungs as she gasped to get it back. Lilith scrambled to her feet. "Is that what I am?" she screamed. "An advantage?" the archer had found her bow again and had an arrow aimed directly at the con queen's face. Her grasp was shaky, and anger painted her bruised face. "Is that why you rescued me from the Grave Desert?"

"I'm beginning to think I shouldn't have rescued you in the first place!"

Quilla regretted the words as soon as they came out of her mouth. She watched as Lilith's anger faded. She let out a stout laugh. A tear spilled from her vibrant green eyes as she lowered her bow.

"Lilith wait!" Quilla rasped in a desperate voice. "I didn't mean it, I didn't mean any of it." But her partner was already headed for the door, her golden heels clicking against the ground.

She turned, her face clouded with hurt. "I'll be gone by midnight, and you'll never have to see me again. That's what you wanted all along, right?" Lilith started to leave, then doubled back. She turned to Quilla for perhaps a final time. "Oh, and your secrets safe with me. I won't tell a soul." With that, she strode out the room, her words still echoing against the walls.

Quilla just stood there, stunned. Then, as soon as she was sure Lilith had left, she collapsed into a sobbing pile. Tears spilled from her eyes; something that she hadn't done in years. Everything ached, it felt like something had been ripped from inside her, something that could never be replaced.

After what felt like hours, she sat up. Her cheeks were sticky with hot tears and her face felt red. She hauled herself to her feet with the help of Ranine's tipped over desk. Her legs felt like shattered glass, as if she would collapse at any second.

This is for the better. The all too familiar voice in her head rang. *You were getting too attached.*

"Shut up!" Quilla barely realized she yelled the words out loud. Another tear ran down her cheek.

Suddenly, she felt a little tinge of anger. It was small, but powerful. Her teeth pressed together as she fed the fire building in her chest. She knew what she had to do.

Chapter Sixty Two
Alohi

Alohi was leaning heavily on her sister's shoulder as she left the bathroom, but instead of the light that usually filled her home, the room was incredibly dark.

The halls were laced with shadows and silhouettes. Plants and tables had shifted in the dark, and her mind had transformed them into monsters.

An eerie feeling sunk into her heart. Ever since she had gotten back from Rock Highland, darkness always seemed to hide something. There was no reason for darkness if not to debilitate the human eye. And the human eye was largely the reason why people themselves still existed.

"Huh?" Ranine furrowed her brow. "That's weird, I'll turn the lights back on." Just as she took a step and her foot immediately recoiled, like she had stepped on something sharp.

"What was it?" Alohi asked, starting to get a hunch that her eerie feeling was right.

"I don't know." Her sister leaned down, trying to examine the thing that had pricked her foot.

Alohi's neck twisted as she heard a click. The lights flashed on, lighting up the room. Alohi felt a tinge of relief, there were no monsters in these halls.

The only new thing was the rose. There was just one, placed so nicely on the floor. But the flower was gone, all that remained were the thorns.

Revelation hit Alohi and Ranine at the same time as they realized what the stems meant. Confusion filled both their eyes as they turned to find exactly what they expected.

"Quilla?" Alohi asked. The con queen was leaning against the wall, balancing her knife on the tip of her finger. A small stream of blood ran from her nose, and she had bruises all over her face. For a second, Alohi thought she might've seen tears on her cheeks. "Are you okay?"

"Alohi." The criminal prodigy's accent was more raspy and hoarse than usual, something she never thought possible. "I would get away from your sister if I were you."

Alohi furrowed her brow, getting more worried by the second. "What? Why? Quilla, what's going on?"

Quilla seemed to shrug off the question, instead turning towards her sister. "Ranine, I really must applaud you." She pressed her palms together gently, giving sarcastic recognition. "It doesn't usually take me this long to crack someone's secret, but you did an excellent job."

Ranine looked as confused as Alohi felt. "What? I don't know what you're talking about."

Quilla pinched her lips, as if deciding what to have for dinner. "Come now, Ranine, you don't have to lie anymore. I saw the birdcage in your closet. It's for a messenger hawk, I believe?" she pulled a small letter from her pockets, turning it so they could both see the dark blue triangle that marked the Empire. "*Dear C,*" she started reading, "*I can confirm that the subject is who we are looking for. The subject has all the correct characteristics, personality traits, and skills. Come at midnight.*" A slick smile curled around her lips. "*Sincerely, Ranine Windlem.* And it's signed." Quilla folded the letter, placing it in her pocket. "No wonder I couldn't find the spy's letters at the docks. You've been sending them out yourself."

Alohi looked at her sister, not believing what Quilla was saying. No, it had to be a lie or a misunderstanding. She couldn't possibly be suggesting that her own sister was from the Empire!

Ranine's eyes shone with shock. Disbelief and betrayal marked her face, but it only remained for a second. Then, an ear-splitting crackle ripped from her sister's throat; it felt like the laugh itself was tearing apart reality as she knew it.

"Woah," her sister rasped as soon as she was done laughing. "I wasn't sure if you were actually going to figure it out!"

Alohi gazed at Ranine, horrified. "What-" she started, not sure if she could finish the sentence. "You work for the Empire?"

Her sister placed her hands on Alohi's shoulders. "Alohi, all these people have done here is hurt us." Kindness sparked in her eyes. "Don't you want some sort of sanctuary, some sort of *revenge*? That's what the Empire gave me, a chance to get back at our father, the Lones, every messed up person in this place!" a gentle smile spread across Ranine's lips. "Come with me! We can be happy together."

Alohi should have felt sad, she should have felt betrayed, she should have just broken down and started crying right there. But instead, she just stood there, it was like she couldn't feel anything. It was too much information, and it had all gotten stuck in the entryway to her brain.

"You're-" she took a breath, her lips not wanting to move. "You're a traitor."

"Alohi it's not like that!" Ranine begged. "I did it for you, for *us*."

Alohi stepped back, the emotions were all hitting her now. It was one big blow, and it was about to knock her out. "No." She mumbled, "No!" tears stung in her eyes, the hurt she was feeling was unbearable.

The expression on Ranine's face had changed, anger filling her eyes. "If you're not with me," Alohi watched in horror as the throwing star appeared in Ranine's hands. "You're against me!"

Quilla stepped in front of her swiftly, shielding Alohi with her body. "If you want to hurt her, you're going to have to hurt me too."

A cruel smile spread across Ranine's face, one Alohi had never seen before. "My pleasure!"

Her sister was the one who threw the first blade, but Quilla swiftly ducked. Next were the con queens knives, being fired not even a second apart. Ranine dodged everyone, drawing more of her deadly stars.

"Don't think I don't know who you are!" Ranine's voice was cold as she fired the golden blades. "Who do you think taught me how to throw these blades? Who do you think C is? Who do you think wants you dead more than anyone else on this planet?"

Quilla stopped dodging, just for a second. Horror filled her eyes with a revelation Alohi was still clueless about. Ranine didn't waste any time, she fired the throwing star right at Quilla's leg.

Blood gushed from the wound on her upper thigh that Ranine reopened. Quilla fell to the ground, clutching the gash as blood flooded onto the floor. Ranine pinned her limbs to the floor, the terrible smile still spread across her face.

"She's alive?" Quilla gasped, tears springing to her eyes.

"*Alive* isn't the right word." Ranine traced the blade of her throwing star against Quilla's cheek. "Cercel was trapped under that rubble for three days before they finally found her. No food, no water, no *light*." Her sister's sick smile grew larger as horror consumed Quilla's face. "She's half insane now, just a shell of her former self. And her only life goal? Capturing *you*!" Ranine dug her forearm into the con queen's throat. "You, the Golden Heir, Ros-"

Quilla flung her knee into Ranine's stomach. "I've heard that name one too many times today!" the con queen stood as soon as she got the chance, but she was too slow. Alohi watched as her sister pinned the criminal prodigy against the wall. Ranine gripped Quilla's wrists so tightly that she must've bruised them.

"You better get used to it, Rosalie Ghan!" Ranine drew her throwing star and pressed it into Quilla's already gushing wound. A scream ripped from her throat, so loud and high that it could have shattered glass. The star went deeper into the flesh and blood spilled all over the ripped cloth of her pants. Quilla's eyes were shut in pain as tears trickled down her cheeks.

Suddenly, Ranine released her grip. All that came out of her sister's mouth was a muffled gasp as Alohi punched the small pressure points in her shoulder blades. Ranine's arms fell limp beside her as she demobilized her legs. The throwing star that she was holding so tightly clattered to the ground, just out of her reach.

Quilla fell to the ground, suddenly looking extremely exhausted.

"Quilla!" Alohi screamed, rushing to catch her friend. "Are you okay?"

All the con queen did to respond was hold up a finger. She breathed heavily, her hair covering her eyes. "One second." She brushed the stray strands out of her eyes with a shaky hand. "I'm fine."

Alohi looked at her with relief; she only felt it for a second. Then all her emotions came rushing back as she looked at her sister, paralyzed on the ground.

"Why would you do this?" Ranine's eyes glittered with powerful anger. "I'm your sister!"

Quilla quickly grabbed a napkin that was lying on one of the coffee tables and gagged her. All Alohi could hear of her once kindhearted sister were the muffled shouts of rage.

She wanted to cry. She wanted to scream out all her emotions and then lay there on the floor for eternity. But she couldn't do that. She needed to stay poised.

All Alohi did was watch as Quilla tied up her sister. Betrayal stung like a fresh wound, and now she was questioning if she could trust anyone.

Chapter Sixty Three
Nikolai

The chaotic voices that filled the assembly hall silenced as soon as the large doors swung open.

Confusion filled all of their gazes when Quilla strode in. The con queen was in worse shape than Nikolai had ever seen. Her hair was messy, and there was a steady stream of blood that came out of her nose. The wound on her upper thigh had reopened and blood soaked her gray, tailored pants. Her eyes glowed with anger, but the puffy redness of them indicated that she had been crying. Either way, he had never felt so scared of her.

Her bruised hands were carrying a tied-up girl. She was gagged and her eyes were just as angry as her captors.

Quilla threw her captive on the ground, and Nikolai was shocked to recognize Ranine. Alohi's sister had more anger painted on her face than he had ever seen, which was strange, considering the two of them never really liked each other.

"Miss Thorne!" his father's loud voice boomed. "What is the meaning of this?"

"Mister Lone," Quilla responded. She was trying to sound poised, but Nikolai could sense the slight shakiness of her voice. "If I may, I believe that Ranine Windlem is the spy." Mutters of disbelief and shock flew around the walls. "I found a falcon cage in Miss Windlem's room, so she could send out letters to her acquaintances in Brighan without using the messaging port. Therefore, not getting caught." Quilla drew a small letter from her pocket, reading it aloud. *"Dear C, I can confirm that the subject is who we are looking for. Subject has all the correct characteristics, personality traits, and skills. Come at midnight. Sincerely, Ranine Windlem."* She folded the letter, a small smile spreading on her lips. "Now, the question is, who is the subject?"

Quilla leaned down to ungag Ranine. Her long fingers were cautious around her mouth, as though trying to avoid being bitten.

Ranine spit as soon as the gag was removed. Her angry eyes looked up at Quilla with enough fury to go around the entire room. Then she laughed, a loud, dry, ear-splitting cackle. "You'll find out soon enough."

As soon as the words came out of her mouth the gag went back in, muffling the sound of her voice.

"Is that enough proof?" Quilla asked, crossing her arms.

Nikolai's father just sat in shock. His jaw hung open and his mustache twitched, disbelief tinting his face. After a while, he cleared his throat. "Well," he started, "I can't say I wasn't hesitant to let you investigate this, but here we are." He turned to Nikolai. "Escort Miss Thorne to our prison."

Nikolai gave his father a curt nod and headed down to help Quilla with Ranine. The con queen looked a lot worse up close. She was covered in bruises and the wound on her upper leg was still dripping blood. They looked at each other, silent understanding crossing their faces. He was relieved that Quilla wanted to get out of this room as much as he did.

"What happened to you?" Nikolai asked as the massive doors closed behind them.

"I was about to ask you the same thing." Quilla rasped back. "Don't think I haven't noticed the changes in the last few weeks."

Nikolai looked down at his gloves. He didn't want anyone to know about his newfound addiction. It was a weakness, a liability, and he couldn't afford that right now. "Let's just pretend that we're all fine."

The con queen nodded in agreement, her eyes downcast. She was holding Ranine's wrist tightly, not daring to let her captive go. Quilla was usually angry, but there was something different about her right now. There was sadness laced with her rage, almost regret.

"Is Alohi okay?" Nikolai asked, suddenly concerned about his friend.

"No." Quilla kicked Ranine's shins. "Would you be? This imbecile right here was the only one she could truly trust, and look at her now." Ranine shot her a look. "Alohi should be proud, though. Without her, I would be dead."

Nikolai's eyes widened. He never knew Alohi to fight. "What did she do?"

Quilla gave her captive another shove. "This traitor was about to drive a throwing star into my heart, but Alohi paralyzed her before she could do it." Nikolai looked down at her leg, Ranine must have made that wound. He never thought that the criminal prodigy could lose.

Nikolai pressed his fingers against his temple. "She deserved so much better."

Their gazes met, both their eyes laced with tears. "We all did." Pain covered Quilla's voice. "You shouldn't have had to become the White King, I never should have had to become the wrath of Hanslack. Alohi should have had a family that loved her, and Lilith-" her voice choked, grief scrunching her face. "Should have never had to meet me."

Concern drifted over Nikolai. Seeing Quilla Thorne, broken and regretful, seemed almost surreal. "Do you ever wonder who we would have been if none of this ever happened?"

Quilla looked at him with a blank stare. "What do you mean?"

"What if-" he started, not exactly sure what he meant. "What if this war wasn't happening, what if we weren't dragged into it?" he sighed, a reality that would never come. "What if we were normal teenagers?"

Quilla gave a small laugh. It wasn't mean, just gentle. "I don't think we could ever be normal." Her lips spread into a small smile. "I wouldn't be, anyway. I was a swimmer."

Nikolai's brow furrowed. "What?"

"Before it all happened." Her eyes were suddenly lit with something he had never seen in them before. "I was just a kid, but I could have been the best swimmer in our country. Even at five years old, I could beat any twelve-year-old. And I loved it! Every time I got in that water it felt like I was alive. I couldn't feel alive anywhere else, I still can't." She swallowed, sadness painting her face. "If everything was still there, if everyone was still alive, I would have been the best by now."

Nikolai gave her a light smile. "A prodigy in all realities."

Quilla laughed as tears spilled from her eyes. "I'm no prodigy."

Even though curiosity stung him, he didn't dare ask any questions. Some people had a right to their secrets, and Quilla was one of them. If she needed to, and when she was ready, maybe he would find out.

"This is it." He told her, pointing to a large door to the side of them. "The prison."

Quilla wiped her tears and shoved Ranine into the dark room. The prison had very little light and smelled of rotting corpses. Sadness was almost a guarantee as soon as they entered the dark halls.

They stopped at an empty cell. Its walls were nothing more than metal bars, and the ground was covered with hay. It looked more like a horse's pen than anything humans were meant to dwell in.

Quilla threw Ranine into the depressing cell, slamming the door after her. "I hope you rot!" she rasped, fury lacing every syllable.

The two glared at each other for a moment, pure rage surrounding both of them. Nikolai felt the cold air in the prison get hot with tension. It seemed it would never end.

After a while, he pointed to the exit. "We need to go."

Quilla gave a curt nod, not looking back at Ranine. But as soon as they took a step, the room shook. Nikolai froze, his hands flew to his swords as another thunderous boom shook the walls.

The con queen had her knives drawn, and her eyes looked ready to kill. "What was that?"

Their heads whipped around to see Ranine cackling in her cell. "You know damn well who it is, Rosalie!"

Nikolai looked at her, curiosity now burning inside him. Who the hell was Rosalie?

Quilla's breathing quickened as more tears rolled over her waterline. "No." She shook her head as her hands started shaking. "No, they're not here. She's dead."

Ranine opened her mouth, the cruel grin once again spread on her lips. Nikolai tapped Quilla's shoulder, he wasn't willing to let Ranine hurt her again. "We're under attack. We need to go!"

The con queen gave a curt nod, and they rushed out of the prison and down the halls, only one thought on their mind. They needed to get out of here.

Chapter Sixty Four
Quilla

The docks of Shina were more crowded than Quilla could have ever imagined. People were rushing to ships in a matter that was in no way orderly. They pushed each other out of the way, desperately trying to get on a boat. The docks smelled of sweat, salt, and chaos. Typically, Quilla would have enjoyed this sort of thing, but right now her mind seemed just as scrambled as those trying to board the vessels.

Nikolai, Alohi, and Quilla were standing at the entrance to one of the boats. He and the politician were waving their hands, trying to get everyone he could onto the already overcrowded ship. They had probably been trained for this because it seemed like they knew what they were doing.

Quilla, on the other hand, was just watching. Her eyes were glazed and her thoughts were filled with denial. She couldn't meet her sister again. It was too soon, she wasn't ready. To think that she might be in this very building was terrifying. Even more terrifying was the thought that she might meet her.

There was no way that Cercel was alive. The rubble had crushed her. Quilla had been standing right there. She had built her life on the fact that her sister had died that night. Her middle name was constructed to remember Cercel. Her first sibling, her first *friend*. And her first kill.

The docks had started to deplete, and fewer and fewer people were scrambling as more and more found a ship.

Another explosion shook the walls, rocks and rubble crashed into the docks. More cracks formed on the walls, eventually breaking and turning to nothing more than rock.

"We need to go!" Quilla commanded Nikolai. He nodded eagerly and scrambled onto the ship. They closed the gate and pushed off the dock.

"Grab a paddle!" Nikolai commanded. Several men and women took one from the pile on the deck and started rowing eagerly. The chaos seemed to be a great motivator. Each person propelled the ship forward with all their might.

Quilla looked in front of them, watching as the stray rocks and debris fell into the water, making enormous splashes. Behind them, the docks had caught fire. Rocks had shattered the wood that made them, and now they were nothing more than a pile of aflame splinters.

Shina was falling apart. The League of Red Doves was in ruins, and though no one knew it yet, it was *all her fault*. Her sister was here, and so was the rest of her siblings. They were probably the most powerful team on the planet, and they were destroying all of this to find her. So many lives were ruined, because of *her*!

Suddenly, Alohi gasped. Her eyes flashed and her face filled with panic.

"What?" Quilla asked, panic suddenly filling her features.

Alohi looked back at the docks desperately. "Where's *Lilith*?"

Quilla stopped breathing. All her senses seemed to fade as an overwhelming panic swept over her. They would have seen her, and she would have been on Nikolai's ship. It wasn't even close to midnight, so she wouldn't have left yet. There was only one place that she could be, in the burning wreck of Shina.

Quilla ripped off her coat and plunged into the murky water. She ignored the screams of reluctance behind her as she swam towards the burning shore.

The water had revived her, its cold touch bringing power to her skin as she propelled herself through the chaotic waves. She could do this forever, she could swim for miles and not stop.

She swerved as rubble came crashing near her. Her hands propelled her backward as the water exploded in a splash.

Quilla quickly swerved around it, pushing herself harder. She kicked faster, and she felt the push of the water becoming more resistant as her arms increased their speed.

More rocks and rubble crashed into the water as Quilla swerved to avoid them. She was moving fast now, faster than anyone could run. All the quick turns and swerves just seemed to be instinct, and she didn't think twice when she made them.

She was almost at the shore now. Motivation pumped through her as she made the final stretch. The gentle touch of sand brushed against her feet, and it was over, she had made it to shore.

As Quilla stood, her eyes lit up with fire. The blaze was everywhere, covering almost every inch of the once stunning docks.

A burning wall stood in front of her. Sweat beaded on her pores, the heat pressing against her skin. There was no way around, the only way was through.

She took a breath, smoke choking her lungs. Without any more thought, she sprinted into the burning flames.

All the water that dripped from her clothes had evaporated. The heat was like nothing she had ever felt. It was like she was walking through the sun. Her eyes were blinded by the constant orange light. It flickered in all different directions, sometimes reaching out to touch her.

The hot wind from the fire blew around her. It felt like the flesh was melting off her skin, but she kept going, teeth grit, eyes focused. Her heels pounded along the burning ground. She could feel flame dancing along the soft fabric of her clothes.

At last, Quilla leaped out of the burning wall. All she wanted to do was collapse, but she couldn't. She needed to keep going. She needed to find *her*.

The white halls of Shina were blackened with smoke. The gray air choked her lungs as she sprinted through the crumbling base. Cracks and explosions covered the once-blinding halls. Rubble was crashing down at unexpected times, in front and behind her.

She leaped over rocks and fire, determination fueling her legs. Fire danced along the walls, it's hot touch brushing against her skin. These halls were achingly familiar to the ones she grew up in. Flames flickered in the same pattern, and rubble crumbled in the same way. Typically, she loved chaos, but this... this was too much.

No. She told herself. She couldn't lose herself in another flashback, not now, any time but now. She needed to keep going.

"Lilith?" she called frantically. The wind of the fire carried her voice away. "*Lilith?*" she tried again, this time louder.

Quilla turned the corner, entering the room that she had once inhabited. "Lilith! We have to-" she stopped, horror exploding through her as she saw the room.

Arrows were stuck to the walls, but they weren't her partners. Instead, they were a shimmering gold. Drops of blood littered the ground in a trail. Desks were tipped over, blankets were thrown off beds. There had been a fight, and it had been deadly.

She stopped breathing when she saw the throwing star. There was just one; golden and identical to the one that she had kept all those nights ago. It was stabbed into the wall, a small piece of paper attached to it.

Quilla strode over and yanked the note off the wall. As she opened it, her legs collapsed beneath her. Tears stung in her eyes as she read the text. Just two words, written in handwriting that was achingly familiar. She hoped she would never have to see it again, she thought she would never have to read it again.

But there it was; two words, written in Cercel's jagged, messy letters.
HEY ROSALIE.

Chapter Sixty Five
Cercel

Cercel felt the cold metal of the throwing star slip from her finger as she fired it at the soldier. The blade landed directly in the center of his heavily protected chest, not touching his skin.

She heard the wind change behind her. Footsteps, though soft, so obvious. She turned and fired another star. It landed in his heavily padded forehead and her competitor walked out of the ring, sulking.

Her legs propelled her into the air as she sensed two arrows coming for her feet. She watched as the airborne weapon sailed under her, sticking into the ground. While flying, she threw two more stars. They landed in her opponent's chests, perfectly squared.

Cercel landed, breathing heavily. "See, Ranine?" she said in a cold accent. "That's how you do it!"

Her apprentice sat watching her, but the girl looked rather unfocused. Her eyes kept wandering, and her lips spread in a bored line. "Uh-huh."

Ranine had been reluctant to learn ever since Cercel and the rest of the Golden Class had to rescue her from Shina. Now, back in the Golden Palace, it was as though her mood had matched the terrible cell Rosalie had crammed her in.

Even Cercel had to admit, her sister's expertise was not to be trifled with. Ranine was a spy backed up by the entire might of the Empire, and to thwart their plans was impressive no matter your background. Of course, they had still gotten something incredibly useful from the expedition.

"Come on." Cercel rasped. "We're sparring."

Ranine simply shrugged, she slumped over to where her padding lay on the ground.

"No, no." Cercel held up a hand. "No armor, let's pretend it's real."

Ranine's eyes widened. Cercel had her attention now. "But-"

"If you ever fight Rosalie, you're not going to have that armor, are you?" Cercel watched as anger filled Ranine's face. It was a powerful motivator, she wouldn't be half the woman she was if not for her unquenchable rage.

"I did fight her!" Ranine's angry voice cut through the air. "And I won! Or I would have if my sister hadn't interfered!"

"You won?" Cercel raised an eyebrow. "Then why did we have to rescue you from that god-awful cell?"

Ranine crossed her arms. "I already told you. My sister paralyzed me, which made it easy for your sister to tie me up."

Cercel glared at her. Her apprentice was stubborn, unable to accept a loss. That cocky nature was going to lead to her demise.

"Fine." Cercel jutted out her jaw. "If you are so talented that you can defeat Rosalie Ghan, then you can undoubtedly defeat her underachieving sister."

Horror sparked in Ranine's eyes. "What-" she stammered. "No, I can't."

Cercel's lips spread into a smile. She tossed Ranine a throwing star. "I'm afraid you don't have a choice." She dropped into a battle stance, fire burning in her eyes. "Fight me!"

Cercel could almost feel Ranine's anxiety as she dropped into her battle stance. Her legs were spread, but not bent nearly enough, and her arms rested gently at her sides. It was sloppy, all that time in Shina had made her soft.

As soon as Ranine took a step in her direction, Cercel swung her legs under hers. Her apprentice hit the floor, hitting her head on the solid concrete.

But Cercel wasn't done. She needed to teach this girl a lesson. Ranine kicked as she was pinned to the floor. Cercel pressed her knee against her apprentice's throat, pushing hard.

"Cerce-" she choked. "Please."

All she did was laugh, running a hand through her pencil-straight hair. "Not so cocky now, are you?" terror painted Ranine's face as Cercel drew a throwing star. The golden thing glimmered in the light.

Her apprentice's face was turning purple, but fear sparkled in her eyes as Cercel traced the blade along her forearm. That look, the desperate plea that crossed people's faces whenever she was near. It was what got her up in the morning, it was what made her train so hard, it was what she lived for.

"Maybe we should give you a scar to match your sisters." Cercel tilted her head innocently as she dug the blade into Ranine's skin. The girl wailed, her eyes watering with tears. Blood spread on the skin as the knife dug through the flesh. The wine-colored liquid dripped all over the concrete, staining its dark blue surface.

"*Cerce!*" all the color had completely left her apprentice's face. Tears leaked from her puffy eyes, and only one thought came to Cercel's mind. *Pathetic.*

Finally, she released her knee from Ranine's neck. The girl sat up, panting. She cradled her bloodied arm, tears still sliding down her face.

Cercel stood, admiring her work. She leaned over her apprentice, intimidation glowing off her. "If you *ever* blow off my teachings again, you will have a deeper cut on your other arm."

Ranine nodded. Fear still swallowed her face and her eyes still spilled tears. Without warning, she doubled over and vomited all over the blue training ring.

Cercel simply walked by her, crinkling her nose at the smell. "Clean that up,"

"Yes, Cerce," Ranine said in a sheepish voice.

Cercel stopped, anger flaring in her own eyes. Her rasp was dark, and her head didn't turn. "Try again."

Her apprentice swallowed. "Yes, General."

A cruel smile spread across her lips. "Better." With that she strode away, leaving Ranine to wallow in her own filth.

She walked briskly through the halls of the Golden Palace. It was her home, the place where she had grown up. And also the place where she had lost everything.

Her path was immediately cleared by the Bronze soldiers who roamed the halls. They scurried to the side and bowed as she strode through, fear similar to the one that spread across her apprentice's face painted their expressions.

Whispers and rumors flew around the Golden Palace about her existence. Some said that death had taken human form, while others saw her as a blessing. Her personal favorite was the rumor that she was the daughter of Satan who got bored in hell and decided to make the living world more interesting.

No whispers tainted the halls now, silence was the only sound. That was what she liked. If so much as a word left someone's mouth, she wouldn't hesitate to gut them, right then and there in front of *everybody*.

She turned when she got to a rather dull room. It was unfortunate that they had to give their guest such a boring living space; but knowing her sister, she had trained this girl to be just as deadly as if she were a part of the Golden Class. If they gave her as much as a pillow, she could kill nearly half their forces.

The rest of her siblings were waiting in the cell. "Took you long enough." Eziekel's accent cut through the air. He was taller than the rest of them, and most definitely the most chaotic. He barely took any time to style his hair, and his dark blue uniform was torn at the sleeves.

"Yeah, Cercel." Lamia joined. "Where were you?" she had the curliest hair out of all of them, and it was tied in a slick ponytail. Her uniform was standard, blue with golden stripes running down her limbs; but she wore a belt with all sorts of needles strapped to it.

"Oh come now." Casimir's sarcastic voice chimed. "You know that she would never bother to tell you where or what she was doing." Her brother's pale skin seemed to glow in the bright light of the cell. The golden beads that laced his dreads shined as his hair swished back and forth.

Finally, there was the girl restrained in the center of them. She looked exhausted, and her hair had come undone and was sprawled out around her. The red steak that highlighted her hair matched the gashes and cuts that bled from her skin. Pain glazed over her face; but no matter how tired she looked, there was always a steady stream of hate coming from her eyes. It was achingly familiar, and it was how she knew she had succeeded.

Cercel smiled as she looked into the girl's shimmering green eyes. "Ladies and gentlemen." Her accent lit up with the powerful feeling of success brimming every syllable. "After five long years, I think we *finally* have a lead."

Acknowledgments

Woah. I did it.

Published at fifteen! Let's go!

There are so many people to thank for the writing, editing, and publishing of this novel. I don't even know where to begin.

First, I'd like to thank my wonderful parents. Unlike my characters, my family relationship is kind, loving, and supportive. Whether it's basketball, writing, or whatever far-off pipe dream I put my mind to, they stand beside me through all of it. Thank you to my dad for putting all your effort into my skills and developing them. You taught me to shoot a basketball when I was eight, and how to not miss a deep three-pointer when I was fourteen. I cannot express enough thanks to my mom, who reassures me that I'm already far above the average when I feel like I'm far below it. You've shared so many coping skills with me and we've shared long, deep conversations in the car that I'm forever grateful for. And- oh right- you taught me how to draw.

Marian, or as me and my brother call you, Grand Tati. I used your birthday money to pay for my editor, and I am very grateful for that. I have also read your writings about the immigration process and I must say, your resilience is more than admirable. You worked hard to give generations of our family a brilliant life, and that work has paid off. Not only did I inherit a rich heritage from you, but a fire and ambition that leads me through life.

George and Suzane. Or, as a very creative one-year-old Olive called you, Eema and Eepa. Your endless questions and support have influenced my life so much. I love laughing about life with you and hearing about your experiences. You are really a hilarious pair and I appreciate that you laugh at my jokes. I know that you guys will always be a second home for me, and I can't wait to answer your numerous questions about publishing and the writing of this book.

Of course, I can't forget my little brother, Miles. Though we fight sometimes, I deeply enjoy our conversations with you and I modeled Quilla and Nikolai's relationship after ours.

My editor, Fay. Your suggestions were helpful and definitely made this book better. While I didn't take all of them, I greatly appreciate the help and consideration you put into your comments.

My proofreaders were beyond helpful. First, I'd like to thank Camila. You were the first person to finish my manuscript and left so many comments the page wouldn't load. The story wouldn't be the same without you, and I love your advice on the plot later to come.

Next is Gwen. Your writing knowledge was incredibly insightful. You taught me so many things but also made sure I felt good about myself. Before you got to it, I didn't know what the semicolon was or how to use it. Now, my book has a total of 125 throughout the entire text.

My coaches follow. Though I never had a writing coach, anyone who has ever coached me at basketball has helped me to an extent words can't express. Every time I write a battle scene, I think of basketball games. I think of what all of you have taught me. The rhythmic breathing, the centering of your balance, telling when your opponent has lost control of their own weight. I learned that all from you. When writing the relationship between Nikolai and Killen, I thought of our relationship and how much I lean on you for guidance.

I couldn't mention my coaches without mentioning my teammates. The competitiveness of our relationship has transformed who I am as a person. Your friendship and encouragement have taught me the meaning of found family.

Amy and Sadie. God, I cannot express how much you guys have helped me. Your reading through my novel was beyond advantageous.

Amy. I honestly don't think I could've made it through the last year without you. Every time I come to you with a question or an accomplishment, your response is always more than I could hope for. You're my biggest cheerleader. You pick me up when I'm down and praise me when I'm happy. Your help with my manuscript was more than needed. The extent of your writing knowledge is impressive and much appreciated. Now and forever, you're the one I come to when I forget how to punctuate. I can't wait to see what amazing things you accomplish in the future and I hope to be included in your life until we both leave the mortal realm.

Sadie. I love every second of talking to you. You have no idea how much I treasure our long hangouts just talking nonsense. Of course, my favorite thing to talk about is writing, and the enthusiasm you bring when talking about it makes me grin and blush. Your comments on my manuscript made me laugh and lifted my confidence in the craft. Every time I'm low, you remind me how amazing I am and how I have a future.

To all the people on this list, you have helped me not only in writing, but becoming the best person I could possibly be. I seriously could not have done it without you guys.

Olive D Wilson loves to write. Whenever she has the opportunity, she pulls out her computer and types. She enjoys writing her own life into the novel, taking aspects of her and friends and putting them on the pages. Her writing has been described as engaging and brilliantly descriptive. She lives in Santa Cruz, California with her mother, father, brother and four pet rats. She spends her free time (just kidding she doesn't have free time). When she's not writing, she makes her way through high school studies while fantasizing about writing.

www.ingramcontent.com/pod-product-compliance
Lightning Source LLC
Chambersburg PA
CBHW062115290726
48975CB00001B/231